The Seventh Son

Also by Sebastian Faulks

Fiction

A Trick of the Light
The Girl at the Lion d'Or
A Fool's Alphabet
Birdsong
Charlotte Gray
On Green Dolphin Street
Human Traces
Engleby
Devil May Care
A Week in December
A Possible Life
Jeeves and the Wedding Bells
Where My Heart Used to Beat
Paris Echo
Snow Country

Non-fiction

The Fatal Englishman: Three Short Lives
Pistache
Faulks on Fiction
Pistache Returns

Edited

A Broken World
The Vintage Book of War Stories

The Seventh Son

SEBASTIAN FAULKS

HUTCHINSON
HEINEMANN

1 3 5 7 9 10 8 6 4 2

Hutchinson Heinemann
20 Vauxhall Bridge Road
London SW1V 2SA

Hutchinson Heinemann is part of the Penguin Random House group of companies
whose addresses can be found at global.penguinrandomhouse.com.

Penguin
Random House
UK

First published by Hutchinson Heinemann in 2023

www.penguin.co.uk

A CIP catalogue record for this book is available from the British Library.

ISBN (hardback): 9781529153200
ISBN (trade paperback): 9781529153217

Typeset in 13.5/17pt Fournier MT Pro by Jouve (UK), Milton Keynes
Printed and bound in Great Britain by Clays Ltd, Elcograf S.p.A.

The authorised representative in the EEA is Penguin Random House Ireland,
Morrison Chambers, 32 Nassau Street, Dublin D02 YH68

Penguin Random House is committed to a sustainable future
for our business, our readers and our planet. This book is made
from Forest Stewardship Council® certified paper.

In memory of Ian Black,
best of room-mates

'The proper study of mankind is man.'

Alexander Pope, *An Essay on Man*, Epistle II, 1733

'The proper study of man is mankind.'

Anon, 2023

PART ONE

2030

1

'Letter for you, Talissa,' said the superintendent, holding out an envelope from his desk in the lobby.

'A letter? Wow. Is this the nineteenth century?'

'Looks important.'

'Sure does,' said Talissa. It bore the embossed initials of the body that would decide her future. HLI. The Helen Lingard Institute.

'Aren't you going to open it?'

'No, thanks, Marlon. I prefer to take my bad news alone.'

'I like the boots. They new?'

'You kidding me? Postdocs don't do new.'

Talissa pushed open the door onto the avenue, the rattle of the new electric tramway, a smell of tar and burnt chestnuts. As she strode over the big paving slabs, the wind pushed the woollen dress against her thighs and her coat rippled out behind her. She skipped down the subway steps in the first hint of winter rising from the Hudson.

Near the study centre was a café where she sometimes retreated. She ordered more than she could afford: plum compote with yoghurt, poached egg and a pot of dark-roast Colombian.

Right, she said softly to herself, as she sipped the first of the coffee. Let's go. She pulled open the letter. 'Dear Talissa Adam . . . Postdoctoral research position . . . a full complement within the limits of our budget . . . short of one pair of hands in the ideal cohort . . . admired your résumé and supporting letters . . . guarantee a place if you were able to externally fund your first year, starting in the fall of 2031 . . .'

The worst. She could call her mother for some commiseration. Or speak to Felix. She could call her best friend, Susan Kovalenko, but Susan's sympathy might make her cry. It was better to champ down on the disappointment by herself, digest it like a python with a kill.

She looked round the café and its bare wooden surfaces. There was a framed photograph of a jazz trumpeter at the foot of the stairs and a vase of gaudily coloured flowers, zinnias perhaps, on the counter. The espresso machine hissed and thunked. Talissa paid and went across to a small park nearby, a scratch of grass with a struggling green ash. In the corner was a bronze that showed a mother and two children, walking away, hand in hand. One child was about five years old, light on her feet and confident; the younger one looked new to walking. Talissa thought of the fossilised footsteps discovered in the volcanic residue of the Rift Valley in Tanzania, where the trail suggested that a child had at one point been picked up by a parent, perhaps because the ground was too hot on its feet.

A plaque said the bronze was a memorial to a steamboat accident long ago, but to Talissa the figures looked like any group of hominins. From the highlands of Uganda to the sidewalks of Manhattan: the hope and duty, the mother doing what she thought was best – but no wiser than the children who'd placed their hands in hers. Talissa's work had made her

4

see all human beings in this way: as primates first, *Homo* second and *sapiens* later if at all.

Sitting on a bench, she wrapped her coat round her. Her PhD had been fully funded; perhaps she'd been negligent in not planning for what came afterwards. Having been awarded her doctorate, she needed to move on; her university offered only a long grind towards a tenure that she might in any case not want. She had been intrigued when she read about the Helen Lingard Institute in Boston, a new organisation that had been started by three people from Caltech with funding from private equity. Their focus was on her area of special interest: the distant but discoverable human past. And now . . . How was she to find something like the seventy thousand dollars that the Lingard offered its postdocs as a salary? Her mother had enough money to live on and to heat her small apartment in the Bronx, but none left over. Talissa's grandparents had come from three different continents, bringing hope and ambition, but nothing in the way of cash.

'What are you going to do?' said Felix later, his voice a fraction less emollient than she'd expected.

'I don't know. If I can't find a postdoc I'll have to do some tutoring. Or bar work.' She leant forward to pick up her beer glass. 'Or I could train as a dancer.'

'Don't do anything rash. You know how you—'

'I may have no choice.'

'I saw Arizona State was hiring. Talissa? Did you hear?'

She smiled. 'I'm not answering that.'

They were nearing the end of dinner in Talissa's apartment. Felix pushed back his chair.

'Where's this going to leave our trip to France?' he said.

*

They had planned to visit Brittany and to see the site where, eighteen months before, a team had found the skeletons of six unusually intact examples of what appeared to be a new human species, *Homo vannesiensis*. Talissa's interest in the subject had started when she was eight years old and her grandma had given her a picture book. It showed people who were heavyset, hirsute but genial, strolling over grassy plains. At college, she had studied archaeology and anthropology on an undersubscribed course; she was quite happy that the focus of public interest and big money had been on genomics. Eventually, however, it began to become clear that the mapping of the *Homo sapiens* code, celebrated as a triumph of scientific ingenuity, had also revealed just how complicated was the miracle of life that it had rendered legible. They had seen into the mind of God, but found that He moved in exceedingly mysterious ways.

By the time Talissa was in high school the public hunger for novelty had already started to look elsewhere, eventually finding what it wanted in the discovery of some new (or rather, very old) humans, who seemed, when reassembled and genetically sequenced, to have been much like the modern family next door. *H. sap* was a bit of a mongrel, it was established, having mated with its cousin, *Homo neanderthalensis*. Then new species of human were discovered: the 'Hobbits' and Denisovans in Flores and Siberia, and now this new people in a cave near Vannes, in France. The long-admired *Homo sapiens* had started to seem less like the last word than merely one of nature's many shots at making humans.

Talissa had first met Felix when Susan Kovalenko brought him round to her apartment one afternoon a year earlier. 'I

6

thought you two ought to meet,' said Susan. There followed an hour of tea and chat before Susan remembered an appointment to see her sister downtown, leaving the two of them alone.

So Susan had produced him, Talissa thought, like a conjuror plucking a card from her sleeve. He was a beautiful man, there was no denying that, with his loosely curled hair and expressive hands. He had the air of a musician whose symphony was not coming out quite right; yet he had broad shoulders and athletic movements. It seemed he was seldom off the tennis court.

Alone together, they were both a little nervous and laughed at things that weren't funny. Then they listened to some music, where it turned out their tastes were different. Felix managed to make this sound fascinating, as though it was obvious that their favourites ought to have been identical. He glanced along her bookshelf and asked some questions. Talissa squirmed a little, feeling he might be looking down on her lack of poetry or European writing, or something. Now that she saw them through his eyes, she had to admit there were a hell of a lot of books about *Homo erectus*. At least they were already at one when it came to their passion for old movies, especially from the nineties.

She offered him wine to follow the tea, but he opted for beer and she found one at the back of the refrigerator.

'Is this all right? I don't know much about beer.'

'It'll be fine.'

She levered off the cap and passed it over, pouring herself a glass of two-day-old white wine at the same time. Afterwards, they went out to a neighbourhood Chinese restaurant.

Everything seemed prearranged. They were destined to be

together and it was only a question of how they played it. Talissa had had only one proper boyfriend and didn't know how to stop herself acquiring another. Nor did she want to.

Over the next two weeks they got together for lunchtime walks or early dinners. Talissa was still busy with her doctorate, but she checked her silent phone every minute, hoping for one of his proper but arousing messages. Felix worked for a small company that sold software to start-ups to help them rationalise their processes. Something like that, anyway, she told Susan Kovalenko. Felix said it was a stepping stone, just to make a little money while he put his game-changing plans in place. He already had some investors lined up for his own consultancy project, the exact nature of which was confidential. Meanwhile, he had a room in a brownstone off Park Slope with two women and their son. He did some childminding as part of the deal and seemed not to mind this chore because he was confident that he would soon be rich and free.

When Talissa finally invited Felix to stay over, she was in a state of uncontrolled excitement. She wanted to see the outline of his abdomen and how it flattened into the groin and the hips; she wanted him to hold on to her, hard. When they came to it, he seemed so transported by excitement that she was fairly sure that some defects about which she was self-conscious – a lack of tone, just here; or there, a splash of pigment in an unexpected place – had escaped his notice. Instead, he whispered to her, explaining, asking her permission and telling her how wonderful she was to him. He seemed to have sensed the things she had most privately desired, some of which she had not admitted to herself.

In the daylight, fully dressed, she looked at him and knew that she had met her life's mate. It was ridiculous; she was too

8

young. But there it was. He was so full of clarity and life; he was the other half of some entity that had been sundered in an older world – in a time, she thought, before even the Palaeolithic. And they were to meet again that evening.

A week after her letter from the Helen Lingard Institute, Talissa had a quarterly bulletin from the Parn Institute in London. The establishment was funded by Lukas Parn, a young Australian-born tech billionaire who had become interested in genomics. Talissa was on the mailing list because she had been turned down for a position on a programme the Parn funded at the University of London. Before finally unsubscribing, she glanced through the message. Among their new initiatives was a proposed study into the role of surrogate mothers in IVF; they had specific requirements of the surrogates they needed, further details on application.

Intrigued, Talissa saw no harm in making some enquiries – from a point of scientific curiosity, at least. She was still turning the matter over in her head when she met Susan Kovalenko in a bar on Columbus, a place they had often hung out in as college students.

'I know you don't like gimlets,' said Susan. 'So I got you an old-fashioned. Thought it would cheer you up.'

'Thanks, but I don't need a pity party.' Talissa looked round the room. 'Didn't we use to come here to get picked up?'

'Maybe you did . . .'

They had begun insulting each other as a way of mocking the tough-girl talk in ninth grade and the habit had stayed with them. It was at much the same time that one of the girls had christened Susan 'Kojak' after a long-ago TV detective she'd watched with her grandpa on vintage repeats.

'How's the DA's office?' said Talissa.

'It's fine,' said Susan. 'I'm getting a promotion.'

'Still behind the scenes?'

'God, yes. Well behind.'

'Look.' Talissa felt suddenly nervous about what she was on the point of asking. 'There's a reason I wanted to see you.'

'You need a reason? After twenty years?'

'Shush. You know the Parn Institute?'

'I've heard of it. Lukas Parn, the Australian cowboy. That the guy?'

'Yup. The Buddha of Bullshit. But rich as hell. Anyway, his London operation is looking for surrogate mothers. They're doing some research project in association with the British public health service.'

'The Parn's work there is in genetics, right?' said Susan.

'Yes, but they do a whole bunch of stuff. One of the things they're interested in is IVF and why its success rate is so low.'

'I know a couple who spent their life savings on it.'

'It's the failure of the embryo to implant that causes the problem. So they want to find out if there's a genetic component to that. Then, if they understand the underlying biology they can maybe get better matches between the surrogate and the donor. Anyway. I did some digging.'

'And?'

'The Parn in London is straight-up,' said Talissa. 'It has a shitload of money and it has proper scientists. A guy called Malik Wood runs it. A big deal academically, got sidelined from research by the money on offer from Parn. They have a visiting professor this year from the Max Planck Institute at Leipzig. They're the real thing.'

'Hold it right there,' said Susan. 'Are you going to volunteer to carry a stranger's baby?'

Talissa looked down at the polished wood of the counter. 'I haven't decided. But I think they'd pay. Not in England, they're apparently not allowed to. But I'll ask if they could make a payment inside the US.'

'It sounds a little . . . out there.'

'I have no money, Susan. Neither does my mother or my boyfriend. I have a career that I care about very much.'

'Boy, don't we all know about that! But listen—'

Talissa put her hand over Susan's. 'Let me finish. The Parn might be a cool place to be around.'

'Well, I guess you could meet some other scientists. People in your line of work.'

'I'm not a scientist, Susan. I'm a historian.'

Susan puffed out her cheeks. 'OK, Talissa, here's what I think. You need a change in your life. I think you're a little stuck. Fine. But you can be impulsive. Fearless is one thing, but . . . You'd need to think about this real hard. Talk of genes always gives me the creeps.'

'Look, I may not be a scientist, but I do know enough to understand that minor, insignificant differences in the genome, embedded over many thousands of years, can lead to minor, insignificant differences in the phenotype – the way people physically are. Put your hand next to mine. There. Tell me there's no difference.'

'Yours is prettier,' said Susan. 'Shape, skin tone, manicure . . . But then your great-greats didn't winter in Kharkiv. That's what made us the people we are. Endurance. It went into our genes.'

'That's not how genes work, Susan. And anyway, your folk had summers in Odessa.'

11

'Not mine. Too poor. Beetroot soup with dumplings. That's where we got our strength.'

'And would that make you less likely to miscarry?'

'Search me,' said Susan. 'I'm going to the bathroom. Can I get another gimlet?'

While Susan had been Kojak, Talissa's high school nickname had been Fearless Frieda, after an animation character who jumped off buildings and outmuscled men. She saw no harm in seeing how much this enormously well-endowed institute in London was prepared to offer.

She messaged the Parn in Russell Square and spoke to a Dr Catrina Olsen, who even in her scrubs looked less like an embryologist than a film star from 1990s Hollywood. Dr Olsen put her on to someone called Sula Kukk, the financial officer, who was encouraging about the possibility of her being paid in America.

Finally, she mentioned it to Felix.

'You know that if I was lucky enough to get picked I'd have to live there,' she said. 'They'd want to keep running tests. And anyway, after a time you're not allowed to fly.'

'So where does that leave me?'

'In Brooklyn, I guess. But it's only for a year. Then if all goes well I'd be back and starting at the Helen Lingard in Boston.'

Talissa felt a sudden panic. 'You can always come to London with me,' she said.

'I can't leave New York. I have all these investors lined up. I had a call last week from an intermediary for a big IT company in California.'

'Which one?'

'I can't say. They want a meeting.'

Talissa fixed her eyes on him. 'You must come and visit anyhow. You can come every six weeks or something. You can stay with me, so there'd be no hotel bills.'

'Have you really thought about this, Talissa?'

'Of course I've thought about it. And I'll think about it a lot more in London before I commit. I'm not going to take any risks, medical or otherwise.'

'Otherwise?'

'You know. Psychological. I won't do it if it doesn't feel right for me.'

Then she could come back to New York, and to Felix.

'I don't like the idea of someone else's child inside you. Another man.'

'I'm not making out with the guy. It's an embryo when they put it in.'

She hadn't thought this through properly. She could see that now. And she was guilty of taking Felix for granted. The fact that they belonged together was so self-evident to her that she had thought them invulnerable.

Felix stood up and walked over to the window. He looked down into the street and said nothing for a minute. Finally, he turned back into the room. 'Is this your way of breaking up with me?'

'No, it's my way of funding my career and helping some people out. If I was trying to let you go, I wouldn't be asking you to come with me to London.'

The conversation had gone badly, but Talissa was too proud to take steps to put it right. She had suddenly lost her bearings with Felix – she who had felt in control of their relationship until that moment, the more loved of the two, if only by the smallest of margins. Then, mid-conversation, a scale had tilted. Their roles had switched and she no longer knew what to say to him: she might come across as panicked or jealous or weak – in which case he would leave for ever. This was the last thing she wanted. They had been together less than a year.

On the other hand, her absence for a few months might crystallise his feelings for her. It would be a stress test for them. And from a personal point of view, there was the prospect of spending time in a city – a continent – she had never visited. A rest from her weekly visits to her mother's airless apartment . . . By the time she came back, Felix would have sorted out his business plans and would be able to see the central part she should play in his life.

She reasoned so clearly to herself that she was scarcely aware of the stubborn reflex that made it hard for her to go back, apologise or change her mind. Two days later, she messaged Dr Olsen to say that once the plane ticket was with her, she'd be on her way.

2

She found a place to stay in Muswell Hill. It was on the top floor of a terraced house that belonged to a Mrs K. Gopal. From some research in New York, Talissa had established that most Londoners were hard up and therefore keen to let their spare rooms. According to her new landlady, this poverty was caused by a run of terrible luck going back more than twenty years: 'One bloody disaster after another,' as she put it. Mrs Gopal was still angry with the 'financial crooks' who'd started the rot and with the 'austerity' governments who'd tried to plug the hole. Talissa listened in the kitchen, hoping the advance rent arriving soon would soften Mrs Gopal's world view, or at least her mood. Mrs G's grudges were attached to events that had happened while Talissa was still in high school on the other side of the world. She wasn't sure, for instance, what was meant by what sounded like 'Brecksit'. And as for what came after . . . Words, fortunately, failed her landlady.

The Parn Institute said it would do its own tests in Russell Square, but before that made an appointment for Talissa at a clinic in Wimpole Street. She paused at the foot of the steps and looked up to the double wooden entry with its leaded lights and brass fingerplates. She pressed a bell marked 'MediPlus' and the door buzzed open.

In the reception area was a long desk, where a woman in a white nylon jacket gave her a form and pointed out a coffee machine. There were four other patients looking at their cell phones as they waited on leather chairs; none of them looked how she had imagined English people would, even if her ideas had been influenced less by anthropology than by period dramas on her streaming service. In reality, this London looked much like New York.

Eventually, she was escorted by a nurse down to the basement. After giving blood, she was shown an elevator to the third-floor 'JPM Scanning Suite'. She took off her shoes as instructed and lay down on a stretcher that chugged her into a white tunnel, where something whirred and chattered above her abdomen. Talissa pictured what it saw through skirt, underwear and covering flesh: the curved ram's horns of the fallopian tubes with their little brushes at the end that swept the eggs along the ducts and down into the ram's face of the uterus itself.

The next examinations, at the Parn in Russell Square, were conducted by a middle-aged obstetrician with a friendly manner. Dr S. Worthington was the name on her badge, and she looked a little more like the Brits that Talissa had seen on screen; she could on a good day have played the mother of the Regency heroine. There was an hour of family history to be gone through first and Talissa worried that her answers were disappointing. Her grandparents had come from different parts of the world; their medical records, if ever they existed, hadn't made it to the Bronx. Where her grandparents' parents had come from, she had no idea. Nor did many other people she knew.

Dr Worthington was reassuring. 'It's really not about your forebears, it's about what sort of environment your womb will provide. Your test results are excellent. Your overall health seems pretty good, too. Do you drink alcohol?'

'Not much.'

There was the snap of a rubber glove, as Talissa knew there would be, and the raising of her knees as she lay back on a paper-covered couch. The last person to have had this view was Felix, Talissa thought, as Dr Worthington slid in a narrow plastic tube that contained, she said, a tiny camera.

'Just a few holiday snaps. Is that all right?'

'Wouldn't be a holiday without.'

It lasted a couple of minutes.

'That's good. Here, take these tissues. You can get dressed again now.'

Talissa resumed her place in the chair. Next, there were questions about her sexual history. She did her best to make it sound regular. What *was* regular? Felix. Monogamy. Yes. STDs? No way. And the history pre-Felix? No need to mention Stan DePina. Focus on Talor Caliskan, two years together and parting as affectionate friends.

'And that's all?' said Dr Worthington.

'Yes. What happens now?'

'There's a DNA test.'

'Do I spit in a tube and mail it to Sweden?'

Dr Worthington smiled. 'No. It's a bit more sophisticated these days. The Parn has some of the most modern equipment. We'll be able to tell you all about your great-to-the-power-of-ten-grandmother.'

'Well, say hi from me.'

'Then there'll be a psychological profile,' said Dr

Worthington. 'Don't worry. It's not intrusive. But we need to understand your motivation. There's a lot of support in the months afterwards, but anything that can be discovered in advance is a bonus.'

'Do you have kids yourself?'

'Yes. I have two girls.'

Talissa looked round the consulting room. 'I feel pretty detached right now. I guess that could change. The experience. The hormones.'

Dr Worthington nodded. 'Detached but aware. I don't think they can ask for much more than that.'

Back in Muswell Hill, Talissa tried to take stock. It all seemed to be going well and she felt confident she'd be selected.

There was a knock at the door. Mrs Gopal had brought her a cup of tea and a samosa.

'I make them myself,' she said. 'You're not vegetarian, are you?'

'No,' said Talissa, though she almost was.

'It's minced lamb,' said Mrs G. 'I do a vegetable one as well, but most people prefer the lamb.'

Talissa bit into the plump triangle and a taste of lean, spicy sweetness filled her mouth. 'God, this is incredible.'

Mrs Gopal smiled for the first time since Talissa had known her; it was as if her fury at hedge funds and Mr Putin had decided to give her a moment's rest.

'It was a recipe of my mother's,' she said. 'She had it from her mother. For all I know, it went back generations in Madras.'

'Is that where your family's from?'

'Some of them. They always called it Madras, though it's

been Chennai for years. My great-great-grandparents met in Tobago. They were indentured labourers. I had a grand-mother from Afghanistan. One from Poland. A grandfather from Hartlepool.'

'Where's that?'

'Don't ask. But people want me to be Indian, really. Then they know where they are. They want me to be wise and gen-tle and to make spicy food.'

'Well, you do. This thing is, like . . . Wow.'

'I just happen to like the taste of chilli. I know I'm English. That's all that matters. But you haven't told me what you're doing in London.'

'I'm an academic. An anthropologist. And I'm . . . looking for funding to continue my work.'

'I didn't know we had any money left in England.'

'I've applied for something that might pay me quite a lot, I think. I think there *is* still money. It's just that it's concen-trated in the hands of fewer people.'

'Don't get me started,' said Mrs Gopal.

'I'll try not to,' said Talissa.

Mrs Gopal sat down on a sofa beneath a window that over-looked a jumble of roofs going up towards Alexandra Palace. Talissa was surprised by this move, but said nothing. It was Mrs G's house, after all, and this room presumably had mem-ories for her – perhaps as the long-time bedroom of her favourite child: the school uniform in the closet, the small shoes in a row . . .

'And how are you going to get the funds in London?' said Mrs Gopal. 'Who have you applied to? A fairy godmother?'

'In a way, yes.' She didn't feel ready to explain further. 'Tell me about your children,' she said.

'I have two boys and a little girl. I say "little". She's twenty-five this year.'

'That's cool,' said Talissa.

'The trouble is, they don't last. The five-year-old becomes a man. A different person.'

'You still have the memory, I guess.' It was hard for Talissa to imagine this far ahead in a life.

'Well, I have the memory of my grandmother, too. But that's all it is. They're both gone. Granny and Sanjiv both.'

'But your son's alive, isn't he? Sanjiv? It's surely just that the child he once was has been replaced.'

'Yes. But by a different person. The Sanjiv I loved no longer exists.'

'Don't you love the new one?'

'Yes. Very much. But I miss the old one.'

Talissa could see no way past this logic. She was beginning to like Mrs Gopal. It was good to have firm views; she could respect that. Perhaps the samosa had also helped. She wasn't sure if her landlady would have religious objections to the idea of surrogacy; she'd seen no Christian crosses or plaster Hindu deities in the house, but Mrs G was nothing if not opinionated. In the end, she decided to risk it and confide in her.

Mrs Gopal greeted the revelation in silence. Eventually, she said, 'Someone else's baby?'

'Yes.'

'It wouldn't stop you having your own children when you want to?'

'Not at all. It would be nothing to do with me.'

'I think it would be. It would be fed from your body.'

'They've done this a thousand times before. They have ways of making it work out well for everyone.'

Mrs Gopal sighed. 'You seem quite unconcerned. Or are you just pretending to be brave?'

'No, no. I feel OK with it. Honest.'

'Will you carry on living here?'

'For the time being. It depends on whether I pass all their tests. I really don't know what the deal will be.'

'I hope you'll stay. You can decorate the room how you like.'

'But doesn't it have memories? Of your children? It feels like it was once your little girl's room. And she was happy here.'

'I told you. They don't exist any more.'

3

While Talissa was talking to her landlady, Alaric Pedersen was preparing to donate the spermatozoa that he hoped would help produce his first child.

As a teacher, he felt obliged to behave at all times with dignity, even when he was miles from the school buildings. He decided to shut out any comic aspects of the situation and to concentrate on being polite and co-operative with the staff. It was a serious matter, after all. His wife, Mary, had had uterine cancer at the age of twenty-one, four years before they met, and the treatment had necessitated the removal of her womb. They had discussed the idea of a surrogate mother throughout the years they'd been married and had been on the point of committing when Mary, in the throes of an uncontrollable affair, had left home for five months.

When she returned, she was troubled by religious doubts. A Christian upbringing had included close study of the Old Testament, which, as she told Alaric, was unusual among Catholics. She always knew the three-letter name of Joshua's father in a crossword and which of Rachel and Leah had first married Jacob. While she often felt watched and judged, she had no actual belief at all – until her love affair, for a long time

22

after which she sensed her god's disapproval. But at the age of thirty-five, and resettled with Alaric for almost six years, she had finally agreed to undergo the process. Their local doctor had managed to secure them a place in a new public-private partnership that was being run between the NHS and the Parn Institute; he told them they were guaranteed the 'dream ticket' – the expertise of the NHS and the up-to-the-minute equipment of the Parn.

The first test was with the NHS, for which Alaric was sent to an address in a far outpost of London, near Edgware. When he went into the Underground station, the barrier wouldn't respond to the electronic chip in his wrist – the gadget he and Mary called the 'blipper'. The time taken sorting it out with the member of staff meant that he arrived ten minutes late. When his turn came, he was shown into a small room with a water dispenser and some plastic cups. On a shelf, there was a pile of what he thought were shrouds.

He tried not to think what his actions might look like to the Year 9s.

The next day, Alaric was back at work. He taught history in the Dulwich–Brixton borders – a truly comprehensive school, he sometimes said, with children from both sides of the tracks. Their interest in the subject was minimal, but he enjoyed giving them an idea that the world had not always been as it was in 2030. 'We're a moment in a long and mysterious journey,' he told them. 'We can only understand where we're going if we know where we came from. But we are not the terminus. Oh no. We are not Victoria.' A promising new girl put up her hand. 'Are we Selhurst Park, sir?'

A Westminster government in the last days of the previous

century had removed history from the list of subjects that children were obliged to study. Making knowledge of the past a mere option was pitiful, Alaric thought. On the other hand, he enjoyed being free of direction from above; it allowed him to invent courses and lessons that might interest them. Some days he'd just make them read – not a textbook, but something like *Animal Farm* that could smuggle ideas into their heads while they were thinking about something else.

Alaric had declined to become head of department because it would mean coming back from holiday a week early in the summer; it would entail chairing meetings and going to a weekly chat with the 'senior team'. It was a thing to do only if you were hoping to move on to a bigger job in a better school. He wasn't. At the age of thirty-eight, he had decided that any energy left over from work would be channelled into a project of his own: an attempt to explain to people of his generation, born round 1990, that they were unusual in having lived in an age where, for a long time, nothing much had changed. 'There are decades when nothing happens and years when decades happen' was the half-remembered saying that inspired him. He was not discouraged when he discovered that its originator was V.I. Lenin. He knew that most people regarded him as old-fashioned and he wanted to show that, at least where history was concerned, he had original thoughts.

Mary worked as a chef at a sports club in Bromley, cooking for tennis and badminton players hot off the court, people trying to stick with the 'healthy option', but drawn to her dish of the day, with hand-made chips. She had been there for four years and was second in command, so she could take some time off when the baby was born. Those early weeks would be vital, they agreed, so the child would bond with her.

24

One thing the Parn recommended was taking a trip with the surrogate before the event: a long weekend or a few days together by the seaside. Nothing broke down barriers more, they said. Alaric had always, since his suburban childhood, loved camping. The smell of canvas, the sound of birds in the morning, the triumph of the camp fire when it came to life . . . In the course of their marriage, Mary had slowly been persuaded of the charm of nights under the stars, especially as Alaric gave her a break by doing all the cooking. He still had a petrol-driven car, an estate with plenty of room in the back for tents and fifteen-litre jerrycans of water; a trip in the old station wagon would be just the thing to get to know this young woman. He'd make his Italian sausage and bean casserole on the first evening.

There was a zest in his step when he left his classroom at break time. He hoped that he'd be able to interest his son in making things together (he always seemed to picture the child as a boy). He had often regretted selling his model railway at the age of fourteen, but if he and Mary moved to a bigger place, with an attic, he could make a replica of an American city – Chicago, say, complete with marshalling yards beside Lake Michigan, with real water in it.

When he checked his phone over a cup of staffroom instant coffee, he was surprised to see a message from the Parn Institute. It was from Dr Catrina Olsen, head of Fertility Programming, and asked him to telephone her within the next twenty-four hours.

4

The next day, at the Parn Institute in Russell Square, Dr Malik Wood was given a message by his excited assistant. 'The boss called. He's in town and wants to see you tonight. Drinks at the Connaught. Six thirty.'

Malik Wood had studied genetics as an undergraduate in England, but a colleague at the Ivy League university where he was finishing his doctorate had lured him into the world of human embryology. He was soon being invited to lecture in establishments so far away he sometimes had to check where they were on the map. The Samson Inoué Centre of Human Embryology in Dhaka was followed by a semester in the Zohar Research Institute at the University of Montreal. He had then become professor of reproductive and molecular genetics at a new research faculty attached to UC Berkeley.

Helping people to have babies was a good use of anyone's time. But these days he no longer found himself at the leading edge of research – he who had once been tipped for academic glory and had been offered posts at Cambridge and Princeton. He ought to have more money and some hard-hitting initials to follow his name. At a party following a lecture at the Royal Institution, a zoologist whispered bad news through fumes of wine and sausage roll: the position he most coveted had gone to Therese Williams.

'But she's hopeless!' said Wood. 'I read some of her papers. They were like undergraduate essays.'

'I know. But people like her.'

Then there came a job offer: as director of the Parn Institute in London. The Parn had money from its thirty-five-year-old founder, Lukas Parn, an entrepreneur who – almost before his voice had broken, it seemed – had made a dozen fortunes from wave power and biotech. Parn had been born and educated in Australia, where his parents had immigrated from Vietnam and the Czech Republic (he had taken a version of his mother's surname); his company was based in America, but he lived most of the time in Berlin. His latest interest was in anthropology. If AI had raised questions about the ability of electronic circuitry to replicate human thought, then the next question, naturally, was what made human beings such paragons. Or as Parn had put it: 'How come *sapiens* is so sapient?'

Dr Wood had a young team under him in Russell Square, where his time was divided between the laboratory and the office; but at the age of forty-two he was peering into the future with a troubled gaze. Human genomics was a fast-moving train that was about to leave him at the station. And then they elected Therese Williams a Fellow of the Royal Society.

Wood arrived at the Connaught four minutes late, to give his employer time to settle. He went through to the bar, which had recently been redecorated in the style of what might have been a Turkish country house.

Lukas Parn sat back among the drapes, like a pasha in his new command.

'What'll you have?'

When people first met Parn, they imagined he'd talk in the geek idiolect of Cupertino and San Jose; they were surprised when he came across more like a Queensland sheep farmer. Wood had met him often enough to know it was a screen that he would lower when he felt comfortable.

'Just a glass of white wine, please,' Wood said. 'Thanks. How was your flight? Have you come from Berlin?'

Parn leant forward and his face caught the light. His skin was smooth, his hair an even teabag brown. Was there a touch of mascara?

'Know much about evolution, Woody?'

'I'm a biologist.'

'Know how the eye evolved?'

'Yes.'

'How?'

'Incrementally.'

Parn puffed out his cheeks and sat back on the crimson plush. 'I want to do an experiment,' he said. 'I want to prove something.'

'That's not normally how exper—'

'One thing I've learned from the AI business. The human species is fucking exceptional.'

'Which human species?'

'There's only one.'

'Only one surviving, yes.'

'Which in itself makes us pretty special.'

'Unusual, certainly. Even gorillas have—'

'Do you think we'll ever find another human species?'

28

'How many more do you want? You're up to speed with the one they found in France?'

'Homo gastronomicus? Yes.' Lukas Parn sipped on his cola. 'There's a lot of crap being talked about how clever all these other human species were. But only we have real cognition. You can't manufacture that. Not even in AI. I spent two point six billion US trying. And you can't pretend some *erectus* knew what he was doing.'

Putting his white sneakers up on the ottoman, he said, 'Think about it. Think about how slowly, how cautiously natural selection works. My neck, by chance mutation, grew a quarter inch longer than yours, so I could reach the last berries. My retina curved one millimetre more, so I could sense how the light was directed. It took millions of years. So when we toddled out of Africa, quite recently, up through Israel, Syria, Turkey, Bulgaria . . . Christ, you'd think they'd sue the fucking travel agent . . . Anyway, this little band of African Sapiens adventurers . . . Tough little buggers.'

'Certainly.'

'And what did we need in order to be more successful than our competitors in Europe? The wild boar and the aurochs and the odd hairy hominin. Weapons? Tools? Muscle? But we're saying that in a few minutes we were building cathedrals.'

'A few minutes?'

'In evolutionary terms, yes. Some tens of thousands of years. Not many. The way I see it, our species is hard to explain in Darwinian terms.'

'But Darwin allowed for saltations,' said Wood. 'Long periods of stability. Plateaux. Then sudden leaps. Punctuated equilibrium.'

'This was more than a leap, mate. From lithics to laptops in the blink of an eye.'

'Can I get you gentlemen some more drinks?' said a waitress.

'Yes, I'll have another Diet Pepsi. Not Coke: Pepsi. Malik?'

'I'm fine, thanks.'

The waitress disappeared.

'Now then, Malik. They tell me you're feeling a bit pissed off. Neglected. Is that right?'

Dr Wood blew out his cheeks and exhaled slowly. 'It's a good job. And I have a great staff.'

'But your research. The glory days are behind you, aren't they?'

'The institute's still at the cutting edge in half a dozen fields.'

'I know. I fund it. But you yourself.'

'Well . . . Sometimes I feel a little restless.'

'Good. Restless is excellent. I have a proposition.' Parn leant forward and put his hand on Malik Wood's knee.

'Oh yes?'

Parn sat back again. 'Did you know I fund a palaeoanthropology research programme? It's attached to the University of London. They do top genetic work. Looking at old bones. Sequencing the genome of *Homo vannesiensis*. That kind of thing. I know people there. In the labs. I have access.'

'I bet.'

'You know all that work they did in Leipzig a few years back. The Max Planck people. Putting together genomes from scraps of forty-thousand-year-old bone. Brilliant stuff. But those PCR machines they used, they're pretty old now. We have better kit.'

'And?'

Lukas Parn's voice had lost all trace of the Outback. 'I'm interested in hybrids. What they can tell us about ourselves. How we got to be the way we are. The inexplicable leap. The "saltation", as you call it.'

'My God. You're not a creationist, are you? You're not going to try to prove that *Homo sapiens* was put together all in one go by God?'

'No.' Parn laughed. 'No, I'm not a creationist. But I'm an exceptionalist. I believe that the superiority of *Homo sapiens* hasn't yet been explained.'

'You're saying Darwin was wrong?'

'Sure. He was wrong about a lot of things. Women. Genetics.'

'But by the standards of what was known at the time, he—'

'Exactly. "The time" was 1850-something. Getting on for two hundred years ago. Anyway, it's not about a Victorian with a beard. It's about genetics, a word unknown to Darwin.'

'How am I involved in this?'

'Your lab. Your touch.'

Dr Wood drank some wine. 'I'll need to know more.'

'You will. In due course. But can I take it that you would be interested in having your salary increased. And a one-off bonus of, let's say, five times salary on successful completion?'

'It depends on what I need to do.'

'Something well within your capabilities. I want you to make a substitution in the course of our new IVF research partnership with the NHS.'

'A substitution?'

'A simple switch. One guy's sperm for another. Before it hits the egg.'

'That's ethically—'

'Extremely important is what it is,' said Parn. 'From a scientific point of view. We're looking at a human hybrid.'

Wood took a swig of his wine. 'But there'd be a massive legal claim if it—'

'If it came to a civil case for breach of contract, I'd bear the damages. I've taken advice from the best here in London. They say there's a remote possibility of a criminal action, but it would be very hard to prove. So most likely they'd offer a "deferred prosecution agreement".'

'What's that?'

'You plead guilty, pay a large fine and promise to be a good boy. After a fixed period of good behaviour you're deemed to have wiped the slate clean.'

'Never heard of it.'

'Fraud trials were too expensive and too complex for a jury to follow. So they developed this compromise.'

'Suppose we all had to pay fines?'

'Don't worry. I'd have you covered. But it won't get that far. Plus, you know how often these mistakes happen.'

'Mistakes, yes, but not deliberate switches.'

'The child would be of incredible scientific interest. And there'd be further rewards for you personally in terms of acclaim.'

'I can't see me being the first author of the paper in *Science* or *Nature*. Not if there's a switch.'

'As things stand now, maybe not. But by the time we're ready to publish, when the kid's eighteen, who knows what

32

the landscape will look like. It won't necessarily all depend on dusty old journals. There'll be other ways of making sure you get the credit you deserve.'

Malik Wood thought of Therese Williams, FRS.

'Go on,' he said.

5

Delmore Redding, the psychologist at the Parn Institute, was a solemn young man with round glasses, a knotted tie and a button-down shirt, which he wore beneath a navy blue slip-over as if in tribute to a Harvard professor of the Kennedy era. His accent had a pleasing hint of North Carolina. His office was on the top floor in Russell Square, where the autumn sun was bending through the almost leafless branches of a sycamore and painting liquid patterns on the bare wall. As she sat down, Talissa tried not to think of her interviewer as an antagonist, someone sent to pry the scabs off wounds she didn't even know she had. She uncrossed her arms and smiled briefly at him.

'Tell me a little about your family,' said Redding. 'Do you have brothers and sisters?'

'No. Just me. I guess I was a handful.'

'And you grew up in New York?'

'Yes. In the Bronx.'

'Do you still live there?'

'No, I live in West Harlem. Made it to Manhattan. Just.'

'Did you get on well with your parents?'

'Yes. We were pretty close.'

He looked at her as if expecting her to say more. Talissa looked back.

'And did you have friends at school?' he said eventually.

'Yeah, I guess so. I was a little . . . Maybe a little geeky, you know? I wasn't the most popular girl, a cheerleader type. But, yes, I had friends.'

'And when you were older, did you have boyfriends? Did you get asked out?'

'Sure thing. But it was all very superficial, you know? They told me I was cute or something, but when we got to really talking . . .'

'Did you scare them off?'

'I wouldn't say scared, no. But they just wanted to fool around and maybe I didn't.'

Delmore Redding made a note on his pad. 'And have you had many sexual partners?'

'I wouldn't want to say.' Did five count as 'many'?

'And your sexual relations, they've been fulfilling?'

Talissa looked down at the floor and noticed Redding's tasselled shoes and charcoal woollen socks. 'I like guys, if that's what you mean. I feel . . . you know, desire for them.'

'And have you had long-term relationships?'

'Hell, no! I'm only twenty-six.'

'But you've had a steady boyfriend.'

'I've had two, to be precise. But sex and love and friendship and respect . . . Wow. You know. Call me in twenty-five years and I'll let you know how I got on.'

They spent ten minutes paddling in some shallow water about 'intimacy' before Redding said: 'Now. On the question of surrogacy itself. Was it something you'd been considering for a long time?'

35

'It never crossed my mind. In vitro, sperm donors . . . There's a whole vocabulary out there most people never use. Never think about.'

Talissa was starting to resent these questions. It was she who had made the offer of lending her healthy body to a stranger: the cross-examination ought to have been the other way round. But she had to answer.

'I do feel protective of other people sometimes,' she said. 'I'll see a child on the subway or in a store and I have an urge to shield it from all the bad things I know may lie ahead. They're so vulnerable. Is that a maternal instinct? I feel pity sometimes, too. For animals, mostly. I'm sorry if that sounds weird. I feel a desire to look after them. And sometimes I feel that same surge of pity for people I just see on the street. But it's not an admirable feeling. I'm not trying to make out I'm a good person.'

Redding nodded. 'And what would you say is your motivation in wanting to carry this child for another woman? Is it pity for her?'

'No. I haven't met her. A feeling of pity would be . . . Out of place. I'm not expecting to perform some kind of miracle. I'm not offering myself because I think it would be a big deal, but because it wouldn't be. And the money would enable me to carry on with my work. That's an important part of it for me. I want to be straight with you about that.'

Also, she didn't say, because I've messed up with my boyfriend and I need time to—

'And what is your work? It says you're an academic. What's your subject?'

Talissa felt a sharp resistance. She didn't want anyone to know that she had been turned down for the University of

London course financed by the Parn. 'I guess you could say I'm a historian. An ancient historian.'

Redding's pen moved across his pad and Talissa sat back, waiting for him to finish.

'Do you have any questions for me?' Redding said.

'Yes,' said Talissa. 'Do I get to meet the parents? Or is it better not to?'

'We've found there's a better result when people become friends. So we do encourage you to get to know them.'

'OK. Well, that would seem to be . . . polite.'

Redding looked up from his pad. 'You don't talk like someone of twenty-six.'

'What do you mean?'

'You sound older.'

'If you say so.'

'Can we just go back to your childhood.'

'Ah! Childhood.'

'Would you like to have had a brother or sister?'

'God, yes. I would love to have had a kid sister. Or brother. I think there was a whole part of me that never got used.'

'What do you mean?'

'A kind of . . . reservoir of protective love that you can't give upwards. To people older than you. You can only give downwards, to someone younger.'

'And is that still frustrated in you? That unused love?'

Talissa thought for a moment, winding the end of a strand of hair around her finger. 'Yes. I think so. I don't think it's, like, rotting inside me. It's not ticking like a bomb. But it is still there.'

'Do you know why your parents had no more children? Was it a financial thing?'

There was another pause. Talissa breathed out. 'I guess it was because my father died.'

'I see. And how old were you?'

'I was eight years old.'

Delmore Redding said nothing. Talissa knew that that was what shrinks did. He also managed to keep his face impassive. She looked at the box of tissues on the table between them. Next to it was a saucer of chocolates wrapped in gold foil. Perhaps if she was a very good girl he would let her have one.

'He'd been sick for a time. I knew nothing about it. I came back from school one day and my mother was crying in the kitchen. There was someone else there. A stranger. I think she was a social worker from the hospital. My mother couldn't speak. So this woman had to tell me.'

Talissa held the arm of the chair. She had probably said enough.

'And you were eight?'

'Yes,' she said, leaning forward.

'It must have been hard for you.'

'Well . . . The thing was . . . I never got to say goodbye.'

There was nothing else to discuss. Talissa felt she had given Redding all he needed to know. It was fine that the Parn wanted to know about her emotional life, but really it was more a question of her womb, wasn't it? Of vaginal pH and the other things that Dr Worthington's holiday photos might confirm.

'What are your plans for the time after the baby's born?'

'It depends on the money. But my hope would be that I'd go back to New York and pick up my research work.'

'I see. They wouldn't mind that you'd taken some time out?'

'Not at all. It's a question of finding a programme where I

can be useful. A placement. And the money, of course. I guess that at that stage putting some distance between me and the parents – and the kid . . . That would be helpful.'

Redding looked at his watch. 'Absolutely. It's been a pleasure meeting you, Miss Adam. You can always message if you have any questions.'

Talissa decided to walk a little through the strange, enormous city. She passed the beetroot-coloured arches of Russell Square station's tiled façade and carried on down the narrow street. On one side were ancient brick houses, tight in their grimy rows, hundreds of years old; on the other side rose tiered modern apartments over a windy plaza of movie theatres and glass-fronted food outlets.

Her idea of this continent was hazy, she had to admit. If someone said the word 'Europe' she thought both of the Russian invasion of Ukraine and of airy art galleries; of a large number of unnecessary languages and ancient monuments. It was a blur of bombs and antiquity, the pillars of the Parthenon blitzed by the Luftwaffe.

In Bloomsbury, the digging works and Road Ahead Closed signs made the streets feel deserted; dry leaves scraped the paving slabs and eddies of dust collapsed between the black railings. Life stirred again in a narrow market. With its Mexican tapas and Japanese sushi bars, this street hardly seemed to be in London at all. And all these little *Homo sapiens*, Talissa thought: the rapid diaspora on whom the intervening years had laid small changes of appearance, but none significant enough to stop their reunion in a few yards of city ground.

Eventually she came to a station, Angel, that she knew was on the black line going north. The reader on the turnstile accepted her dollar-loaded wrist chip and she went down into the tunnels, thinking about the baby-to-be.

Another being helped into the light wouldn't alter the flux and reflux of the ravening species, but its existence would bring joy to its parents and employment to her. What more, really, was there? Love and joy. Work. Joy *from* love.

6

During the eleven o'clock break, Alaric went to a far corner of the school playground where he wouldn't be overheard. He fished out his handset and called Catrina Olsen's direct line.

'Thank you for ringing, Mr Pedersen. Forgive me if I ask you a couple of questions for security. I think you provided us with some hard-to-guess answers?'

'Fire away.'

'Let me see . . . What was the favourite locomotive in your train set when you were a child and what was your nickname for it? Gosh, these really are quite niche, aren't they?'

'Mallard. I called it Nigel, after Nigel Gresley, who designed it.'

'That's fine.'

'Is everything all right with the sample?' said Alaric.

'What? Oh. Yes, absolutely fine. Top of the range.'

'It's just that since I've never . . . you know, fathered a child, I didn't want to take anything for granted.'

'Quite right too. No, the reason I was calling is that I think we have the ideal surrogate for you. She's a young American woman.'

'American? But does she live here?'

'She's visiting. She'll be here for a year.'

'Then she'll go back to America?'

'That's the plan. It works well for us. After the birth we suggest that the surrogate mother has no contact with the child for a period of twelve years. After that, it's a matter for you. There are also statutory entitlements at age sixteen, though the law's changing. But obviously, if she's on the other side of the Atlantic and immersed in her work, that's ideal. A clean break.'

'I see. What else makes her ideal?'

'Age, health. Also, she's a positive and independent person. Her psychological profile was good. Then there's the family backgrounds.'

'The what?'

'We've taken into account the DNA profiles of you all. Where you come from, where your parents and grandparents are from, and so on. There's good variation.'

'Is there an ethnic aspect to this?'

'We don't use that term any more. The fractional differences between the phenotypes of human populations are insignificant. Differences in hair colour, skin pigmentation, eye shape and what have you. They're largely the result of genetic drift, maybe some sexual selection. "Historic Habitat Adaptation and Drift" is the accepted phrase for it now. Known as HAD.'

'That's catchy. When you say insignificant—'

'I mean from a scientific point of view. Socially, of course, it can still be rather different. But that's not our concern. We keep an open mind. If it turned out that the offspring of a mother with long roots in one part of the world developed slightly differently from the child of a parent with ancestry on the other side of the world, we'd be interested to look at why.'

'I understand,' said Alaric. 'I teach in a school with kids from all over the world, so I'm used to it. You're oblivious to difference. Except for those times when you need to be super-aware of it. Sounds hard, but you get used to it.'

'Exactly. HAD is a very small part of what we're looking for. But the background family differences between all three of you in this instance are helpful.'

'We're a mixed bag, you mean?'

'Diverse in the best sense,' said Dr Olsen.

Alaric let out a sigh. He had had a primitive fear of not being a man – that his sticky sample would be underpopulated. He'd looked up the statistics. It was not just numbers, it transpired, but also a function called 'motility', which for some reason made him think of a disabled person's scooter. Now it seemed that it was all right. Not only were his spermatozoa numerous and active, but his and Mary's DNA was ideally wide-ranging. He wanted to pat their nomadic ancestors on the back.

'When can I meet her? The surrogate. What's her name?'

'Talissa Adam. I think you've already discussed with my colleagues the idea of spending a weekend with her?'

'I thought we might go camping. And if she's American, she won't know this country very well, will she?'

'I think that's a great idea.'

In the evening, when he'd shared the news with Mary, Alaric messaged Talissa. It was hard to know where to begin.

Dear, dearest . . . Ms Adam . . . 'Dear Talissa, if I may' . . . Even 'dear' was a bit analogue. Eventually he got down some sort of note. It ended: 'And my wife, Mary, has managed to get that weekend off work, plus one day of annual leave, so do let us know if that would work for you.'

The message made Talissa laugh. Alaric was thirty-eight, she'd been told, but going on sixty-eight by the sound of him. She didn't confirm the dates because she was still waiting to hear how much the Parn Institute would pay. If it was not enough to subsidise her first year at the Helen Lingard, there would be no camping weekend and no baby. She sent a holding answer. 'Great to hear from you still sorting the last details will confirm dates ASAP Best regds TA'.

She had never been camping before. Once, when she had been on a dig in Idaho, the van had broken down and had not been able to take them back to the hostel, so six of them had taken turns in a ridge tent that was designed to house the equipment. The bugs and the pygmy shrews had enjoyed themselves, but the idea that you would camp for the fun of it seemed bizarre.

The day after Alaric's message she had a meeting with Sula Kukk, the financial officer at the Parn. A click of the mouse had revealed that Sula meant 'gannet' in Estonian. In person, she was more ursine than birdlike, large and slow of movement.

'We can offer you accommodation that matches our assistant professor level,' she said from behind her desk. 'We have some recommended properties, but you'd be free to choose.'

'That's cool,' said Talissa. 'But what about the fee? As I think I explained in my interviews, I'm looking for a sum that would help me continue my research work.'

'How much do you need?'

'A postdoc salary for a year.'

'We can make arrangements for our American headquarters

44

to make a direct transfer to a research establishment. That shouldn't be a problem. How they channel that money back to you is none of our business.'

'Thank you.'

'But I'd need to speak to Dr Wood. He's at a conference in Helsinki at the moment.'

'I could save you on accommodation,' said Talissa. 'I have a room with a friend in Muswell Hill.'

It was pushing it to call Mrs Gopal a friend, but she did feel she was becoming closer to her.

'Is it within half an hour of here?'

'Yes.' On a good day.

While she waited for Dr Wood to return from Helsinki, or at least to read his messages, Talissa had an idea. Suppose she asked Alaric and Mary if they could use the weekend to go to France and visit the site of *Homo vannesiensis*. It was unlikely that she'd be able to go down into the excavation, still less get a glimpse of fossil, all the important bones having been removed, but it would be interesting just to see an historic site opened up.

Some minutes on the internet established that while France was only about twenty miles away, Vannes was on the wrong side of the country for the Channel Tunnel. Still, Alaric sounded like the sort of man who might enjoy a logistical challenge and a long drive.

7

Talissa arrived in Tulse Hill at nine in the morning. From the heights of Alexandra Palace, via Underground and Overground, mile after mile of grey morning, tiled tunnels, shunting yards and terraces seen through unwashed train windows . . . She wondered how far, if she'd started out at her local subway station in New York, she would by now have travelled. Florida, pretty much.

She was a little afraid to admit that she had never been camping before; it was her anxiety about the bathroom and sleeping arrangements that preoccupied her as much as the thought of meeting Mary and Alaric. Here it was, though: number 25 on a glass-panelled front door up a paved garden path, beside which stood garbage bins on wheels. There were only two bells.

'Talissa? Come on up!'

Her first sight of Mary. A smiling, homely person with a wary eye.

Mary hugged her. 'Come in, come in. Put your bag down there. Did it take for ever? We should have come and picked you up but the thing is we're already halfway to Folkestone here, so . . . Coffee. You must have coffee. Or tea.'

'I hope I'm not late.'

'Not at all. And we have a flexible ticket for the Tunnel anyway. Would you like something to eat? I'm making scrambled eggs. Alaric! Talissa's here.'

Talissa sat down while Mary went in search of her husband. The living room had a bookshelf along one wall that was filled with history books and detective stories; on the mantelpiece were photographs of older people, Mary's parents possibly, posing in front of what looked like paper screens.

A sandy-haired man in outdoor clothes and white sneakers came in. He looked at Talissa warmly as he held out his hand, though she saw some shyness in his eyes. Mary came back into the room with a tray she put down on a table.

'Come on, you must have some,' she said, handing a plate to Talissa. 'Are we all packed up, Al?'

'These eggs are great,' said Talissa. 'How'd you get them so—'

'Trade secret,' said Mary.

'Butter,' said Alaric. 'Roughly half a pound. Have you got the checklist?'

'Right here,' said Mary. 'Is that all you're bringing? That little rucksack?'

'Yes, I . . . I don't have any . . . camping clothes,' said Talissa. 'And I wasn't sure what the weather's like in France.'

'Same as England, pretty much,' said Mary. 'I'll put another jumper in my bag for you. And a waterproof.'

Mary took the wheel and Alaric insisted Talissa sit alongside her in the front. Feeling like a child, Talissa relaxed and let the grown-ups take control. Her parents had never owned an automobile and neither had anyone else she knew in New York; almost every car she'd sat in had been a yellow cab.

On the train, a woman in a uniform urged their vehicle forward till it all but touched the one in front. Mary got out and opened the rear door, from which she produced a thermos of coffee. Alaric began to do a crossword. Once they were in France, Alaric switched his watch over to his right wrist, to remind him to drive on that side. Mary took the navigator's seat and Talissa moved into the back. It was not long before they were in flat French countryside with incomprehensible signs.

'Have some more Evian,' said Mary. 'You can get quite dehydrated in the car. Here you are. Then you can have a little sleep while we listen to one of Alaric's interminable history books. Or podcasts.'

'Sure thing.'

'Otherwise you'll have to hear his running commentary on the historical significance of the place on every signpost.'

'Hey! That's not—'

'You'll learn a lot, Talissa. It's better than college.'

Talissa settled back on the seat. After a time, the early start did begin to catch up with her and she closed her eyes, letting the words of the audiobook and Alaric's commentary merge in her head. Rouen: Joan of Arc on fire . . . Compiègne, a railway carriage in a wood . . .

She awoke to find they had stopped at a gas station. Alaric filled the car while Mary bought baguettes and cheese from the store.

'The key to finding a good place to camp,' said Alaric, restarting the engine, 'is not to be in a rush. So we don't drive after three o'clock. We should be deep in the *parc naturel* by then.'

The grey stone houses along the road looked primitive and

the villages sullen or withdrawn. In one, a group of three young men with bicycles stood outside a shuttered café, smoking. Mary and Alaric chattered about sunset, streams and wind direction.

They turned at the church onto a narrow road and drove on for ten minutes into ever-deepening woods and quietness.

'Do you need to get permission to put up a tent?' said Talissa. 'I mean, who does the land belong to?'

'It's fine,' said Alaric. 'France is a big country compared to England. Not so many angry farmers. As long as you don't frighten any livestock and you pick up all your litter.'

'What sort of livestock?' said Talissa.

'Hippopotamus. Giraffe. Wild buff—'

'Stop it, Alaric!' said Mary. 'He's teasing. Sometimes there are sheep or cows. But not here. We're in woodland, not grazing country.'

Alaric took the car off the lane and down a track into deeper woods. 'I think this is as far as we can go,' he said.

They got out and stood beneath a canopy of leaves. Apart from the ticking of the engine as it cooled, there was no sound. Alaric put his finger to his lips and all three of them listened to the silence. It was as if the branches above their heads had sucked not just the light from the sun but the noise of the world through the trunks from the earth below.

'Did you hear that?' said Mary.

'Hear what?' said Alaric.

'A trickle of water.'

'Well, the stream should be close. Just over that way. Let's get the tent up in this clearing and then we can think about a fire. And dinner. It'll get cold soon.'

'Can I help?' said Talissa.

'No, thanks,' said Mary. 'We're old hands. You go and stretch your legs after that long journey. By the time you come back we'll have everything sorted out.'

Talissa moved off, reluctantly. She had on some hiking boots she'd borrowed from Mrs Gopal, her daughter's cast-offs, but was aware that her jeans and sweatshirt, bought from a barrow on Canal Street, were too urban for the forest. Still, Mary and Alaric obviously wanted some time alone, so she'd put some distance between them.

She walked for five minutes, then clambered up a bank to find a place to sit. She could still just see a reflection of the sun in the windshield of the distant car. As she looked round, she noticed a fir tree that was taller than the others and stood alone. It would make a good landmark, she thought, as she walked towards it. From its shade, she could still see the mound on which she had sat and she knew that from there she could safely find the car. In the other direction, there was a passage through the undergrowth that led out into a more open space. It looked worth exploring. Once there, she found that the woods thinned into a field. While there was still cover, she squatted behind a tree and emptied her bladder of all the Evian that Mary had wished on her. Pulling up her jeans and checking that she could still see her lonesome pine, she set off again.

On the far side of the field there were signs of a terrain less wild, something like a park. Talissa tramped on, her black hair blowing out behind her. She was usually aware of landscape and nature only in so far as they had academic interest, as habitat or hunting ground; her own existence had been spent in a numbered city grid. Beyond the hedgerow was an iron fence, after which the ground fell away to a lake. At the edge of the water were some fallen beechnuts in their hairy

50

shells. She bent to pick one up and levered out the brown mast, whose tip she nibbled in her front teeth. Just like a *Homo vannesiensis*, she thought. The sun was going down and she decided to make her way back.

As she turned from the waterside, she saw a building on the rising ground: a grey stone place of innumerable rooms that even her French was good enough to know would be a *château*. It was about five minutes' walk away, too far to risk in the fading light, and anyway, she might be shot as a trespasser. Did French landowners keep guns, like Texans? She was sorry not to explore further, though: the building was decrepit, exuding, even at this distance, a tantalising sense of history and absences.

When she got back to the clearing, she found that a tent had been erected. The khaki colour of the canvas blended into the trees and someone had moved the car itself out of sight. Thin smoke was rising from a circle of gathered stones. Mary was setting out some collapsible canvas chairs; Alaric came out of the trees, dragging a couple of dry branches, which he began to break up and feed into the fire. It was starting to grow dark, and from the inexhaustible rear section of the estate car there came gas lamps and battery-powered torches.

'Right, Talissa,' said Alaric. 'Your job's to hold this lamp over the pan so I can see what I'm doing.'

Talissa did as she was told, occasionally stealing a glance through the tent flap to see what awaited her at bedtime. From his pocket, Alaric took out a piece of polished wood, from which he unfolded a blade. 'Opinel,' he said. 'French carbon steel. The best.' On a flat piece of bark, he chopped an onion and put it into a pan with leaves of thyme he shredded from their stalks and some oil from an old tonic water bottle. Then came the sausages, separated with a few lethal cuts of the knife, and the scent of fennel as they hit the oil. Mary unscrewed a bottle of red wine and passed it round in some enamelled cups.

'You look frozen,' she said. 'I'm going to get you that extra jumper now.'

Talissa swilled down some of the wine and tried not to cough. Alaric moved the pan to a cooler part of the fire to let the sausages cook through and sprinkled in a little of his wine to stop them burning. Talissa found the aroma quite exciting, as the overtones of alcohol mixed with the onions, herbs and charred skin of the sausages. When he was happy that the meat was cooked through, Alaric poured in a tin of cannellini, added some salt and a squeeze of garlic paste, stirred it in and moved the pan to one side, till it bubbled as gently as he wanted. Then he settled back in his chair to watch.

Over dinner, Talissa asked them what they hoped the baby's life would be. She was surprised by how much of it seemed to consist of hoping for the best.

'And you feel the world is all right for another child?' she said. 'You don't worry that we're burning up the planet? Another mouth to feed? And human beings apparently by nature so violent?'

'Well, I do worry,' said Mary. 'I worry that the child might be unhappy and that we won't be able to care for it in some way. I've seen how wretched life can be. All over the world. In our own country, too. But somehow . . . I don't know. For me, I think it's a way of saying yes to the world. I don't understand what we're doing here, in this life, but then nor does anyone else. But I feel fortunate to have been given a chance to breathe this air, for a short time. I want to be a part of nature, of the process. Especially since I so nearly wasn't.'

'I understand,' said Talissa.

'And you?' said Mary. 'Do you worry?'

'No. I wouldn't be a part of this scheme if I did. I have thought about it, though. And I think in the end it's . . . insignificant. It's just an act of love.'

'What more can you do?' said Alaric. 'Not have children? Sign out and say, That was not for me, that Life thing. Here comes the darkness again. Goodbye, everyone. Or hope to make a small addition. A good person, well loved.'

'I like that,' said Talissa. Emboldened by the wine, she almost squeezed his arm.

'Will you have children of your own one day?' said Mary.

'Oh boy. I don't know. I'd like to, I think. But only if I was sure of the father. I think a dad should stick around.'

'Tell us more about you,' said Mary.

'What?'

Mary laughed. 'Your life. You know. Who you are!'

Talissa smiled back, as she gave an edited version.

'And were you always a bit of a brainbox?'

'I was a slow starter. Then it took me a while after Dad died to focus again. But I got there. It's a question of finding something that interests you. Then the work's not work at all and you find you've done twice as much as you were asked.'

'And do you do much in the lab?'

'No, the DNA stuff is very specialised. I'm more of a big picture girl. Tools, art. Family trees. How they fit together. Which is why this new French find is so important. I do have to understand the basis of genetics, but the detail of what those guys do with their machines is beyond me.'

It was nearly ten when they made a move towards bed.

'We've cleared you a space here,' said Mary. 'And we've

given you the air mattress and this super-warm sleeping bag. I hope you'll be comfortable.'

'And what about you?'

'I've got this foam thing and Al likes to sleep on the ground. It's his Inuit blood.'

'So we're all in here . . . together?'

'Yes. Is that OK? We only have one tent, but it's quite roomy. Here, have some of this.' Talissa felt some tissue paper being pressed into her hand. 'Take this torch and just . . . You know. The woods are your friend.'

Talissa went off into the darkness, in the same direction as before, and squatted behind a tree. Emptying the bladder was one thing, but what about the bowel? She brushed her teeth and hoped that she could last until they reached a town with plumbing. And how was she to change her underwear the next day? Would she hide in the woods or wriggle in the sleeping bag? Dear God, please let them not be 'naturists'. There had been no talk of showers and clearly she'd be sleeping in her clothes. When she got back to the tent, she found that Mary and Alaric were already bedded down. They called out a friendly goodnight as she climbed over them and unzipped her bag. The wine seemed to numb her senses and she found herself drifting off with the smell of canvas in her nostrils.

The sound of a creature a few inches from her face awoke her. She was separated only by a layer of fabric from . . . A hippopotamus. No. But some large snuffling creature. A wild boar perhaps. A wolf. They'd reintroduced wolves, hadn't they? Like Montana. It had not disturbed the even breathing of the others. Talissa lay there for some minutes until her heart returned to normal. For a further hour she lay un-moving, all thoughts of sleep now gone. She looked at her handset to find it was still only 02:17. They would doubtless have a campers' early start, but there were still hours of the night to get through. Soon after three, she decided to get up. Taking a battery torch and Mary's thermal jacket from where it hung outside, she tiptoed away from the tent and up her previous path into the woods.

It was a relief to be away from the intimacy of others, as they rustled and grunted like creatures in a cave. The air outside was cold, but not unbearable; the trees and the undergrowth were reassuringly lifeless. She felt a stab of homesickness for the sidewalks of Harlem, but the night, now that she was walking briskly through it, held no fear. From the solitary tree, she struck off towards the field and the park beyond. It was only when she reached the lake that she knew where her feet were taking her. She crossed an overgrown lawn and came to a side door into the building. It was barred by two wooden planks nailed into a cross, but a minute later she found that the main entrance at the front of the house was jammed open. A chain with a padlock hung loose and weeds were growing up through the worn stone of the threshold. She shone her torch inside and pushed open the door. The double-height hallway bore the signs of having been partitioned into what might have been offices. It was hard to tell from the state of disrepair, with paint in blisters and wallpaper hanging like dry bandages peeled from a wound.

She felt the excitement of her vocation: the scent of humanity in a mysterious habitat, with something waiting to be understood. Her torch beam washed the walls and showed two staircases, one with smashed banisters and missing treads, but the other looking strong enough to take the weight of a slight, inquisitive American. The building had been converted, that was clear: from a once majestic residence to an institution. But what kind? And how many layers were there to dig?

Down a long corridor she came to rooms with numbers stencilled on the doors. Some seemed to have been dormitories, with the remains of iron bedsteads; others were more like narrow cells. The air was pungent and damp. Most of the walls were painted green up to a line at waist height, with flaking white above. In one of the larger spaces an old invalid chair stood alone beneath a broken window, with bent spokes protruding from the wheel.

A normal house, with its owners regularly out at work or on errands, was empty half its life, even before it was abandoned to the weeds. But this place was not normal. It felt as if some catastrophe had emptied it. On the second floor, there was a warren of smaller rooms, some missing their floorboards, showing joists that supported only air; there were internal windows in the corridors as if the inhabitants had needed to be watched. A small butane cylinder lay on the floor of one such room, and next to it the cardboard package of what looked like pizza. On the wall were spray-canned graffiti, in words she couldn't understand. Were they French or simply meaningless, like the swollen Esperanto of the subway? In any case, these vandals had obviously come later, after the place had been deserted.

She went out onto the landing, where a half flight of stairs led to a closed door. As she went up towards it, she heard a muffled banging from the other side. It seemed too random to be someone trying to communicate, but too rhythmic to be a window unfastened in the breeze; and anyway, it was a windless night.

The door was stiff, and Talissa had to put down the torch

while she pushed at it with both hands. She took half a pace back. A man was in the room, broad-chested, quite short, unkempt.

She felt no fear: more a sense of pity, a desire to help.

Bending down quickly, she grabbed the torch and pointed it into the gloom, but there was nothing left to see: only another empty room, with a narrow bed and bars on the window. A china lampshade hung on a flex from the ceiling.

The darkness must have misled her. The torch was powerful, the batteries new. Its beam showed nothing. Pulling the door shut behind her, she went back down into the hall. In a corner were some stone steps leading to what must be a basement. To prove to herself that she had not been frightened by what she'd seen, that she was still Fearless Frieda, scientist, she went downstairs.

Much of what was there had previously been stores and cellarage. There was a honeycomb of small rooms with stone wine bins, now empty, their openings closed over with cobwebs. Behind a door with stencilled markings, she found a room of shelving units. Some rotted cardboard packaging bore just discernible markings of a red cross, as if they had been medicines. There was a pair of large electrodes, shaped like the mouthpiece of an antique telephone. She could make out the words '*Ministère*' and '*Santé*'. There was a loud bang behind her.

A door slamming, she was fairly certain. Clearly, some air pressures had been altered by her opening and closing of other doors . . . It was time to get back to her new friends asleep in the tent. But as she was leaving, she saw that the corridor dropped half a level into a lower passageway, almost a tunnel. It was too intriguing to ignore, and she went down into it. The brick floor was wet and the walls were sweating a grey moisture. The darkness, even with the torch guiding, was intense. The tunnel seemed to reach a dead end with a metal door. As she came closer, Talissa saw that it belonged to an old elevator. She had seen such things in hundred-year-old buildings in New York.

What was odd was that she had seen no elevator shafts in the building higher up, no sign of any access on the first or second floors. Her torch picked out a small metal square in the elevator frame. She put her face close to it. It was grimed over with moss, but when she rubbed away the dirt with her finger, she saw the shape of an upward arrow. She pushed it. At once there came a clank and grinding, then a hungry whirr as though the mechanism had grabbed some source of power.

Something was coming down into the basement, and coming at speed. This time, she didn't linger, but turned and ran back up to the hall and out of the front door into the park.

8

After they had taken down the tent, or 'struck camp' as Alaric put it, there was some tidying up to be done. The stones that had ringed the fire were hurled into different parts of the wood and the tyre tracks of the car were smoothed over with a spade. It made Talissa feel sorry for researchers of the future who would puzzle over this primitive hearth. Occupational debris there was not.

In a small town, they stopped at a café with a bathroom out back. Talissa was too relieved to be critical of her first sight of mainland European plumbing. There was even hot water in the stained basin, if you waited. Refreshed, she joined the others and dipped a croissant into some coffee.

It was early afternoon when they arrived at the resting place of *Homo vannesiensis*. Local officialdom prevented them from getting more than a glimpse through barriers and tapes. Two young women in high-vis jackets stood guard over the path that led to the cave where the main find had been made, fifty feet below. It was still accessible, they said in English, by boat or on foot from a neighbouring beach, but only at low tide and with an appointment at the *mairie*. The best they could offer was an information kiosk on the top of the cliff, with photographs of the archaeologists at work, close-ups of femora and mandibles and links to further reading.

In the car on the way back, Talissa told them that the site had first been identified by two teenage brothers walking the family dog along the beach one evening. They had noticed a flint among the granite rocks at the foot of the cliff. The nearest flint formations were fifty miles away, so it must have been brought in as a butchering tool. About a quarter of a million years ago.

'Good spot,' said Alaric. 'Scout cadets, I expect.'

'I remember it well,' said Mary. 'There was a huge fuss in the news.'

'Of course,' said Talissa. 'It was an important find.'

'And that tabloid headline,' said Alaric.

'What was that?' said Talissa.

'Well,' said Mary, 'after they'd done some research, they suggested that this human would have had quite pale skin and would have been loutish and aggressive. The headline said something like, "Say Hello to Our New Great-Grandad . . . White Vannes Man".'

Two days later, back in London, Talissa was called by Dr Catrina Olsen and invited to a meeting in her office.

'It's all about the timing,' Dr Olsen said. 'Would you like a biscuit?'

'Timing?'

'Yes. When we implant the embryo, we need the precise point when your womb will be the most hospitable. It's the eighth or ninth day of your cycle. Once we have a date, we know when to start giving Mary her treatments. Then her

60

ovaries will mature every egg available to them so they're ready on exactly the right day for you.'

'How come?'

'She has injections and oral treatments to make that happen.'

'And what about the father?'

'He's on standby. We tell him to bottle things up for a bit so he can produce a decent volume. It's easy enough for men.'

'I see,' said Talissa. She thought of Mrs Gopal and her sad face when she'd said of her young children: 'I told you. They don't exist any more.'

'So,' Dr Olsen was saying, her blue eyes sparkling, 'we ask if you'd take some hormone replacement medication to synchronise your cycle with Mary's.'

'But why? If you know when my eighth day is coming, why can't you start her treatment so it syncs?'

'Well, it makes us able to be more precise. And women's cycles do vary a little from month to month.'

'Mine doesn't,' said Talissa. 'You could set your watch by it.'

Eventually she persuaded Dr Olsen to depend on her punctuality.

'We can manage,' said Dr Olsen. 'But we'll need to do the occasional blood test to double-check which hormones are active.'

'That's fine,' said Talissa.

'Do you have any other concerns?'

'None at all. I mean, I presume the implantation won't hurt.'

'No. It's a very narrow probe that's inserted. Long, but thinner than a knitting needle. So it's not like a—'

'Got it.'

*

61

Back in Muswell Hill, she explained it all to Mrs Gopal, who had become intensely interested. Talissa had discovered that her landlady's first name was Kavya, but some diffidence prevented her from using it, even as they became close over long talks in the kitchen while Mrs G prepared another of the dinners she insisted on sharing.

She showed Talissa how to cook rice by flavouring it with stock and spices and cinnamon sticks, then leaving it alone on a heat diffuser over the lowest flame without ever being tempted to lift the heavy lid. There were instructions on how to use coconut milk to make a curry out of cashew nuts or even garlic.

'You make it out of garlic? Just whole garlic cloves?'

'Oh yes, it's one of my favourites. It's not an Indian dish, it's from Sri Lanka. Don't forget the half lime at the end.'

Talissa enjoyed it when they talked about cooking. Mrs G was also good on families and the strangeness of life; she just needed to be kept off politics.

On the day before the implantation was due, Kavya Gopal made Talissa a special dinner with half a dozen vegetable dishes and a couple of crackling poppadoms alongside. Nothing too strongly spiced, she said, to avoid any indigestion. When Talissa departed for Russell Square in the morning, Mrs Gopal gave her a slim paperback.

'You always have to sit around in these places,' she said. 'Here's something to take your mind off things.' The book was called *Beside Myself, Beside the Sea: Tales from a Tamil Nadu Childhood*. Talissa seldom read anything that was not related to work and found the collection so beguiling that she only just made it out through the closing tube train doors at Russell Square.

She gave her name to the receptionist and waited in the ground-floor area, which was filled with orange-upholstered sofas and armchairs, scattered with soft, sage-green cushions. There were some fashion magazines on the coffee table, but no indication of what the purpose of the building was. Talissa seemed to be the only patient there. The others who came and went, bleeping themselves through the glass turnstiles, were clearly staff members: geneticists and researchers on their way to the main labs and offices on the ground floor. The chairs in the waiting area were comfortable, the water from the cooler was fresh and cold; an abundance of money seemed to have smoothed the edges of existence.

A few days earlier, Alaric and Mary had had their appointment. Mary was the first to be called from the waiting area. She and Alaric hugged, a little tearfully, as they wished each other luck. Twenty minutes later, it was Alaric's turn.

'This way, please, sir,' said a nurse, and escorted him through a white door marked 'Private'. They were in an internal corridor with several small rooms protected by locks with punch-in number codes. It was clean without being sterile; you wouldn't necessarily have known it was a health facility at all, thought Alaric. There were no half-finished coffee cups on top of swing-bin frames with saggy black liners; it was not like the place where he'd made his first donation. The nurse knocked at a plain white door and waited. When there was no reply, she pushed in the code.

'How's your day been so far?' she said.

'So far, so good. But the best is yet to come,' said Alaric.

The room was small and bare, with a small computer screen on a wall bracket. There were no magazines.

'How long is it since your last emission?' asked the nurse.

'Oh, ages.'

'More than three days?'

'Much more.'

'Good. Now I just need to double-check some details to make sure there are no errors.'

'I should hope not,' said Alaric. 'Don't want to be fathering a child with someone else's wife! Poor kid. I mean, poor woman and—'

'Your wife's name is Mary Pedersen, as shown here on this pot?'

'Yes.'

'And this is your name and date of birth?'

'Yes.' Alaric's birthday was 4 November, but he managed not to make a firework joke.

'Good, so now we stick on a barcode and you're all set. You can use the material available here. Let me just switch it on. We have a subscription to this channel. It's a little bit more upmarket than some. Here we are.' She handed him a small plastic pot with Mary's name on it. There was no funnel or wooden scraper as there had been at the NHS clinic.

'Just put the pot in this dish and press the call button here when you've finished.'

She went out and closed the door.

In his office, Malik Wood checked the contents of his jeans pocket, pulled on some pale blue scrubs over his day clothes and went downstairs to the laboratory.

Looking up from her bench, Ayesha Cross, the senior embryologist, said, 'To what do we owe this—'

'Just making sure you're all happy in your work this morning.'

A few minutes later, the call button from the donor room caused a light to come on.

'Don't worry, Ayesha. I'll get it,' said Malik Wood.

'All right, Dr Wood. Thank you.' She raised an eyebrow.

Wood went down the corridor to the locked donor room, knocked and listened. He put in the number code and went into the empty space.

The pot was in the kidney dish, full to a depth of about a centimetre. Wood pushed down the waistband of his scrubs and from the pocket of his jeans beneath pulled out an identical but unlabelled pot that was full to a similar level. He took the original offering and stuck a yellow note on the outside so he wouldn't see the donor's name. Then, with his fingernail he peeled off the clinic label and barcode, and transferred them to the pot he had brought in. He smoothed the corner of the adhesive label where he had raised it with his nail so it sat smooth against the plastic. He shoved the initial pot (Alaric's, though he still hadn't seen the name) and the yellow stick-on inside his jeans pocket, pulled up his scrubs and went back to the laboratory.

'Here we are, Ayesha,' he said, holding out the replacement sample. 'Don't forget to cross-check the labels.'

'Thank you, Dr Wood. What service.'

Although IVF was a minor part of the Parn's activity, the embryology suite had been built to Malik Wood's specifications. In the course of an international career, he had seen facilities where large tanks marked 'Sperm 2' or 'Embryo 3' had been parked in the corridor or once, unforgettably, in the cafeteria. They could do better than that, he insisted. He was ashamed of the week his office had been used as a sperm bank while building work in the proper store was completed. Someone took a picture of the interim arrangement and pinned it up as a memento of how not to do things.

In addition to the passenger lifts, there were electric dumb waiters for shifting samples quickly between levels. On the lower-ground floor, behind double wooden doors with iron inlays, was the finished storage area in which potential humans of the future were held in liquid nitrogen at minus 196 degrees.

The important action took place on the first floor. A small operating theatre where the mother's eggs could be collected was joined to the lab by a hatch through which they would be passed in bloody liquid form in a glass tube. They were then poured into a small petri dish, where they could be counted under a microscope. Numbers were shouted back and forth through the hatch. 'We have six eggs!' 'Eight!' There was an air of urgency.

The chosen egg could be surrounded by the father's cells, leaving the most determined swimmer to penetrate the membrane, as in nature. Dr Wood, however, preferred the 'ICSI' method by which one of the embryologists injected a single sperm into an egg, using a Magnon Eclipse T*i*4 micromanipulator. The ejaculate was washed in a centrifuge and resuspended in a watery solution to leave only the spermatozoa. These could be viewed through a microscope and counted with a hand-operated clicker. Some looked frisky, some indolent; about half didn't move at all. But from the manic to the inert, Dr Wood told his team, they gave a snapshot of society.

Working the micromanipulator was simpler than it looked, he told anyone who asked – to the irritation of Ayesha Cross and others who actually did the job. The little red joystick was geared so that quite strong hand movements resulted in minuscule adjustments at the sharp end, under the lens. Once the piercing had taken place, the chosen sperm was hydraulically despatched down the needle's core by the rotation of a chrome-covered knob on the left-hand side of the machine. The process was repeated several times. The fertilised eggs were then arranged in a circular plastic dish that was placed into an incubator the size of a desktop printer with six vertical compartments, each one bearing the name of a patient. On a small screen on the front of the apparatus, time-lapse photographs showed the division of the cells and the formation of an embryonic *Homo sapiens*. The embryo would break out of its shell on the seventh day, but before then, on day five, the chosen candidate would be put back into the surrogate. The other embryos were sent to be stored in the cold tanks downstairs for future use. 'You can always have fraternal twins,' Dr Wood told the mothers, 'but we prefer that you have them two years apart.'

Talissa was deep in a story of seaside Pondicherry when she was finally called and taken upstairs.

'If you'd just like to pop in here and use the toilet first,' said the nurse. 'Then I'll take you through.'

The room where it was to be done was internal, with no window, though it had a hatch, which opened into the lab next door. There was a large reclining chair, like a dentist's, with additional leg rests. Beside it was a table with instruments and an ultrasound screen.

'Now if you'd like to pop your clothes off. Everything below the waist. You can keep your top on. Then pop them over here. I'll be back in a minute with Dr Olsen.'

Talissa 'popped' her jeans and underwear onto the stool, then sat in the dentist's chair, on which someone had laid a protective sheet of paper.

The wall opposite was blank. She had expected pictures of happy babies, beaming mothers, even teddy bears. Perhaps the modest success rate of the procedure made it unwise to raise people's hopes; but there was something a little off-putting in the bare, magnolia-painted plaster of the wall.

There was a knock on the door, and Catrina Olsen put her head round.

'Can I come in?'

'Absolutely.'

'This is my colleague Alex du Plessis, who'll be watching the screen with us. And Ivy you've met,' she said, indicating the nurse.

'Yes.'

'Everything's gone swimmingly through there,' said Dr Olsen. 'So we're ready when you are. Do you have any questions before I begin?'

'I don't think so. We've been through it all so many times.'

'Of course. So if you put your legs up here. That's right. Now shift your tail bone so . . . No, not that way . . . Forward a bit. *That's* it. You comfortable?'

'Yes.' As much as she could be.

Dr Olsen crossed the room to the hatch. When she returned, she was wearing a surgical mask, gloves and what looked like goggles. She sat on a stool. 'A tiny bit of cream here . . . Just relax . . .'

Talissa thought how Felix would hate to be witnessing this. She felt the thin probe and thought of how she herself had been conceived in a bed in the Bronx, probably late one night. She thought of how much her father might have liked to see a child of hers. She imagined Kavya Gopal's children, no longer what they were, but changed into other versions of themselves, the prototype lost in time. And although she was happy to be helping, she felt also a momentary, unaccountable grief.

PART TWO

2031

1

To Alaric's delight, it was a boy. He was born without incident in a room on the top floor of the Parn after a labour
lasting eight hours, in the course of which Talissa needed
only mild pain relief. When the placenta had been delivered,
she was examined and cleaned up; there was no need for
stitches, the obstetrician told her, and after drinking some
herbal tea she fell into a deep sleep while the baby was given
a first feed of her colostrum. An hour or so later, Mary went
in and pushed back a strand of hair from Talissa's forehead,
choking on her emotion but determined not to wake this fearless young woman.

Mary went and sat in the sunlight in a room down the hall,
overlooking Russell Square, holding the baby while a nurse
handed her a bottle. Alaric sat beside her, his eyes shining,
stunned with pride.

'Ugly little bugger, isn't he?'

'Shh,' said Mary. 'He's perfect.'

Talissa was discharged the next day and took a taxi up to
Muswell Hill, but Mary slept in a second night while they ran
tests on the baby. Alaric came and brought her some sandwiches he'd made at home with Cheddar and sliced tomato.

'Have you heard from Talissa?' he asked.

'Yes, she rang this afternoon. She said she was feeling great. She had to come back here for another test or two, but she's already got her ticket home.'

'I'll miss her,' said Alaric. 'I've never met anyone quite like her before.'

'We'll stay in touch, I'm sure. And after twelve years she can meet the little guy.'

'If she wants to. She'll probably have a family of her own by then.'

'Do you think?' said Mary. 'She doesn't strike me as the maternal type.'

'That's an odd thing to say, in the circumstances.'

'But you know what I mean.'

'I do. It's what made her so right for the job. She told me once it was just like looking after a friend's house while they're on holiday.'

'Talking of houses . . .'

'Yes,' said Alaric. 'I collected the keys this morning. You do understand, don't you, that it's not such a great area.'

'Yes, yes, we've been through this. But the garden. Long enough to kick a ball in.'

'Yes.'

'And an attic. Big enough for—'

'For anything, really.'

Mary laughed. 'All aboard!'

'We'll see. Have you decided on the name?'

'Yes, I have,' said Mary. 'If you're OK with it, I'd like to call him Seth.'

'Seth? Was he someone in the Bible?'

'He was the son of Adam. After Cain murdered Abel in the

field. Adam, when he was a hundred and thirty years old, had another son, a sort of replacement for Abel.'

'Legend! How do you know all this?'

'Bible study. In one version, Adam also had four boys with Lilith. So Seth was his seventh son.'

'Who the hell's Lilith?'

'Adam's first wife. A real hot number, according to one of the Hebrew apocrypha.'

'If you say so.'

Mary laughed. 'But really it's just because I like the name.'

'So do I,' said Alaric. 'Seth Pedersen. Sounds reliable. Nice guy. Lend you his lawnmower.'

In Muswell Hill, Talissa packed her bag to return to New York. Kavya Gopal watched her, sitting on the bed.

'Have you got somewhere to live?'

'Yeah, I have a place in Boston starting in October. It's kind of a loft in the Allston district. It's a student neighbourhood, but it looks pretty cool. Until then I'll stay with my friend Susan. It's not long.'

'What about your boyfriend?'

Talissa laughed. 'We'll have to see how that goes. I don't think you really liked him, did you, Kavya?' She had finally managed to call her landlady by her first name.

'He's very handsome.'

'That's not enough, is it? What did you really think?'

'He only visited twice, so I couldn't really—'

'Don't tell me you're not going to have an opinion! Not just when I'm leaving.'

Mrs Gopal smiled. 'Maybe he thinks about himself too much.'

'I guess most people do. It's about how you disguise it.'

'Some things you just can't . . . Anyway, my American friend. Are you feeling strong?'

'Strong? Yes. I never felt better. I slept a lot in that room at the clinic. It was super-comfortable. I got some exercises to do. But they were happy with me. A young mother, you see. Just made for the job.'

'And how do you feel about the baby? About saying goodbye.'

'I didn't say goodbye, Kavya, because I never said hello. I never even really got a look at him.'

'And that's OK? Are you sure?'

Talissa stood up. 'I told you. I never engaged, like, emotionally. It was someone else's kid. Their project, their life. If ever I wavered for a second, I just told myself that it was none of my business. I was the house-sitter.'

'And will you ever get to meet him?'

'When he's twelve years old, they say. If I want to.'

'And will you want to?'

Mrs Gopal also stood up, so she was facing Talissa.

'I can't . . . I can't say.'

The older woman opened her arms for a moment. Talissa moved in gratefully and held on to her.

'Your heart's beating so hard,' said Mrs Gopal.

Talissa stepped back. 'Bullshit! Let's do this thing. Let's pack.'

'It's time for some tea. You won't have proper tea when you get home, will you?'

'Not like your tea, no. But you'll bring me some when you come and visit, won't you?'

Kavya Gopal looked out of the window. 'I expect so. You'll have forgotten who I am by then.'

76

'Nonsense. How could I forget? When you talked me through my first contractions? To say nothing of my first samosa.'

'I'll come to Boston if the taxman hasn't taken all my money. Who voted for these idiots?'

'Would you give me a hand with this zip, Kavya? I've picked up so much junk. Honestly . . .'

The new house was further out of town, but closer to Mary's work and only five minutes more on the bus for Alaric to get to school. It had a pebbledash finish and ugly uPVC windows at the front, but it had plenty of space inside. Alaric fitted up a room for Seth next to his and Mary's. They'd bought an old wooden cot with flaking paint from a junk shop and he stripped it back to the pine, then rehung the side so it slid up and down more easily. The walls of the room had to be rubbed down before they could be repainted, so the air on the landing was filled with dust. 'It's all about the preparation,' he told Mary when she complained. 'Any fool can slap on paint.' Then he bought yards of MDF from the local superstore. For days, he measured, marked and sawed, before he set about making a toy cupboard with soft-close hinges. More clouds of, this time slightly toxic, particles billowed out of the room; but every screw was countersunk so no rough edge should scratch the fingers of the little prince. It was painted red and blue, the colour of the local football team. It was a miracle of rare device, he told himself, as he sat back on his heels; now they needed only trains and cars and wooden building bricks to fill it.

Since she herself had difficulties with dairy products, Mary fed Seth on a soy-based formula that the Parn had recommended. It seemed to go down well with the baby, and his early health checks were normal. He slept through the night in a wicker basket on a stand by her bed and sometimes she put out her hand to feel the regular swell of his breathing. She marvelled at the solid width of his ribcage. After the windows of his room had been left open for two weeks and she was sure there were no paint fumes left, she entrusted him to the cot. When she went in at six the following morning, exhausted from worry, she found him still asleep with the cellular blanket unruffled round his shoulders. She lifted him up under the arms and he opened his unfocused eyes and gazed toothlessly at her, or anyway, in her direction.

There was a call from an NHS health visitor, with a notebook in a red easy-wipe cover, who weighed Seth on a portable scale. The trips to the Parn involved more modern machines and what seemed to Mary an extraordinary amount of blood, albeit taken in single drops from a fingertip. Seth seemed not to mind the pinprick so long as there was a bottle to follow. On the top deck of the bus home, Mary pointed out the sights to him – though he only ever looked at the finger itself, not at the sights to which it tried to guide him.

The weeks melted into months, the rhythm of Alaric's work easing the passage of time. Mock exams; half-term; set reports due . . . His colleagues asked after the baby and eventually, when he was four months old, Mary brought him in to the staffroom, still swaddled and with a face swollen red from sleep and crying. The women said how sweet he looked, the men gripped his fingers and asked again how old he was. 'He looks like his mum,' said Rose Paxton, the glamorous head of science. 'Looks like every other kid,' said Bob Tainsley when they'd gone.

Soon after his first birthday, Seth took his first steps in Eden

Park. It started evenly enough, then there were spurts and staggers before he regained his balance and his dignity, like a drunken sailor on shore leave. Mary returned to the kitchen at her sports club, but her varying shifts and Alaric's long holidays and early finishes meant they needed little outside help.

Mary bought clothes from recommended shops and young mothers' groups, aware that she was one of the less young ones. Just as all the talk of her 'eggs' when she was preparing for the treatment had made her feel like a battery hen, now the mothers' talk of 'socialising' their children made Seth sound like a puppy. But she was happy to take him to playgroups and nurseries, where he met other children with their different hair and skin and clothes and voices and individual ways of being. Mary sat on the edge of the room and watched, feeling like a visitor to a Victorian menagerie as they ran and fell and fought. Seth seemed more self-reliant than most, quite focused on the game he wanted, but reluctant to co-operate.

When he began to talk, his voice was high and pure. The imperative was his mood of choice and Mary became accustomed to doing as instructed. He was a solemn little boy. It was not that he couldn't laugh when he saw something funny on a screen or in the room, but in his interaction with his parents he seemed to feel no urge to smile.

Alaric casually introduced him to storybooks and films about trains: diesels and steam engines with rosy cheeks, though Seth treated them all with indifference. What excited him was next door's cat, a stray called Nettle, in whom no other human had ever shown an interest. Seth would point out the cat in the garden and try to stroke her if she came over the fence, though she ran away when he approached. To make up for the persistent rebuffs, Mary bought him a soft toy cat with black and white fur that was subject to his scrutiny and rough handling. It lived on the solid chestnut boat bed that Alaric had bought from a salvage yard and reconditioned when Seth outgrew the cot.

Between the ages of three and four, he began to show affection for his parents, becoming anxious when Mary prepared to leave the house. 'Don't go out,' he ordered when he saw her putting on her work clothes. 'Stay with Ess!' – which was the name he gave himself.

He liked wrestling with Alaric and being suspended over the banisters or thrown down with pretend force on the bed. Visitors to the house were treated with suspicion, and he would stare at them, unblinking, till they left.

'He's starting to develop a character all right,' Alaric told his colleagues at work, without saying that the character Seth was developing was rather an odd one. His affection for the child was such that he could barely admit this to himself, though in the course of a check-up at the Parn, Mary did muster the courage to ask if they were sure that Seth was (she had checked the word) 'neurotypical'. The doctor assured her that in some respects Seth was rather advanced and that any divergence from the norm was unremarkable.

Eventually, there came the question of school. The local primary seemed fine to Alaric, run by a stern matriarchy and with pupils from all over the world. Seth was one of the youngest in the reception class and to Mary's anxious eye appeared to be among the smallest, too. He was a thickset boy with wide ribs and short legs that neither of his parents wanted to take responsibility for, though Mary told her husband that his own mountain-dwelling ancestors had surely played a part. The hundreds of small children who swarmed between the modern buildings over the playground with its rubberised asphalt represented every variation of humanity and recognised no differences between themselves. Only the parents who came to walk them home worried that their child might be singled out for having some identifying mark that made them a fraction too different.

Seth himself was unconcerned with such things. Football was what mattered. He watched it upstairs on a screen. He recognised the red and blue stripes of Crystal Palace from the colours of his toy cupboard and felt a passionate delight in their movements. He beat the floor with his hand as he urged them on.

2

Boston was fine, even if it wasn't New York. From her room high up in a block on the south side, Talissa gazed out towards the Charles River. She was expecting Felix for the evening and wasn't sure how to behave.

They had seen each other on her return from London, but she could tell at once that something had changed, irreversibly. He had talked for a long time about someone called Jada, a woman he had apparently become close to. Her family was difficult to deal with, he said, because of 'cultural differences'.

'You could have come to London more often,' Talissa had said.

'I came when I could. Any time work allowed. But I didn't feel at ease in your apartment there.'

'Why not? I made the room all homey for you. I bought your favourite beer. Or don't you like that one any more?'

'No, it's fine.'

'What was it then?'

'I knew your landlady was judging me. She was saying bad things about me.'

'Don't be crazy. You're bigger than that.'

Talissa thought she knew what had happened. She had put her work before her emotional life: before *him*. Felix must have felt that she had shown where her priorities were. She could hardly blame him. He had also told Leon, who told Susan, who at once passed it back to Talissa, that he felt betrayed. She had, after all, had a child with another man.

She had tried to win him back by gentleness and flattery, by being kind and not hoping for too much. She was not going to give up on the other half of her because of that one misjudged conversation in which she had become suddenly self-conscious, like a tightrope walker who looks down. Yet from her side, that was how it looked.

She remembered bits of conversation from the early days, when they lay still after making love. 'What are you listening for?' 'Your breathing,' he said. 'If there's any catch in it I know I haven't done my job.' 'And now?' 'As clear as a southern breeze.' These were the moments when she had felt filled with a peace that could never be broken – but which through her impulsiveness she had apparently squandered.

This could happen, it seemed. You ruined it, your one big chance at love, by inexperience, at the age of twenty-six. The rest of your life would be a shadow play.

Her two-year position as a paid postdoc had been renewed by the Helen Lingard Institute, though this was now her final year and she had been promised an assistant professor job when she returned to New York in the fall. She had her own loft apartment in Boston now, only one room, but spacious, with a screened-off sleeping area, a queen bed and a balcony with a river view, if you strained your eyes a little. The HLI was on Prospect Street in Cambridge, between the headquarters of HubSpot and MediPlus, and took about a half hour's walk from where she lived, over the bridge with its new cycle and pedestrian paths that had halved the traffic going past the old Mobil gas station. She used the time to gear herself up for the challenges of work. The research group consisted of six people and she sometimes felt she was the least gifted of them all. There was a competition to impress the boss, Kristof Landor, a Hungarian émigré of terrifying intellect with a way of moving his head suddenly on its axis, like a hawk.

At a party in Landor's Back Bay house, Talissa had met a cousin of his, Aron, who worked in construction. 'They got the brains. My side of the family got the brawn,' he told her over a large bourbon, clutching his glass in a paper napkin. For a year afterwards, she met Aron in the small apartment at his head office or in a white clapboard inn near the golf course at Brookline, where he seemed happy to indulge her playful fantasies. His own demands were always the same, that she pretend to be a dental nurse as he gazed down her shirt front. He liked to use the language of his business when they fixed their next rendezvous. 'Site visit Tuesday?' The construction business offered no end of erotic double meanings; they made her smile, though she drew the line at having their liaison described as a 'servicing agreement'. Aron Landor was a simple guy, Talissa thought, which was one of the reasons she enjoyed his company, until his wife became suspicious. 'This project's done, missis,' he told Talissa in the end. 'I'm real sorry. I'm handing in the keys.' 'I know,' she said, kissing his cheek. 'It's been a pleasure, mister.' And so it had been, to fool around with no thought of children, no entanglements, just a pulse of secret anticipation at the HLI on the days when she'd be heading out to see him. It had helped her to think less about Felix and the fact that their love affair had lasted only ten months.

As the big dinner day came near, she had begun to worry that she couldn't remember what Felix liked to eat. Beer was what he drank, craft beer to be precise – Desperado, Copperneck and others easy to track down in the specialist stores in her neighbourhood. She made a salad with butter lettuce and grilled shrimp and a dressing she'd invented, with sides of cornbread and yellow tomatoes of a strain that had been rescued from extinction, the deli guy said, by growers in Oregon. On a last-minute impulse, she dashed to the spice store and also made a cashew nut curry, consulting the recipe that was still on her handset. She squeezed in half a lime at the end and raised a glass to Mrs G.

She had almost forgotten how beautiful he was. That soft skin, the thing her genes had first cried out for; then the loose curls and the narrow wrists that led to those hands . . . broad but with delicate fingers that, when he was in the mood, were able to carve thoughts in the air. She felt as if she might faint, and made up her mind to appear indifferent.

He kissed her, turned away and looked out of the window.

After a minute, Talissa said, 'What are you staring at?'

'See that car down there?' he said.

'Which one?' She crossed to the window.

'The black town car. The one parked in front of the warehouse.'

'Yes, I see it.'

'Who does it belong to?'

'How should I know? I never saw it before.'

Felix went and sat down on the sofa.

'Let me get you a beer,' said Talissa. 'You seem a little distracted.'

'We're on the verge of this huge deal, you know.'

'That's good. Did the big investor come through?'

'They turned against us.'

'But there's others?'

'There's a lot of interest. We're taking offices in Murray Hill.'

'That'll be expensive.'

'People let you down.'

During dinner, he seemed to find it hard to concentrate and changed the topic, seemingly at random, but perhaps in accordance with a logic that Talissa couldn't see.

'Are you still in the same place with your Brooklyn couple?' she asked, trying to get him onto familiar things.

'They didn't renew. They'd been planning to move in a friend of theirs all along. They didn't tell me.'

'So, where are you living now?'

He looked at her hard, as if for the first time. 'I live in Queens.'

'Is it a nice place? A house or what?'

'It's OK.'

'Do you like the shrimp?'

'What? I don't like shrimp. What's this?'

'It's cashew nut curry. I got the recipe from my landlady in London.'

'She was not a good person. She told lies.'

'Don't be ridiculous. Kavya was like a mother to me. As long as you kept her off politics, she was great company as well.'

'She was always saying bad things. She was a schemer.'

'Bullshit. You shouldn't talk like that about people you don't know.'

Felix was looking at the underside of a plate. 'Where are these from?' he said.

'They came with the apartment.'

'I think they're from Dresden.'

'Maybe that's the style. I didn't know you were a ceramics expert.'

'People pay millions for these waterfront properties. We sold one to the MediPlus chief executive. For twelve million. He's going to put a pool in.'

'What do you mean you sold it? You in Boston real estate now?' Talissa laughed.

'That woman told me.'

'Which woman?'

Felix didn't answer.

Talissa stood up and poured herself some wine. 'Would you like to know what I've been up to?'

There was no reply, but Talissa told him anyway, omitting the visits to Brookline and the old-style underwear that was apparently standard for a dental nurse.

'So I aim to be back in New York in September . . . Did you hear that? Felix?'

'OK.'

'Would you like some dessert? I got this from the French patisserie. Or I have organic cheese from a local farm. In Fairhaven or somewhere.'

'I'm not hungry.'

When she came to look more closely, he did look thin.

'How's Jada by the way?'

'She was unfaithful.'

'I'm sorry to hear that. Though I guess it spares you those "cultural issues".'

'I'm with Desirée now.'

'Who's Desirée?'

'Jada's sister.'

'Jesus. Is that a good idea?'

Felix didn't answer but stood up again and walked over to the window. 'Sonofabitch is still there,' he said.

Talissa went and stood beside him. A terrible fear was creeping up in her. 'My love,' she said, putting her hand on his arm, the beautiful arm that used to hold her. 'Will you tell me just what's going on?'

Felix said, 'They must have called ahead from Penn Station when they saw me get the train.'

'But why are they following you?'

'My phone's bugged. My messages.'

'Have you called the police?'

'They have the police in their pocket. What do you think those lobbyists are doing up on Capitol Hill? Making sure they pay no tax. That's just for the little guys. The girl on the checkout. They pay the taxes so the system stays in place.'

'You sound like a hippy or something.'

'It's how it works. They don't just read your messages, you know.'

'And how do you know this? Who told you?'

'I'm smarter than they think.'

Talissa poured herself more wine. Whatever she had expected, it wasn't this. Felix talked for another hour in his urgent yet toneless voice, yawing and banking in the breeze of his thoughts, driven on by some narrative reasoning that was hidden from Talissa, though compelling to him. She tried to help by suggesting connections between the men in the car, the woman who told him things, the investors who had let him down and other actors in his life. He was too impatient to explain and brushed her questions away. For Talissa, it was like coming in on the end of a long spy movie and trying to catch up on who was on which side and who'd said what to who and why and what the hell it all added up to.

By the end of the evening, it was clear to her that there was no point in searching for the lost pieces of a complicated jigsaw. What had gone missing was Felix.

The next day she called Susan.

'I don't know, T. He was always a little weird, wasn't he?'

'What do you mean? You introduced us!'

'Yeah, I know. He was OK back then. His dreams and schemes were kind of what made him attractive, weren't they? They were part of the package.'

'He was so romantic.'

'That's what I'm saying. But then, I guess . . . things kind of got the better of him.'

'What does Leon say?'

'I haven't seen Leon in almost six months.'

'But they were close, right?'

'Yeah, in a guy way. I'm not sure they ever, like, really confided.'

'I don't know what to do,' said Talissa. 'I feel there's something badly wrong.'

'You think? It's not just macho bullshit? They have their pride, you know. And if it's not worked out for him in business, he'll have to make up some weird excuses.'

'It's not like that. He believes this shit. He believes it so much he can't concentrate on what's actually in the room.'

'OK, honey, I'll take your word for it. I haven't seen the poor guy in months. Don't cry, T-T.'

'I'm not crying. But I am upset.'

'Of course you are.'

'We were lovers. We were . . . I knew he was flaky. I didn't always trust him. But I . . . I took his part. I wanted it all to work out for him. I loved him.'

She'd never said these words before, she thought, not even to Felix.

'I know you did, honey.'

Talissa breathed in.

'You still there?' said Susan.

'Sure. But if I interfere, he might think I'm trying to get back with him or something.'

'But you are, aren't you? Does he still have feelings for you?'

'I don't know. He started talking about something else straight away. He didn't really engage with me all evening. He never asked me how I was.'

'So. No feelings.'

'Not for me,' said Talissa. 'Not for anyone, I think.'

'Hasn't he got someone else?'

'Well, there's someone called Desirée, who's the sister of his ex. Jada. But I wasn't that convinced.'

'Who the hell is Jada?'

'Someone whose family he had "cultural differences" with. Don't laugh.'

'I never met the woman. Never heard of her.'

'Perhaps it was a secret affair.'

'Listen,' said Susan. 'I'll call him.'

'Won't he think that's weird?'

'No. He was my friend first, remember? It's OK. I'll suggest we meet up. Maybe invite Leon, too. I should see Leon anyway. I don't like to leave things hanging. So I'll meet with them and call you back.'

'I like you, Kojak.'

'Thanks. How's your love life anyway?'

'I have no love life. I'm an anthropologist. I view people scientifically.'

'What about that builder guy? Has he hung up his power t—'

'Call me.'

It was a joke going back to the ninth grade that Talissa was a femme fatale with insatiable appetites while Susan was the chaste and practical one. It had not been true then and it was not true now, thought Talissa – though as she'd passed the age of thirty, who knew? A friend of her mother's had told her that her romantic life had only started to blossom in her fifties.

For the moment, she felt no need for someone. Occasionally she wondered if, without Felix, she was better off alone anyway: the absence gave her something to idealise and long for. When she was a sophomore, a college counsellor had told her this was because her father had died when she was young and she had become determined that no one should replace him. 'OK,' said Talissa. 'If you say so. But I only came by to get a vitamin supplement.'

She didn't think about Seth. Mary had messaged and sent a photograph in the first week, but Talissa had asked her not to send any more. There was something about the way Seth looked that made her feel unhappy: he was familiar yet unfamiliar. Perhaps it was only that he looked so little like her. The picture made her feel anxious and she put it away in a drawer.

Anyway, the protocol was that there should be no contact until he was twelve and it was there for a reason. He was Mary's son.

Susan called to say she had met with Leon and Felix. It seemed they had had a lot to drink in a bar in Tribeca, then gone to a steakhouse in Brooklyn. Felix didn't make much sense, she said, but wanted to be left alone. He had moved to an apartment on Park Avenue, apparently. After dinner, she and Leon took the subway north together. Leon said he thought Felix had been referred to a psychiatrist, but he'd seen him only once; he was pretty sure the Park Avenue apartment didn't exist and that Felix was still in Queens. She and Leon had another drink back at her place and one thing had led to another, so the evening had not been a complete write-off, Susan said. 'I'm pleased to hear it,' said Talissa.

In June, she packed up her stuff and, in the Allston tradition, left what she didn't want out on the street for next year's undergrads to help themselves. In the summer, she took a backpack and a small tent up into the Adirondacks, having discovered that camping was really not that bad. She didn't cook on a fire as well as Alaric did (less practice, she told herself), but she slept for eight hours a night and it was cheap as hell. She fell in with some other people, nature freaks, and they explained the bird life. She told them about excavations and a pioneer woman archaeologist who used to sit on top of the trench and shout down to the students: 'Dig faster! Faster!' In October she moved into an apartment in Harlem, not far from where Susan was living with Leon, and began her work as an assistant professor, with some teaching and her own research into *Homo vannesiensis*.

It was a hopeful time of year, when the wind came off the Hudson and blew her coat back against her as she walked towards the subway.

3

At school, Seth had no close friends. He was shorter and stockier than most, his skin a little paler than the average, though not enough to make him stand out. In the playground, he kept to himself, unless there was a game that appealed to him – a game of pirates, for instance, in which he could be relied on to repel boarders. His heavy forehead and dark eyebrows made it look as if he was thinking things through carefully, though his weak chin suggested it was unlikely he'd reach much of a conclusion. While the other kids didn't think about such things as facial features, they did get an impression from him, and it was one they liked: solemn, but not hostile. And to get a smile out of Seth was an achievement. He was recognisable in the corridors and stuffy classrooms, with their Tupperware boxes full of marker pens and half-finished art projects pinned to the doors. The school tried not to push its pupils in the old disciplines, but encouraged them to find their own interests; some of the classes had an 'open-door policy', meaning any child could wander in.

Mary and Alaric were thrilled by the experience of watching their child grow: from shorts to long trousers, from words to sentences, from expressions of want to moments when he could reason and respond. When Mary gave him his favourite food, sausages, he would grace her with a smile, or at least a loosening of the jaw muscles and a light in his eyes. She fed him in much the same way as she catered for the people at her sports club: with a show of healthy stuff to start with, but then heavy on meat and potatoes. He could eat two rump steaks if he was offered, though cheese disagreed with him. Gradually, Alaric was able to interest him in trains. He bought a set in a toyshop in Regent Street. It was themed on a children's book about dragons, but the rails didn't fit together and the trans-former kept short-circuiting. The assistant took it back without a question and added it to the pile of returns behind her counter. Online, Alaric found an old Hornby set in its original box, and, despite doubts about its age, he bought it. The track was small enough to set up in Seth's bedroom, where they both sat on the floor. As instructed, Seth turned the knob on the trans-former two notches. His eyes filled with wonder as the train began to move. It was not an interest in what trains did in real life, Alaric could see; it was joy at inexplicable motion.

Seth was in Year 6 when Miss Chapman took the children in her class to the local swimming pool. There was a classroom assistant in the shape of Weston Bernard, a hefty youth with a red polo shirt whose short sleeves rode up over biceps swollen by the gym. Miss Chapman undertook the safety lecture on the coach; Weston repeated it emphatically when they lined up outside the building. The school had booked the hour, so there were lifeguards on duty and no other swimmers in the lanes of the big pool or in the shallow water of the infant area.

The children emerged from the changing rooms into the warm, chlorinated atmosphere, some nudging and giggling, one or two running on confidently. Miss Chapman had a towel round her waist over her plum-coloured costume; she looked down at the water in the gutters and on the floor as if worried about the germs in that soupy air. She stepped into the paddling pool with the non-swimmers, discarding the towel as she went down the steps. Weston had new board shorts with an orange palm-tree design over his pale legs. He went into the shallow end of the big pool with the minority whose parents had signed a statement that they could swim. He counted them in by name and made each swim a width alone before allowing them the freedom of the depths.

At the end of the allotted half hour, Miss Chapman blew a whistle and the children left the water. They rearranged themselves according to which changing room they had used. As they hopped on the sticky floor, hunting for locker keys, sharing towels, there came a sudden shriek of panic that made them all stop, wet-haired and half-dressed. There were whistles and the sound of a klaxon from the pool area.

Miss Chapman wrapped her towel round her waist and Weston slipped into his rubber sandals. 'Stay there,' he shouted to the boys. The pair were in time to see one of the lifeguards, a man, dive into the deep end of the pool. A second, female, lifeguard leapt in from the other side.

Miss Chapman gripped Weston's arm. 'My God. What's happened?'

Weston, who was himself not much of a swimmer, ran along the edge of the pool, sandals flapping, and jumped in.

The water under the high board was churning. Arms flailed, heads bobbed and sank. Miss Chapman stood, unable to move, her hands raised to her face, her fingers in her mouth.

Eventually the shoulders of the female lifeguard in her

white T-shirt broke the surface as she began to kick hard towards the side. In her arms, as she swam on her back, was a child whom, with an athletic twist of her shoulders, she deposited on the tiles. Miss Chapman, unfreezing, ran round to where the boy lay and bent over him as the lifeguards clambered out of the water. It was Seth.

The male lifeguard pushed her away as he knelt down over the motionless child. He turned Seth on his front and pressed between his shoulders. Seth coughed and exhaled water. They sat him up and he opened his eyes. He stared about him, as if confused.

Miss Chapman wrapped her arms round him and began to sob.

The female lifeguard stood up and looked into the pool, where Weston was making slow progress in the deep end. 'Keep an eye on him,' she said to her colleague. 'Don't want two in one day.'

'My God, my God,' Miss Chapman kept saying.

'Might have known it would be him,' said Weston Bernard as he himself was given a hand out.

'He was in your group,' said Miss Chapman.

'Only for changing,' said Weston. 'You had him for swimming.'

'He can't swim,' said the male lifeguard.

'That's obvious,' said Weston. 'That's why he was in her group.'

'He must have got lost in the changeover,' said Miss Chapman.

'He'd been in the big pool before that,' said the female lifeguard. 'I saw him holding on to the side. We'll have to fill in a report.'

'Don't worry. We can put our heads together,' said the male lifeguard. 'It was an accident. The important thing is—'

'That he's all right,' said Miss Chapman.

'Just swallowed a lot of water.'

'Had a fright,' said Weston. 'Perhaps he'll learn.'

'Are you all right, darling?' said Miss Chapman, hugging Seth to her.

Seth belched out more water and said something that sounded to his teacher like 'S fell.'

The school played down the incident when reporting it to the parents. Alaric was known to be easy-going, but as a teacher himself was sure to be a regular participant in checks and safety tests. He might be critical. Mary was liked by the staff, including Miss Chapman, but was not someone you would risk antagonising.

Fortunately, Seth himself seemed relaxed about almost drowning. Miss Chapman sat him down and explained how he must think ahead, not just pull himself along the pool by hanging on to the side, but try to think what the dangers might be: he, a non-swimmer well out of his depth . . . Imagine.

'I won't swim again,' he said.

'That's not what I'm saying, Seth. I'm saying you need to work out what the risks are. Think ahead. And listen to the teachers.'

He nodded, as if humouring her. 'Yes, miss.'

When they had been briefed about the incident by the school, Alaric was inclined to put it behind them. 'It's very unfortunate,' he said, 'but at least the safety procedures worked.'

Mary was not so sure. 'It's not that I want to blame Miss Chapman or the local authority. As you say, it worked. Up to a point. I'm more worried about Seth. The way he just put himself in that situation, knowing he couldn't swim.'

'He's a daring lad.'

'It's a failure of imagination.'

They had a short discussion about whether courage and a lack of foresight were the same thing.

'The important thing is that we keep an eye on him,' said Alaric. 'Especially now he's growing bigger.'

'He seems to be on the verge of puberty already,' said Mary. 'Is that normal?'

'I think it gets earlier all the time,' said Alaric. 'Something to do with nutrition. To judge from my generation and the boys I teach, the mean age has come down by a year in the last twenty-odd years.'

'But Seth's only eleven.'

'I know. But there was a boy at my school who at that age was equipped like a man. And not just any man, but—'

'I get the picture. But eleven . . . I don't want him to be a man already. I feel he's hardly had a boyhood.'

Alaric laughed. 'He's never been exactly childish. Dear boy.'

'Which reminds me,' said Mary. 'Next year he can meet Talissa.'

'Have you been in touch?'

'No. But I do think about her.'

'Do you think she'll want to come and visit? Or has she forgotten all about us?'

'Both,' said Mary. 'If you see what I mean.'

Alaric went back to the spare room, where he worked on his book, *History Awake: The Challenge of the New Century*. He had dropped the idea that the world had gone to sleep for about fifteen years after the fall of the Berlin Wall. The facts didn't support the thesis. The Cold War had ended, true enough, but Russia then evolved, via Wild West gangsterism, into Stalinism Mk II. In 2001, Islamists attacked America, who invaded Iraq in 2003 and plunged the Middle East into war without end. Banks and hedge funds bankrupted the world but had their losing bets paid out from ordinary people's taxes. A scientific consensus agreed that the planet would shortly burn itself out unless humans changed the way they lived. You couldn't really characterise all this as 'nothing happening'.

His new idea was that most of the changes the world had undergone in the last fifty years, while often eye-catching, were superficial, and that the underlying concerns of humanity had remained the same.

'What's really altered in our lifetime?' he asked Mary. 'In the way we live from day to day?'

'Well,' said Mary, 'when you and I were children, say in 2000, the internet suddenly began to work properly. Then everyone had smartphones. How about that?'

'It was just one gadget. For the rest, it was still Russia, terrorism, Christmas cards, terrible game shows on television . . . It was still the world of my infancy. But now with mobiles.'

'OK, so then, in the second part our lives,' said Mary, 'climate and energy crises. Potentially world-ending.'

'But we never *see* this great Dogger power station,' said Alaric. 'All those turbines in the sea. Or the nuclear fusion labs. I'm not even sure where they are. People still eat baked beans and worry about their pensions and the Man U–Tottenham result. The only *visible* difference is the number of private cars. Quieter roads.'

'I think you're forgetting ADEPT,' said Mary.

The provisions of the Anti-Discrimination and Equality of Populations Treaty, passed by the United Nations in July 2040, had been adopted by member countries to varying degrees. The Unites States passed a Thirty-Fifth Amendment; the European Union issued binding directives. The British Parliament, with no constitution to amend and with its application to rejoin the EU having been rejected, continued to dispute the merits of the treaty with itself.

'I'm not sure about that,' said Alaric, 'how much it's really—'

'Come on, don't you think ADEPT has finally moved the world into a post-identity phase? And surely that's a change. For the better, too.'

'I hope so. But some people say it's just another attempt to get those with real grievances to give up their struggle. It's worked in some countries more than others. At different rates, in different ways.'

'But that's history, isn't it?' said Mary. 'Hard to pin down. It runs through your fingers. You know that.'

'I suppose I do. Never the terminus, always the way station.'

'Exactly.'

'Perhaps we really are Selhurst Park,' said Alaric. 'But you have to keep going.'

4

The message was forwarded from the Parn Institute in London.

Hi Talissa

I've been wanting to be in touch for years, but I've stuck to the rules. How are you? I know that you have to do some follow-up tests with the Parn this summer, so I guess you'll be coming over. Unless you can do the tests at the US branch?

You're also allowed to meet Seth for the first time. Let me tell you first up that he's an absolute dear. Alaric thinks he's like me, I think he's a bit like A, but most of all he's himself. In a good way! He was quick to walk but slow to talk. He's still rather quiet unless you prod him along. He's gentle, and loyal to us and affectionate in his way.

He's a little small for his age ('old eggs', Alaric keeps telling me), but he's strong and healthy and grown-up in other ways. He hit puberty at eleven. Just to warn you. He didn't make many close friends at primary school but the other kids liked him, you could tell. He's a bit reckless and I lost count of how many times the school had to ring to tell us that he'd wandered off or had an accident. But there's nothing naughty about it. He's just a dreamy boy. He loves Crystal Palace football club (football's what you call 'soccer', Al tells me). He pretends to like trains to please A. So that allows A to buy more track for their set. Seth's quite good at making scenery. 'We'll make an engineer of him yet,' says Dad.

He passed all the necessary tests and started at secondary school (high school) last September and is in the football team on Sundays. We love him more than life itself and we raise a glass to you every day, sometimes twice a day if I'm honest, to thank you for what you did. Being parents is a joy and we owe it all to you.

Seth understands that there was another mother who carried him inside herself. He's quite OK with it and the Parn follow-up service has been very comprehensive. Of course, you'll check with them yourself, but I can promise that if you do meet it wouldn't be difficult or upsetting for him. He's not that welcoming to visitors, but I'd make sure he made an exception in your case!

Please say yes, come and see us and we promise not to take you camping. Unless there's another old human site you want to see of course. (Al says Ashers End counts as 'Palaeolithic'.)

With love from Mary x

Talissa had thought about Seth more often than she had expected. She didn't miss being part of his daily routine; she was happy that his parents were taking care of him. But she did want to look at him, this creature who'd emerged from her and had for a moment fed at her breast. She remembered, even from those short minutes, the sweet smell of his head. Now it was as if she had reached the moment in a love affair when the one jilted accepts there can be no speaking or touching but they long, nevertheless, to set eyes on the beloved – just once to *see* them.

She'd read many life stories of young women, often teenagers, who'd given up their babies for adoption. Most of them had been able to put the child out of their mind, because the need to survive overrode all else. Others, it seemed, fell apart. They had thought the wound was cauterised or healed, but over the years it poisoned them. For every mother and child who became friends on reuniting, there was another pair for whom a meeting led to bitterness.

The timing of Mary's message was good. Work was settled and a summer vacation was due. Talissa's romantic life had been confined to affairs of the Aron variety. She preferred hot assignations to adapting herself to all aspects of someone else's life and pretending they were destined for one another, or that she liked his friends. At the age of thirty-nine, she thought it was unlikely she'd have children of her own, which made her more curious to know about the one she'd carried. The only aspect of her life that made the trip to London difficult was the dog she'd adopted the previous summer. Pelham was named for the district where he'd been picked up, in the Bronx, near where her mother lived. He needed exercise and affection, but Susan Kovalenko had assured Talissa she could manage. There was a fraught farewell on the stoop of Susan's brownstone, with boxes of dog food changing hands. Susan hurried Talissa off towards the subway in case she missed the plane. 'Go on,' she said. 'I'll make sure he only listens to NPR.'

*

The plane bumped over the Atlantic like a cart going over a farm track, but, holding a glass refilled with business-class champagne, Talissa found it exhilarating. She reclined, lay flat, had a vibrating back massage and a saucerful of warm nuts before falling asleep in the middle of an old Ryan Gosling movie.

She dreamed, as she often did, of the abandoned house in a Brittany park and the man she'd seen inside.

On their return to London, she'd looked up the French word she'd seen on a package in the cellars and found that *santé* meant 'health'; so the *Ministère de la Santé* that had supplied the place was the Ministry of Health. The house had clearly been converted from a private residence into a hospital. But however long it lasted in its new role, the tides of failure had washed over it. Money ran short. Weeds grew through the front door. No one had been cured.

She knew no one would go back to the building and discover that man there in the same way that she had. Perhaps there was a factor of time involved. He was there then – on that day, *her* day, not Saturday or tomorrow.

Her thought process here was irrational, she knew, but she wondered if reason was the only way to truth. All her teachers at college had stressed the importance of data and logic: the scientific method; if she and her classmates showed a failure of process, they lost marks. But no grading system could allow for human variation. You could switch off the non-scientific parts of your brain while you were working, but they were only in sleep mode. When Newton was not using mathematics to describe the laws of celestial motion, he was busy with alchemy. Gravity and its logic would make him

105

immortal, but he devoted more time to the futile hope of turning mercury into gold.

Talissa was woken by the flight attendant and told to put her seat in the upright position.

She had fixed to spend a few days with Kavya Gopal in Muswell Hill, but before that thought it rude to turn down Mary's invitation to try their refurbished guest room. With a slight headache from the champagne and too tired to negotiate the transport systems of south London, she took a taxi from Heathrow and hang the expense. The journey was quick; there were hardly any private cars on the roads.

The street was like parts of Queens – cheerless, the houses cheaply built, but not a terrible place, she thought, for a kid to grow up. She blinked and braced herself as she went up the crazy paving to the front door.

'Dear girl!' She'd forgotten how affectionate Mary could be; there were tears in her eyes, and then on her cheeks, as she hugged Talissa. 'You haven't changed at all. You're still so lovely.'

Talissa hugged her back. 'I'm nearly forty.'

'You still look twenty-six.'

'Well, you're looking real good yourself.'

Alaric emerged from a door off the hallway. He had grown plumper in the belly and the sandy hair had receded a little, but the manner of shy determination was the same. There was a fussing over her bag and suggestions of tea or something stronger as they showed her through into the sitting room. It was nine o'clock in the evening London time and they had kept dinner waiting for her.

Alaric showed her upstairs to her room and explained how

everything worked. When he'd gone, Talissa looked at herself in the mirror, splashed water on her face, then brushed her teeth. Nine o'clock in Ashers End maybe, but sometime in the small hours of yesterday for her. She took two aspirin, straightened her clothes and headed for the stairs.

In the sitting room, Alaric handed her a glass of red wine.

'Dinner will be five minutes,' said Mary.

There was the sound of footsteps.

'Here he comes,' said Alaric.

The door opened.

'Seth, this is Talissa. Who you've heard so much about.'

Talissa stood up. Seth was shorter than she was, but manly for a twelve-year-old – solid, pensive-looking, black-haired and with what looked like a shaving cut on his upper lip. She scanned his face, instinctively, to see the features of his parents pushing through. She could see neither. Unsure how to greet him, she started to hold out her hand. Seth advanced and put his arms on her shoulders, then kissed her on the cheek. She was pleased, though there was something learned about the gesture.

'It's so great to meet you at last,' she said.

'It's nice to meet you, too,' said Seth. It was surprising to Talissa that his accent was what she thought of as 'British'. From *her* womb, her blood supply?

There was a feeling of triumphant goodwill in the room, as if Mary and Alaric were thinking, but were too modest to say: Look what we've done with the baby you gave us. Isn't he great? All Talissa's friends' offspring had been presented to her on a similar current of pride and it was easy to go with it. Seth's face remained impassive, but the beaming smiles of his parents were enough for all of them.

After dinner, when she went up to unpack, Talissa came across the gifts she had brought. A recent book about American history for Alaric, and for Mary a presentation pack of spices and marinades from her favourite deli on the Upper West Side. She left them on a table outside their bedroom.

When Seth came back from school the next day, Talissa went for a walk with him to Eden Park.

He took a football and bounced it on the pavement as they walked.

'Are you happy at your school?'

'Yes. I like it.'

'Do you have friends there?'

'Yeah, they're all friends.'

'And what's your favourite subject?'

'I like D T.'

'What's that?'

'Design technology. We make things.'

'Anything else?'

'I quite like history. Dad gives me extra lessons at home.'

In the park, Seth ran with the ball at his feet and kicked it into a goal with metal posts that were rusting at the base. His movements were solid and sure.

'You ever hear about baseball?' said Talissa. 'That's what we played as kids.'

'I think I've seen it. You try to hit a home run.'

'That's it. I used to like that, though I never played after I was about fourteen. I was a good pitcher. That's the one who chucks the ball. Maybe you could come to New York one day.'

'Yes, I could take a plane.'

'It's worth seeing. Tall buildings. What kind of food do you like?'

'Burgers are my favourite. Or sausages.'

'You like hot dogs?'

'Yes, but Mum says they're bad for you.'

'You need to go to the right place. They have to be grilled. Ever heard of Coney Island? It's where they used to have a big amusement park with lots of rides. A long time ago. It's been kind of run-down for ages. But there's still a guy I know down that way who makes the best hot dogs. Grilled. With fried onions and German mustard. I used to take the subway with my friend Susan.'

Seth began to bounce the ball on his instep. Talissa could see he wasn't interested in her reminiscences.

His face was set as he looked down at the football. The low brow and dark, fixed eyes gave him a kind of beauty, she had to admit. His breath came hard. Bang, thud, went the ball, bang, thud. Up and down, spinning on the instep of his foot. Bang, slap. He took it on his thigh, then his chest. He trapped it under his foot, released it and ran on to the pitch, where he sprinted towards the goal and kicked the ball hard. It rose and caught the underside of the bar, smacked down onto the line. Seth ran round the goal with his arms upraised.

They walked over the green space, a fenced-off part of which belonged to a school. Seth went ahead occasionally and sometimes hung back as though he were listening. Talissa wasn't sure what her job was, but presumed she was meant to tire him out. It reminded her of her walks with Pelham in Morningside Park.

On the way back, they stopped at a café, where Seth asked for a burger.

'Won't you have dinner soon?'

'It's OK. Mum won't mind. I'm always hungry.'

The thing came, overcooked, in a flaccid bun with brown onions hanging out of the side, but he seemed to like it. Talissa asked for coffee, which was stronger than they had in New York, and not as hot. She put it to one side.

It was hard to keep the conversation going with Seth. She tried to get him to talk about his life, but he didn't seem interested in himself. When she asked about his plans for the future, he responded as if the question were in some way invalid. Despite this, Talissa sensed that he was content with his life. Mary had told her that when they had all had to fill in some forms for vaccinations, under 'Occupation', Seth had written 'Child'. It had been a long time since she was in sixth grade herself and she had perhaps forgotten what it was like to be this young.

As they were returning to the house, going down the sidewalk with Seth bouncing his ball, he stopped and grabbed her arm. 'Wait!' Talissa looked up and down the street for a speeding ambulance or some hazard that would make it dangerous to cross.

'It's Nettle.'

'What?'

They stood still for perhaps thirty seconds before a tabby cat stuck its head out of the laurel hedge that ran along the front of the house on their right.

The cat hopped down and allowed itself to be stroked by Seth.

'How on earth did you know that—'

'Shh. Do you want to stroke her? She may not like it.'

'No. I'm good, thanks. More of a dog person.'

There were warm embraces when Talissa left the next day. Mary pressed a small wrapped present into her hand. 'If you don't like it, or you think it's sentimental, please don't worry. Just chuck it out. It wasn't expensive.'

Embarrassed, Talissa said, 'I'll open it later.'

'Of course. And thank you for the all spices and the—'

'And the book,' said Alaric. 'I'd read some reviews. It sounds good.'

'Do you promise to keep in touch?' said Mary.

'I think that's my cab.'

'But do you promise?'

'I promise,' said Talissa as she hugged Seth.

Apart from a few grey hairs neatly threaded through the black, Kavya Gopal seemed unchanged. 'Hello, my young American,' she said, opening the door.

'Not so young now, Kavya.'

'You're a child. Do you know how old I am?'

'None of my business,' said Talissa, though she had worked it out: sixty-three.

They stood, looking at each other for a minute on the doorstep, holding one another's hands, looking each other up and down before Mrs Gopal stood aside to let Talissa into her cluttered hallway.

'I have another lodger, but he's out at work till late. I told him he had to get out of your room, so he's in Sanjiv's.'

It was not long before they were sitting at the kitchen table, looking out through the steamy window over the yard with its dustbin cupboard, the brick wall and, beyond it, the spire of the radio mast at Alexandra Palace.

Kavya Gopal stood up from the oven. 'I don't know if you

remember these,' she said, transferring something from a baking tray onto a plate.

'Not the samosas?'

'I wasn't sure you'd remember.'

'I've thought of them every day for twelve years. In the seminar room, in the field, in the—'

'Don't exaggerate, girl. I may have lost my touch.'

But she hadn't. 'It's that sweetness,' said Talissa.

Mrs Gopal smiled. 'A little from the peas, a touch of cinnamon. But mostly it's from the lamb. I know where to buy it and how to mince it fine.'

A second pot of tea came onto the table as Talissa was brought up to date with Sanjiv, Kalpana – and Aidan, who'd apparently been named after someone in the Hartlepool branch of the family and worked in sports administration.

'Now tell me about your boy,' said Mrs Gopal.

Talissa sat back in her chair. 'What can I say? He wasn't how I'd imagined.'

'What do you mean?'

'I think I expected him to have fair hair, perhaps, like his dad. At least to look like a cross between his parents. And somehow to be more childish. It's as if by waiting this long to see him I've missed his boyhood.'

'Was he friendly? Was he polite?'

'Yes. He was polite. A little solemn.'

'In what way?'

'It was as if he'd been taught how to behave with people outside his family. There didn't seem much real warmth.'

'Same as Kalpana. She was shy. She didn't like other people at all. We had to teach her to be nice.'

'Yes, it was a little like that.'

'But she grew out of it. Did he seem clever?'

'He seemed . . . practical. But he thinks high school's a waste of time.'

'Boys. They don't like it. Mine were the same.'

'It was all quite strange.'

Mrs Gopal looked hard at Talissa. 'And did you love him? Did you feel a mother's love?'

'No. Thank God. That would have been too much. I felt . . . concern. I wished him well.'

'That was it? No love?'

'You're not supposed to feel love. He's not my child. I leased him a room for nine months. That's all. Like you did with me.'

'You felt nothing else?'

Talissa looked down at the kitchen table. 'Yes, I felt something else. Something powerful. But I couldn't put a name to it.'

At her host's suggestion, Talissa went up to her old room to rest and fell asleep as she had often done before, lying among the cushions. The room that had once been young Kalpana's was tranquil and sleep-inducing. No wonder the girl hadn't liked visitors.

At dinner that night, the conversation swung away from the personal, and Mrs Gopal began to lament what had happened to her country.

'There's some good signs at last,' she said. 'But for twenty years we were a backwater. The man with the silly hair who lied about the Brecksit . . . And then the hopeless people who came after. It was like living under Modi or . . . your one. The man like Gollum.'

'Trump?'

'Shh! Don't say that word. I thought of leaving England.'

'Where would you have gone?' said Talissa.

'That was the trouble. I didn't like the look of India and we'd cut ourselves off from Europe.'

'And it was all the fault of the man with the silly hair?'

'Don't mention *his* name either. It's forbidden in this house.'

'I don't even know it,' said Talissa.

'Good.'

'When are you going to come and visit me in New York, Kavya? My apartment has a spare room, you know.'

'I hear bad things about America.'

'What bad things?'

'The White House killings for one. Only last year, was it?'

'Yes. That was bad.'

'They never found who was responsible, did they?'

'Not exactly, but they're pretty sure it was a group called Vector.'

'And who on earth are they?'

'It's a long story. After Tr—, I mean Gollum, people stopped believing in the truth. He showed them how they could believe their own lies instead. So they made up other stories and called *them* the truth. Do you remember QAnon? And Make America Great Again?'

'We heard the names in Muswell Hill. An age ago now.'

'Well, twenty years or so. Anyway, they were conspiracists. The internet allowed them to flourish because proper journalism had collapsed. People wouldn't pay for real news when they could find sensation for free. Vector kind of mutated out of that mess.'

'So they're just liars?'

'No, it's more sinister. They hated ADEPT, you know, the UN resolution.'

'That I do remember. It was good.'

'Then Vector made common cause with a few groups we'd all thought dead and buried. Fifth-generation Ku Klux Klan types. It took some time. It was like raising the dead. But the coffins creaked open.'

'In this country that kind of person's banned.'

'They're crazy, the Vector people. They're delusional. But there's still only a handful of them. It shouldn't stop you coming to visit me, Kavya. Do you like dogs?'

'I don't mind them.'

'You won't be indifferent to Pelham. He won't let you be.' Talissa opened her handset. 'Let me show you a picture.'

When, five days later, Talissa unpacked her bag in the bedroom of her apartment in Harlem, she came across a package wrapped in blue tissue paper. Of course: Mary's gift to her.

Inside was a small cardboard box, more paper, and a gold-edged glass locket with a curl of black hair in it. A note said: 'A little keepsake of our lovely boy, with all our thanks and love from A and M'.

She lifted it up and held it to the light. It was Victorian, she guessed, prettily done, hand-made glass with a fine gold chain. It was the kind of thing you'd pick up in one of the better antique markets: probably of no enormous value, a hundred dollars or so, but charming all the same. She put it in a bottom drawer of her dressing table, with some old ticket stubs and souvenirs.

Within a few days, she was back in her routine of work, and dog care, and the occasional night out. But the thoughts of Seth never left her: neither the odd emotion she had felt for him and failed to explain to Kavya Gopal, nor her feeling of unease.

One morning, shortly before Seth's sixteenth birthday, while she was looking for an old passport, Talissa chanced across the locket in its drawer. She was taken aback by the power of the anxiety she felt on seeing it again. For years she had been determined to detach herself emotionally from Seth and from his parents; to keep her distance was both 'scientific' and a way of protecting herself from any sense of loss. Yet her body and her blood had fed the child. On an impulse, she removed half the hair inside. She chose the strands that still had some root tissue attached. She placed the hair in an envelope and took it into work with her. She asked Mark LaSalle, a young colleague, to pass it on to a friend in the genetics lab with a request for a DNA test. The result came back two weeks later in the shape of an attachment to a message from Mark to Talissa's private ID.

Hi Talissa

You need to contact them for a password to open this as the whole thing's protected. It's all double-blind and automatically printed out from the lab, so no one has actually seen this result. It's erased from the lab records in six days unless you ask for it to be stored. For that, you'd need authorisation from professor level and a second password. The specimen has been returned to us here.

Mark.

That evening, Talissa had a code sent to her handset and opened the attachment. After a long jumble of numbers and acronyms, the results were displayed in small type. They included input from *Homo u.i.* [Unknown Introgressor B4] and from *Homo sapiens vannesiensis*. But the key figures were at the end: '*Homo sapiens*: 43.5 p.c. *Homo sapiens neanderthalensis*: 51.5 p.c.'

Talissa stared at the polished wooden floorboards of her living room, then out of the window on to the street, to the brownstones opposite. A Neanderthal.

5

The school buildings were joined by a covered bridge where teachers patrolled reluctantly between lessons.

Seth liked the flow of human traffic that carried him from one class to the next. It relieved him of the need to make decisions. In the form room, where they gathered every morning after assembly, he'd found a desk in the back row between Wilson Kalu and Sadie Liew, two others who kept themselves apart. Wilson was serious and quiet, but met Seth's eye each morning with a trusting half-smile; at Christmas he'd invited Seth, alone of the class, to come home and meet his family.

They had recently acquired a puppy, a small brindled creature with white feet. Seth sat on the floor with the dog, speaking quietly to it, watching it explore. It was so silent and soft-footed in its white socks it was as if it was trotting through snow. Seth had to be gently dragged away from watching, up to the dinner table.

Here they had not just turkey and potatoes, he told Mary when he got home that night: they had beer and rice with spices he'd never tasted before. Wilson's parents gave Seth a present wrapped in red paper: a Crystal Palace shirt. Wilson looked on and caught his eye when he opened it. 'Never seen you laugh like that before, Pedder,' he said. It was his shortening of Seth's last name, a way of claiming him.

Sadie Liew had ended up sitting next to him by accident – a new girl joining halfway through the term, assigned the only spare desk – though by Year 10 it was clear to Seth that she loved him. She was anxious in science lessons when he did experiments with another partner; she kept him a place next to her in the canteen. The girls had to wear the regulation skirt or trousers, but, apart from that, anything they wanted. Sometimes Sadie left the buttons of her blouse open so he could see the strap of her underwear when she leant across. Some days it was pink, some days it was very white. He didn't know if she did this on purpose, so he tried not to look; it made him feel peculiar.

It was thought that he shouldn't be in Alaric's class for history, so he was taught by Mr Tainsley, who said his work showed promise. 'But, Seth, you need to take more pride in what you do. You could be the best in the class if you wanted. I think you remember more than Rubina. You can write as well as Callum. But you never finish the project. Don't you want to do well in the exam?'

These teacher's chats were something he just sat through, nodding his head. So long as he said nothing and didn't disagree with them, they'd soon stop talking and leave him alone again. All the comments urged him to take himself more seriously. But when they said these things, he just felt apart from all of it – separate. He noticed that he looked more grown-up than most of the boys and wished he didn't: Alaric had shown him how to shave and doing it each morning was a chore.

The best part of the week was football. Outside the forty

119

minutes of PE on Friday mornings, there was no school sport; but when two boys had been given trials by Charlton Athletic it was clear that football was a part of life for many of them. A young English teacher called John Rankin got permission to put together a team to play other schools' under-16s on Sunday mornings in the park. Seth played in midfield and was able to use his left foot as precisely as his right; an equivalence that had been a drawback in the classroom was an advantage on the pitch. Watching his team on screen had given him a combative attitude; he tackled the opposition players with a grim precision, his eye stuck to the ball. Best of all was what Mr Rankin called his 'positional awareness' – the way he made himself available for a pass. Some of the boys were in awe of this skill, but it didn't make him popular with them; he wouldn't join their celebrations of a goal, and this led them to distrust him.

A group of children who all lived on the same estate began to pick on him. He'd find his way barred in the corridor by a boy much taller than he was. Two girls emptied the salt cellar onto his spaghetti in the canteen, then walked off laughing. There was something in their eyes, though, that wasn't just hatred. Seth sensed some fear in them. One day when he went to his locker, he found that the catch had been levered open so the door hung loose. Inside, his Crystal Palace shirt had been cut in half with scissors.

He didn't tell anyone. He climbed up to the attic, where he talked to Alaric about the track they were building. Sometimes he'd go into the garden and coax Nettle over the wall from next door. If Mary was on the evening shift at work, he and Alaric would have dinner together and watch a film until she got back. Alaric ran seasons of what he called 'the greats', introducing Seth to Tom Cruise, Sandra Bullock and others from his own childhood.

Seth seemed to have stopped growing at about five feet six and still slept in the boat bed Alaric had restored. When he lay down, he fell asleep at once, unmoving, and woke only when his mother shook him hard by the shoulders in the morning.

Every six months until he was eighteen he was obliged to go to the Parn Institute for some IQ and verbal tests, followed by an hour's interview with Professor Delmore Redding, now the senior psychologist. This process had been part of the contract signed by his parents and he'd grown used to it.

The parts he feared were the sensory trials that came first. Everything about them made him uneasy. He was given a chair in front of a screen, where a black plastic hood was lowered over his head. When it was in place, resting on his shoulders, there was no ambient light, only two small holes opposite his eyes. With one eye covered, he had to identify dots in a visual field by clicking on something like a computer mouse. This made him nervous because his fingers couldn't move fast enough to record all the flashes. This was not because he lacked dexterity but because he saw so many lights. After a time, he was allowed to rest while they lifted the hood and taped some gauze over the other eye.

'That's the end of first act,' said the assistant, a man of about forty in a white jacket, whose name badge said 'Mike Battista'. 'Time for an ice cream while the house lights are up.'

Seth was disappointed when no ice cream materialised.

The tests continued, using light from different parts of the spectrum, going beyond a normally visible range into infrared and ultraviolet. Seth felt he was doing badly because he was preoccupied by the idea that there was someone else in the room. Mike's voice was high-pitched and slightly mocking in tone. Yet Seth twice caught another sound, at a lower level, as if Mike were whispering to someone.

During auditory tests, some noise-cancelling headphones played sounds from a range of frequencies. Sometimes he was asked to click when he heard anything; at other times Mike took the headphones off and asked him to describe the sounds. For part of these trials he was blindfold; apparently they wanted to see how much his auditory and visual capacities were linked.

It was often hard for Seth to explain some of the things he sensed, to say whether they were sounds or pictures. It was the same thing when he had been sure that Nettle was going to appear in a few moments; he simply knew. This part of the morning seemed to go much better, but again Seth sensed the presence of another. It was not that he heard Mike whispering or made out a third voice asking questions; it was more that the air became thicker.

The last part was the smell tests. For this he wore both blindfold and headphones with low white noise that could be penetrated only by the researcher's direct feed. He was also strapped into a tight-fitting mask, through which different aromas were fed.

'And this one? What's your score out of ten?'

'Nothing.'

'What?'

'I can't smell anything at all.'

'Really? That *is* interesting. Nothing at all?'

'No.'

'This one.'

'Eight.'

'What did it make you feel?'

'Hungry.'

Seth jumped. He had felt something touch his arm, like a finger testing his flesh.

'What was that?'

'What?' said Mike.

'Something touched me.'

'No, no. I'm over here behind the screen.'

He listened carefully and thought he heard breathing.

'Are you ready to carry on?' said Mike.

'I suppose so.'

'Thank you. Focus now. This is an important one.'

There was a faint hissing in the mask.

He had to think much harder. It was pleasant, yet not entirely.

'Six?' he said. 'Yes, maybe six.'

'What did it make you feel?'

It made him feel the way he did when Sadie Liew leant forward over his desk. He didn't want to say so.

'Strange.'

'Strange in a good way?'

'Sort of. But also . . . unhappy.'

'What?'

'Like a puzzle you can't solve.'

The white noise meant he couldn't hear Mike Battista's laughter.

When they'd finished, he could order in any lunch he liked. Most people got salads from Brunswick Square Gardens, but Seth asked them to send out for a double burger, no cheese, from a restaurant called Holborn High Steaks, one of the few places in London that still specialised in meat.

As he was walking upstairs to the lounge on the top floor to wait for the delivery, he overheard Mike speaking into his handset, his voice carrying up the stairwell void.

'Sure. Of course I'm pleased you're pleased, Lukas. What? No, I don't think so. It's fine. But another time I'd be grateful if you didn't touch him.'

Half an hour later, Seth was woken from a light sleep in an armchair to be taken down the corridor to see Professor Redding.

The preliminaries – windy chat about his health, his parents – were always awkward until they got down to something more concrete.

'Right,' said Redding. 'Friendships. How's it going?'

'I'm friends with all the children.'

'Any one in particular?'

'Wilson's still my best friend. Najma, she's nice.' He was thinking of what Talissa had told him about her friend Susan Kovalenko: 'You need someone real close. Someone you can confide in. Then three or four you can have a laugh with. That's enough.'

'You like the girls in your class?' said Redding, looking through his round glasses with his head on one side.

'Some of them.'

'Do they like you?'

Seth thought about the look in the eye of the girls who'd poured the salt on his food. 'They're not very kind to me.'

'Do they say bad things? Do they tease you?'

Looking out of the window, over the square, Seth saw the leafless sycamore that Talissa had seen years before. Eventually, he said, 'I think maybe they do like me but they don't know how to show it. They don't know what to say.'

124

Redding waited, hopefully. Seth said nothing. The silence lengthened and Redding broke first. 'Do you have feelings for any of them? Do you feel attracted?'

'Some boys do, I know.'

'And you?'

'I'm not sure. I think I feel scared.'

'Go on.'

'I mean, sometimes I look at maybe Osanna or Sangita and they seem . . . like grown-up women. Their clothes and hair and . . . They seem powerful. To have something over me.'

'And?'

'But I feel they'd want something back. Something I don't have. A feeling I can't give.' Seth looked down at his feet. 'I don't know what I'm saying.'

'These things are complicated.'

'Yes.'

'And are you still playing football?'

'No. I gave up because it made the others hate me.'

'You gave up? I thought you were the star player!'

'I told Mr Rankin I was injured.'

'How long ago?'

'I didn't play at all last term.'

'Didn't he check on your progress?'

'He asked a couple of times. But it's on Sunday. It's not an official school thing. And anyway, the teachers aren't meant to be friends with us outside school.'

'What did your parents say?'

'Mum's not interested in sport. Dad was sad about it, but he doesn't want to interfere.'

'I see. His position's delicate, isn't it?'

Seth breathed out heavily. 'One of the boys in the football team, he knows about how I was born. I don't know how.'

'Did he tell you?'

'No. But he calls me "Test Tube". And then in chemistry lessons he says things like, "Look, here's your dad, Seth," and holds up a tube.'

'How does that make you feel?'

'Lonely.'

'All the time or just when they're teasing you?'

Seth looked round the room, then down to the saucer of foil-wrapped chocolates on the table. 'They've made me feel different,' he said. 'When I go into the classroom it's as if I'm invisible. I can't be part of them, of what they are. It's not that I envy them or really want to join in with their jokes and things. It's just that I don't want to be alone.'

'I don't quite understand.'

'It's not that I like them,' said Seth. 'But I want to have the chance.'

'What chance?'

'The chance to belong.'

'And what would that mean?'

'It would mean I could make my own mind up about things. About life. As it is, I can't really get to decide anything. You know, maybe I should ask Sangita or Osanna to come out after school. But I can't. Because it's like I just don't have a way in.'

'Is it that you feel pushed apart from them?'

'No, it's more than that. They think I'm worth less. Inferior.'

'That must be hard to take.' Delmore Redding spoke softly, but Seth heard feeling in his voice.

He looked at Redding. Like all the children of his age, he was blind to differences of appearance. But at that moment it

126

occurred to him that Professor Redding might have come from somewhere that his grandparents had been mistreated. They'd learned this in old Mr Tainsley's history class. Was that why Redding's voice had a tremor in it?

'I know they're wrong,' said Seth. 'I know they're stupid to think so. But if you're on the receiving end, you can't prove it. How can I show that I'm as good as they are? Just because my mum had cancer once, a long time ago.'

Redding looked at his pad. 'Can we change the world?' he said eventually.

'What?'

'Well, Seth. We have one life and we have to decide. If the other people don't want you, if they think you're worth less than they are, are you going to let it break your heart?'

There was a silence while Seth thought about it. 'I don't want to be the best, I just want to live like other people. To have a chance . . . to . . .' He looked at the floor.

'To have a ticket to the game?'

'What?'

Seth didn't tell his parents about his Crystal Palace shirt. He didn't want to admit how hard he had tried not to weep. Palace were his club. Although Alaric had painted his cupboard in their colours, it was Seth who'd discovered them, by himself; it was he who'd followed them every day, imagined himself sliding passes through into the stride of the centre forward. It was he alone who'd loved them. What had been done to his shirt – to him – was violent. Perhaps they hadn't meant it to hurt so much or so accurately. Surely if they'd known that it would be a spear into the heart of his private world, they wouldn't have done it.

127

Yet when he sat in the bathtub that evening he felt that in some way he perhaps deserved it. He had secrets, he had pride. He thought he was as good as they were. Perhaps, without admitting it, he believed he was better. But the others had found him out. Now there would be more pain to come and maybe it was right that there should be. One day, when he'd taken his punishments, it would end.

Mary could see something was wrong, but hesitated to intervene. He was such a baffling child anyway – so independent, so assured, yet in other ways quite disconnected from the world she herself worked her way through every day. She had never been a parent before. How was she to know what was normal? In a matter-of-fact tone, she asked one or two mothers at the school gates what they felt about their boys. All of them were surprised by their sons – by how little they seemed to be a mixture of their parents or even a reboot of just one. For religious or cultural reasons, a few of them pushed hard to shape their boys a certain way; but most of them shrugged and let their offspring become whatever they were apparently destined to be. It was like buying a seed packet with no label from the garden centre, one mother sagely told her: whether it turned out to be a tomato or a cauliflower was not yours to question; your job was to help it become the best tomato or cauliflower it could be.

When she'd left Alaric all that time ago, then returned to him, it had taken Mary years to reorientate herself. She felt so guilty for the pain she'd caused that she barely registered the fact that both of them, in different ways, had become more confident in their partnership. She had shown some independence, to put it crudely, and Alaric some staying power. The timing of the Seth adventure had been right for them.

Now, in the light of Seth's individuality, that sense of purpose seemed to stall. She was filled with love for him, fearful for his future, but troubled in the course of many wakeful nights that she was not doing as well by him as a mother should.

6

In the hours that followed her opening of the DNA results, Talissa felt as if she was caught in a room on fire where every exit turned out to be blocked.

There had been a mistake . . . There had been a crime . . . The weight of it was more than she could bear. She needed to confide. In Susan. In Mark LaSalle. Even in poor Felix. She'd been told by Susan, who'd heard from Leon, that Felix was in and out of some mental health facility. For the first time, she regretted not having a man who shared her life at home; the closeness of a lovers' bond would have covered such a secret, kept it safe.

She walked up and down the stripped floorboards of her apartment, reeling from one wall to another, like the lioness in the Bronx Zoo.

Or Kavya Gopal. Yes, Kavya would be good. But she was on the other side of the world. Or her mother. She'd have a long perspective; she was old enough to be selfish and therefore calm. But no: she was also becoming forgetful and might not understand.

The problem was the discovery was so large that once she shared it, once it was out in the world, it could never be reined in. Then she began to consider what it might mean for Mary and Alaric. Who was going to tell them? She pictured the look of disbelief on Mary's face and the dumb agony on Alaric's. They didn't have the capacity to take in such news. Finally, she thought of Seth himself. Bouncing the ball on his foot, sensing the presence of the cat in the bushes, scared of girls, eating his burgers, barely smiling, making his way through school like all the others. Word of this must never reach his classmates. In high school she'd been teased for an entire year for having the wrong shoes.

In the middle of the night, and not before, it came to her that she should contact the Parn Institute in London. She went into the living room and looked at her screen. The lavish home page unfurled. 'Our People'. Catrina Olsen was still there, with the same mugshot. Malik Wood remained the director, now a little grey above the ears. If there had been some bizarre mistake, these people ought to be told about it. Maybe they already knew, but had decided to keep it quiet. They'd sure done enough blood tests.

Perhaps the first thing to do was to check the result, make sure it was neither a blip in the machinery nor a practical joke of some kind. If she asked Mark LaSalle for another test, he might become suspicious; on the other hand, she could scarcely send the hair sample elsewhere and expect the degree of confidentiality that she'd had from an academic lab.

At six in the morning, she remembered reading a book by a Swedish palaeoanthropologist whose main concern in extracting DNA from ancient bones had been how easily they became contaminated: by bacteria, by the DNA of other species who had shared their resting place or by their modern-human handlers. In Leipzig, they'd constructed sterile rooms where many retests had been run by postdocs in full protective gear before they'd got results they could rely on. A Nobel Prize had followed. Talissa crafted a modest message to Mark LaSalle that gave no suggestion the results had been surprising but in which she chastised herself for being care- less in the presentation of the sample. The lock of hair had been left lying around. Who knew, perhaps Pelham had even sneezed on it. She couldn't live with her better scientific self without a confirmation of the result. Therefore she was going to bring a second sample, one which had been more rigor- ously looked after.

Knowing Mark a little, she added a PS about coffee or a drink to thank him for his time.

So, ten days later, she found herself in a real old-fashioned steakhouse on Lexington and 47th, Mark LaSalle's choice of rendezvous.

Mark's reputation was that of what the head of department, Debra Hillenbrand, called 'a second bassoon'. He was not the brightest on the team, but he got the work done. Talissa had worked with him on some finds in Idaho and they had both done research into *Homo vannesiensis*, as well as teaching undergraduates. He was eight years younger than Talissa, and had done his first degree at Northwestern, his family being long-time Chicago people, descended, so he said, from French trappers.

Professor Hillenbrand was ambivalent about Mark. 'He's nice to look at,' she said. 'He's the kind of guy who when I was starting out was a menace to have around. Too keen on the opposite sex. Or as we called it then, "misogynist". That word stopped them in their tracks.'

With the professor's caution in her ears, Talissa had kept a distance between herself and Mark, though his regular looks were not of a kind that appealed to her in any case. If a man were not actually beautiful, like Felix, she preferred him plain but dynamic, like Aron Landor.

'I ordered a martini for you,' said Mark, as she sat down. 'I hope that's OK.'

'Sure thing.'

'Straight up. With a twist.'

'How did you know?' She seldom drank martinis, but she was in Mark's debt and wanted to join in.

'No sensible person wants ice cubes to displace the liquor. The twist was a guess.'

'And I'm a sensible person?'

'Maybe not. But you're a clever one.'

'Right.'

Talissa did some fussing in her purse. The evening seemed to be going at a hundred miles an hour already. She was glad she had opted for a simple dress and scant make-up.

'So,' she said. 'Thanks again for your help with the DNA thing.'

'Did you get the second result OK?'

'Sure, I got the code last night and opened it up. It was exactly the same as the first result.'

'So. No contamination.'

'Yup. All good and regular.'

'So, was this a little side hustle of yours?'

'Yes. Nothing to do with our programme. It was just a favour for a friend.'

'You know that public labs are not allowed to test for species percentages,' said Mark. 'Only a few academic labs like ours can do that.'

'I do. I remember the fuss when the law was passed. I never quite understood why they had to be so fierce about it.'

'It was hard enough to get the health care system to fund DNA testing at all. They had to fight to prove that knowing someone was likely to develop heart disease or breast cancer was a money saver in the long run. Early prevention.'

'Of course, but why couldn't the tests also show that you had some founder-American or Chinese or whatever in your ancestry?'

'They just thought that information would be prejudicial. Could be harvested and used against people.'

Talissa shrugged. 'Well, I guess it *is* kind of private.'

'Yes,' said Mark. 'It also means so little. My grandma did a commercial spit test, when they first came out, and discovered she was five per cent Ashkenazi Jew. She thought that changed who she was! My dad had to explain to her very slowly that there was not a gene for "Jewishness". It was just that at some point, many hundreds of years back, a couple of her ancestors had stayed in the same place for a long time and bred within a restricted population, accounting for a minute and insignificant genetic change. That was all that was caught by the test.'

'And what did Grandma make of that?'

'Dad told her she was too old for a bat mitzvah now. So. I ordered some clams on the half shell to start with. Then I thought I'd have the rib-eye. What about you?'

'Oh wow. I think I'll just get the baked eggplant.'

'You don't eat meat?'

'Not much.'

'You should have said.'

'No, I shouldn't. This is my treat to say thank you. Would you like wine with it?'

While their food was on its way, Talissa listened to Mark talk about his family back in Illinois and thought about Seth. She had forgotten the federal law on DNA testing. It meant that if Seth were tested in America, he would find out nothing about his ancestry. She would need to check that a similar restriction applied in England.

In addition to the littleneck clams, the waiter brought some oysters and some cold Chardonnay. With the steak, they drank a red wine that tasted like plum jam and Mark persuaded Talissa to try a corner of his giant rib-eye. How much Seth would have liked it, she thought, with the side orders of cornbread and French fries, dusted with thyme and served in a metal cone.

'Look at this! I feel like we're back in another century,' said Talissa.

'Are you OK with that? I think it's, like, their specialty here. To make you feel like Jack Nicholson might walk in with Michelle Pfeiffer on his arm.'

'Hope Michelle was a carnivore,' said Talissa. 'But, yeah, I like it.' The wine had made her feel benevolent.

'So how's your home life?' said Mark. 'If I'm allowed to ask?'

'It's great, thanks for asking. Just me and Pelham at the moment. We like it that way.'

'Pelham? Is he . . . an anthropologist too?'

'No. He's a dog.'

'Oh. I thought he—'

'But a very handsome one. Like a greyhound, but smaller. With long whiskers and big brown eyes. A beautiful blue-grey coat. He kind of talks to me. He's playful, runs like the wind, but likes the sofa best. He's very devoted.'

'I bet. And were you . . . If I can ask. Were you ever married?'

'Pelham and me? I wish.'

'No, I mean—'

'Not yet.' Talissa smiled. 'You?'

'Me? No, no. Not at all.'

'Why do you ask?'

'Oh, nothing. Just that, well, people notice that you're . . . God, I don't know how to put this without losing my job.'

'Poor Mark. Life in the femisphere.'

'Personable? Is that an OK word?'

'I think so,' said Talissa. It was presumably what Aron Landor had had in mind when he whispered in her ear, though it was not exactly the term he'd used. She felt a tug of nostalgia for the smell of sweat and cement dust.

'What a relief,' said Mark. 'Thanks, Dr Adam.'

'I'll make a note of it on your next appraisal.'

Despite herself, she felt a small erotic charge at the thought of admonishing Mark while he stared at the floor. He drained his glass and put it down in a hopeful way. Talissa was ready to leave, but felt it might be rude. More wine came, and Mark LaSalle got down to business, telling her about his life's disappointments and the way he felt misjudged. What is it about me, Talissa thought, that makes people feel they can confide? Susan used to tease her that she had a distant manner that she'd cultivated to keep people, men especially, at bay. But that wasn't at all what happened. Mary and Alaric had trusted her from the moment they let her into their flat. Kavya Gopal had told her about her deepest feelings for her children within an hour of her arrival.

'. . . only three long-time girlfriends,' Mark was saying. 'I really don't think that's extreme. By any metric.'

'Sure thing.'

'But it's a minefield, you know.'

'I thought any straight guy in the city could have his pick of—'

'Not any more. And in any case, I'm not any straight guy. I'm a romantic.'

'Of course you are.'

'Seriously, Talissa. I mean, maybe once back in caveman days, guys could just sleep around and it was all good. But I honestly don't think it's been like that in this century.'

Starting to be tired by the dating conversation, Talissa pushed him into childhood and his family. Unlike her, he had brothers and sisters. They'd moved out of the South Side to Evanston and had a big family life with Thanksgivings and graduations, unsuitable boyfriends and family quarrels . . . She had ceased to take it in; but Mark was a decent kind of guy, she felt, rather modest when you thought about it, and had perhaps been wrongly portrayed as a potential creep at work.

In the days that followed, her sense of panic receded far enough to allow her to formulate a plan. Humanity had a genocidal history of tearing itself to pieces over differences of appearance in its own kind. They had fought and killed for language, historic grudges, skin colour and other matters of no scientific significance in people of the self-same genotype. If her fellow humans could be this violent to their own people, how would they treat someone who was *actually* different? The record of what they had done to other species was discouraging: kill, eat, 'domesticate' or put in a zoo. That was about it.

The only thing to do now was to contact the Parn Institute in London. Her regular communication with them had stopped some years ago, but she could reopen it with an approach to the sympathetic Catrina Olsen. After all, it was Catrina who'd impregnated her. And together, they might shape a plan to protect the boy.

7

'You are joking, I presume,' said Lukas Parn.

Malik Wood had been summoned to Berlin and was sitting opposite his employer in his apartment on Görlitzer Strasse, on the second floor of a block that had once been on the east side of the Wall.

'No, I'm not,' said Wood.

'So the birth mother of the hybrid is a palaeoanthropologist specialising in the Neanderthals?'

'Not quite. Her speciality is *Homo vannesiensis*.'

'But why have we ended up with someone who works in the area?'

'If she hadn't been in research, she wouldn't have read about the trial. She saw it in our newsletter.'

'But this is her specialty.'

'She's not a geneticist. Mostly she just teaches the under-grad course. Methods of dating. Family trees. She's not a high-flyer.'

'She's an assistant fucking professor. That's what she said in her message to Catrina Olsen.'

'Exactly. Not a full professor. Probably never will be. It

was not intended for her to be the mother in any case. It's not as if one of them was specifically chosen.'

'So who screwed up?'

'No one,' said Malik Wood. 'We had eight patients under the scheme. The chances of the mother being this Talissa Adam were seven to one against. I knew there was an implantation taking place that morning at about eleven, but I didn't know any names. When I swapped over the sperm I covered the label so I wouldn't catch a glimpse. That way, I didn't know the name of the parents, let alone the surrogate.'

'Go on.'

'It was controlled. So in the years to come we could view all the test data objectively.'

Parn blew out some air through his lips. 'But there's a record of which one it was?'

'Yes. Date and time and a barcode. It's encrypted and only I have a password.'

'And does it match the kid with the bizarre test results?'

'I haven't checked. But I'd be thunderstruck if it didn't. Also, the way he looks.'

'Brow ridge, barrel chest, high voice? Hairy?'

'A suggestion of all these things, yes. But not extreme. And he has less of a brow than you'd think. Less than Charles Darwin, as a matter of fact.'

Parn frowned again. 'It sounds like it's out of our control.'

'Listen, Lukas, have you read the literature on how many surrogate babies have found out later in life that they were fathered by the wrong sperm? Lots of doctors have been sued for negligence. Their labs are full of students fighting for bench space, sticking barcodes on any spunk jar they find.'

'That's not the Parn way.'

'That's what I'm saying. Everything we did was measured. And don't get me started on the big hospital in London where they'd run out of sperm donors and the head of department stood in and did it himself. He had nine children.'

'That's a lot of jacking off.'

'Not at all. He did it the old-fashioned way. With the women's consent.'

'Jesus.'

'I know.'

After a pause, Parn said, 'But her job must have shown up in the background interviews. The psychological profile. It must have been flagged that one of the mothers was a potential nightmare.'

'I've gone back over her application and over Redding's notes. She's officially described as an unemployed academic. When Delmore asks what her subject is, she says ancient history. I've listened to the recording and seen the transcript.'

'Well, she's a liar.'

'She was unemployed at the time, hadn't got a postdoc place. She used our fee to self-fund one the following year in Boston, where she stayed on and was then paid by the institute in the usual way. She did well. What she actually said to Delmore was, "I guess you could say I'm a historian. An ancient historian." It's not a complete lie.'

Lukas Parn stood up and walked to the window. 'I've drilled down through her history,' he said, 'and it seems she even applied to work as a researcher on one of the programmes we were running with UCL.'

'Well, if our sweep didn't show that up it's probably because the firewalls between all the different areas of what the Parn does were too effective. Also, there's a mass of confidentiality around all job applications. Data protection.'

'So we're a victim of our own professionalism.'

'Look,' said Wood, raising his voice a little. 'What difference does it make? Any mother who discovered it before we were ready to release our findings to the world . . . that would be a problem. The fact that she has some expertise is really neither here nor there.'

'Listen,' said Parn. 'I know people don't like me. They're jealous. But I believe in science, I really do. And while I may not have your skill in the lab or your knowledge, I am a professional. My organisations don't screw up.'

Malik Wood didn't answer. It was important to be on the front foot when talking with Lukas Parn, but you didn't want to push it.

He walked to the window and stood next to Parn. They looked over the railings of Görlitzer Park. There was a view of patchy grass over a boundary wall that was covered in raw graffiti. He found it distasteful that Lukas Parn chose to live in Berlin, in this ostentatiously modest apartment with its Trabant-era furniture, while his big millions were splashed over residences in Connecticut and on the Sydney harbourfront.

'So,' said Parn, sounding a little calmer. 'How many people know now?'

'Just the original group. The big three. You, me and Redding.'

'And now this woman. The surrogate.'

'Yes. She hasn't spoken to Catrina yet, but we should take it that she's somehow found out. Her message suggests as much. Something about an "unexpected development".'

'Are you sure there's no one else?'

'Dead sure. Of course, some of the kid's test results are pretty weird and I can't rule out the possibility that the guys who do the trials may have had some queries in their own minds. But they've raised nothing with us.'

'Why not?'

'We pay them to listen and record accurately, then move on to the next task. Outside the master hard disk, there's a lot of automatic self-erasing. Data doesn't hang around or get duplicated.'

Lukas Parn nodded. Malik Wood began to breathe again. When Parn's Australian accent faded into Zurich with a hint of Berkeley, Ca, it meant the danger was passing.

'OK, Malik,' said Lukas Parn. 'Get back to me by seven tomorrow evening with an action plan. Do we pay for her flights? Do we enlist her as a fellow researcher? Give her money. How we deal with any future leak. The press. God help us. All the details. All the angles.'

'Right.'

'What was the name of that woman who got the job you so much wanted? Then became a Fellow of the Royal Society.'

'Therese Williams.'

'That's right. Remember Therese. An FRS is still not beyond you. So long as you don't fuck it up now.'

'I'll try.'

'Get yourself a hotel. In the meantime, do you feel like a currywurst?'

'No, thanks. I had something on the plane.'

'Tell you what. I know a place where they do whole deep-fried chicken. That's all they do. You'll love it. They've had the same menu for a hundred years. They got pictures of old Nazis eating there.'

'Oh for fuck's sake.'

'It's history. Not airbrushed. It's in Leuschnerdamm. Five minutes by car.'

While in Berlin Malik Wood reluctantly picked the meat off his crisp, leather-brown chicken beneath photographs of smiling SS officers, Seth Pedersen was going through his termly report with his form teacher, Rose Paxton, in the Dulwich–Brixton borders.

'It's the same old story, isn't it, Seth?'

'What, miss?'

'You look as though you're concentrating, but all your subject teachers say the same. You don't see it through.'

'Yes, miss.'

'In my physics class you sometimes seem to have a real understanding about how things work.'

'I seem to know. Before you explain. Those experiments with weights and pulleys and stuff like that.'

'But your written work doesn't back it up.'

'I'll try harder.'

Rose Paxton crossed her legs, causing her skirt to rise for a moment. Seth looked away, with the same sensation in his chest he had when Sadie Liew leant over his desk.

'Your art report is really not acceptable.'

'What does it say?'

Taking out some glasses from a case on the desk between them, Rose read: ' "Seth has made it only too clear that he has no interest in landscape or portrait." Is that fair?'

'I did like some shapes and colours Mr Mills showed us. Cubism it's called. But what's the point of art?' said Seth.

'I think you'd be better off asking Mr Mills.'

'Don't you know then, miss?'

'Well, I'm no expert on the history of art. But from a scientific point of view, I can say for sure that it was one thing that marked us out from other creatures from an early age. A desire to depict the world we live in.'

'I don't understand.'

'Human beings have always wanted to reflect back the world they see. Starting with pigment drawings in caves, then going on to . . . well, all the great artists I expect Mr Mills has told you about.'

'Why would you want to do that, though?'

'Do what?'

'What you said. Reflect the world back.'

'It's really not my field,' said Rose Paxton, taking off her glasses. 'But I don't want to see a report like this again.'

'Yes, miss.'

'Are you happy at school, Seth? Is something troubling you and making it hard for you to concentrate?'

'It's OK.'

'Is someone being unkind to you? Are you being picked on?'

'No, it's fine.'

'You must tell me. You're a bit more grown-up-looking than the others. Children can be very cruel.'

'It'll stop one day.'

After their chicken lunch, Lukas Parn and Malik Wood went for a walk in Treptower Park.

'You've seen all the data on the kid, haven't you?' said Wood.

'Yes. He seems more Sapiens than I'd expected.'

'Well, that's nature. A billion binary choices between Mum

and Dad as the embryo develops. One kid's like Mum, the next one's like Dad. Maybe Mum's alleles had a big day.'

'That's a shame.'

'The alternative,' said Malik Wood, 'is that Neanderthals and Sapiens are hard to tell apart. After all, the total difference between the two species is only ninety-six amino acids.'

'Explain?'

'Well, the difference between you and me is thirty. That's enough to differentiate a human individual of the same sex. The difference between you and a female like Catrina Olsen is sixty. That's how close we are to Neanderthals: you to Catrina plus half as much again. Just half.'

Neither spoke for a bit. Then Parn said, 'You don't think you messed it up?'

'In what way? The process worked brilliantly.'

'In preparing the Neanderthal sperm. Could there be bits of other DNA patched in there?'

'No.'

'Walk me through it again.'

'You sure you want to hear? You do know that all this has been possible, hypothetically, since about 2020?'

'I do. But tell me as if to a kid. I want to see if there was something you missed.'

Parn was wearing the look of a patient but concerned inquisitor, an expression that uneasy staff in offices around the world called his 'Rodin', after *The Thinker*.

They sat down on a bench in the shadow of a towering Soviet war memorial to the battle for Berlin in 1945.

'I only know what arrived in London,' said Malik Wood. 'Your palaeo people did the spadework, right? So you tell me. Did you start with what was available online?'

'No,' said Parn. 'We started again. My palaeo lab got a bit of bone from behind the ear of a Neanderthal. I forget the anatomical name.'

'Petrous, presumably,' said Wood. 'A new sample? How did you manage that?'

'Paid for it. Museum curators are human.'

'Ah. The Parn way.'

'OK. So, look, Malik, it's not my special area, but as I understand it . . . The extract was then put in a salt solution, centrifuged, tidied up and the fats taken out, leaving a liquid with single strands of DNA. Right? I'm not quite sure of the next step.'

'Well, you simply supply the other strand,' said Wood, 'because it's complementary. Our old friend the double helix. Base pairs are always the same. Then you have a library. Then that's amplified millions of times by PCR. The public got to know about the PCR process years ago when they were tested for COVID-19. Same idea.'

'Right,' said Parn. 'So then we had the basic genome. On computer.'

'Yeah,' said Malik, 'but that's been available for years. Why did you go through it all again?'

'We wanted the best. We have the facilities. The labs, the money. Also, we wanted confidentiality. We didn't want our name on the lending-library ticket if we'd checked into some publicly available database.'

'OK.' Wood was used to Lukas Parn throwing his money around. 'So then what?'

'We'd now got the fullest sequence of Neanderthal DNA that's ever been put together. Then my lab guy went to a place in Zurich. They inserted it into the scaffold of a Sapiens genome. Next it was synthesised into long runs – very long runs, they told me – and compared to standard Sapiens. Then they were swapped around with gene editing. You'll know how that works.'

'It's easy,' said Malik Wood. 'Imagine you have two translations of an ancient text. One has been censored and had all the good bits cut out. You examine them in parallel and make the substitutions, match and patch, to get to the original. Of course, it includes making chromosomes. We've known for ten years now that Neanderthals had twenty-three pairs, like us. Since the Shanidar Z6 find.'

'The one they called Picasso?'

'Yup,' said Wood. 'And then your Zurich people must also have gone for a Y chromosome to get a boy.'

'That's right,' said Parn.

'Why did they do that?'

'Because the boy bit is dead simple. Only a handful of useful genes on the Y. The rest is junk. Beer and football. Don't tell Olsen and the girls.'

'I think they may already know.'

'This stuff was then sent to you guys in London. So you take the story from here.'

Before answering, Wood looked up at the colossal statue behind where they sat. It showed a Soviet soldier clasping a rescued child, while under his broadsword, at his feet, lay a broken swastika, crushed by his righteous force.

'What do you think the Berliners make of that when they walk past with their sandwiches every day?' said Wood.

'I imagine they blank it out.'

'Do you think?'

'I do. And for the kids, it's too long ago. It's history.'

'Don't they teach history in Berlin?' said Wood. 'I mean, that lunch place with the SS pictures. And the nightclubs in the Stasi cellars. Aren't they ways of remembering?'

'No, I think they're ways of forgetting. By normalisation. Entertainment. And anyway, how many generations will it take? How much sorrow can be borne?'

'But this statue,' said Wood. 'It's as if in Washington DC they'd been obliged to install a giant memorial to the North Vietnamese, smack in the middle of Pennsylvania Avenue. Showing a Vietcong guerrilla clasping a burnt child and crushing beneath his victorious sandal a napalm canister and the American bald eagle. Do Berliners *like* having this here? As a kind of self-chastisement?'

Parn shrugged. 'I haven't asked them. But I'm no big fan of the North Vietnamese. My father was a kid at the fall of Saigon.'

'I'd heard.'

'Now tell me what your guys did in London.'

'Well,' said Malik Wood, 'I had the help of a biochemist from Imperial. The Neanderthal sample was injected into a denucleated Sapiens cell.'

'What cell?'

'Any cell.'

'Yeah, but how do you get a tadpole, a little sperm, out of that?'

'By artificial meiosis. Just as in our body we make sex cells, sperm and egg, from other cells – you and I are doing it right now – so you can induce that process from outside. It's a question of adding the right hormones to the cell, I think, something about a gonadal environment, which causes it to split and recombine the bits of its granny and grandpa in the usual way into a nice healthy gamete – an egg or, in this case, sperm.'

'Right,' said Parn. 'Is he OK, by the way, this Imperial guy? Is he reliable?'

'Yes. He's a geek. It's the lab work that thrilled him. He had no idea there'd be a practical outcome. He signed a bunch of confidentiality stuff. Plus he received a large bank transfer.'

'And you ended up with things that looked like spermatozoa?' said Parn.

'Yes. Millions. They were then suspended in a sticky semen substitute that was indistinguishable from the normal stuff. We even added a drop of top-quality synthesised aroma.'

'So the final sample in the pot looked like the man had just rubbed one out?'

'Yes. The embryologist who implants it into the ovum had the whole thing magnified to the umpteenth under the lens and she raised no questions.'

'Who was the embryologist?'

'Ayesha Cross.'

'She the one you were fucking? Then dumped?'

'It was a long time ago.'

Parn was silent, gazing down the rectangular beds and pathways of Treptower, where the office workers were finishing their lunch break.

8

That evening, Talissa went over to Susan's apartment for dinner, taking Pelham with her. It was a twenty-minute walk through Harlem, past some old Spanish places and some newer Russian ones. She had heard back from Catrina Olsen, offering a meeting in London in ten days' time; but the weight of the secret still pressed her.

'Hello, beautiful,' said Susan as they walked in. 'And hello, Talissa.'

Susan knelt down to fuss over the dog, who made some noises in return before hopping onto a deep brown sofa under the window.

'Make yourself at home, kid,' said Susan. 'Oh. You have. Right. Have a drink, T. There's some wine open. Or Leon'll make some cocktails when he gets in.'

'I'll wait. Who's the fourth?' said Talissa, looking at the dining table.

'Surprise.'

'I've had enough of your surprises.'

'One more won't kill you. How's things?'

'Well . . .' said Talissa.

'Work? That professor? Firebrand, or whatever her name is? Riding you hard?'

'No, she's fine.'

'Men?'

'I'm past all that. I've told you. I'm post-sexual.'

'Bullshit. Must be students, then.'

'I don't know, I feel I'm on the verge of doing something crazy.'

Susan sat down on the sofa, next to Pelham, and stroked a velvet ear. 'Tell me.'

'I'm going to London on the thirtieth. To see some old friends.'

'Your landlady?'

'Among others.'

'That'll help. You like it there. Will you see the parents?'

'I think not. It's probably best to leave them to their lives.'

'What about the boy?'

'Same thing.'

'So it's just a holiday.'

'Hey, Kojak, why don't you come along? You've never been.'

'We don't all get long vacations like you. DA's office never sleeps.'

Talissa felt the need to tell becoming intolerable. She was about to do something she'd regret.

'Do you have any aspirin?' she said.

While Susan was in the bathroom, the front door opened and Leon let himself in. He went to change out of his work clothes and returned with a tray of cocktails. Talissa swallowed the aspirin with water, then weakened and took a drink. The crisis passed.

Leon's story of his day at work, interspersed with a few questions directed at his guest, made Talissa feel better. He worked in an office in midtown doing something he didn't much enjoy, which was one reason he was quick to change into jeans and an old T-shirt as soon as he could.

Talissa had just accepted a refill of her drink when the bell rang and Susan went to get the door.

'I think you two know each other,' she said, showing in Mark LaSalle.

'Sure thing.' Talissa felt wrong-footed, though relieved that it wasn't a stranger. 'But how did you know?'

'You mentioned Mark's name about fifty times when we last met.'

'Yeah. Well, we had some business a little while ago,' said Talissa. 'Anyhow, good to see you, Mark. How's life as the last of the carnivores?'

'Lonely. How are you, boss? Not seen you since last week.'

The mood loosened and Susan opened another bottle of wine. Leon and Susan asked Mark about his work; out of modesty and fear of confusing them, he deferred to Talissa, who pushed it back to him.

'So that's the big question in our field,' he was saying.

'And have you found the missing link?' said Leon.

'It's not a chain,' said Mark. 'It's more like a photograph of a tree with a dozen boughs, hundreds of branches and thousands of twigs. Unfortunately, the picture's been overexposed and many parts of the tree are just a white blur. What's in focus are two fruits hanging from the tip of thin, adjacent twigs. Sapiens and Neanderthal. We're looking for the slightly thicker twig above them, from which the individual twiglets separated.'

'And that's a blur?' said Leon.

'Afraid so. They used to think the daddy was a guy called *Homo heidelbergensis*. But we think he's too young.'

'Any other suspects?' said Susan.

'Well, there's a guy called *Homo antecessor*, but we think *he* was too old.'

'Sounds like there were a lot of human types around.'

'There were. Maybe a dozen. It was a real hit-and-miss business to arrive at the survivor. Us.'

'So where did this common ancestor live?' said Leon.

'We don't know,' said Mark. 'Could be anywhere. Africa, Europe, Asia.'

'Or the good old USA?'

'No. We didn't get any humans till the Exodus Event, when a few hundred Sapiens, people at last like you and me, went out through North-East Africa and colonised the world. About sixty-five thousand years ago. They got to America over the land bridge with Russia. On foot. No Bering Sea then.'

'So how come this daddy guy might have been in Europe before the big exodus?'

'Because there'd been lots of unsuccessful trips out of Africa before. Early versions of the human had tried to settle all over Eurasia. Then the next wave, slightly different, would come out and maybe breed with the previous lot. But none of them survived. Like *Homo erectus*, they died and left their bones in the ground.'

'Presumably some went back to Africa,' said Susan. 'Don't you think? The homesick types?'

'Maybe,' said Mark. 'And maybe that shuttle, that gene flow, to and fro, was helpful in allowing the most robust version to emerge.'

154

'Us?' said Leon.

'Yup. But now things are confused by this new discovery in Brittany. *Homo vannesiensis*. We're not sure where he fits in.'

'Wow,' said Susan. 'Am I descended from a Frenchman? *Passez-moi le Camembert*.'

'Camembert's from Normandy,' said Leon. 'Even I—'

'I doubt it, Susan,' said Talissa. 'But the dates are interesting. And we can date more accurately than we used to. Much more accurately than with DNA.'

'OK,' said Leon. 'Science makes my head hurt. Shall we talk about the Yankees now?'

It was nearly midnight by the time Talissa stirred Pelham from his bed beneath the window and said her goodbyes. Mark said he'd walk back with her, since his subway station was in that direction. When they got to her brownstone, Talissa found that she had invited Mark in for a last drink.

'You were so sweet the way you explained all that stuff,' she said, sitting on the sofa next to him. She had drunk about three times what she was used to and had to close her eyes to stop the room from spinning.

'Not too technical?'

'A child could have followed.'

When she looked up again, she found herself admiring Mark's patient modesty and his dark brown eyes more sincerely with each passing moment.

'This is a truly terrible idea,' she said, leaning forward and kissing him.

'I know. I've never done this before. Not with a colleague who—'

'Of course you haven't. Come this way.'

She wanted to feel the panic of her secret knowledge being

physically crushed. She longed to indulge the kind of urge that wouldn't have given a second's pause to their common ancestor. She pulled off her top and felt the night air on her breasts. God, I'm like a fucking bonobo was the last thing she remembered thinking as she pushed down her underwear.

The meeting with Catrina Olsen took place in her office in Russell Square.

'I think there's something not quite right with Seth,' said Talissa. She wanted to feel her way, to see what Dr Olsen knew.

'That's what you said in your message. I did alert Dr Wood in case he could help. But I couldn't give him any details.'

'No . . . I didn't say too much in the message. I wanted to discuss it in person.'

'Of course. We pride ourselves on following up. Ten years, twenty years. We're always here.'

Talissa breathed in hard and tasted the last of the chilli eggs and tea with which Kavya Gopal had sent her out into the world that morning.

'Well,' she said. 'When we went through the process, all those years ago, were you aware of anything unusual?'

'I've looked through my notes and—'

'You keep notes?'

'Yes. I just write things down at home. The computer systems here are full of firewalls. Also, the files have a limited life. After a fixed period, they self-erase.'

'Yeah, I'm familiar with that system at home. Is that the Parn's choice?'

'Confidentiality is key for us, but mostly it's the law of the land. There was a big new privacy law in 2038 and more data protection acts a couple of years back. Pen and paper's not a bad backup.'

'And what did your notebook say?'

Catrina picked up a piece of paper. 'Nothing remarkable. It recorded an "American surrogate, aged twenty-six". It says, "She was humorous and detached. Career-minded, returning to USA. High score on DR psych test. Procedure regular and without incident." DR is Professor Redding. Or Dr Redding as he was then.'

'I remember him. Button-down shirts.'

'Then there's a follow-up about the pregnancy and the birth. All good.'

Dr Olsen's features glowed with reassurance and expensive face creams. Had she also had a little artificial help? Talissa wondered.

'What did the Parn conclude from its collaboration with the British health service? The scheme I was part of.'

'Nothing amazing, I think. Malik Wood did publish a paper on the findings. As I recall, it was quite technical, mostly about oestrogen levels.'

'No breakthrough in embryology research?'

'No. But you have to keep trying. We did another partner scheme five years later and found some interesting things about early miscarriage.'

Talissa wished she had better interviewing skills. In the DA's office, Susan would have picked up a few tips on how to corner a witness; she would have known what to ask next.

Catrina Olsen was a medical doctor, so must have sworn a number of ethical oaths: she was unlikely to be party to something underhand. And there was, beneath the creamy skin, a sense of dedication. Talissa recognised someone else who had put her work first.

'Do you have kids yourself?'

'I do,' said Dr Olsen. 'Two boys. Teenagers now, with enormous feet.'

'And . . . do you find them surprising? Or predictable?'

'Utterly surprising.' Catrina laughed. 'They seem so unlike us. I put it down to the way the world has changed. Information. How we access it. And diet.'

Talissa remembered a conversation in which Mary had said similar things about Seth, though less blithely. After a moment, she said, 'Is it quite unheard of for a child born by in vitro to discover that its father was not who it was meant to be?'

'I wish it were,' said Dr Olsen, 'but I've heard some horror stories. Most clinics in London are oversubscribed and under-funded. Some of the basic admin work is done by students. But I can absolutely assure you that it's never happened here. There's no chance of a drunken hospital porter slapping on the wrong label.'

'All right, Dr Olsen,' said Talissa, trying to force a DA note into her voice. 'I'm going to ask you a question. But before I do, I'd like you to swear that you won't repeat it. To anyone.'

Catrina Olsen laughed. 'Repeat what? The question itself?'

'Whether the answer's yes or no, you must never tell any-one that I asked. Not your husband, not your director. Least of all him.'

In Catrina's face, Talissa saw primitive curiosity at war with professional certainties. In the end, her confidence in her long-time employer was victorious.

'All right,' she said, smiling. 'Ask away.'

'And you promise never to——'

'Yes, I promise.'

'Did you know that the father of one of the eight children in the scheme was of a different species?'

Talissa stayed a few more days in London. She was hoping for an interview with Malik Wood, but he was still in Berlin, she was told, and the institute couldn't give out his contact details. There was no need to rush home. She was trying to work out what her drunken night with Mark LaSalle might amount to and thought some time away would help. Her long kitchen confabs with Kavya Gopal were another reason to linger.

For the first time, Mrs G approved of what her own government was trying to do.

'I'm all in favour of these picks,' she said.

'I beg your pardon?' said Talissa, putting down her tea.

'They've introduced a system called Personal Identity Cards. We call them PICs for short.'

'What are they?'

'They're a way of trying to make life fairer. It's like an ID card, except that it records details of where you're from, where your parents came from, their income, how long they've lived in the country, if they went to college, your own education, your birth gender and something about your race.'

'Race? They can't still be using that word! It's unscientific.'

'The government have a new term for it, but I forget what it is. But you know what I mean.'

'I do. But if you used that word where I live . . . Oh boy.'

'My husband and I used to call ourselves "mixed-race". It was a badge of honour in those days.'

'History's like that,' said Talissa. 'Martin Luther King referred to his brothers and sisters as "Negroes". When I was a kid, they still talked about "people of colour". Can you believe it! Anyway, tell me about the PICs.'

'It's a system to put right anything that's been a disadvantage in the past. It was our belated response to ADEPT. You know, the United Nations thing that—'

'Of course.'

'I think it's worked quite well,' said Kavya.

'So how did your kids do? Sanjiv, for instance?'

'Third generation in this country gave him half a point. Parents not at college a full point. Nothing for being a boy.'

'What about me? Would I get anything because my dad died when I was a child?'

'Yes. You're what they call a half orphan. You'd get something for that. Five's the best. If you're a Fiver, you can walk into anything.'

They sat at the kitchen table, adding up their scores. 'Anyway,' said Kavya, 'you lose two for being American.'

'Stop it! But has the scheme been any good for your kids?'

'Aidan doesn't need PICs. He's a finance director now.'

The steamy Muswell Hill kitchen, as twice before, gave Talissa a respite from her life, and she was reluctant to leave. Only the thought that she would soon become a burden persuaded her to pack her bag and head for the airport two days later.

On the plane, she thought about Catrina Olsen's response to her question. Shock and disbelief had struggled for a while on her face as she tried to find words; but the incredulity was slowly undermined by a visible, seeping panic.

'I'm afraid so,' said Talissa, when she thought Catrina had struggled long enough. 'Your boss. You know . . .'

'Malik?'

'No. The one above him.'

All the colour had by now ebbed from Catrina's face. 'Parn . . .' The word was barely audible.

'Those guys,' Talissa said. 'Artificial intelligence . . . Solar-powered spaceships . . . Immortality . . . All that big dickery.'

Catrina held up a hand.

'The money means they live by other rules,' Talissa went on. 'Not the law. Then they say it's for the good of human-kind. Dear God.'

'But how could they . . .'

'Do you want me to explain the science? I expect you'd understand the details better than I do.'

'I know it's been technically feasible for a time. But the laws. The ethics. I *mean*!'

In the end, Talissa had felt sorry for Catrina and tried to reassure her that nothing would leak out. 'My priority is to protect the child in question.'

'Of course,' said Catrina, struggling to stop tears running down her face.

9

Pelham had been dropped off in the apartment by Susan on her way to work and was sent into a spin when Talissa got back from JFK that afternoon. Her safe return from the store triggered a welcome-home gift, but a week away taxed all his resources, as he ran round the apartment in search of tributes to lay at her feet.

When she had settled him down, Talissa checked her messages and was startled to see one from the office of Lukas Parn inviting her personally for a weekend in Connecticut. It was well crafted, with no sense of threat, though the question of why he should want to see one of eight women in a long-ago surrogacy trial was not touched on.

Ten days later, she took the train. It was not long before the smell of pizza and the glare of subterranean Penn Station were forgotten in the wash of sunlight on quilted green fields. At East Norwalk, she and Pelham were met by a man at the barrier.

'Dr Adam? I'm Steve. You can put the little feller in the back here. Let me take your bag now.'

They climbed into what looked like an armoured assault vehicle, painted white, and moved off silently from the parking lot.

'Your first time in Connecticut?' said Steve.

'I've been a coupla times.'

'Prettiest state in the Union.'

After a short spin on the freeway, they spent ten minutes on a smaller road, then turned onto a track. They passed through an old turnpike, then some white-painted gates that opened at their approach, after which there was a half-mile drive through giant oaks and redwoods.

'Feels like California, don't it? Could be in Sequoia National Park. Had them brought over special.'

They came to a ridge, from which Talissa could see down towards a tree-fringed lake. It reminded her of the park attached to the chateau where she'd camped with the Pedersens. To the far right, in the distance, was a stone circle of prehistoric design.

Even if the trees had had to be imported, she could see why Lukas Parn had chosen the site. From the lake, a flight of ducks took off in ragged formation; beyond the upright stones the air glittered with the thinned light off Long Island Sound. The vehicle turned suddenly onto a drive, at the end of which stood a mansion in the antebellum style: shuttered, with long verandas. Talissa smiled. Just because it had been manufactured didn't mean it wasn't elegant. She dropped down from the assault vehicle onto the gravel.

'This is Alice,' said Steve. 'She'll take care of you from here on in.'

A young woman in short pants and sneakers smiled and held out her hand. Talissa was pleased by the casual outfit; she'd thrown in only one dress on top of the jeans and T-shirts in her own bag. She followed Alice inside, through the hall and up a wide staircase, imagining the rustle of crinolines, then down a passageway hung with oil paintings to a pair of oak doors.

'Hope this is OK for you,' said Alice. 'You can call down for anything you like, though there's most things you might want in the little pantry there. You close the curtains with this button here if you'd like a nap. Lukas says he'll see you downstairs at six if that's OK. Would the dog like something to eat?'

'No, it's OK, I brought him some food. And the bathroom?'

'It's through those doors there. And the spa and pool are down below. The pool's at 79.5 degrees, but I can make it warmer if you like. It only needs a minute. You take the elevator to minus one. Would you like me to fix you a massage?'

'No, it's fine, thanks. I'll just . . . settle in. I have a book I need to finish.'

'A book? Right.' Alice closed the doors behind her.

In the pantry were two fridges. The first held rows of white wine, as well as Salon champagne and some craft beers. Talissa took a Diet Coke and found some pre-sliced lemon in the second fridge, on whose lower shelf were various deli plates. She nibbled some buffalo pastrami, then took the whole dish guiltily to the nightstand with her drink.

The bed was big enough for half a dozen. Talissa sat propped up in the middle and gazed through the window down towards the stone circle, through which some sheep were wandering. Once, at a conference in Chicago, when the Holiday Inn was overbooked, she'd been moved by the organisers into a Four Seasons room overlooking Lake Michigan. By comparison, the Parn suite was a Five Seasons. It would be good if Mark were there, she had to admit. Mark had discovered that Professor Hillenbrand thought he was below par intellectually and a potential menace to women. Alarmed by the knowledge, he did everything he could, in public and private, to prove her wrong. This made him, Talissa had to admit, a very easy companion: alert in conversation, yet responsive and altruistic in the bedroom. He was no trouble at all.

It turned out she was more tired than she'd thought and the pillows in their starched cases began to whisper bluegrass lullabies in her ears. After an enlivening sleep and a shower beneath a Niagara of lightly scented water, she drank some tea, put on the dress and some silver sandals and went out into the grounds with Pelham, on a tight leash for the sheep's sake. She was drawn towards the sea, where she let the dog run up and down the beach, dipping into the shallows and shying back, affronted each time by the cold, then shaking himself before cantering off again with an incredulous smile.

When it was nearly six, she walked back to the house, gave Pelham a sachet of Call of the Wild bison mix, told him to stay off the bed, shut the door and went downstairs.

'Dr Adam. Hi. Step this way.'

Lukas Parn was a funny-looking little guy, Talissa thought, as he gripped her hand. His face looked like a leather mask that had spent too long in the tannery while fake eyelashes were stuck into his lids. His hair sprang from its follicles with a black, synthetic vigour. At least his short denim pants and bare legs looked credible, as did his second-day T-shirt.

He led her through to the immense saloon, whose floor-to-ceiling doors gave onto a terrace and a lawn that overlooked the Sound. He sat cross-legged in an armchair and waved Talissa towards one of the sofas.

She sat, feeling, even in her simple cotton shift, a little overdressed.

'You like it here?' he said.

'It's great. Is this where you live?'

'No, I live in what was East Berlin, but I try to spend time here when I'm in America. Do you play golf?'

'What? No. There was no golf where I grew up. The Bronx.'

'Shame. I have eighteen holes. I had to buy some land for the thirteenth and fourteenth. Got it from my neighbour. Charged me a fortune.' Parn laughed.

'What can I get you to drink?' asked Alice, who had come silently into the room on her bare feet.

'Usual for me. Dr Adam?'

A warning flickered in Talissa's mind. Something mild. 'A beer, maybe?'

'Wicked Ship coming right up.'

When Alice had left them with the drinks, Parn said, 'Good of you to come, Dr Adam. Accepting an invitation from a stranger.'

'Nice of you to invite me,' said Talissa, nudging her pawn forward in turn.

'You were in touch with my place in London, I understand.'

'Yeah, I visited two weeks ago. I spoke with Dr Olsen.'

'Good. She's been there twenty years. Knows everything about embryology.'

Talissa drank a little of the beer.

'And did you have a concern you wanted to talk about?' said Parn.

'Some assurances.' She had practised this conversation.

'Assurances?'

'To do with privacy.'

'Whose privacy?'

'The child I carried as surrogate mother fifteen years ago.'

'We have the highest standards of confidentiality. We set the bar.'

'Well, that's a start.'

'You seem anxious. Do you know something I don't know about the kid?'

'That depends on what you know.'

'Perhaps we should talk about this over dinner. I have some plans that might interest you.'

'OK.' Talissa felt relieved that she had given nothing away so far.

Half an hour later, Parn was showing her round his stone circle. 'It was inspired by Avebury in England,' he said. 'The stones themselves came from Iceland.'

On the grass in the middle, there was a small table with some chairs. Alice appeared between two monoliths.

'What would you like for dinner, Dr Adam?'

'What are we having?' said Talissa.

'Whatever you like. We have everything.'

'I'm going to get a hot dog with mustard and some chilli tacos,' said Lukas Parn. 'And another root beer. Then cherry and walnut ice cream.'

Talissa found her mind empty. 'Maybe a salad?'

'What kind of salad?'

'Oh God.' Her mind grew even blanker. 'Do you have samosas?'

'I'm sure we do. With salad?'

'Yes. And . . . anything else Indian. Anything.'

'A selection of Indian dishes, with salad. You got it.'

She had been expecting something like the candle-lit castle dinner in the first reel of a Dracula movie. But the picnic table was not even laid and her host was picking at a scab on his foot.

'So,' Parn was saying, 'when the sun rises over the Sound there, the first rays strike that omphalos. Then it throws a shadow. I had an astronomer work out the geometry so they could be placed to the millimetre. What's your birth sign?'

'What?'

'When's your birthday?'

'May.'

'Taurus or Gemini?'

'*What*?'

Parn laughed. 'Come and sit down. Take this chair so you can look over the water. It's calculated that at the exact hour and minute of my birth the sun's reflection from the silica quartz particles in Omphalos Maximus, the big one over there, triggers a laser in the ground to project an image of a Sagittarius over the entire henge.'

'And to think for my birthday I got a cupcake from the students.'

While Alice shuttled back and forth with the food, Lukas Parn said, 'Let me tell you a little more of what we've been doing. You know my background?'

'Near enough.'

'Good. No need to recap. I'm an originator. A philanthropic disrupter.'

Talissa managed not to say 'Of course you are.'

'Life fascinates me. I don't want mine to end. Maybe we can fix that. I believe so. Meanwhile, past lives interest me too. Creatures we'll never see again. Or thought we wouldn't.

You probably remember a man from a few years back called George Church?'

'I know the name. At Harvard, wasn't he?'

'He said he could recreate a woolly mammoth from fossil DNA.'

'I remember.'

'My people in Wyoming actually did it. In 2028. We kept it quiet.'

'You're telling me.'

'The bastard died. It was a herd animal. Turns out it didn't like to be alone. We tried to create a mate, but there were a lot of mutant disasters. Creatures from the black lagoon, had to be disposed of pronto. Also, he didn't like the climate. Plus there were problems with its immune system in the modern world.'

'I see.'

'We're doing a lot of scanning and mining in Siberia right now, though. See what we can find beneath the permafrost. Climate change has been a blessing.'

'Any other creatures you've recreated?'

'An aurochs. But it died too. Our most successful was a thylacine.'

'A what?'

'Tasmanian wolf. Killed off by the Poms after they'd wiped out most of the humans. But not long ago. Very close to my heart. I lived in Hobart for a time as a kid. It looks like a dog, though it's a marsupial. You know. Has a pouch. Ours is still alive in a compound in Wyoming, somewhere off Route 59.'

'Is it OK?'

'He's quite happy, I think. Fucks a lot of local canids they bring in.'

'Lucky thylacine.'

'How's the dinner?'

'It's good, thanks. How's the hot dog?'

'Hot,' said Parn.

'And canid?'

'Ha! Now, to get real. It may be that one day an extinct species will live again. I don't know. That's all a bit Disney for me. What I'm interested in is the human animal. How we got to be like this and why we are so different. I think that interests you as well.'

'It's a part of my job.'

'I don't quite believe the usual explanation. Routine evolution by natural selection.'

'What are you suggesting?'

'I'm suggesting that we need to study more to find the scientific answer. The obvious way is by comparison with other human species. Isolate the differences. The benefits of understanding what I call the Great Saltation, or the Big Leap, if you prefer – the thing that made us only a little lower than the angels . . . If we knew how that worked, what the code was in genetic terms, the health benefits would be incredible.'

Talissa said nothing. Darkness was falling over Long Island Sound.

'Are you cold?' said Parn. 'We can go back inside if you like.'

'It's great out here, but . . . Yeah. Maybe.'

Back in the house, Parn took Talissa down a corridor to a second saloon, slightly smaller than the first. He turned on a light switch to illuminate a picture gallery, among which were soup cans and film stars.

'These are my pride and joy,' he said. 'The Warhols. Good, aren't they?'

'They're like posters,' said Talissa. 'We had one on the wall in my freshman year.'

'Let's try in here,' said Parn, opening a door in the corner.

He pointed to a canvas. 'You recognise the painter?'

'It looks familiar. Is it French?'

'By way of Russia.'

A moon-faced child was floating through the sky above a peasant settlement.

'Chagall?' said Talissa, the word forming on her lips some-how. Where had that come from?

'Good,' said Parn. 'Do you like his work?'

She didn't. It looked to her like a greetings card gone wrong, but having been so blunt about the Warhols, she backed off. 'It's . . . cute,' she said.

'Anything else you like in here?'

Talissa cast her eyes round the room. She went to most of the big shows at the Met, but had no claim to expertise. None of Lukas Parn's pictures touched her; they seemed to have been picked out to reflect his acuity in buying them. By the window was a small oil of a pewter jug. 'That's nice,' she said. 'That little one.'

In the main saloon, Parn offered more drinks, but Talissa declined. He himself rang for a cappuccino.

'Do you mind if we go back to the Big Leap?' he said. 'It's nice for me to be able to talk to someone who knows a bit of "ancient history".'

Why had he said the words like that, with spin? Talissa was glad she'd drunk only two small beers. 'Of course.'

'So,' said Parn, 'we think of Neanderthals living in Europe

and Asia for some hundreds of thousands of years, developing slowly, very slowly. Stone tools, wooden spears. Maybe some pigment art. Boy, were they in no rush.'

'I think it took all they had just to survive. Incredible extremes of climate. A chaos of ice ages and warming. Volcanic eruptions. No time for Warhols.'

'OK. Then finally – finally – a new human species, Sapiens, is formed in Africa. And a few thousand of them travel up through the Middle East and conquer the world.'

'Possibly no more than eight hundred, some scholars now think.'

'The number goes down every year! You'll be giving me their passport numbers next. Imagine! That crazy little caravan. Those desperadoes.'

'I have imagined them,' said Talissa. 'More often than you can know.'

'Men, women. Children born on the march . . . the old ones dying . . . some maybe staying to make settlements . . . it's like *The Grapes of Wrath*, for Christ's sake. On a bigger scale.'

'A smaller scale, in fact, we now think.'

'But they were modern in their brain and in their self-awareness. They had the consciousness that you and I have. The thing that sets us apart from all other creatures.'

'So we believe,' said Talissa. 'But we don't know for sure that they already had it.'

'Explain.'

'Well . . . Perhaps one of them, a lonely, frightened nomad, confronted someone from another human species somewhere in what's now Iraq. And in that moment of alarm first discovered self-awareness by trying to guess the intentions of the other.'

Silenced at last, Parn put down his coffee cup.

'Well, maybe,' he said. 'The consensus now is that the capacity for consciousness, the genes that code for the necessary connections in the brain, had been around for tens of thousands of years. Like feathers in birds before they were used to fly. It was environmental pressure that caused this circuit to become active. Perhaps it was living in larger groups. The need to learn, to teach and to remember.'

Talissa looked out over the darkened lawns towards the sea. 'I'm not a neuroscientist,' she said.

'Suppose it *was* Darwinian,' said Parn. 'You know. By the book. A mutation in the brain of one individual that caused the faculty to form. So. Huge and obvious advantages, heavily selected for, widely passed on. But there were still probably some steps along the way. Joe Sap going up through the Gulf states into the belly of Europe sixty-five thousand years ago wasn't self-aware in the same way you and I are. I suspect there were other operating systems that got updated. Maybe he was on what you might call HS5, while you and I are running on HS12.'

'We don't know that.'

'No. We don't. But my feeling is that somewhere round HS5 there was a major breakthrough. The Big Jump. Neanderthals had set the standard rate of human development at one mph. Now these Sapiens are going at Mach 1. Speed of sound. And maybe the earlier programs are still in the guts of the machine. In the hardware. In the genes, in other words.'

'We'll never know that. Not in our lifetimes.'

'Not in yours anyway. Sorry. That was a tasteless joke. So. What we really need to know is whether other human species had the same faculty of consciousness that we have. And if they had the upsides of it, did they have the downsides too.'

'What do you mean?'

'The bad stuff. The pre-emptive massacres. Think of Joe Sap plodding up the Euphrates and suddenly meeting his first human of a different species. You're saying that by trying to figure out what the other guy was going to do, he may have discovered the whole idea of planning and volition in himself.'

'Maybe.'

'But suppose Joe doesn't like the idea of this other guy having plans that Joe can't read. Makes him scared. So he decides it's best to kill him. World War One. When no one wanted to declare war, but no one wanted to be caught out either. So they killed ten million to be on the safe side. Or Iraq Two. Same idea. Or all the killing in between. The whole history of humanity. Murder as precaution.'

Talissa smiled. 'Other drawbacks?'

'Well,' said Lukas Parn. 'Dementia. Psychosis. The Sapiens diseases. Madness. The second thing that makes us different from all the other primates.'

'Too much guesswork now,' said Talissa. 'I'm a data-driven scientist.'

'So am I, so am I! That's why I'm hungry for more facts. I want to find out if other human species had the same kind of mental consciousness. Then we can begin to see how Sapiens became exceptional. At what point and how we became able to build cathedrals. And if other human species, given time or the Big Jump, could have done the same – if they'd survived. And to understand how the Sapiens wiring went wrong to allow in all the malfunctions. A few demented young, whole shitloads of demented old.'

'Most animals get deaf and woozy when they're old.'

'But they don't go crazy. Delusional. Not in the same way.'

'It's a big project.'

'I like big projects. Then, once we know, maybe we can figure out a way of helping humankind.' Parn stood up. 'Shall we go and look at the sea before we go to bed?'

He pushed open one of the French windows and led the way across a terrace and down over the lawns, under which soft, hidden lights were triggered by his steps. At the point where the grass met the sand dunes, there was a wooden platform with a rail. As they leant on it, Lukas Parn began to point out and name the stars above them, while Talissa wondered how she was going to wrench the conversation round to Seth.

'. . . gas giants, more than a million light years away . . .' Parn was saying. 'Hard to get your head round astronomy, isn't it?'

'Had you down as more of an astrology guy,' said Talissa.

'What?'

'You know, "Virgos are loving and loyal and fond of stationery" kind of thing.'

Parn laughed briefly. 'People get me wrong. They expect me to be a geek. Sure, I used to talk that tech bro stuff, especially when I was microdosing ayahuasca. Synergistic decacorns . . . incubator AI singularity . . .'

'You did what?'

'Exactly. I dropped it partly because it scared people off. But the real reason is that I don't care about the "speed of science". OK, the Chinese have a working space escalator. So what? I bet you don't even know where it is. It makes no difference to you and me how they shuttle up the goods to their little space station. What matters is human nature. What are seven billion people going to do with their lives when AI already does their jobs better? First we need to understand ourselves.'

'Maybe.'

'And I'll tell you something else, Talissa. Money. People can be dismissive of the power of money. Old Europe, for instance. They're snobbish about it. But money can buy you views like this. Stars, soft grass. Art, comfort, happiness.'

'And *are* you happy?' said Talissa, curious despite herself.

'God, yes. My wealth enables me to focus on discovery. Philanthropy.'

Through the seat of her dress, Talissa felt the press of a stranger's hand. She jumped.

'You could be part of that,' said Parn smoothly, as if the hand belonged to someone else. 'We could work together and—'

'I'm sorry?'

'I don't often meet people who hold their own with me. Even if you were a bit rude about my pics. You're also, if I'm allowed to say these things, a very—'

'I need to check on my dog. Excuse me.'

'Breakfast is at nine in the sunroom.'

Talissa ran across the lawn in her silver sandals.

A knocking dragged her from unconsciousness among the down and pillows. Alice put her head round the door.

'Breakfast in fifteen.'

'I think I'll pass, thanks. Not really a breakfast kind of gal.'

'Lukas has a surprise for you.'

'God.' She hauled herself upright. 'I have to take the dog out. Maybe twenty minutes. See how I feel.'

'Tea or coffee?' said Alice. 'Or something else?'

The sunroom was on the south side of the house, in a wing pushed out towards the sea. A maid was in charge of what was clearly the big food event of the day. Lukas Parn wasn't there, which gave Talissa time to prepare what she was going to say while the pancakes and fruit platters came and went. 'Would you like some corned beef hash now?' said the maid. 'Or would you like a mimosa?'

Talissa winced. There was nothing she liked less than orange juice and sparkling wine, unless it was the phoney name it went by. 'No, thank you. I'm all done,' she said, and took Pelham on his leash out onto the lawn.

In the distance, she saw Lukas Parn sitting on a rustic bench in an arboretum above the lake. She walked over briskly and, having clipped the loop on Pelham's leash to a bend of the woodwork, sat down beside him.

'About last night,' he started.

'This morning is what matters,' Talissa said. 'We didn't get to the point. Maybe we don't even need to spell out the details of how it happened. The safety and well-being of a child are what we need to talk about. I'm here to get some assurances.'

'Go on.'

'I've discovered that one of the children born fifteen years ago in London is more than fifty per cent Neanderthal. The boy I carried for two innocent people.'

'How did you—'

'None of your business. I'm not going to describe the kind of trauma this was for me. Or what this would mean to his parents.'

She felt Parn's eyes steady on her face. She gripped the edge of the bench. Parn said nothing.

'Someone in this story,' she went on, 'is a monster. And it sure isn't the poor boy. I haven't looked into the legal situation yet.'

'I have.'

'Please be quiet. In any case, it would presumably come under English law. Let's leave that to one side. Let's talk about confidentiality. If what your people did was to get out publicly, you'd be ruined. Finished. Maybe you'd go to a federal jail in New Jersey, maybe you'd be banged up in London. Who cares?'

'If what you're implying is true – and I'm admitting nothing – it's likely to be seen as a tort not a crime. Therefore remediable by the payment of damages. No Sing Sing.'

'I don't care. The important thing is that your name would be on it. You could never work again. No more the big innovator. No more being ... what was your word ... a "disrupter". No more big dick stuff of any kind. You'd just go back indoors and count your money. There'd be nothing else left for you to do in the rest of your life.'

'I can promise you that no names will ever reach the public from our end of things. That was never the plan.'

'What was the plan?'

'Research. For the good of humanity. And finally to publish the huge scientific implications. Think back to what we were talking about last night.'

'And you thought it ethical to create a hybrid without consulting anyone involved?'

'We're all hybrids. We all have traces of those early introgressors and antecessors. Little smudgy fingerprints. One day we'll map the full lineage, all the gene flow between different human species.'

'That's not the point.'

'What is the point? What's more important than research? Than science?'

'The life of this child.'

'Come off it, Talissa. Let's think back fifty thousand years to somewhere in Spain or Uzbekistan. Here's the Neanderthal settlement. Some sort of corral maybe with shelters and a fire. Here come the children of Joe Sapiens, just out of Africa. They meet. They communicate. They breed. We know this happened many hundreds, even thousands of times because the evidence is in our genes. Yours as much as mine.'

'That has nothing to do with today.'

'Of course it does! Joe Sap is drawn to lovely Miss Neander. It's true love in the Steppes. Roast aurochs for dinner, then it's a regular fuckfest. What's their child like? I'll tell you. He's like the one now living in London. Genetically that's who he is. And he's the ancestor of both of us. Many thousands of these hybrid people lived and bred all over Eurasia. And from them, you and I are descended. Are you saying there was something wrong with them, these brave people? That our grandparents were worth less than us?'

'No, I'm not. I'm—'

'Because that would be "racist", wouldn't it? If we still used that word.'

Talissa stood up, feeling that the conversation had got away from her.

'It's quite simple,' she said. 'This must never get out. The boy must be protected. From what I understand, he's a normal kid who lives a happy life and gets on OK in school.'

'Not surprising,' said Parn. 'Either his mother's genes got lucky or, more likely, the difference between the father's and mother's contributions was too slight to make much differ-ence in the phenotype. In the way he is.'

'I know what a phenotype is,' said Talissa. 'What I'm tell-ing you is that if ever this does get out, I will go straight to the nearest news station and tell them what your people did.'

'And suppose it leaks from your end?' said Parn. 'After all, you've presumably had a DNA test done. So that's immediately . . . How many people would you say in the lab and in the office? I'd say that's half a dozen potential weak points. By comparison, we have a circle of three. All of whom swore in blood before the event.'

'The deal remains the same. It gets out, you get named.'

Lukas Parn stood up and began to walk towards the house. 'I'm sorry about last night. I was carried away by my enthusi-asm. It happens. But I'm hoping to start a new research centre up the coast, near Narragansett. If ever you got sick of your job, I'd be looking for someone to oversee it. Parts of the building are a little run-down, but there'd be a budget to remodel.'

'Just give me your word again. On total confidentiality.'

'You have my word. I don't want a leak any more than you do.'

'And if anything does start to get out you'll do everything you can to protect the privacy of the kid.'

'Sure will.'

Talissa wasn't sure how much Parn's word was worth, but she felt it was the best she could do.

'Will you stay for lunch?' he said, as they neared the house. 'I've got this string quartet coming in from Boston. To play in the stone circle.'

'No, thanks. I don't like that kind of music.'

*

180

When she unpacked her bag back in her apartment, Talissa found a small rectangular parcel, embedded in her refolded clothes. She bridled to think of someone rummaging in her laundry. Between the paper and the bubble wrap was a card. 'This is the surprise that Alice mentioned at brekkie. It comes as a gift with my best wishes and admiration. Lukas. PS Narragansett . . . Have a think.'

Beneath a layer of tissue was a painting, the one of the pewter jug she had admired. On the back of it was a sticker that read 'William Nicholson. Leicester Galleries, London, 1934'.

She retrieved the wrapping from the bin so she could send the picture back.

PART THREE

2047

1

Talissa heard no more from Lukas Parn after she had, with a hint of regret, returned the painting. Weeks went by and the need to confide the secret of Seth's parentage began to feel less acute. Months passed. Nothing happened. On bad days she felt like a character in a film noir who becomes implicated in a crime from whose coils she will never be free; her dreams were soured by impending discoveries of vile deeds she could not remember being part of, but for which she faced the chair.

The best salve was her correspondence with Mary. As they had predicted in Russell Square, the separation of mother and surrogate by the Atlantic was helpful, with Talissa in the role of foreign godmother. Seth, Mary said, was pleasure-seeking and impulsive, with no thought of consequences and no fall-back plans. On his first and only ski trip, he had disappeared off the back of a mountain, leaving Wilson Kalu and his younger sister alone as darkness fell; he had gone sailboarding on a reservoir in south London without a life jacket, regardless of the fact that he had never learned to swim. On the other hand, he had, to everyone's surprise, been offered a place at an ancient university. Aged seventeen, he had shown an interest in engineering and some aptitude for it. Any shortfall in his exam grades was to be made up for by PIC points connected to his parents, his maintained school and the means by which he had been conceived. In a year's time, he would apparently be living among ivy-covered quadrangles of old stone and scant sanitation. 'Of course, Alaric puts it all down to that bloody train set.'

Talissa's relationship with Mark LaSalle moved into a frictionless phase; she had even taken him to the Appalachians for a week of camping, to which she had become addicted. 'I'm going to make you my Italian sausage and bean casserole tonight,' she said. 'If you play your cards right.' He had claimed, with a straight face, to enjoy the experience.

The pleasure she took in Mark's company was genuine, if nothing like the elation she had felt with Felix, who, according to Susan, had gone back to hospital.

'Leon tells me he's gone to a different place,' she said. 'In Vermont, I think.'

Talissa had messaged Felix regularly, but it had been a long time – almost seven years – since she had seen him. The Massachusetts state facility in which he'd been an inpatient for six months had sounded too grim to visit; then when he was back home in Queens there'd seemed no need. The Vermont place was said to be more cheerful and less dependent on stupefying drugs to keep the patients ticking over.

So one day at semester's end, she flew to Burlington and took a cab up through the hills, in the direction of Canada. The grey road with its yellow stripe went past logging tracks and painted cowsheds as it ran through the woods. She'd made an appointment with a Dr Ramos, the resident psychiatrist, who was familiar with Felix's case. The taxi turned down a track between conifers and deposited her outside

Greenhills House. In her street clothes, she felt out of place. 'Too bad I don't have a milkmaid's outfit,' she muttered out loud as she went up some steps into a large building that had been breeze-blocked into the trees, then covered with sawn local timber to give it a more homey, log-cabin feel.

Inside it was like a faltering motel, with no one on reception. Eventually, she was shown down two corridors to an office and asked to wait. She looked out of the back window over a paddock towards some pine woods. The door from the passage swung open and a man in denim work clothes came in. He had grey hair and a round belly, but no toolbox. Talissa smiled up politely. Through his beard he muttered something she didn't catch. There were two armchairs and a cheap coffee table, on which was a bowl with two apples and a half-finished glass of water. The man lingered, shifting his weight, and coughed. Talissa looked again and saw that it was Felix.

She stood up and gripped his forearms. Felix and not Felix. But he knew her. She could tell by the way he nodded his head. Then the years broke through her. She put her arms round him and began to sob. Christ, Christ, *Christ* . . .

He diffidently touched her head.

It took her time to compose herself. Laughing, pushing back the hair from her wet face, she sat down in one of the chairs while Felix took the other.

There was no point in asking him how he was. 'I heard from Susan you were here,' she said in the end. 'Looks like a good place.'

'I've been here a long time.'

'But you go home to New York when you want.'

'I do what I like.'

His voice was flat. She looked at the hands that had once thrilled her with their movement in the air, the hands that had held her. The fingers were stained with nicotine.

'So . . . I guess your days are peaceful here.'

Felix shook his head. 'I've met a man who has business interests,' he said. 'In Arabia. He makes a lot of money.'

'That's good. Saudi Arabia? I thought we'd broken off relations.'

'In my father's house are many mansions.'

'What do you mean?'

'The sands of Arabia.'

She tried a different tack. 'Susan and Leon are back together. I think this time it's for good. Which is just great. They're so obviously made for each other.' There was no response. 'Leon's such a cutie too. You still see him from time to time?'

'Yeah.'

'They have this real nice apartment not far from where I live now. Leon's mysterious job must be going well. Did you ever understand what he does?'

Felix looked down.

'Did you know I have a dog? Pelham. He's a great little guy. He talks to me. Then if I'm staying home and I've finished work, we'll watch a movie together. On the couch.'

'Right.'

'He only likes animations, to be honest. He falls asleep in the other stuff.' She paused. 'Felix?'

His eyes moved to meet hers.

'What do you do all day?'

'My aunt comes to visit. She doesn't like it if I'm not here. The guy upstairs is a pain in the ass.'

'What does he do?'

'He's up all night trying to see what's going on. He has a telescope. He says it's for looking at the stars.'

Talissa glanced down at the table, the shiny supermarket apples. She could guess how they tasted. She inhaled through the tightness in her chest. Fearless, wasn't she? Or meant to be. Go on, then.

'Do you know who I am, Felix?'

'I've told my aunt about him.'

'You don't have an aunt, my love. Do you know who I am?'

'She won't let me.'

'Tell me who I am.'

Felix's face was expressionless as he looked out of the window. 'I know you.'

Talissa bit her lip. 'And do you remember . . . what we were? How we knew each other?'

Seven years, she thought, is not long in the history of love.

He looked back into the room, his eyes on her face for a long minute. But there was no focus in them and he said nothing, until suddenly: 'I went to Canada once. Drove up from here. We went to a Dippy's Donuts.'

'And?'

'They'd run out of donuts.'

'That's Canada for you.'

He said nothing.

After a minute, the silence began to upset her and she felt the tears beginning to rise again. She started to speak, hanging out ideas in the hope that one of them would make him rise.

'. . . in the department. Can't keep going on in the same place. Sometimes I think I might go back to Boston. Ask the Helen Lingard if they'll take me back. Do you remember coming to see me there?'

'In Boston?'

'Yes! We had dinner in the apartment. Shrimp and . . . something. Salad, I think. It was . . .'

She looked for an answering light, but he had vanished again into a labyrinth behind the eyes. For him, there was something more urgent than her attempts at conversation.

'I guess it was a while ago,' she said softly.

For another five minutes or so, she tried. But the effort was making them both tired and the urge to give in – to let reality take whatever shape it was insisting on – was too great. She hugged him one more time and made her way to the front desk, keeping her eyes fixed on the long, sterile corridor ahead of her.

When she told Susan about the visit, she tried to make it sound positive. She stressed the rural setting and the fresh fruit.

'Yeah, Leon told me it was the best place on the East Coast,' said Susan. 'Not that that's saying a whole lot, I guess.'

'He's lucky to be there. I don't know who pays for it.'

'It's some partnership with a drug company. Felix got onto it through a ballot at the public end. At the big place where he was before.'

'Has Leon been to see him?'

'A coupla times. Felix only goes there for a rest. I think it's a three-month stay. Then he's meant to manage on his own, back in New York.'

They were eating Chinese food in Talissa's apartment.

'I don't know what to do,' said Talissa. 'I can't help him. I don't want to interfere with his life. I'd prefer to let it all fade into history. To keep my memories intact. But I feel sorry for him.'

'Did he seem sad?'

'He seemed . . . flat. It's hard to say if he feels pain like you and me. You just can't tell. The shrink said they try not to use strong meds. But occasionally it's necessary, to flatten out the worst.'

'And what's the worst?' said Susan.

'Voices. Ideas of persecution. Just, I don't know, living in another world. A different reality. It seems like a kind of tundra. But with electrical storms.'

They looked at one another over the cardboard cartons on the table. 'I often think back to what he was like when you first met,' said Susan, sticking in her chopsticks. 'He was a bit grandiose even then.'

'Yeah, but he was in the room. And everyone should be ambitious. I liked that about him.'

'Plus, he was super-hot,' said Susan.

'He was beautiful.'

Talissa thought of his belly and his matted hair.

'What did the shrink say?' said Susan. 'Does he think he might get better?'

'No, not really. He said it's like he's switched onto a different operating system. For good.'

'Is that all he said?'

'No. He explained the whole thing, as far as they understand it.'

'And?'

'It's complicated.'

'Listen! It's me you're talking to!'

Talissa laughed. 'OK. But this is the bit where I usually tell the kids they can look out the window for a while.'

*

Dr Ramos had a small office on the first floor. To judge from the view over the woods, it was almost directly above the room where she'd just been with Felix.

With his moustache and his short-sleeved white shirt showing hairy arms, Ramos looked like the professional tennis players she had watched on TV with Felix, one of those guys who hustled in the early rounds but seldom made it to the second week.

'So, Ms Adam. What did you make of him?'

'Well . . . He's not the man I knew.'

'I understand,' said Ramos. 'And who is he now?'

'He's someone else.'

'It's what happens. Felix suffers from what in the old days they called schizophrenia.'

'What does that mean?'

'I can't tell you about Felix in particular because you're not his next of kin.'

'But in general?'

'Our brains carry the potential to switch programs. Like a computer that decides of its own accord to suddenly change and run on a different operating system.'

'Why does it do that?'

Ramos laughed. 'We don't know.'

'Even roughly?' said Talissa.

'Ripple dissolve . . .' said Ramos, making a wave motion with his fingers. 'Let's go back two hundred years. All sorts of people they call "lunatics" are first gathered in these huge asylums. Each state has one. Among these thousands, the doctors can make out an interesting group. What in Latin they call—'

'I don't speak Latin.'

'OK, what they call "young madness". Hits you around twenty or twenty-one years old.'

'Felix was older than that.'

'I know. Unusual, but not unheard of. Anyway. You hear loud voices, but there's no one in the room. You become convinced that there are powerful but secret systems running the world. You're their plaything. They read your thoughts and broadcast them to the world. That kind of thing. You're persecuted. Often you're driven to kill yourself.'

'Right.'

'Then in about 1910 some Swiss guy stops calling it young madness and christens it schizophrenia.'

'Does it really matter what it's called? It's a thing, right?'

'Sure it matters. That word implies your mind is split in two. But it's the exact opposite. Felix's thoughts and beliefs are far more unified than ours. We can see both sides and change our mind. He never can. So the wrong name leads to a century of misunderstanding.'

'But what causes it in the first place?'

'Fast-forward now.'

'We're through with the ripple dissolve?'

'Yup. Fast-forward to about 1960. We have a primitive grasp of genetics. Looks like this thing runs in families. At least, if a parent or aunt has it, you're much more likely to get it. So off go the lab guys to try to finger the guilty gene, or combination of genes. They draw a blank over decades. Genetics is still rough and ready. Anyway, there's a hitch. In identical twins, one may get it and one doesn't. So it's not just genetic. There must be a secondary cause.'

'Like what?'

'Life. Experience. Stuff that happens to you. Especially

what junk you throw into your system. Drink, drugs and so on. Seems they can flip the switch and make your brain change program. Provided you already have that predisposition.'

'Complicated,' said Talissa.

'Fast-forward again. With better genetics they discover a lot of the so-called identical twins were not actually identical, but fraternal. Just looked alike.'

'So it *is* genetic after all?'

'No. The Nazis murdered all the Germans who had it. That should have eradicated it. But by thirty years after the war, it was back to pre-Nazi levels. Higher, in fact.'

'So then what?'

'Well, there's a long, long civil war between the biological guys who still say it's basically a thing like multiple sclerosis, like a little blister forming in the brain. But instead of sitting on the brain cells that regulate the movement of your legs and arms, it forms on the cells that control your thoughts. I'm putting this quite crudely, but—'

'Crude's good.'

'Meanwhile, the other camp say: No, it's all to do with life experience and we need to listen to what these patients say. Their stories, the things they tell you, they're not just neural exhaust, or nonsense: they're an attempt to explain their world. Then it becomes political. Democrats go with the life-experience theory – bad housing, street drugs, immigration – Republicans with the genetic, God's curse, tough luck and so on. Roughly.'

'Politicians are not scientists. Can we fast-forward again?'

'OK. Let's go to 2025. The human genome's fully mapped. Now genome-wide surveys begin to identify a few of the genes common to the sufferers. But there are hundreds of them! And maybe many more to come. This coincides with a complete loss of faith in diagnostic categories.'

'How come?'

'The professional bodies in charge of psychiatry give out this handbook to us doctors. There's a ten-point test for this disease. To receive the diagnosis, a patient needs to have exhibited a minimum of five of the symptoms acutely in the last six months. So two people can be diagnosed with the same illness without sharing a single symptom.'

'Sounds a bit of a—'

'Clusterfuck? By 2030, they've ditched almost all the labels. There is simply a long spectrum of madness, from Mrs Happy, at one end, to Mr Life-in-a-Back-Ward at the other. But the difference is only quantitative. Think of a one-to-a-hundred scale. I'm about an eight. I have some low moods that are unrelated to my life circumstances. A couple of irrational phobias. I'd guess you're about a five. Felix is a ninety.'

'But what about all the advances in brain scanning and so on? Surely they must have helped?'

'Not much,' said Ramos. 'As long ago as 2035 we could map the whole brain and its hundred billion neurons. But mapping's one thing. Understanding what the hell's going on there will take another maybe fifty years. Minimum.'

'And meanwhile we're all crazy.'

'Pretty much. You buy a car off the lot. The chassis is fine. The wheels don't fall off. But the new stuff, the stuff that hasn't had time to bed in . . . Oh boy. Sure as hell the fancy electronic warning systems will go wrong, it's just a question of when. Young madness or old madness. Youthful dementia, like your Felix, or senile dementia, like half the population.'

'And why are we like this?'

'It's who we are. It's our special frailty. In the genes. No other primate has it. Mind you, no other primate walked on the moon. So maybe it's our special power too.'

When the cab eventually came to collect her from Greenhills, Talissa had an urge to ask the driver to go the other way – not to the modern airport with its sweating departure gates, but north into the woods.

At work, she'd battled against the temptations of a certain way of thinking, in which impulses and thoughts were allowed to go where they wanted, regardless of logic. Her occasional recourse to this mindful but unstructured state was one reason why she'd given up trying to rationalise what she'd seen twenty years ago in a closed room of a derelict chateau in Brittany. A man, a kind of man: of her species, or possibly of another. Or an illusion. Perhaps even a *de*lusion, of the kind Felix suffered. She found it impossible to know. And she was aware that each revisit altered the memory a little. The more she scratched at it, the more she reshaped the outline.

It was ceasing to matter to her, because she was content to embrace uncertainties without always reaching after reason and fact. This response was 'unscientific', said her professional conscience. But according to most philosophers she knew, or had heard of, to be contentedly unsure was the mark of a mature mind – because only small intellects are frightened of the unresolved.

As Talissa leant back against the car upholstery, she closed her eyes and let her mind wander.

She saw the scene that Lukas Parn had briefly invoked. A Neanderthal settlement somewhere on the Asian steppe. Fifty

196

thousand years ago. To this, she began to add detail from her own knowledge . . .

A dignified and hardy people, hunters with a sense of family and group. A dozen or so in this one. Ready to move over the landscape, to follow food or shelter, but fixed in ritual: people who care for their young and bury their dead among flowers. A form of speech, uttered loudly, sometimes in a high voice at odds with the deep chest from which it comes. A palisade, some shelters made from dried hides stretched over sharpened wooden poles. Dead animals butchered by honed flints and roasted on fires, then passed around. Marrow scraped from the cracked bones. A way of life that hasn't changed for tens of thousands of years: a people resilient through earth-altering changes of climate and landscape. A hardy human species persevering in a just habitable niche.

Then a shout from the edge of the palisade. A small group is seen approaching in the dusk. What are these creatures, these people who seem new yet familiar?

They come closer in the dying light, three female, four male, in animal furs. Their hands are bare and open, with no weapons. They are all smiling. Why? As they come closer, it's clear they are humans, nothing to be frightened of – though they are a little taller, narrower, with darker skin on their limbs and faces. They seem tired from travelling. To take in more air, they use their mouths because their nose openings are so small.

It's not their size or their strength that makes them daunting. The local men could fight and kill them easily. It's something else they have. They will never not take what they want. If it needs a day or a month or a lifetime. They're driven by a force the older people cannot match. It's pointless to deny them.

At this moment, as the winds begin to howl, it seems that lust is destiny. The strangers enter the corral and take the offered food, the women with their breasts hanging free of their coverings, the agile, smiling men tearing flesh from a bone with their teeth . . . In all the local females there is the clamour of desire.

Eventually one of the new men comes, sated with food, still smiling. In a dark corner, by a tree, he chooses a mate, puts his hands on her breast, then pushes the fur he is wearing to one side so she can see it, holding itself up, away from him, like a craning creature of its own desire. She kneels and spits on it, moves the saliva up and down with her mouth, her fingers, to prepare it. He spreads the cleft of her apart, kneels and laps it like an ox before he pushes in. Soon there's so much pressure on the part of her that wants it most that she's reduced to nothing but a point of fire.

She'll move onward with them, when the sun comes up, and leave what she's known behind. Tomorrow and the next day, these nights of giving in, the fall.

2

Seth's college was one of the oldest in the university. A man who looked like an undertaker showed him to a staircase in the corner of a cobbled quadrangle. He saw his name, in white capitals, S.K. PEDERSEN, on a black background painted onto the stone arch of the doorway. He carried his two bags up the stairs and unlocked a rough oak door with the iron key he'd been given. An inner, more normal door opened on to a vaulted room with an old leather sofa, sideboard and armchairs. Stone-mullioned windows overlooked the courtyard at the front and, on the other side, a three-acre garden of lawns and specimen trees with a winding lake.

A course induction timetable bleeped on his handset. He looked round his new lodging and found another door, which led into a bedroom with a wardrobe and a bed under a purple cover. Through yet another doorway was a scullery with a hob and a kettle. There was no sign of a bathroom. He went up the winding stairs and found more lodgings like his own, the names of their inhabitants, J. ROCKINGHAM and M. GOSLING, painted in white on black on the lintel. Up another flight was a kitchen, beyond which was a sign saying 'Bathroom'. Inside were no baths, but there was a lavatory and a cubicle with a tiny shower head. Using only tools from the shed, his dad could have upgraded the whole thing in twenty-four hours.

At seven, he put on his black gown, as instructed, and went like a wary bat over the cobbles to a building that divided one quad from the next. The stained-glass windows made it look like a church, but the porter had told him it was where they ate. It wasn't like the canteen at school, or like the cafeteria at the sports club where his mum worked. The old tables were joined together to stretch the length of the hall in three long lines. Candles flickered in silver holders and the other students stood behind long benches, waiting for the word to sit. Then waiters in short white coats brought plates of egg flan and fresh vegetables in a gravy made from meatless stock.

Next day, there were more messages on his handset. The Brunel Building: Introduction by Dr Miriam Stenson. The Challenge of Engineering by Professor Ibuki. Year One sandwich lunch, Woodrow Parlour.

Seth ignored them while he went to look round the streets; he was interested in building, but not so much in lectures or timetables. He thought the best way to absorb more knowledge was simply to spend time in this place from another era.

The boards near the porters' lodge had printed paper notices. On a whim, he contacted the 'secretary' of the college football club, then messaged home to ask for his old boots. Two days later, he found himself, with a dozen others, at a sports ground on the far side of the river. The secretary gave them some drills with a few old footballs he emptied out from a string bag. Then they had a five-a-side game over half the pitch and, though he hadn't played for years, Seth began to enjoy himself. He didn't know the names of the others to call out for the ball, but they seemed to find him anyway. Afterwards, he was one of three told to report for first-team training at 2 p.m. on Fridays.

'Our first match is against Corpus next week,' said the captain, a third-year from somewhere in Scotland. 'You look a wee bit like Lionel Messi,' he said to Seth, 'so you'd better have this.' He handed over a shirt with the number 10 on the back. Since Messi hadn't played for Crystal Palace, Seth had never heard of him; but he looked him up later and discovered he'd been famous years ago: one of the best of all time, it said. Corpus turned out to be quite weak and Seth set up a tall, skinny girl called Rosalie Wright to score a goal after only a few minutes. All the others in the team were boys, and they went home 3–1 winners (Wright 2, Pedersen 1, the intra-college bulletin reported). The others were friendly enough, though there were no celebrations afterwards; they didn't meet again till the next training session.

The days were easy, Seth found: rising at ten, when the sun pushed through the curtains, making tea in the scullery with ingredients he'd buy through a hatch near the dining hall, then going out to Tarvino's, an Italian coffee bar whose espresso had a rich, almost sweet taste. If he was in the mood, he'd look into a lecture afterwards. He liked the talks on twentieth-century history, and there was a lecturer on German literature who wore a long gown over her black skirt and spoke in a way he found interesting. By then he was hungry. It had been difficult to find a place that still had meat on the menu, but in the course of his wanderings he found a discreet café called The Veal Thing, which was far away from most university buildings, near an electronics factory. There was also a diner where he munched through steak pies with the workers on their break. Afterwards, he went to a small cinema near the marketplace that showed films made long ago. These were more arty than the ones he'd watched with Alaric; most of them were about men and women who found themselves in emotional tangles that made Seth laugh. He liked the lighting and the atmosphere and the strangeness of the characters' concerns, though he hated the music. Why, when he was relishing the sound of cicadas or tyres on gravel, did they have to put in a screech of strings?

He was used to not having friends. He'd never trusted Sadie Liew's interest in him and though he did like Wilson Kalu, he'd lost touch when Wilson went to university in Manchester. Seth saw it as a natural parting of their lives, not his to quarrel with. He saw hardly anything of the other engineers, who disappeared to classes while he was still in bed. He was on speaking terms with a couple of the men from the electronics factory at The Veal Thing, but the people he saw most were the football team. He was the only first-year student in the First XI, yet they treated him with a kind of respect that was new to him; they didn't call him 'Test Tube'. Seth forgot to turn up to an extra practice and was disciplined by being made a substitute for the semi-final. He was brought on at half-time and his college won 2–1.

A week later, he was dozing on the big leather sofa in his room when there was a knock on the inner door and Rosalie Wright put her head round.

'Thought I'd make sure you hadn't forgotten the training,' she said.

Shit. He had. 'Come in.'

Rosalie was already in her shorts and trainers, carrying a sports holdall, though she hadn't yet tied her straight, reddish-brown hair back and it fell evenly over her shoulder blades. 'Can I put this bag down somewhere? It's not till three, but I'm up to date with all my work, so I thought I'd just check up.'

'Sure. Would you like some tea?'

'I'll make it. In here, is it?'

Rosalie clattered about in the scullery and came out with two cups. She felt in her holdall and brought out a packet of biscuits. 'Energy bars,' she said.

They sat either side of a boarded fireplace that had once burned coal, then gas, now nothing. Rosalie swung her long legs over the side of the armchair and chatted about the worrying weakness of their defence.

Seth was impressed by how at ease she was. She came from a different part of the country, somewhere further north. Her voice was melodic, but with a slight gurgle, as if she was try-ing not to laugh. She chatted on about the game, her last goal ('He's just give us the ball and we've banged it in') and said nice things about Seth's abilities. When she leant forward to pick up her teacup, her oversize football shorts stretched open for a moment and Seth could see that she was wearing noth-ing underneath. He wasn't sure if he'd seen right at first, but when Rosalie swung her legs back over the arm of the chair he could make out the fine, russet-coloured hair rising from a central point, though the view vanished when she sat up straight again. He hadn't seen Mary with no clothes on since he was a child, and in the pornography he'd seen the women had no hair at all. He was fascinated because what he'd just glimpsed of Rosalie seemed so animal, yet at the same time delicate.

'Anyway,' Rosalie said. 'We all want to know how you

learned to play like that. Did you have trials or something at school? For a pro team?'

'Two boys at my school had trials for Charlton, but not me.'

'Were they better than you?'

'I don't know. They were the year above. I never saw them play.'

After a few more minutes, Rosalie said, 'You'd better get changed, hadn't you? And I need to get my game pants on. Give us the bag, will you?'

'I'll go into the bedroom,' he said. 'You can change in here.'

He gave her time to dress before he re-emerged. They walked down to the playing fields, with Rosalie now wearing white stretch shorts, with a panther logo, beneath her team kit. 'Nice panther,' Seth said, pointing.

'I know. I've got a pair of navy ones, too. I don't put them on till the last minute or the lads on my staircase tease me.'

After the practice, they fell into conversation again as they walked past Pembroke on the way home. Crossing the front quad, Rosalie said, 'I think I left a bracelet in your room. Can I come and have a quick look?'

'Sure. Where exactly did you leave it?'

Back upstairs, they drank water, made more tea and finished the biscuits as they talked about the coming final. Seth found that words like 'offside' and 'through ball' now carried a charge when Rosalie used them.

'What are the showers like here?' she said. 'The water pressure on our staircase is a joke.'

'Not too bad.'

'Can I borrow a towel?'

Mary had packed him a spare, which he found in the

bottom of his wardrobe. When Rosalie came back from the bathroom, wrapped in the Crystal Palace towel, she grabbed her boot bag from the sofa and laughed. 'I know I've got some clean things in here somewhere . . .'

'You can change in the bedroom,' said Seth.

But it was only a minute before she put her head round the door and said, 'Seth, can you come in here a second?'

When he went into his own bedroom, he was at first too taken aback by the sight of a sports bra and the panther logo 'game pants' on the bedspread to register the fact that his Palace towel was lying alongside them.

'Right,' said Rosalie, kneeling down in front of him and tugging at the waistband of his shorts. 'I think this could be part of our regular warm-down, don't you?'

Seth didn't know what to say, so stroked the hair on the top of her head, which was still damp and smelled of lemon shampoo from the shower.

There seemed to be a huge number of clubs that you were urged to join, but Seth was reluctant to commit. Anyway, you could turn up uninvited to these things. On the basis of a single visit, the Sino-Russian group in Cat's had asked him if he'd like to be its treasurer.

One chilly morning, the two third-year students in the rooms above – J. Rockingham and M. Gosling – invited him to 'go to the races' with them. He was surprised to discover this involved horses. They travelled by train to a nearby town, then by coach to the course, while John Rockingham explained the fundamentals of betting. Seth enjoyed wandering among the bookmakers down by the white rails and soon got the gist of their sign language. Martin Gosling, who was wearing a felt hat for the outing, took him to the paddock, where the horses were led round in a circle.

'What do you think?' said Gosling.

'I like that one. Number four. Plus someone just put a big bet on it.'

'How do you know?'

'Those men by the rails are trying to deal with it by placing other bets between themselves.'

'The bookies? You get what they're saying?'

'Yes.'

Gosling consulted his card. 'Betsy's Rabbit. A. McGowan up. The weight's against him, but McGowan's a good jockey. The horse was second last time out on going that was described as "good to firm". What do you like about him?'

'Big lungs,' said Seth.

'True,' said Gosling. 'And not sweating up, unlike the favourite. You still seeing that football girl, by the way?'

'What's that got to do with it?'

'Nothing. Sorry. Just wondered. She comes past our room sometimes in a towel. She looks nice.'

'She is nice.'

Gosling put on the bet and Betsy's Rabbit won by three lengths, the jockey not even going to the whip. After this, Seth was invited to the races as a cross between seer and lucky charm, and although his selections lost as often as they won, he did seem to have a better eye than the others. John Rockingham told him it was the first time they'd ever ended in credit over the course of a term and they took him to a Greek restaurant to celebrate.

They all drank wine, which Seth had previously had only at Christmas. Afterwards, as he climbed the stairs to his room, he had to grasp the handrail in the wall. He had forgotten that Rosalie Wright had invited herself round for what she called a 'pre-training session' and she was waiting on the sofa in a short dress to show off her legs, even though it was November and she was wearing woollen tights and zip-up leather boots against the cold. Seth excused himself and went to the scullery, where he vomited in the sink.

Rosalie laughed when he came back into the sitting room, sweating and pale. He remembered nothing till the next morning, when he was woken, naked in bed, by the bleep of his handset. 'Hope you feel better this morning. Don't forget training! Promise I didn't take advantage last night. R xx'. Beneath the words, however, was the image of a wink.

Inspired by the Greek wine, Seth began to visit some of the pubs for which the town was famous. He had a beer with his pie at lunch, though it made him sleep through the film he went to afterwards. The college itself had a bar in a new building near the river and he decided to explore it by reading the names on the bottles that were ranged in tiers behind the counter.

'I'd like some Campari please,' he said, picking one at random.

The bartender, a young woman he thought was a student, looked at him curiously. 'How do you want that?'

'Oh, the usual way.'

She poured out half a tumbler. 'I've never served one of these before. Do you have ice with it?'

'I think so.'

He took the red drink to a chair and sat down with it. It was sweet and bitter at the same time, like cough medicine with herbs. He began to like it. By now he was learning to drink slowly so that he wouldn't be ambushed by his legs suddenly going numb. John Rockingham came and sat at his table and asked if he had any tips for Newmarket. They were joined by Arusha and Mireya from the second year. John suggested they go to the Duke of Clarence, near the Higgs Laboratories, because the beer was better; the girls said they didn't do alcohol but they'd come along anyway.

For the first time in his life, as the four sat close together around a small table with cast-iron legs, Seth found himself included. He told them about a very old French film he'd just seen, which featured a twelve-year-old boy roaming round Paris and bunking off school: he saw his mum with another man outside a café in a square. The print was so old it was fuzzy.

There was then some talk about what they did in the vacations and John said in the summer he liked to go to an uninhabited island off the coast of Scotland. 'There was once a priest there. About three hundred years ago. A missionary, maybe, though I'm not sure he found any converts. Then there were a few hardy crofters. You can only get across when the tide's right.'

'What's it like there?' said Mireya.

'It's calm. All humans left a hundred years ago. You can stand there with the seals on the shore and the birds overhead and nothing else. You listen to the wind. It's like being back at the beginning of time.'

Arusha laughed and began to tease him for being so easily impressed, but Seth found himself intrigued by the sound of the place.

'Aren't the main islands wild enough already?' said Arusha.

'You can always go one better,' said John. 'If there's a

wilder one, you have to see it. You have to go and colonise it. That's what humans do!'

Seth was picturing himself among the birds and seals, for- aging for edible plants along the shore. He wouldn't mind being alone.

His reverie ended. 'Shall I get a drink for Martin?' he said.

'He's working tonight,' said John Rockingham.

'No. He's coming. He's here.'

A moment later, Martin Gosling came into view through the glass door and made his way to their table.

Rockingham looked at Seth. 'How on earth . . .'

Seth couldn't explain how he'd known Martin was arriv- ing; he just knew. He tapped the side of his nose, as he'd seen people do, and said, 'Betsy's Rabbit.'

The evening went along fine until the music started and he could no longer hear what anyone was saying. The boom and pulse of it made him feel anxious, as though something vio- lent was about to happen; he couldn't understand how the other people carried on talking.

He stood up from the table and left quickly, happy to be outside again in the sound of bicycle tyres going over the wet streets.

Alaric and Mary were proud that their boy was at university, though surprised at the amount of money he was spending. 'All these eating places,' said Alaric. 'I suppose they don't serve meat in his college,' said Mary. 'And the pubs and bars!' 'He never cost us much before, Al. There'd be months when he put nothing through his blipper at all.' Alaric sighed. 'I wish he'd be in touch occasionally. I'd like to know what the lectures are like. And the practicals.'

Seth had been to only two practicals. He found they were focused mainly on data processing, which held no fear for him, but little interest either: he wanted to be looking at pre-stressed concrete and daring bridges. The preliminary course was obligatory, however; at the end of it, you were meant to be better able to choose your speciality.

His field of study for the time being was Rosalie Wright and the narrow backstreets of the town, both of which he found rewarding. Sometimes he combined the two and persuaded Rosalie to go to clubs and bars that other students didn't visit, though she wouldn't drink more than one beer and didn't like to be away from her biology studies for long. The only place she'd happily waste time was Seth's bedroom. Her own lodging was in a new block specifically designed for third-year students around a social hub, though she found it 'too much like a Soviet space station'. She preferred the sixteenth-century atmosphere of Seth's building with its sooty wainscoting and aroma of old sherry. When the heating came on at full blast, as it sometimes unexpectedly did, she liked to strip off and walk round his rooms, like a domestic animal looking for a comfortable perch, proud of her long, collapsible limbs. When she was settled, she'd toss back her clean hair and pat the cushion next to her. Seth thought her matter-of-fact attitude was something to do with the way her studies required her to look at plant and animal reproductive systems all day long. She certainly seemed fascinated by his own organs and subjected them to close attention, lifting and examining with scientific detachment. 'It's not quite like any of the ones I've seen before.' 'Have you seen a lot?' 'No, but don't forget I sometimes had to shower with the lads after a game.' 'In what way's it different?' 'I don't know. Just . . .

different. Nicer.' All she asked was that he do the same for her, instructing him in the use of his fingertips or tongue in unexpected places. 'That's nice, just like that,' she said. Her voice was calm and informative, like someone recommending a modest holiday resort against its more famous neighbours.

Seth was not embarrassed or ashamed to do what she asked. The only difficult moments came when Rosalie seemed to want more from him. She would lie against him or look hard into his eyes and ask him what he thought or what he felt. It didn't seem enough to say that he felt fine, or even happy. Once she asked him outright if he loved her. He was surprised by the question, thinking his 'love' belonged, if at all, to Mary and to Alaric. 'Of course I do,' he said, but the words sounded strange to him.

Rosalie tried to interest him in music, taking him to college folk nights and visiting bands in paying venues, but gave up in the end and went with him to the dark cinema instead. 'You're like Freud,' she said. 'What?' 'In Vienna, which was then the musical capital of the world. He wouldn't let his bairns have lessons and had the piano taken away from their house.' They also talked about football. Rosalie had an elder brother back in Newcastle (her home town, as Seth now emphatically understood) and had taken his place in the school team. Seth didn't stop to think how fortunate he'd been to find her; he just knew that Rosie would be there again tomorrow with her melodic voice and her really quite remarkably long legs and her unembarrassed yet specific sexual requests.

Shortly after the start of his second term, Seth was asked to go and see the Senior Tutor, a zoologist called Briony Riske, in her office at the far end of the garden, beyond the duck pond's furthest pool.

A young man he had never seen before was also present in the room. Dr Riske introduced him as Amol Shastri, a student protocol adviser, whose presence was obligatory under college statutes.

Dr Riske breathed in deeply and gathered her gown about her shoulders. Seth could see she wasn't enjoying this.

'About your work, Seth,' she began.

'Yes?'

Colouring a little, and consulting data on a small screen by the desk, Dr Riske then gave a fair imitation of Rose Paxton, old Bob Tainsley and all the other form teachers he had ever had. There were no complaints about his ability, but a number of questions about attendance and work completed.

'I didn't know that lectures were compulsory,' said Seth.

'Not all of them are, but . . .' Dr Riske looked at Amol Shastri.

'The basic background is compulsory. The rest are optional, but you need to register which ones you've chosen. It's your first step towards specialisation.'

'And then the practicals,' said Dr Riske. 'Is there some reason you've only attended three?'

'I thought they were optional as well,' said Seth.

'It's laid out in the induction literature.'

'Did you read the induction?' said Shastri.

'I don't remember. But I'll read it again.'

'One other thing,' said Dr Riske. 'The most important thing, in fact. You apparently didn't turn up for the first-year exams.'

Seth looked out of the window. He hadn't known that there were exams. Rosalie hadn't mentioned anything.

'Can I sit them now?' he said.

'No.' Dr Riske stood up. 'Listen, Seth. It's not unusual for first-year students to struggle. It's a big change from day school and living at home. I'm going to ask a second-year engineer to keep an eye on you.'

'It's part of the mentor system,' said Shastri. 'He'll be your college uncle.'

'All right,' said Seth.

'But I'm afraid if things haven't looked up by the end of term, we'll have to rusticate you,' said Dr Riske.

'What does that mean?'

'Send you home.'

'But I love it here! My room and everything. I fucking love it.'

Dr Riske concealed a half-smile behind the wing of her gown as she showed him to the door.

When Seth was well out of earshot, she turned to Amol Shastri and said, 'I thought I'd seen it all.'

Shastri nodded. 'It's not that he isn't bright enough.'

The second-year engineer who was told to 'keep an eye on him' was called Rick Sharpless and he took the job seriously. He asked Seth to leave his outer door open when he went to bed so he could come in and make sure he was awake in the morning; he looked in again at six in the evening to check Seth knew what was needed for the following day. He also told him where the college launderette was and how to get a free wash. He wasn't Seth's idea of an uncle.

Rick made it clear that he disapproved of the amount of time Seth spent with Rosalie.

'You probably shouldn't drink so much alcohol, either,' he said. 'Three beers a week is the recommended maximum. They're keeping a check in the college bar.'

'That's why I go out.'

A few days later, Seth saw Rick in discussion with Rosalie in the college café. When he went to join them, Rick looked uneasy.

'We were just talking about football,' he said.

'He thinks we spend too much time on it,' said Rosalie. 'I told him it was none of his business. Anyway, it's the summer term next, so we won't be playing.'

Before the vacation, Seth was asked to see Dr Riske again and she told him that his improved attendance record had been noted but that he was still on probation.

It didn't matter, because once he got back to Ashers End, the whole world of university seemed to vanish from his mind. He helped Alaric to plumb in a new basin in the spare room and make good. Mary arranged her shifts so that she was at home most evenings and able to cook his favourite dinners. They asked him about his life at university and he told them all about his huge room and the tiny shower on the top floor. He couldn't mention all the things he'd done with Rosalie Wright or his interviews with Dr Riske. He did tell them that his college had won the football cup final 2–1 against Trinity and that he'd had two assists. He also said he'd made friends with the two boys on the landing above him and this was the news that finally seemed to put their minds at rest.

'I'm making shepherd's pie for tomorrow,' said Mary,

which was Alaric's cue to ask where you got the shepherds these days. Everything seemed to be all right again, and on Sunday he helped his father extend the marshalling yards for the freight trains in the attic.

When the summer term began, he found it hard to readjust. He thought he should go to some practicals and he wanted to see Rosalie, but he wasn't sure how to resume this life. There was no football to be played. Three weeks later, he went for a short visit home for Mary's birthday. He discovered on his return that he'd missed a big party to mark the six hundredth anniversary of the founding of the college, in 1451. There had been marquees and bands, jugglers and fire-eaters; there was dancing till dawn and beyond.

A few days after that, Martin Gosling told him that Rosalie had been there until the last knockings and had spent most of the time with Rick Sharpless.

One day in June, in the middle of final exams, Rosalie was walking across the front quadrangle when she bumped into John Rockingham.

He stopped to talk to her. 'How are you? I'm sorry we don't see you on the landing any more.'

'Yes. I know.'

'What happened?'

Rosalie wanted to get on with some revision, but politeness made her stop and talk. 'Well. He's a canny lad, Seth. I really like him. But I'll be away at the end of term and he'll have to fend for himself next year.'

'Did something go wrong?'

'No. We had a lot of laughs.'

'What was it, then?'

'What's up, man?' she said with a laugh. 'I thought you were only interested in horses.'

'Fair point,' said John Rockingham.

'I'm sorry. I really am.' Rosalie pushed the back of her hand across her eyes.

'Was it to do with that anniversary party?'

'God, no. You can't make a whole drama out of whether someone asked you to a college dance.'

'Seth doesn't always think things through,' said John. 'But he'd never hurt anyone. Not knowingly.'

Rosalie looked up towards the Wren cloister, where the college clock told off the centuries. 'Look at this.' She held up her wrist. 'He gave us this bracelet one day. It was a lovely thing to do. And when we were in the room with him and chatting and messing about it was dandy. Other times, like in the vacation, I don't think he gave us a thought.'

3

A year after Seth had graduated, a rumour began to circulate. At first, it was shared only between people hungry for sensation and stayed within their orbit. It stated that a human of an older species, thought to be *Homo vannesiensis*, was alive and walking undetected down the streets of an American city.

It was a typical summer story. News outlets adopted and explained the very British joke about 'white' and 'Vannes' and 'man', and brutish manners at the wheel. 'White Van Man Lives!' became a catchphrase in the public mind. Populist networks included daily updates on their bulletins and invited evidence of 'sightings'. Thousands of elementary-school children sent in photographs of their classmates.

The handful of scientists who were consulted for their opinion were dismissive, saying that the latest Big Foot or Yeti rumour was not going to make them lift their eyes from their real work, even in a slow July. 'It's like the old days of the *National Enquirer*,' a Yale professor sighed. In August, a man in Sioux Falls, South Dakota was pursued by drunken college students and held down while they pulled out some of his hair with a view to having it DNA-tested. The students were arrested and fined; the man in question brought an action against the city police for failing to protect him.

Watching a newsfeed one night, Talissa became aware of the incident when it was included as the tailpiece to the main bulletin, framed as a student prank. It caused her a moment of panic, but seemed a long way removed from Seth. Then, a few days later, FBC, the last remaining news organisation with the resources to fact-check its stories, ran a short item. They had contacted a palaeoanthropologist from Harvard, who gave an opinion on the feasibility of the clone idea (low), and the head of the human genomics department in Cambridge, England, who believed it was technically possible. With no further facts coming to light, the item became holiday-season fodder for loudmouths and 'prompters', then began to fade away.

In September, however, a little-known news organisation called Galatia started to pursue the story with more vigour. Galatia was financed by Christian fundamentalists with cavernous pockets. By the end of October, it had turned its attention to the various activities of the Lukas Parn Foundation; by December it had established that one of Parn's establishments had bred a thylacine which had been kennelled in a remote part of Wyoming. They published photographs that purported to show the animal in its compound, though it had died at the age of three, lonely despite its hectic sexual life and unable to adjust to the modern world.

Under pressure from the media, Sheila Rahm, the Parn's vice-president, public relations, gave a statement in New York confirming the thylacine experiment and revealing that they had in addition bred an aurochs and a woolly mammoth, neither of which had survived. She concluded by saying: 'These

218

were experiments in the name of scientific research, though we are not yet ready to publish our detailed findings. The Parn Foundation is dismayed by the sensational tone of the recent coverage. We hold ourselves to the highest scientific standards. I would like to make it clear that we have no plans to try and revive any other extinct species.'

The implication of the Parn Foundation made Talissa think again. Could it be that someone had leaked or discovered something? If so, how had it travelled so far from the facts? A clone not a hybrid, and the wrong species at that? Was all news reporting really *so* inaccurate? She still had Lukas Parn's personal message ID, but hesitated to use it.

The other possible person to consult was Susan Kovalenko. She might well be hurt at not having been asked before; but sitting at her desk, with Pelham snoozing on his beanbag alongside, Talissa wondered if this might be the moment to be bold – fearless, even.

Then, as she began to type, she saw there was a new message for her.

It read in harsh italics: '*We know what you did*'.

There was no given end point for the message, but after the words was a Sun Cross symbol: a plus sign in a circle, which had been used in Bronze Age religions and had recently been adopted by the Vector group – possibly, it was said, because it was rudimentary enough to be within the drawing capabilities of all their members.

At the same time, half a dozen cars were pulling up on the gravel parking lot of an expensive small hotel in the shadow of the Luberon mountains in Provence. It was late afternoon, but the heat was still pressing. The guests were told by a young woman in a grey linen uniform to leave their bags and walk up the short avenue of olive trees to the terrace of the restaurant, Le Panier de Paille, where drinks were waiting for them.

Lukas Parn had chosen the place on a whim, drawn by a swimming pool that was not the usual rectangle but a salt-water lake sculpted into the limestone slope beneath the main terrace. He had booked out all sixteen rooms, though his party numbered just five. In addition to himself, there were Malik Wood and Delmore Redding, making up the original 'Big Three'. Catrina Olsen had resigned from the institute after she had discovered from Talissa Adam what had taken place; she had refused a severance payment on the grounds that it was an attempt to buy her silence and her original contract of employment was already restrictive enough. The others at the hotel were Sheila Rahm, the head of PR in New York, and a barrister from Gray's Inn, London, called Celeste Usman, whose expensive opinion had pleased Lukas Parn.

The first night was down to 'orientation', which meant more drinks on the terrace, followed by dinner.

'Woody, you do the ordering,' said Parn. 'Get me a Pepsi. I know they have it because we got some sent ahead.'

'All right,' said Malik Wood. 'But my French is not up to much.'

'I can speak French,' said Celeste Usman.

'OK, what's French for corn dog?' said Parn.

'*Chien de maïs*. Literally. But I doubt they'll have that.'

'Oh, I think they will.'

'Oh God, not a currywurst, please, Lukas,' said Malik Wood.

220

'You guys,' said Parn. 'You just don't understand the service industry. The clue's in the name.'

In the end, they all ate roast langoustines on a bed of 'courgette caviar' and the *agneau de Provence en plusieurs cuissons*.

'Lamb and mash,' said Parn, cutting up what was on his plate. 'I can live with that.'

The wine list insisted on organic regional suppliers and respect for '*terroir*'.

'I'm not having you drinking the local neck oil,' said Parn. 'We've got work to get through tomorrow. You don't want a biodynamic hangover.'

After a brief talk with the English-speaking sommelier, Malik Wood persuaded him to open up his reserve cellar. 'Let's have the Château-Grillet,' he said. Celeste Usman was the only one to keep up with Malik Wood as a sequence of bottles were ferried in by the impassive staff.

They moved to the veranda in front of the main building, where a bottle of Armagnac and five miniature tumblers were left on a table with candles in glass sleeves and two cans of Pepsi on ice.

In the morning, after a muted breakfast in the back courtyard, they gathered in Parn's suite, where the sitting room had linen-covered sofas arranged round a low stone table, on which sat jugs of coffee and iced water. The room, while opulent, was windowless. Parn instructed them all to sit, though he himself remained standing.

'OK, to kick off, I've got some news for you,' he said. 'We haven't just come down here to eat some fancy food and drink too much alcohol. Have some water, Malik, you look like a fucking ghost.'

Wood did as he was told, his hand trembling from his share of the magnum of red that had followed the white wine.

'Here's the thing,' said Parn. 'On Friday night I heard back from our people in Irkutsk. We've made a breakthrough. They've found an immaculately preserved cave site, an actual settlement of Neanderthals and early modern humans living together. It's miles from anywhere, that's the problem, but we got some ultra-strong scanners where the permafrost was thinnest and they kept coming back with these interesting shadows. Then we mined. Looks like there was some big geological incident.'

'What sort of incident?' said Wood.

'Fuck, I don't know. It was a long time ago, mate. A glacier, a landslide. Those guys were always living through it.'

'A volcano?' said Sheila Rahm.

'No. There are no volcanoes in the area. But the result is a bit like Pompeii, a settlement frozen at a moment in time. Men and women trapped in a yedoma ice cave. There's even a dog.'

Parn was nervously active in the way that unsettled his staff around the world. He always had one piece of information more than they did – sometimes, like this, shocking or impossible to dismiss. But he revealed it all in a rush, from the corner of his mouth, so they could barely take it in before they were expected to be fully up to speed with it.

Malik Wood noticed a thin rime of white around the base of Parn's nostrils, something he had become familiar with in the course of big meetings and press conferences.

Parn went to a projector at the end of the room and pressed a button. On the bare plastered wall, there appeared a photograph, quite indistinct, but in which they could make out different skulls, ribs and femora, with handwritten labels – 'Sap (F) 22b' or 'Nean (M)19a' – superimposed on the layered silt.

'What's the date?' said Sheila, a notebook open on her knee.

'It's forty-six thousand years before the present. We've got a squad of Russian helpers. Ex-army. It'll take years to dig everything out and date it. Obviously, it's all super-secret at the moment. I'm pumping cash into the security of the site. Luckily, it's such a godforsaken place that no one goes there of their own free will. The locals say that even the birds fly upside down so they don't have to look.'

'But it has a relevance,' said Delmore Redding. 'To our hybrid.'

'Sure does. It shows that we cohabited with Neanderthals. We didn't rape their women or keep them in brothels or as slaves.'

'Or vice versa, presumably,' said Sheila.

'Exactly. Neanderthals were stronger, physically, but they didn't kill off the new people. Us. There was something to be had from collaboration. From breeding.'

'That's what Sapiens was always good at,' said Malik Wood. 'From maybe eight hundred and fifty individuals in the Exodus Event to a peak world population a few years back of almost nine billion. That's a lot of sex.'

'All right,' said Parn. 'Let's talk about our young hybrid. We've now had more than twenty years of observation. Malik, can you give us the headlines? Keep it simple, keep it short.'

'I suppose the main finding is this,' said Wood, putting down his cup with a rattle. 'The thing we thought defined modern humans – us – was in fact available to other creatures. Neanderthals had a consciousness very much like ours,

223

and in some ways superior. I think we will be able to show one day that there were several levels, or perhaps flavours, of human consciousness. It's not a single entity. Also, that different people alive today may have inherited different versions of it.'

There was a pause. Then Delmore Redding spoke. 'The absolute bedrock of civilisation,' he said, 'is that if today a Peruvian, descended from the Aztecs, met a founder Australian or a Namibian of a long-established habitat or—'

'We get the point, Del,' said Parn.

'—they would all assume and recognise the same thought processes in the other, whatever the differences in appearance. That's what makes us human. That's the absolute bedrock.'

'Correct,' said Wood.

'And you're saying that isn't true?' said Redding.

'I'm saying that all these people you mention may be running on slightly different systems.'

'That's an extremely dangerous view.'

'It takes an adjustment,' said Wood. 'But I don't believe it's reductive. You have to open your mind to the idea of diversity. People have different hair colour and that's OK. They can also have slightly different mental processes without being different species and without any loss of dignity, or any threat to their human rights. There isn't just one magic faculty that makes us who we are.'

'And we have this from the kid? The London hybrid?' said Sheila. 'What's his name, by the way?'

'Don't know,' said Malik Wood. 'We still follow up all eight kids in the trial. One is massively different. He – or she – is known as Number Seven.'

'As a matter of fact,' said Parn, 'I think Delmore knows the name, but let's not go there. Malik, can you, for the sake of the non-scientists, give a very brief explanation of where we've reached?'

'I'll try. But there's only so much you can do to make it completely simple. So brace yourselves.'

Malik Wood drew a deep breath. He spoke of the Garden of Eden and the moment at which Adam and Eve became aware of being naked – a sudden change of awareness when they had eaten the apple: a parable of what actually happened in evolution, perhaps. He talked of how a child of maybe three or four years old first starts to know that it is a named individual who will wake up the same person tomorrow, not just a ball of pain and want, but a repeating entity. Briefly, he touched on other creatures and their levels of consciousness, the way that chimps and corvids could use tools, how a certain species of bird knew how to start a forest fire to drive out prey. He invoked Shakespeare, who, he said, more or less invented the idea that each human was different, but also to some extent predictable, according to both their inheritance and their sense of themselves: Malvolio was not Ophelia. Above all, he said, it was consciousness that had made us a little lower than the angels but far above all other species; for centuries it was believed to be *the* defining human attribute.

'So for a long time, people thought there was a separate entity, a self or a soul, like a pilot in the brain. Religion embedded this idea. It was called dualism, and for ages it was the orthodoxy. Until the last century, when the consensus changed and we began to believe that our brains are actually just a bunch of neurons, same as the brains of other species – and that the idea of a "self" is a delusion. We are one unified collection of cells, not two. The sense of a pilot or a soul had been helpful in the story of our survival. But it was at best a "necessary fiction". It was unscientific to believe it was a separate entity. Dualism became a laughing stock.'

Celeste, the lawyer, moved discreetly on to her third cup of coffee; Sheila's pen was at the ready, but she was still not writing.

'Fair enough, Woody,' said Lukas Parn. 'I have a feeling the shit's about to hit the fan. Are you about to use the words "nucleotide bases"?'

'No,' said Wood. 'Late last century, the idea came up that consciousness was a "spandrel".'

'What the bloody hell is a spandrel?'

'You don't need to know. I prefer to think of it as a logo. Fashion-conscious people pay thousands of dollars to have the right badge on their shoes or watches or handbags. Sometimes it's just a little star or circle – or initials even. But it's cool, it sends your friends a message. It says you're pals with some big star. You're rich. It's what gets traded, it's the defining thing. But it has nothing whatever to do with the shoe, which is designed as sole, upper, closure, arch support and so on.'

'Excuse me,' said Parn, 'but what have shoes got to do with—'

'Consciousness is what distinguishes us from thrushes and tapeworms, sure, but it's inessential,' said Wood. 'We'd be fine without it. It is in fact an "*un*necessary fiction". It's a logo.'

'But,' said Parn, 'if it has no use, how come it has survived all the ages of human evolution?'

'Well, for a start, our evolution is not yet long at all, compared to that of other human species. And second, the genes that code for the synapses in the brain that give us the faculty are probably located in the genome next to other much more essential genes. It is those other genes that have been positively selected, not the logo.'

'Such as?' said Delmore Redding.

'Disease resistance would be my guess.'

'Wouldn't the genes for the logo be elsewhere on the—'

'No. Genes can easily hitch-hike on a part of the genome where they might seem out of place. They are just survivors, entirely selfish. They'll cling on anywhere.'

'But the logo genes might be selected against?' said Redding. 'If they don't really help us?'

'Absolutely. In due course they probably will be. But it looks like they've found a secure little ride. They're clinging on tight. For the time being.'

Malik Wood drank some more water. His hangover seemed to be retreating. 'OK,' he said, 'I'm now going to give you a dramatically simplified version of how the logo actually works. Please don't take notes or I'll get drummed out of every professional body for gross oversimplification.'

'Is that a thing?' said Sheila.

'No,' said Celeste Usman. 'Not in law.'

'Anyway,' said Malik Wood. 'Handsets away.'

A German neuroscientist called Alois Glockner, he told them, had had access to a massively powerful SADS (synaptic activity dual spectroscopy) scanner that could show what went on in the actual synapse. Complete chaos. Too much. But through connections in the commercial world, he got hold of a program that helped him run the scans at super-slow speeds. Then he discovered something: that there was a moment when all the data coming in from the senses cohered with data from the major organs. For a moment there was 'binding', then for a microsecond 'ignition'; so the creature, whether dolphin, crow or human, had the sensation of being an entity. The moment passed too quickly to be useful. But Glockner put his name on it.

'Glockner's Isthmus,' said Redding. 'I remember that.'

'Yes,' said Wood. 'And it was unitary. Just sensory. No dualism. So that was all good. The next bit was an accident. And like the first Victorian breakthrough, it was the result of an industrial accident.'

A Greek docker in Piraeus had fallen from a height and impaled his lower jaw on a piece of iron sticking from a concrete slab. It had gone up through his palate into his brain, where, sawn off by paramedics from the concrete, it stayed lodged while hospital doctors tried for several days to find a way to help. Far from losing consciousness, the man was hyper-alert. Instead of being only periodically self-aware before lapsing into the more normal version of 'screen-saver' consciousness, he was fully 'on' all the time. Beatrice Rossi, an Italian neuroscientist, believed the bar was pressing on the seat of the neural substrates of consciousness, holding a valve open. With the help of a colleague, Elena Duranti, she SADS-scanned the locus intensively over three days and showed that there was a loop between Glockner's Isthmus and a site of episodic memory. So the faculty that had set humans above all other creatures was not in fact an entity but a link between two pre-existent functions, things that had existed apart for millennia – like Normandy and Sussex before the invention of the boat – until a chance mutation in an individual had provided a connection.

228

'All quite Darwinian from then on,' said Malik Wood. 'The loop gave a temporary advantage to its first possessor and her offspring. So it was heavily selected for.'

'I remember reading about the discovery at the time,' said Sheila Rahm.

'What's convincing is the slight sense of anticlimax,' said Wood. 'After all these years of searching, not a priceless treasure – not even an entity, just a *link*. Boy, does nature love pairings. Our most basic requirement, water, is not even an element!'

'You would know,' said Parn.

'So what I'm saying, ultimately,' said Wood, 'is that the Rossi–Duranti loop is quite clumsy. I mean, all credit to those who found it, but the faculty itself is intermittent. You are self-aware when you choose to be. But by far the biggest problem with the loop was that any genetic variation at the point of meiosis opened up the way to insanity.'

'You've lost us, Malik,' said Sheila.

'OK. To oversimplify again. When you, or your cells, make a sperm, which some of us are doing at this very minute in this room, you recombine the genes you've inherited from both parents. Same thing with an ovum, though they seem to get made all at once. Each time, a different combination of Granny and Grandpa. It's fabulously hygienic and good news for your offspring. But at a molecular level, it's also very delicate. Single errors around any of the genes that code for the loop can lead to other sorts of consciousness. So the loop is not just a random neural accident, giving only intermittent powers. It's worse than that. One single typo in its genetic blueprint or one misstep in the exchange of parental alleles jams open the door to psychosis.

And that's why *Homo sapiens* has the other defining feature. Madness.'

Lukas Parn stood up. 'Thank you, Malik. I don't know if everyone could follow that.'

'As much as I need to,' said Sheila. 'But what I want to know is what has this to do with Number Seven?'

'That's a bloody good question,' said Parn.

'OK,' said Malik Wood. 'This bit's easy. Romantic even. Picture a Neanderthal settlement somewhere in Europe. They've had a niche for hundreds of thousands of years. They're few in number, but they're a success. Through ice ages and geological upheavals. They have language, tools and some burial customs. One day a bunch of other humans – a little slimmer, darker, taller, but recognisable and attractive – rolls into town. Sapiens.'

'Look out, it's the Crazy Gang!' said Lukas Parn.

'Exactly,' said Wood. 'Here come these irresistible people. They have a way with them. They're sexy, they do things a bit differently and in many ways better. Sharper weapons, whatever. The Neanders don't know the new guys are also crazy. Most of them are fine. Imagine you're a Neander. You don't know that one in a hundred of these new guys hears the voices of people who aren't there and believe their thoughts are dictated by the planet Zog. You don't know that many of them will go demented in old age. Because you haven't seen them get old. Most of them get killed by predators or die of disease before they reach that stage.'

'This is a bit comic book. Could you be more scientific?' said Delmore Redding.

'Christ,' said Wood. 'I'm trying to keep it simple! In evolutionary terms there are probably immunity advantages that modern humans will get from Neanderthals, who've been in Eurasia for ever. Equally, modern humans will bring resistance to certain African diseases and pass those on to these old Europeans they're now mating with. But there are probably two sides to the coin. Miss Neander may give Mr Sapiens a chance of getting paler skin and therefore a better shot at not dying from rickets or vitamin D deficiency, but she may also give him a susceptibility to viruses.'

'I think I preferred it when it was less scientific,' said Sheila Rahm. 'Tell us about Number Seven.'

'It appears from our studies that Number Seven has a different version of consciousness. It's human, it's sophisticated, it's robust. But it's different.'

Malik Wood looked round the suite. Each of the others was sitting still. Delmore Redding looked as if he wanted to speak but had decided to wait.

Savouring the moment, Wood drank some more water. Delmore Redding cleared his throat, but Wood held up his hand.

'From a hundred SADS scans of the brain and from the enormous number of psychological tests done by Delmore's staff, I can say that Number Seven has a high IQ by modern human standards. He went to a normal school and has just graduated from Cambridge. Or was it Oxford? Doesn't matter. He has an additional or different sense. A kind of synaesthesia between sight and hearing which allows him to detect the proximity of other creatures. He may have other sense variations, including one or more senses that are not compounds of our own, but entirely different.'

'Christ,' said Parn.

'It's what we hoped,' said Wood. 'If the eye grew by minute

adaptations over millions of years and gave us the whole idea of sight, imagine how other mutations could open up new fields of perception. Historically, we thought there were only five senses because we'd only developed five sense organs. Probably there are hundreds. If we had the right receptors, maybe space and time would not be a mystery.'

'Is his sight receiving light from different parts of the spectrum than ours?' said Redding.

'Probably. As you know, we Sapiens can see only a small part of it.'

'Christ, Woody,' said Parn. 'What else?'

'In sensory terms,' said Wood, 'he seems unresponsive to music. Or most of it. That's not necessarily genetic, of course, but it is suggestive. More important is this: in cognitive terms, he appears to lack the ability to make forward hypotheses.'

'In simple English, please, Malik?' said Sheila.

'He doesn't foresee consequences over any length of time. Of his own actions or the actions of others. He just doesn't project forward outside a context. He was told as a kid that next door's cat, who he used to play with, was dying, but was amazed to find it dead a week later. He also has no interest in art, or what you might call the human urge to reinterpret the world. To reflect our life back on itself in order to understand it better.'

'Does he have empathy?' said Sheila.

'Yes,' said Delmore Redding. 'As much as you or me.'

'But isn't that a projection?'

'Yes, but it has no time element,' said Wood. 'That requires a different function of the brain. And a link. Our old friend.'

'OK, Malik. To summarise?' said Parn.

'The evidence of the scans and the tests is that he does possess

Glockner's Isthmus. But he does not have the Rossi–Duranti loop. Or rather, he has a different version of it. Instead of being a valve, he has a straightforward connection that stays open. And while one end, like ours, starts at Glockner, the other end is attached to a different memory site. More autobiographical, less episodic, which may explain the lack of temporal planning. So what we're saying is that he is humanly conscious but in a more consistent way, with, so far as we can see, no corollary weaknesses. No susceptibility to delusions or to hearing voices.'

'And which came first,' said Parn, 'his version or ours?'

'Good question,' said Wood. 'My guess is that there was a loop, then a connection, then a loop again. But of course there was so much backwash between the continents, so much breeding between early humans in Eurasia and early *Homo sapiens* expeditions out of Africa over the millennia that it's hard to map exactly. But it's likely that a medium-primitive Sapiens version became embedded in a local Eurasian population and that the successful Exodus Event group of Sapiens thousands of years later may have had their genome refreshed with their own genes from earlier exoduses reinserted by their gene flow with Neanderthals.'

'You've lost us, mate,' said Parn. 'But basically you're saying that today a bloke in Siberia might be conscious in a slightly different way from one in Uruguay.'

'I am. But I'm also saying that in no way is that a problem. Any more than saying one of them is two centimetres taller or has skin a couple of shades paler is a problem. As I said at the start, you can't make a fetish out of minor differences.'

'Yes,' said Delmore Redding. 'It may be illogical and wrong, but history is full of people who have exploited these unimportant differences. To evil ends sometimes.'

'That's true,' said Wood. 'But we're scientists. The biggest genetic variation between any two humans on this planet is between two villages in the Congo ten miles apart. That's a fact. Like bonobos and chimpanzees becoming different species when a river separated the original parent population. Either of our Congolese has more in common with a person from China than he does with his next-village neighbour. This is really important to understand. That's why the discoveries we've made by way of Number Seven aren't fuel for what they used to call "racists". On the contrary, they are an overpoweringly strong argument for the celebration of difference.'

'And as you told me once,' said Parn, 'the difference between you and me is thirty little things, between you and Sheila is sixty and between you and a male Neanderthal, ninety-six.'

'That's right,' said Wood. 'Those little things are called "amino acids".'

'And are we studying the hell out of those ninety-six?'

'You bet we are.'

'All right, everyone,' said Parn, standing up. 'That'll do. You've all been present at a historic event. Even by the standards of the Parn. Keep it strictly to yourselves. Remember the confidentiality agreements you've signed. But enjoy. Be glad you were here.'

Parn sneezed explosively.

'Thank you, Lukas,' said Sheila Rahm.

'You're welcome,' said Parn. 'I think it'll make a pretty interesting paper, Woody. I can see that FRS just round the corner. Number Seven's going to make us all rich and famous. But you especially.'

Malik Wood drained his glass. 'Sure,' he said. 'Though the paper's going to take a bit of placing.'

'I've found somewhere I think will take it,' said Parn. 'Peer-reviewed, but pretty broad-minded. Christ, they've even published Therese Williams.'

4

London was barely recognisable as the city Talissa had first visited. In a planned reversal of use, the silent buses drove down lanes kerbed off thirty years earlier for cyclists, while the rest of the roadway, once used by cars, was crammed with pedal bikes. It reminded her of a school history book with a photograph of 'Old Beijing'. The only noise came from the thudding of the barges on the old Fleet river and other just uncovered waterways.

It had to be made, this visit, the first time she had seen Mary and Alaric since she had discovered the truth about Seth. She'd kept in touch and knew that Alaric was on a term-long sabbatical from his school and that Mary had changed job, leaving her sports club to work for a company that catered large events. Seth, she also knew, had graduated with a degree in engineering.

Talissa was dreading the moment. It was no consolation to think that she would be the first human being in history who had to deliver such news. Before leaving New York, she had also rung the private number Catrina Olsen had shared after leaving the Parn. They had agreed to fix a time to meet once Talissa was in town.

In Ashers End, Mary held open the front door at the end of the path. She stretched out her arms as Talissa approached, her head on one side.

'You *still* haven't changed! What is it with you? Look at me all grey. And you . . . Come inside and tell me your secret.'

'Good genes, I guess,' said Talissa, following her into the hall. 'Sure can't be the way I live.'

Seth was away, it turned out. He was visiting John Rockingham in Newmarket, Mary said, where they were sure to be talking about horses.

We know what you did . . . Talissa braced herself. It was better that Seth wasn't there. She had to tell his parents before they found out from a less considerate source. I'll do it now, she thought, before we get too comfortable.

But Mary had prepared a special dinner, whose herb and onion aromas were already in the air, while Alaric was opening some wine.

'Where are you staying, Talissa?' said Mary, putting the first of the dishes on the table.

'With my friend Kavya.'

'Is she the one who did so well out of PICs?' said Mary.

'Not really. Her son could cash in, but he refuses to use them.'

'Refused,' said Alaric. 'Past tense. The new government's dropped them. Quite right, too.'

'Al's cross because he scored so low,' said Mary.

'Nonsense,' said Alaric. 'I just thought there was a confusion, that's all. Between important things and frivolous things.'

'Go on,' said Talissa.

'Well.' Alaric's voice became teacherly as he poured some wine. 'Slavery and the Holocaust were historic crimes against humanity. It's not for us to say how long we have to try to make amends — with identity cards or anything else. It's for the descendants of those who were wronged to decide. A murderer doesn't set his own jail sentence. But a hundred and fifty years of slavery ... What do you think? Maybe two thousand years of payback?'

'I guess.'

'They're one thing, those crimes,' said Alaric. 'We have a sacred duty to remember. The other thing is quite different. Saying my grandfather had slightly redder hair than yours, therefore I'm entitled to a better job than you. That's not sacred. That's the narcissism of small differences.'

'That's a good phrase,' said Talissa.

'Yes, I read it somewhere,' said Alaric. 'Freud, I think. But what I mean is that people need to stop making an obsession of tiny variations in appearance that are the result of simple genetic drift. That was the thrust of the ADEPT thing.'

'How do you know about genes all of a sudden?' said Mary.

'Rose Paxton explained it to me.'

'And who's Rose Paxton?' said Talissa.

'The head of science,' said Mary. 'Al was infatuated with her.'

'No, I wasn't!'

'All right, you weren't,' said Mary. 'I think the last straw for Al was when the PICs people gave Seth half a point because my family's from Japan.'

'Bloody insult,' said Alaric. 'If anything they should have deducted a point.'

Talissa found herself looking at her hostess. She hadn't given Mary's background much thought before; the Parn enquiries had been all about her own family history. Then she

238

remembered, from their previous flat, a photograph of two older people posing in what could have been a Japanese interior.

'Whereabouts?' she said.

'Two of my grandparents were from a small town near Osaka,' said Mary. 'One was from Hiroshima. I think that's why Al fell in love with me. A hotline to history.'

'And the fourth one?'

'Paris. He was French. He met my grandmother when she came over as a student. But I was brought up in Brighton.'

'That's a cool family,' said Talissa.

'I thought so,' said Alaric.

'And we've ended up living next to the big Crystal Palace radio mast,' said Mary. 'The glamour.'

'Our own Eiffel Tower,' said Alaric. 'In honour of Mary's *grand-père.*'

'And where's your family from, Alaric?' said Talissa.

'Don't! It'll take for ever,' said Mary. 'With a lot of fjords and a surprising twist. There was a grandfather born in Nazareth.'

By the time dinner was finished at midnight, there was no longer any chance of confiding to Mary and Alaric the news that would change their lives. Jet-lagged yet relieved, Talissa promised she would visit them again in two days' time.

As the night train headed north towards Muswell Hill, she leant her head against the window. She would deliver the message better when she was rested; she'd have time to prepare the exact words. She had forgotten how much she had become a part of the Pedersens' lives. Alaric with his bean and sausage dish, Mary saying, 'The woods are your friend' . . .

They had seldom met, yet they had been loyal to her for more than two decades. The look of delight on their faces when they caught sight of her after a break . . . And now in return she almost loved them.

She shifted in her seat and let her mind drift as the stations went by. She herself could have married, she thought, and lived a life like theirs. Maybe. Mark would probably have gone for it. She could have pushed Aron Landor into leaving his wife. Though without the thrill of subterfuge, was he someone you would really want to spend all your time with? Or Felix. She had loved him for sure, body and mind, one fine day. But she had messed it up. Through sheer . . . inexperience. How cruel that the crucial question had been asked of someone too young to get the answer right. Now it was too late to have a child, but she still felt susceptible to a passion that could reset her world; she was still open to love.

Susan had once assured her that the kind of man you met depended on the kind of man you wanted to meet. 'You always set your satnav for Adventure, not for Home,' she said.

'Are you saying that if I'd gone out on the town in a settling-down frame of mind, I'd have met different guys?' said Talissa.

'Yes. Or at least, you would have *chosen* different guys, that's the point.'

'And what about you, Mrs Wiseacre?'

'I set my satnav for Adventure every time. But it always landed me at Leon.'

Up in her old room in Muswell Hill, Talissa lay down among the batik-covered cushions on the bed. She wanted to clear her mind and sleep, but her brain kept asking questions. Was there a way in which giving birth to Seth had satisfied – or cauterised – any desire she must once have felt to be a mother to her own child? And without that urge, had she been drawn to a different kind of man and lived a life that was not truly hers?

She turned onto her side, her synapses firing on a surge of American time.

What would her father have thought of all the decisions she had made? He had told her to be brave, to try everything. That much she remembered of him – when he'd taken her to the park in winter, his hand crushing her smaller fingers in their woollen gloves, when he'd pushed her on the swing and urged her to go up on the climbing frame. But probably dads wanted their daughters to have children, didn't they? Some urge beyond reason, not unkind.

Occasionally, at home in Harlem, she lit a berry-scented candle at her desk because she knew he'd loved the smell. When she inhaled it, she missed him with an ache in all her limbs. What she missed most was everything about him that she could never remember.

In the morning, Talissa sat at the familiar kitchen table. Kavya Gopal presented her with sliced banana with a squeeze of lime and told her to eat up while she cooked some chilli eggs.

A news alert came through on her handset. It was from the plausible FBC in New York. 'Galatia, a fundamentalist Christian news organisation' it reported, 'is claiming that the so-called White Van Man is not a clone of *Homo vannesiensis*, as had been thought, but a hybrid of Neanderthal and *Homo sapiens*. The individual is thought to be living somewhere in Europe. Our London correspondent, Todd Brown, has more.'

'Are you all right?' said Kavya.

Talissa put the handset away in her bag. She held her head between her hands and screamed.

She felt Kavya's arm round her. 'What is it? *What is it?* Tell me.'

Then it came out through moans and gasps and Kavya's baffled interruptions, a torrent of confusion and fear, of bad choices, vanity and misplaced affections. Talissa felt as if the whole misbegotten venture of humanity was trying to find release through her exploding head. 'What are we?' she sobbed on Kavya's shoulder. 'What have we done?'

She pushed the older woman's arm away, repelled by human touch, even at its kindest, wanting instead to feel the wood of the table against her cheek.

Then she stood up, pulled open the back door and ran down the side of the house into the street.

In Ashers End, Alaric was drying the glasses from the night before. When he'd put them away, he'd have the whole day clear to work on his book.

'I'll be back at five,' said Mary. 'I've got to make canapés for a party in town tonight.'

'OK. Nice seeing Talissa, wasn't it?' said Alaric. 'Though I thought she seemed a bit tense. Probably the jet lag.'

In Newmarket, Seth was at the gallops with John Rockingham, watching a two-year-old they'd heard good things about.

'Beautiful creature,' said John. 'Lovely, easy action.'

'Yes,' said Seth, 'but she seems to have a cough. Can you hear?'

'She's on the mend,' said the trainer, coming alongside them. 'And we've got six weeks yet.'

*

In Harlem, Susan Kovalenko was asleep, but she had caught some news the night before.

'I must remember to tell Talissa about the white van man,' she said.

'It's so her thing,' said Leon. 'How long is she in London?'

'Just a week.'

'So we get to keep Pelham for a bit longer.'

Felix was lying in his one-room apartment in Queens. There were four different medications on the nightstand. It could happen that he took them twice; other days, not at all. The yellow capsules were to stop the man upstairs from shouting. The blue one kept his own thoughts from escaping onto the street.

In Russell Square, Malik Wood had called an emergency meeting in his office.

'I think we need to control the narrative,' said Sheila Rahm, by video from New York. 'This is going to be a London thing, so I'm getting on the next plane. Until then, you need to get yourself the best damage-control person you can find.'

'Ahead of you there,' said Malik Wood. 'I've had plans in place since I met with Parn in Berlin. Say hello to Clive Brewer.'

He indicated a short man in a patterned suit, sitting on his sofa next to Delmore Redding. Brewer smiled and raised a hand.

'What I suggest,' said Sheila, 'is that one of you needs to go and speak to the parents. Tell them whatever story you've prepared. It was all a mistake. Shit happens. It was an important experiment for the good of humankind. Whatever.

243

Discuss how they break it to the kid. Presumably they'll want to do that themselves. But speak to them first.'

'I can do that,' said Brewer.

'Maybe not you,' said Malik Wood. 'No disrespect, but this needs someone who's been involved all along.'

'Where's the surrogate?' said Sheila.

'In New York,' said Wood.

'The first thing to do,' said Clive Brewer, 'is to get the kid to go public. Let him own it. Find the biggest audience. Do a one-off interview.'

'But he won't want to be seen, will he?' said Sheila.

'They'll use FAT. Face-altering technology,' said Brewer. 'It's quite an old process, but it's become much better in recent years. And it's fail-safe. They've never had an identification.'

'It's too risky,' said Wood. 'I've had Parn in my ear all day stressing the need to protect the kid's identity.'

'I can get a deal with the broadcaster,' said Brewer. 'It's a one-off exclusive. People see the kid, or a version of him. They understand his need for privacy and respect. They back off. I'll get my VA to check the latest viewer figures.'

'It would have been a natural for the old BBC,' said Delmore Redding.

'I still don't like it,' said Wood.

Brewer ignored him as he looked up from his handset. 'OK. It's Flip Talk. No surprise there. I'll get on to Jade Johnson. She owes me plenty.'

'Can we have an update on our legal position?' said Sheila Rahm.

'OK,' said Malik Wood. 'Lukas Parn was advised that it was not a criminal matter, but there might have been a breach of contract. A tort. The contract was not specific, but they could reasonably argue that a Sapiens father was implied.'

'More than implied,' said Sheila. 'From what I understand, they were told that they were to become parents at last. Both of them. Personally. The fulfilment of their dream.'

'The point is,' said Malik, 'that Parn believes he can take any hit. In damages. And if it came to a crime, they'd go for a deferred prosecution, so he could pay a large fine and promise to be good.'

'We'll need a team to present to the public,' said Brewer. 'Malik and Delmore, that's fine. Good optics. But you need a woman.'

'Catrina Olsen would have been ideal,' said Malik.

'Let's get on to her,' said Brewer. 'See if you can persuade her.'

'She won't do it. She's furious with us.'

'Who else knew about the experiment?'

'Only Lukas Parn,' said Malik. 'It was his idea. But he only does positive grandstanding. The breakthroughs.'

'All right,' said Brewer. 'This is going to be a bumpy ride. Parn may have to get over his shyness and go public. Until then, let's find someone caring and trustworthy to join the team. Preferably female.'

'Well,' said Sheila Rahm. 'What about Ayesha Cross? She actually worked the manipulator, didn't she? In the lab. Seems like a nice person, too. You look doubtful, Malik.'

By the time she had regained control of her emotions, Talissa no longer recognised her surroundings. She was in a street of small houses, a long way from Kavya's. Once, there would have been cars parked along the kerb; now there were hefty garbage bins on wheels.

She called Catrina Olsen. 'Can I come and see you? Now?'

'You've heard?' said Catrina. 'It's best if I come to you, I think. Where are you?'

'I don't know.'

'Click on your "Locator". OK, I've got it. What on earth are you doing up there?'

'I don't know. I just . . . walked till I collapsed. Can you come?'

'Of course. Go to the café behind you, the Colney Bakery, on the main road. I'll see you there in about half an hour.'

Talissa tried the door, but it was closed. On the other side of the main road was a park, visible through railings and a line of trees. Looking to kill some time, she walked along the pavement till she found some gates. At a slightly lower level was an enormous old brick building, hundreds of yards long, utilitarian but with a fancy bell tower. A uniformed porter sat in a wooden hut by a barrier at the top of the drive and she decided not to go any further.

By the time Catrina arrived, the café had opened. They were the only people in the glum interior, which smelled of disinfectant. A cleaner was mopping the floor, banging against the furniture.

Talissa took Catrina's hand on top of the small table.

'It's good that you're in London when this comes out,' said Catrina. 'You've at least got me to talk to. I presume you've still not told anyone at home?'

'No. But when these Galatia people started sniffing around, I thought it would be only a matter of time. They'd clearly

246

got a source. I thought I should tell the parents myself. Rather than have them called by some reporter.'

'What made you sure?' said Catrina.

'I had a message from someone at Galatia.'

'God.'

'Yeah. I got Parn to give me his word he'd do everything to protect Seth's identity, but even so . . .'

'There'll be a steady drip, drip, don't you think?' said Catrina. 'Even if everyone acts in good faith, which is a big "if" with Parn. It'll be very hard to keep it watertight.'

Talissa let go of Catrina's hand. She sucked in some air over her teeth. 'What the fuck have we done?'

'Not much,' said Catrina. 'You and me. It's what other people have done.'

They drank some coffee. Catrina stared at the tabletop as if an answer might be in the grain of the wood.

'What are you doing now?' said Talissa. 'For work?'

'I'm a consultant. I could retire, but I like the work. I prefer it to the Parn.'

'What will happen to the people there?'

'I hope they go to prison. But I wouldn't bank on it. Lukas is bound to find a lawyer to get them off.'

Neither of them seemed able to talk about Seth.

'How are your boys?'

'Oh, quite grown-up now,' said Catrina. 'Ben's a musician, Anders works for an IT company. They're both happy in their way.'

Talissa saw a sparkle return for a moment to Catrina's eyes.

'I'm glad they're OK. By the way, what's that huge building on the other side of the road? In the park?'

'It's apartments, I think,' said Catrina. 'It was originally built as a lunatic asylum in the nineteenth century. Colney Hatch. It was famous in its day.'

'It's gigantic.'

'I know. I think it grew too big to manage.'

There was a silence. Eventually, Catrina sat up straight. 'My dear Talissa, we need a plan.'

'I know. Let's try to get through this together. If you're up for that.'

'I am,' said Catrina.

5

Talissa rehearsed the words as the silent train headed south from Muswell Hill. She had met Seth — several years ago, admittedly, but she knew him to be an ordinary boy, if a little unusual. He was no freak, and there was consolation in that. Second, her work had increasingly revealed the mongrel nature of the world's humans: one subspecies now, for sure, but with a pariah-dog pedigree. Perhaps that scientific fact would take the edge off what she had to say. But she was not lecturing people who already understood such things; she was dealing with Alaric and Mary, parents of an only son.

Alaric opened the door and fussed round her, offering coffee and warm cheese canapés left over from some function. Mary would apparently be back soon; Seth himself, it seemed, was still away.

'What are his plans?' said Talissa, as she sat down.

'Seth doesn't really do plans,' said Alaric, putting down a cup of coffee on the table. 'He started a postgrad course, but he didn't like it. Did a couple of placements with big companies. Nothing's stuck yet.'

'I guess the world's always going to need engineers,' said Talissa.

'I think so. But getting launched. It's difficult. We don't know whether to let him go his own way or try to help.'

'What else is he interested in?'

'Horses. I think maybe he'd like to breed them. An odd thing for a boy from Crystal Palace.'

'Football?' said Talissa, remembering her walk in the park with the schoolboy.

'Yes, he does still follow it. But it's too late for him to be a player. For a professional club, anyway. Even in a lower league.'

'I guess university put an end to that.'

'God, yes. The big clubs sign them up aged ten.'

As they chatted, Talissa remembered a piece of advice she had read somewhere long ago. If you have bad news to break, do it in stages.

When Mary was finally home, and was sitting down with them, she began.

'It's so great to see you guys again. But there's something I think you need to know.'

'We're all ears,' said Mary. 'You're not getting married, are you?'

'No, no. The news is . . . not very good. I have a, like, suspicion . . . More than a suspicion. It's to do with Seth.'

'What about him?' said Mary.

'With these procedures, even with all the modern technology, there can be mistakes.'

'But Seth's a healthy and—'

'To do with paternity. It's a busy lab, so many samples and embryos and eggs and . . . incubators. Human error.'

'Are you saying I'm not the father?'

Alaric's voice was so plaintive that Talissa couldn't meet his eye.

250

'I'm saying we must all remember what a great kid he is.'

'How do you know? After all this time?'

'Has something suddenly come up?' said Mary.

Talissa had decided it was best not to mention the DNA tests she'd organised back home. She stalled for a moment.

In the silence, Mary said, 'If it turned out it was someone else's sperm, we'd love him just the same. He's who he is.'

'Yes. That's the important thing,' said Talissa.

The quietness filled the room again, like fog. She could tell they knew there was more to come.

Alaric said, 'I always thought . . . I always wondered . . . No, I didn't! What am I saying? I'm making stuff up now. But are we sure? How do we know?'

They had reached the part of the conversation for which no amount of rehearsal could prepare them.

'I don't think anyone can know for sure who the actual father is,' said Talissa.

'We could do a DNA test,' said Alaric. 'I know it's controversial these days, but I'd have thought the Parn could organise something. They're still monitoring him, after all.'

'That could rule you out, Al,' said Mary, 'but it wouldn't tell us who the father is. Not that I care at all. As far as I'm concerned, Alaric *is* Seth's dad. But how do we know, Talissa? What have you found out?'

'Those people at the Parn,' said Talissa. 'I don't think they were honest. Ever.' Still breaking it by stages, she told herself.

'What do you mean?'

'I'm not sure it was a mistake. I think someone switched a sample. Maybe no one knew which sample or which surrogate, so they could dress it up as science. Double-blind and all that.'

'That nice embryologist,' said Alaric. 'The one who, you know, put in the . . . What was her name?'

'Catrina? No. It wasn't her. She was in the dark.'

Talissa felt the weight of her life's choices bear down on her. This was the moment. She closed her eyes, then opened them and looked up at the ceiling of the square front room. She noticed for the first time a stuck-on cornice.

Still staring upwards, she said, 'You know that Lukas Parn finances a lot of work in genetic research.'

'Yes. I think so,' said Mary.

'And palaeoanthropology. Have you heard about a character called White Van Man?'

'It was me who told you about that silly name,' said Alaric. 'In France that time.'

'There's been a rumour going round that someone created a clone of him.'

'I saw that.'

'But that's not true. What does appear to be true is that there is a living hybrid. A cross of two human species. Not a clone, and not *vannesiensis* at all. But a mix of Sapiens and Neanderthal.'

Mary, who was leaning forward on the edge of the sofa, let out a cry. 'Not . . . Not our . . .'

Talissa nodded.

Alaric stood up and said, 'I knew it. I knew there was something. Those bastards. Those utter, fucking—'

Talissa held on to the edge of the chair. 'Let me explain what I know,' she said.

On the way back from Newmarket, Seth found his screen full of messages from someone called Clive Brewer. Why was this stranger urging him to get in touch? He turned off the handset.

A young woman in the carriage was looking at him, stealing glances over her book. She was wearing a kilt over black woollen tights. He caught her eye and the skin of her face coloured a little as she looked down, but not before she had given him a half-smile.

This sort of thing had started happening to him since he'd left university. Thirty-five-year-olds in business skirts, teenage girls in jeans, even people old enough to be his mother – they seemed to want to rest their eyes on him. If caught, they smiled in different but similar ways.

It was a nuisance. He felt he was missing out on something. But he couldn't ask them what they wanted. There was no way for him to approach this woman in the kilt. It was not in his nature and it was possibly against the law.

He hadn't slept with anyone since Rosalie Wright. That had all been easy, because Rosie knew what to do. She didn't look away, she just told him what she'd like from him next, in his own time. Maybe he'd never again meet anyone like her.

The woman crossed her legs, causing the kilt to rise. Seth turned his head and gazed the other way, out of the window.

When he got home, he found his father pacing up and down in the small back garden.

'Are you all right, Dad?'

'I tried to call you.'

'Sorry. I turned it off. I was being bombarded by some stranger.'

'Come inside.'

'Where's Mum?'

253

'She went to work. They have a dinner thing. In Holland Park.'

In the kitchen, Alaric went to a corner cupboard and took out an unopened bottle of whisky.

They sat opposite one another at the table. Alaric stared at Seth in a way that he hated himself for doing. He could still see a little of Mary there, as he had on the day of the birth. Now he also looked for evidence of another kind. The nostrils, wider than his own. A ridge above the eye sockets – not enormous, but, now he came to look at it, more pronounced than most. The legs that had given him a usefully low centre of gravity on the football pitch. He'd always been aware of these things, but never thought much about them. Feeling like a Nazi doctor, Alaric turned away and took his drink over to the window. None of these features were beyond the scope of an exchange of genes between two regular parents. Surely.

'How are you doing?'

'I'm fine, thanks. Why are we drinking whisky?'

'Do you not like it?'

'I've only had it once. With John Rockingham. When he was telling me about his uninhabited Scottish island. Trying to recreate the atmosphere. Would you like to go there with me one day?'

'No fear,' said Alaric. 'I like towns. How was Newmarket?'

'It was windy on the gallops. We saw some good horses, though. John wants to buy a share in one.'

'We had a visitor today. Talissa. You remember her?'

'Yes, of course. She took me to the park. When I was, like, twelve.'

'Did you like her?'

'Yes. She was . . . kind.'

254

Alaric found a smile had stolen up on him. Seth was still himself. 'Did you trust her?'

'Of course. She's your friend. You and Mum. Right?'

'Yes. I like her, too,' said Alaric. 'And I also trust her. She told us that after all this time some doubt has come up about your birth.'

'What?'

'It seems I may not be your father after all.'

'I don't understand.'

'Maybe there was a mix-up at the clinic.'

Seth said nothing.

'So,' Alaric went on, 'it's probably worth clearing up. If you don't mind, we'd like you to take a test. Talissa says the embryologist at the time, a woman called Catrina, can get it done in an ultra-modern place that tells you everything.'

Still Seth said nothing.

'Seth?'

'You painted the cupboard in Palace colours. You dressed up as Father Christmas at my first school when I didn't know anyone. And I think it was you who sent those new football boots when I was at college. I couldn't care less what any test says.'

'Let's have some more whisky then.'

Seth held out his glass.

When the result came back from a private laboratory, it followed the law in giving no details of the species composition of the subject, offering only statistics on ancestral habitats and disease susceptibility. The lab owed Catrina a favour, however, and after she had signed a confidentiality agreement they agreed to reveal more data. It confirmed what the New York test had found, that the subject was 51.5 per cent

Neanderthal. She printed off the key part of the result and then, as she had agreed, double-deleted the file.

She read out the numbers to Talissa and they arranged to meet again at the Colney Bakery, their now agreed centre of operations. Over a toasted sandwich, they decided to form a two-person shield in front of the Pedersens. For the first time since *We know what you did*, Talissa felt an element of relief. She was no longer alone.

Catrina had offered the use of her flat near Marylebone High Street to Alaric, Mary and Seth and got them to re-route all incoming communications on their handsets to an end point that she and Talissa could also access. She herself had moved into a spare room with her younger son in Highgate.

'Somehow,' she told Talissa, 'we have to control the process.'

'We'll be up against the Parn's PR army.'

'We have to work with them.'

'I still have Parn's private ID,' said Talissa. 'I can call him.'

The story rumbled on. In the absence of new facts, reporters turned to opinion and interview. There was a clip of a Professor Targett, head of London's 'prestigious Museum of Human History', commenting, 'This could reset our understanding of who we are and how we got here. But only if the individual agrees to co-operate.'

The next day there was an interview with the Archbishop of Canterbury, the Right Reverend Dr Penelope Farmiga, who seemed less excited than alarmed. 'We must respect the individual in the eyes of God,' she said, 'and grant him dignity and privacy.'

'But he's not really a man, is he?' said the interviewer. 'He doesn't have the same entitlements as you or me.'

'He's a human being, as I understand it,' said Dr Farmiga.

'Let's go for a walk,' said Catrina, pushing open the doors of the Colney Bakery.

The air was edgy with the coming of winter.

'That was bad,' said Talissa.

'I know. I'm afraid it's going to get very rough. I've had a lot of stuff coming in from someone called Clive Brewer, the Parn's PR man. They want Seth to do an interview. A one-off thing. Probably with Flip Talk, and with syndication in America and worldwide. Then there'll be some sort of privacy deal.'

'Do you trust him?'

'He warned me that the press'll come after you as well.'

'What do you mean, "come after"?'

'Force you to talk. It's what they always do. When someone has a problem, they pretend to be their friend. Get them to confide. Then they stitch them up.'

'How do you know this? I thought you were a doctor.'

'Anyone can see how it's done.'

'What do you think we should do?'

'I think you should go home,' said Catrina. 'Then maybe find somewhere to hide for a time. Make sure no one but me can reach you on your handset.'

'But I promised to stay and look after him. The shield, remember?'

'I'll manage,' said Catrina. 'I don't think there's anything you can do now, Talissa. You've done the hard bit by breaking it to the parents. To be honest, I think you're more of a liability now. A way of getting to him. Or *at* him.'

'But if I go back,' said Talissa, 'that's my flight allowance used up. The federal government rations our long-distance trips.'

Talissa felt saddened by what Catrina had said. She'd need time to think about it, to talk it over – with Kavya, perhaps. But she also felt exhausted by the weight of what she had carried for so long.

They stopped at the gates down into the park, from which they could see the apartment building, converted from the old asylum.

'That place,' said Talissa. 'It's so, like . . . gigantic.'

'I think it had to be,' said Catrina.

'Were Victorian Londoners that insane?'

'I looked up the history after we first met here,' said Catrina. 'They say it took five hours to visit all the wards. The male corridor was a quarter of a mile long. With locked rooms every ten paces.'

'Why did they shut it down?' said Talissa.

'It was the policy of the time,' said Catrina. 'Fifty or more years ago. Something called "care in the community". They thought the patients would be better off outside.'

'And were they?'

'I don't know. I'm not sure how much "care" they really got. Or how much of a community they found.'

'I had a boyfriend once . . .' Talissa trailed off.

'And?' said Catrina.

Talissa looked at the Italian bell tower, thrusting up into the sky.

'Never mind.'

6

Lukas Parn was sitting in his Berlin apartment.

'I gave you my word, Talissa,' he said into his handset. 'We're a powerful organisation and we'll do everything we can to protect him. Just relax. Take it easy. Goodbye.'

Opposite him was a sharp-eyed old woman whose Prague vowels occasionally scratched the surface of her acquired Australian English.

'I don't understand what you thought you were doing,' she said.

'I wanted to help Dad,' said Parn, closing the handset. 'That was my main motive.'

'It's too late for that.'

'I know.'

'All that research . . .'

'The brain implants were hit-and-miss. They did restore some memories in some people with dementia. But in others, they gave them memories of things they'd never done.'

Milena Parn drank some tea. 'He's very near the end now.'

'Thank God. Listen, Ma. We all make sacrifices in the name of science. For the greater good. We use animals in laboratories.'

'Humans are not mice. You know that.'

'But think of what we do to one another anyway. In war. We've murdered each other by the million. No one remembers the life of one poor kid shot in battle.'

'His parents do.'

'Not if they're long dead too. Plus, my people didn't kill anyone. Far from it. We actually gave life.'

'And what have you discovered?'

'I'm not going to bore you with the science. But I think we ought to be able to identify some differences between the two species and these could give us indications of where the causes of Sapiens dementia lie. In the young psychotics and in the old people.'

'And then?'

'They'll develop therapies. Treatments, preventions. If we can get at the genetic basis, the therapies will work much better. We'll be treating causes, not symptoms.'

'No one can play God. Not even rich men.'

'Don't be like that, Ma. We can see that future generations do better.'

'Would it stop them going to war?'

Parn stood up. 'Who knows? Maybe it would. Do you want to go out to lunch?'

'No. I'm not hungry.' Mrs Parn fiddled with the clasp of her bag. 'I won't be seeing your father again. They told me not to come back. I've said goodbye.'

'How was he when you last saw him?'

Milena Parn thought for a moment. 'I think the last time I saw him was twenty years ago. Really saw him. Before he went crazy and thought I was his long-lost sister. Have you any idea what that was like? Not being recognised, I mean.'

'A little.'

'After I'd given him my life. It made it all seem so . . . pointless. All the years.'

Parn sat down again. 'It was a long time.'

'He was the sensitive type, you know. When I first met him. He was very handsome, but nervous. He remembered the fall of Saigon, when he was a kid. The sound of the bombardment. People forget about that. They think it was just helicopters. But all the French houses were shaking as the Vietcong shells came in. His sister died in the rubble.'

'I thought the Americans—'

'No, they'd long gone. I sometimes wonder if it left a mark. Seeing that as a child. Then starting again in a foreign country. They were in Darwin at first, you know. The Northern Territory. Of course, they were lucky to get in at all. It was easier if you came from Europe, like my family. That's why we took my surname.'

'So,' said Parn. 'How long would you like to stay here in Berlin? I have to go to London soon, but Ilse can look after you.'

'How's the young woman in the case? The surrogate mother?'

'Not that young any more. But she's OK, I think.'

'And what does she think of the trick you played on her?'

'I can't reach her. I've tried often enough.'

'You liked her, didn't you?'

'To be honest, I hoped she'd become a friend.'

'A girlfriend?'

'Maybe.'

Mrs Parn shook her head. 'And did you ask her out?'

'I invited her to stay in Connecticut.'

'And?'

'I gave her a painting she admired.'

'But did you give her flowers?'

'She wasn't a flower kind of girl.'

'So you offered her money.'

'No. I mentioned some research funding.'

'That's money.'

'I was in a hurry.'

'That's why you're lonely, Lukas. People don't want to be rushed, they want to be appreciated.'

'She was kind of prickly.'

'What happened to the painting?'

'She sent it back.'

Milena Parn pushed her cup and saucer across the table. 'Maybe I could manage something. A sandwich, perhaps.'

'I'll send Ilse out. I suppose you want Vegemite.'

'I'll have whatever's convenient. But no mayonnaise. Some Dijon mustard on the side if they have it. Not avocado. I leave it to you.'

When Parn returned from speaking to his housekeeper, his mother said, 'Are you going to be in trouble for this? People seem very angry. I keep hearing about it.'

'That's what I'm going to London for. I had a conference a while ago with a woman in Gray's Inn. A barrister. She said we might have to pay damages for breach of contract. But the last I heard it's with the Department of Public Prosecutions.'

'And what do they do?'

'They decide if a law may have been broken. Then they put it before a judge to see if they think there's a case. And he or she may throw it out or they may send it for trial. At the Old Bailey.'

'That sounds bad.'

'It probably won't come to that. It'll be OK. In a civilised country, scientific enquiry can never be against the law.'

'It's the people, Lukas. Their feelings. You've never understood that. The young man in question. His parents. The surrogate you tried to make friends with. What do you think they feel?'

'I hope they feel proud to have been part of something historic.'

'It's not too late to try to understand.'

'It's not too late for me to sell real estate in Alice Springs. We are where we are.'

Everything was happening too fast, Seth found.

The flat they'd been lent was near some interesting shops on Marylebone High Street, but he wasn't allowed to visit them. Groceries were delivered to the door on Dr Olsen's account. Mary was given unpaid leave by her employer and carried on as normally as she could. She tried to protect Alaric and Seth from all news except what was filtered by Catrina. Alaric settled to work on his book, but found he couldn't concentrate. He had some eggshell paint delivered and started to redo Catrina's woodwork.

There was a call from Catrina herself at the end of the week.

'The baying of the hounds is a bit scary. The Parn have this PR guy called Clive Brewer they want you to meet. He's lined up a one-off interview on Flip Talk with their top presenter. In return, he says they'll handle all the press and they promise Seth won't have to do anything else at all. They'll protect him. Be the filter for all queries. Plus the Parn will pay huge compensation to you in order to avoid any civil case. I think we're talking millions.'

'I don't know,' said Mary. 'I don't know anything at all about how this stuff works. And I don't need compensating.'

'Let's meet and see what you make of him. We can do it remotely.'

The next day, the smooth face of Clive Brewer appeared on Catrina's desk screen. Alaric, Mary and Catrina herself took up the other quadrants; Seth didn't want to join in.

'Here's the thing,' said Brewer. 'You don't get an hour of prime-time Jeremy Rede every day of the week. I've had to pull up a lot of trees here. But they're up for it. A full hour, no ads. It's pretty much unprecedented.'

'What we need in return,' said Catrina, 'are guarantees. About privacy. And respect.'

'Yes,' said Alaric. 'And we need to know that this is an end to it. That afterwards Seth can go about his life.'

'I'm on it,' said Brewer. 'What we already have is a chance for the lad to tell his story. In his own words. Let people see how normal he is.'

'I've never seen the show,' said Alaric, 'but Rede sounds a bit of a—'

'I'm going to give you some statistics here,' said Brewer. 'My numbers people have done a lot of work on the reach here. Multimedia stuff. Qualitative as well quantit—'

'Thank you,' said Catrina. 'We'll think about it. I do see that there's an advantage in putting Seth on air. They can see that any unusual features in his . . . background are of no consequence. And that to say otherwise would be cruel and bigoted. Possibly against discrimination laws as well.'

'Let me get you some stats,' said Brewer.

'But it all depends on the good faith of the interviewer,' said Catrina.

'No one can deliver Rede,' said Brewer. 'He's a mav. But Jade Johnson owes me. The head of content there. I'll let you know what assurances I get.'

The night before the interview, Seth lay down in bed and pulled up the covers. Was he really so interesting to the world? He thought about his childhood and wondered if he should have done things differently. With Sadie Liew, for instance, or with the boys who'd menaced him at school. He felt he'd fitted in all right at university. It was true that he'd been a loner, but that was only because he didn't like getting up early. In his last year, he'd met a few engineers. Other friends: Rosalie, the horse-racing guys . . . No one seemed to think he was that interesting, let alone unusual. He had no thoughts about what might await him the next day. He couldn't have conjectured and he didn't try.

In the morning, he left the house by the back door and went to the end of a cobbled lane of disused garages, where a black saloon was waiting. Catrina had told him that for the duration of the event he was to be known as Simon Green.

He spoke his new name and the destination code into the dashboard mic. The car moved off silently. They drove west out of central London onto an old arterial road, past the derelict Hoover Building. He put on the surgical mask, head-covering woollen hat and shaded glasses that were waiting on the seat.

The studios were part of a group of buildings that looked like a government installation, behind a checkpoint with a security guard. Seth was deposited outside a glass double door, where a woman with a clipboard was waiting. 'Mr Green?'

Seth nodded. He was shown into a bright atrium with red sofas and huge framed photographs of presenters and famous people on the walls.

'Let's get your pass fixed up, shall we?' said the woman. 'Over here.'

At a reception desk, Seth signed himself in as Mr S. Green and was given a lanyard. They went through internal doors to a bank of lifts. On the third floor, the woman said, 'I'm handing you over to Vicky now. She'll look after you from here. Have a good one.'

A woman with red lipstick and another clipboard shook his hand. 'Hello,' she said. 'You got here all right, then?'

'Yes.'

He was told to wait in a windowless lounge with more famous photographs on the wall and invited to help himself to coffee from a thermos and anything he fancied from a tray of Danish pastries.

Vicky came back and said, 'I'll introduce you to Jade in a minute. She's in charge. Then we'll take you through to the FAT lab, where you can choose what you want to look like. Are you a fan of Jeremy's?'

Seth couldn't tell her he'd never seen the show. 'Yes,' he said.

'He can be naughty, but he's got a heart of gold. I think you'll get on well.'

Seth poured himself more coffee. He wished it had been like the heart-starting nectar from Tarvino's, opposite his old college. This stuff, sipped beneath his raised mask, was hot but weak and he was beginning to register the fact that he had hardly slept. His system needed to be kicked awake. He hoped they wouldn't ask him anything too difficult.

The FAT lab was down the corridor and had three chairs in front of a mirrored wall, like a hairdresser's.

'Come and sit here, love. I'm Diane.'

A friendly woman sat him in a padded chair and fitted a helmet over his head.

'You can take off your mask and things now.'

From the various images projected on a screen inside the helmet, he chose a mixture of two: one who reminded him a little of Talissa and one who looked like an older Wilson Kalu. They were then mashed together into a persona that was impressively different from anyone he'd ever seen. For the voice, he chose a rich bass, far from his own light tenor, with a faint East Asian, possibly Japanese, cadence. For all his anxiety, he felt an urge to smile at this terrific new person he'd invented.

He walked back to the windowless lounge, but found he'd left his mask and hat and glasses in the FAT lab. Once he'd retrieved them and put them on again, he watched a screen in the lounge that showed a live feed from the studio, where technicians came and went in front of three empty chairs. The door opened and a woman with mustard-coloured culottes bustled in.

'Hi, I'm Jade Johnson,' she said. 'Head of content. So you got here OK?'

'A car brought me.'

'So this is not live, obviously. Otherwise the press would be all over the place. This is for tomorrow's show, but we'll be trailing it once you've had time to get clear. Make sense?'

'Yes, it seems to.'

'So I'd just like you to relax. Jeremy will do the interview, of course, but Joanna will be in the studio, too. She's the best. She'll keep him in check! So if you're happy, Terry will collect you in two minutes and walk you through.'

Seth felt like a parachutist when the dispatcher pulls back the door in the fuselage. He watched the clock on the wall until a young man came in and asked him to follow.

They went through some heavy, soundproof doors and into a warehouse, behind some black screens – 'Mind you don't trip on these cables,' said Terry – then out into a blazing light and a set that Seth recognised from the screen. Two of the chairs were now occupied, one by a smiling woman in a short skirt and one by a man in his forties with wavy hair and a red tie under his suit.

'You sit here, please,' said Terry. 'There's a microphone in the arm that'll pick up everything. No need to look down.'

Meanwhile, the man, who Seth presumed was Jeremy Rede, was answering questions from a voice in his earpiece. He looked boyish yet out of condition, with heavy jowls. His small eyes gleamed.

As Seth settled into his chair, a glass box was lowered over his head till it sat lightly on his shoulders. 'Take off your mask now,' said a floor manager. Through the glass, Seth could see the version of himself he'd chosen in close-up on the monitors. Huge cameras with circular bases on wheels rolled in to surround them.

'OK,' said a camera operator. 'I'm locked on you at this level so we don't show anything that's not gone through FAT.'

'Quiet in the studio,' said a disembodied voice. 'Running up and . . . Go.'

'Good evening,' said Rede, looking at the lens opposite. 'Today we have nothing less than a world exclusive for you. An interview with a new species, no less. *The Jeremy Rede Show* welcomes White Van Man, also known as Simon Green.' He smiled warmly in Seth's direction.

On the camera opposite Seth, a light came on.

'Good evening, Simon,' said Rede, leaning forward. 'Welcome to the show.'

'Thank you.'

'For the benefit of those who've spent the last six months on planet Mars,' said Rede to the camera, 'Simon was born twenty-four years ago in a London clinic. A test-tube baby whose father was not his human dad, but the recreated DNA of a Neanderthal. So, Simon. What do you make of the rest of us?'

'What do you mean?'

'Well, you're a little bit different, aren't you?'

'Isn't everyone different?' said Seth.

'But some are more different than others! I did a test back in the day when you still could and I was ninety-nine per cent *Homo sapiens*. Yes, thank you, Joanna, I was a bit surprised, too. But, Simon, you're not like us. How does it feel?'

'I haven't had time to think about it.'

'Your DNA is telling its own story, though. You must see the world a little bit differently.'

'I don't know how you see it.' Seth felt the weight of his sleeplessness. There didn't seem much he could say in answer to these questions.

'Well, let's think about it,' said Rede. 'Let's just brainstorm it here for a moment.'

'Uh-oh,' said Joanna.

'I mean,' said Rede, 'what does your Neanderthal half do for you, do you think? Does it make you strong?'

'What?' Seth shook his head.

'All right. Put it this way. Are you good with computers?'

'I had to do some coding at university.'

'Of course. The dreaming spires.'

'I think that's Oxford,' said Joanna.

'Let's get down to the nitty-gritty,' said Rede. 'Do you feel attracted to Sapiens women, Simon?'

'I can't answer that,' said Seth.

'Fair enough. Take five. Let's rewind. To the beginnings of time . . . Somewhere round about forty thousand years ago, the last of Simon's ancestors on his father's side died out. Maybe in a cave in Gibraltar. They went extinct, like the megafauna – by which I mean the giant lions and ten-foot-high kangaroos and the woolly mammoths. Bang. All gone. And now, through the miracle of science, here he is again! With some modern human thrown in.'

Seth looked at the studio floor. He saw its grain and pattern. Encaustic, he thought, like the ones in the spare bathroom at home.

'Come on, then, Simon. Give me a hand here. You have the gift of speech in the language of Shakespeare. You've got to tell us what it feels like to be from a different species. You're the first person who ever could.'

Seth shook his head. Rede threw a glance at his co-presenter, then turned back to Seth, smiling patiently.

'Can I ask you when you first discovered that you were not like other men? Can I ask you that?'

'Just recently I heard there were some unusual test results, but I haven't thought much about them.'

'Why not?'

'It's as if you had a blood test that said there was something odd about your red cells. So long as you felt fine and the doctor was OK with it, you'd just carry on, wouldn't you?'

' "Just carry on", says the most remarkable guy of the last forty thousand years!'

Seth drew back a little in his chair.

'When you were a kid at primary school, did the other kids tease you? Call you names?'

'Why?'

'You know what kids are like. Did they comment on the way you looked?'

'It didn't matter what you looked like.'

'OK. But did you at least get a big score on your Top Trumps?' said Rede.

'My what?'

'Your PICs. Intersectional points. We used to call them Top Trumps on this show after the old children's card game.'

'I don't know. I never saw a PIC. I don't know if my parents filled one in for me.'

'But surely you'd have scored off the scale. Maybe you guys missed a trick there.'

Seth shrugged.

'And you're saying that your parents never told you that you were different.'

'I wasn't different. They only did this test a few days ago.'

'But I understand the clinic did tests till you were eighteen. A whole bunch of them on the way you think and feel and see and understand.'

'I've never seen those results. They were mostly about the mothers, I think. You'd need to ask the clinic.'

'Oh, we have. They say you think in different ways. You can't imagine things the same way we do, make plans. That you have different senses. As many as eight. Your brain's arranged differently. Is it like having superpowers, Simon?'

'Nothing seems super to me. Nothing I can do is as amazing as what we can all do with our eyes. Seeing.'

'I'm told you have a way of picking winners at the races. Now that's a superpower I wouldn't mind!'

'You can say that again,' said Joanna.

Rede laughed modestly and for a moment Seth warmed to him.

'I like horses,' said Seth. 'I have a feeling for them, but I don't have any magic way of knowing which one's going to win.'

'But you're ahead of the game, right? In your betting life?'

'Maybe by a few pounds. But there's nothing odd about that. I just look at them, their quarters, hear their breathing, that kind of thing. Horses are wonderful creatures.'

Seth began to relax as he talked about his feeling for animals, a sense of kinship, first with the cat next door, Nettle, then with dogs – Wilson's brindled cross – and how he'd been taken to the races by some friends at university. The betting and the making money, he said, were secondary to his feeling for the beasts themselves in the paddock: the huge muscles of their necks and their placid, long-lashed eyes; the way their response to the heels and hands of the riders was somehow on their own terms . . .

'Perhaps your forebears did some horse whispering in their caves,' said Rede. 'And I think the fossil remains indicate they ate them, too. And talking of eating, the scientists think your ancestors may have enjoyed the taste of their own—'

Joanna leant forward in her seat. 'Thank you, Jeremy. Let me ask you a question, Simon. When your parents discovered the truth about you, what did they feel?'

' "Feel"? I can't say what they felt. I don't know. And I don't have the words for it. The words maybe don't exist.'

'But,' said Joanna, 'did their attitude change? Did they, maybe, back off? Did they disown you a little?'

'They would never disown Ess.'

'What? What's Ess?'

Seth didn't know why he had used his own childish name for himself.

'Let me ask you something else,' said Jeremy Rede, rejoining the conversation. 'Do you feel you have full protection under the law? Under human rights legislation, for instance?'

'I've never thought about it.'

'Because,' said Rede, 'I'm wondering if you're covered. In the context of the legislation, I mean. There are laws against discrimination, aren't there? But they're designed to protect people who came from other countries, not from other species.'

Seth began to feel a strange fatigue. The interview was like playing one of those old screen games where ogres jump out from rocks and battlements, wielding spiked balls on long chains. This Jeremy Rede was out to hurt him – in the same way as Rick Sharpless or the boys who'd blocked his way in the school corridors. That much he could see. But he couldn't make out what exactly Rede was trying to get at – what he wanted from him.

He yawned, then gathered himself for a last effort and sat forward in his chair. 'Do you want me to say something terrible?' he said. 'Is that what this is?'

'You can say whatever you like,' said Jeremy Rede. 'Be my guest.'

'Do you want me to tell you some awful secret?'

'Anything you like,' said Rede with a glance to Joanna.

'Whatever way I have of being human,' said Seth, 'whatever tiny different genes are doing what they do inside my head, I'd rather have mine than yours.'

'And why is that?' said Rede, cocking his head to one side.

'Because you seem so . . . crude. You seem like . . .' Seth had to think hard. Then a picture came into his mind. Something he'd seen in a children's book. 'Like a dog on its back legs in a circus tent.'

'You heard it here first,' said Rede, laughing. 'History is made as a middle-aged *Homo sapiens* is described as "crude" by a half-Neanderthal!'

Jeremy Rede drew on his experience to keep the interview running, doing most of the talking himself, but after thirty minutes received an instruction in his ear to wind it up. Seth replaced his mask, hat and glasses, shook hands with both interviewers and made his way behind the blackened flats, being careful not to trip on the cables. He waited in the windowless lounge.

After a few minutes, Terry took him down to the exit, where the car was waiting.

7

In a Gray's Inn office, Lukas Parn stood impatiently until the clerk showed him through to a cluttered, book-lined room. Celeste Usman pointed to a chair on the other side of the desk.

'Thank you for coming in.'

'I like it,' said Parn. 'It's like going to Harley Street. Old buildings, modern skills.'

'Just so I can make sure we're on the same page. I understand the surrogate mother accepted a payment in New York in full and final settlement of any contractual claim. Is that right?'

'Yes,' said Parn. 'She took advice from lawyers recommended by her university. This whole thing was a bit out of their wheelhouse, to be honest. All she wanted was enough to make sure her mother was OK. We settled on a six-figure sum. Mom's in a larger apartment in the same building with all her utility bills paid and Talissa has some cash in the bank for once.'

'And the parents?'

'We made a big seven-figure offer to settle out of court, but they don't want to take any money. They haven't signed off on anything, but they say they're happy with the way their son is. They call him a blessing.'

'All right,' said Celeste. 'So now. The trial. You've all been cautioned, I presume.'

'Yes, they came to see the three of us – me, Malik Wood and Delmore Redding. They read us our rights a couple of weeks ago. I was pissed that the arraignment hearing was so short. The judge seemed to wash his hands of it.'

'I think that was always likely,' Celeste said. 'He was going to send it for trial because there's a legitimate public interest. It's not that the justice system wants to find you guilty, it's more that they want the issues to be aired. They'll want a jury too.'

There was a knock on the door.

Celeste showed in a large man in a suit with the white bands of an advocate. 'This is my colleague, Thomas Rennard. He's going to lead.'

'What about you?' said Parn.

'I'll be the junior. Thomas has more experience in this area than I do. He had a very good result recently in *R* v. *Amazon*. You probably read about it.'

Rennard pulled up a chair and helped himself to a chocolate biscuit from a plate the clerk had brought in earlier. He looked like a man who denied himself little.

'So, Mr Parn,' he said. 'My colleague has given me the background. I understand we took our trousers down at the hearing.'

'We did what?'

'You agreed that the error took place in your clinic.'

'Yes. I was advised that —'

'Good advice.'

'I'm still hoping to protect the identity of the individual.'

'Don't worry about that,' said Rennard. 'There's a new law almost every month to protect the privacy of victims in criminal cases. Neither Number Seven nor the parents will be within a hundred miles of the court. We'll just focus on whether this was an accident.'

'What are our chances?' said Parn.

'Well,' said Rennard, 'it's interesting. There have been quite a few civil cases for negligence. Crowded workbenches in the clinic and so on. But the prosecution will claim this was deliberate. That's a first.'

Parn said, 'Could I just explain the scientific benefits that—'

'No,' said Rennard. 'Forgive me. I need to explain a little. The prosecution will need to show that someone in your clinic knowingly made a substitution. If you tell me that was the case, then we can't plead not guilty. Not if you tell me that you did it. However good the intentions. But if you tell me you don't know how the mistake happened, then that's a different matter.'

'What I'm trying to say is—'

'Stop,' said Rennard. 'Excuse me, but I'm going to make a rather odd request, Mr Parn. Which is that from now on you don't tell me anything. Anything at all. I think that's the best way. Your organisation is known to have had an interest in hybrids. Your own PR person – a Ms Sheila Rahm – admitted that you recreated individuals from the genomes of two extinct species, a type of wolf and a mammoth, I believe. That's one thing. But what the prosecution needs to prove in your case is that one of the accused or someone acting on their behalf knowingly made a donor substitution with a human embryo. I ask you, Mr Parn, how on earth are they going to prove that?'

When the case opened in Court Number One at the Old Bailey, Talissa was watching on a link from her apartment in New York.

To her, the court looked like an old church, with its arches and high wooden panelling. The oak benches for the lawyers and the press were ranged like pews. She was fairly sure that above the central seat of judgement – one of five leather-padded thrones on the dais – she could see a hanging crucifix. Beneath the cross sat the lone trial judge: 'The Right Honourable Lady Justice Rampersad, aka Dame Iris Rampersad' read a caption as wide as Talissa's screen. The judge herself took up little room: a slender individual with an unsmiling eye.

In front of her was a bank of screens at which she glanced through the bottom of her reading glasses. Occasionally, she prodded at them with a forefinger. There were other screens of varying sizes in the court, but there were also documents in boxes being wheeled down the gaps between the pews. Some of the files formed low battlements along the tables, behind which lawyers bobbed up and down. Others craned forward to whisper into the ears of those who sat in front. To Talissa far away, they seemed like soloists in an orchestra that Dame Iris was conducting. She was disappointed that none of them wore wigs.

For the prosecution, a tall, gaunt man leant forward to address the judge. 'Alexander Mayne, KC' read the caption. 'My Lady,' he said, 'I intend to show that the defendants' behaviour met all three definitions of fraud under the Fraud

278

Act 2006. There was fraud by false representation. Fraud by failure to disclose. And fraud by abuse of position.'

'Thank you, Mr Mayne,' said the judge. 'You will be aware of substantial amendments to the act in 2034.'

'Indeed, My Lady. I intend to rely on them.'

The camera showed Parn, Wood and Redding, all in suits and ties. Parn was whispering in Wood's ear while Redding stared straight ahead.

'My Lady, the defendants have exercised their right to silence,' a burly lawyer was now saying. 'Thomas Rennard, KC' read the caption. 'It has further been agreed between both sides that in the interests of their privacy and well-being, no member of the family involved, nor the surrogate mother, will appear.'

Lady Justice Rampersad nodded and raised a permissive hand.

Witnesses were called. Catrina Olsen took the stand in a trouser suit with her hair scraped back, wearing thick-rimmed glasses. Talissa smiled.

'Could you summarise for us your opinion of the defendant Lukas Parn?' said Mayne.

Catrina thought for a minute. 'I would say he is a very brilliant man and that he has many admirable qualities. But he is someone who believes his great wealth puts him above normal considerations.'

'What sort of considerations?'

'Moral. Legal. Behavioural.'

'I see. And what of Dr Wood?'

'My Lady, I object,' said Rennard, rising awkwardly to his feet. 'This is mere gossip.'

'I think that in view of the defendants' refusal to testify,' said Mayne, 'the jury is entitled to have a sense of what they are missing. I would further submit that Dr Olsen is an expert witness and thus allowed to offer an opinion.'

Dame Iris leant forward. 'The court is not much moved by old-fashioned ideas of admissibility,' she said. 'We prefer weight. I am going to allow the evidence in, though in due course I shall give the jury an appropriate direction.'

'Thank you, My Lady,' said Mayne. 'Dr Wood?'

'A superb scientist,' said Catrina. 'But also vain. He left mainstream research for a very highly paid job and has always wanted to re-establish his academic credentials.'

'And Professor Redding?'

'A straight arrow,' said Catrina. 'Good at his job. But not a very strong character.'

Talissa went to the kitchen to make some tea and when she returned found Thomas Rennard in full flow.

'So you were unaware that the embryo you put back was not genetically that of the actual parents?'

'That's right,' said Catrina. 'Everything was normal.'

'Did you at any time see anyone making a swap or interfering in any way with the process?'

'No.'

'Thank you, Dr Olsen. Your view of the characters of the defendants was most colourful, but, ladies and gentlemen of the jury, this case will turn not on character sketches but on evidence. Or the lack of it.'

The next witness was Ayesha Cross, who recalled Malik Wood personally bringing in a sperm sample from one of the eight fathers.

'And you remember this,' said Alexander Mayne, 'because it was unusual?'

'Yes, the director of the clinic wouldn't normally do that.'

But under cross-examination from Rennard, Ayesha Cross admitted that she didn't know which of the eight babies in the test had resulted from this sample and that she had not seen Malik Wood interfere with anything. Pressed, she also agreed that Wood occasionally acted 'playfully' in order to 'keep up morale'.

The following day, the prosecution called an expert witness, Professor Selma Sanderson, the head of an Edinburgh fertility clinic. Questioned by Mayne, she said she thought it was inconceivable that such a mix-up could have happened by mistake.

'And yet,' said Rennard, when his turn came, 'you concede that mistakes regularly happen in such clinics and that the sperm samples would have been indistinguishable to the naked eye? We know that other organisations run by Mr Parn had an interest in palaeoanthropology and that it has for a long time been possible to create such a substance from a reconstructed Neanderthal genome. I put it to you that an administrative oversight – a muddle, in other words – is a far more credible explanation of what happened.'

'I doubt it.'

'Please look at this.'

A photograph dated 2029 came up on a display screen facing the jury. It showed large chiller tanks labelled 'Embryos' and 'Sperm' on the floor of an untidy room. The remains of a sandwich lunch were visible on a desk behind them.

'How many samples are in each tank?' said Rennard.

'Thousands,' said Professor Sanderson.

'And this picture was taken in the Parn Institute's clinic in London?'

'I believe so. That's the secretary's office. It became quite well known in our little world. I think they were having building works done at the time. Finishing the storeroom. It was all very tidy after that, I believe. The samples were professionally looked after.'

'No further questions.'

The following day, Ayesha Cross was recalled. 'Ms Cross,' said Thomas Rennard, 'you have testified that Dr Wood personally brought into the lab one of the sperm samples in this trial and that this was unusual.'

'That's right.'

'What was your relationship with Dr Wood?'

'It was good.'

'Come, come, Ms Cross. It was more than that. You were lovers, were you not?'

'Briefly,' said Ayesha Cross, after a pause.

'And Dr Wood ended your liaison.'

'It was an unwise relationship. It was . . . unprofessional.'

'I would like the court to look at display B, please.'

On the screen was a reproduction of a message sent to the Galatia news desk from a generic end point. It said, 'WRT your investigation of White Van Man suggest you look at Parn–NHS partnership London 2030 onwards. Subject Number Seven.'

'Before you answer my next question, Ms Cross,' said Rennard, 'I would like you to know that we have done extensive research on the origin of this message and are prepared to call expert witnesses. I would further remind you that you are under oath.'

'I understand.'

'Did you send that message?'

Ayesha Cross looked down. 'Yes. I sent it.'

'No further questions.'

The trial lasted three days, some of which Talissa missed by being at work. The next time she was able to watch live, Alexander Mayne was on his feet.

'Ladies and gentlemen of the jury,' he said, 'my learned friend makes a great deal of the absence of material evidence. What does he expect? A surveillance camera in the sperm donation room? I think not. Phone records, as we have conclusively demonstrated, show increased traffic between the three defendants in the days before the procedure. Can we give you chapter and verse of what they said? Of course not. We don't tap phones. This is not East Berlin a hundred years ago. My learned friend calls the evidence "circumstantial at best", but in the absence of confession or eyewitnesses, circumstantial evidence is sufficient in English law.'

Thomas Rennard in turn stressed the failure of the prosecution to suggest an adequate motive. 'Pecuniary gain? I think not. The institute has invested greatly with no financial return and has shared its data free of cost with the National Health Service. Some sort of power trip or God complex? Even Dr Olsen, who was sharply critical of her former superiors, stopped short of suggesting that. Professional renown? Career advancement? No learned paper has yet been published, though my clients remain sanguine on that front – and determined to share the fruits of their labours.

'My learned friend relies on the testimony of Ms Ayesha Cross, who says she remembers Dr Wood himself bringing in a sample to the lab. The same Ms Cross was Dr Wood's jilted lover and on her own admission betrayed the trust of her employers to the press. I suggest to you that her testimony is worthless.'

The judge began her summing-up for the jury. 'You are not to read anything into the defendants' refusal to testify,' she said. 'That is their right.'

To Talissa it seemed obvious from a quick look at the jury that they might well take a different view about the silent three. A part of Talissa wanted the Parn people to be brought low. She had no doubt that they had deliberately switched the sample. On the other hand, if the whole thing could be passed off as a bizarre mistake it might make Seth less of a phenomenon to be stared at or pursued.

When the jury returned the next day, Talissa found herself excited to hear the words familiar from courtroom dramas.

'And how do you find the defendant Mr Lukas Parn?'

'Guilty, My Lady.'

The camera stayed on the face of the forewoman of the jury, even as the public gallery vented its surprise.

'How do you find the defendant Dr Malik Wood?'

'Guilty, My Lady.'

The camera moved for an instant to Alexander Mayne, KC, straight-faced, resisting congratulation from the bench behind.

'How do you find the defendant Professor Delmore Redding?'

'Guilty.'

Before the sentences were passed, the lawyers were allowed to plead. Buoyed by his success, Alexander Mayne moved up a rhetorical gear, though he had little of substance to add.

Thomas Rennard stood up to make his plea in mitigation.

'My Lady, the life of the young man who is at the centre of this trial has not been easy. Or rather, it was an ordinary life until public scrutiny brought that to an end. I feel sure my learned friend would join me in wishing him privacy and peace of mind in the future.

'The data collected by the Parn Institute has been of very substantial scientific value. It has moreover been recorded in an exemplary way, we have heard, with none of those involved knowing which of the children involved was a hybrid. It is not so much on the nature of our cousins *Homo sapiens neanderthalensis* that the life of this young man has shed light as on the nature of ourselves, *Homo sapiens*. We have seen that our senses are limited and that other humans had different and in some ways superior ways of gathering information about the world. We have seen how our outstanding mental and cultural achievements have come at a cost. That, to quote an academic comment on the case, "The connections that enabled Beethoven are unstable. But they are closely related to the neural circuitry of delusion, a mental condition which so far as we know is specific to us modern humans – unique, indeed, not just in the genus *Homo*, but in the primate family and for all we know the entire animal kingdom." No other creature has such an unstable relationship with reality.'

Bringing his focus onto the circumstances of the case, he stressed the anonymity, the lack of any ad hominem motive, the fact that 'the left hand did not know what the right hand was doing' and that the defendants were motivated at all times by a desire to improve the lot of humanity.

Rennard coughed and looked at his notes. 'My Lady, there have been many human species over the years. At one time there may have been as many as a dozen. We are the last one

285

left alive. It is as if the turkey were held to be the epitome of all birds, the chihuahua the final expression of the canine. Our way of being human, My Lady, is a very odd one. By studying our cousins and former breeding companions, we understand more about our strangeness and more about the things that afflict us. And we may hope that our descendants, while honouring the achievements of our past, may be able to curb the lust for violence and find a way to cure the illnesses that appear to be their fated corollary.

'The triumph of our kind lay at first in our fecundity. From a handful out of Africa to the billions of us now across the world. Our minds are focused on our own existence minute by minute. With other humans, this was not so. They may even have thought of themselves first and foremost as "he" or "she", not "I". Or in fact none of these at all. The chances of natural selection and cross-breeding brought us where we are today. A world in which other humans bred with our efficiency and left a greater genetic legacy would have been different. Still human, but in a different way. Perhaps no Venice or Einstein. But other cities, other minds as great, perhaps less startling but more peaceful, more sustainable and more in tune with our fellow creatures. The Sapiens consciousness, we have heard, may eventually be selected against by evolution. It is inessential. We have heard it called a spandrel and a "logo". It is an opportunist, a hitch-hiker, like so much of our genome. It may one day die out, leaving the world with a better kind of human being.

'We stand at the moment like men shining a torch into a darkened room. The beam of light is thin. It may be that we will never understand how we came to be what we are. That the evidence is just too old, too degraded or too hard to find.

It may be that the shutters can never be torn down to admit the full light of day. But thin beams of light are all we have. And they are won at a tremendous cost of time and intellect and money and dedication on the part of scientists. I put it to you that the Parn Institute has done more than most to help us – if not to provide the cures and answers, at least to frame the questions. I further put it to you that the sentences in this case should reflect that unprecedented contribution.'

8

Talissa watched the sentencing with a mixture of horror and relief. Dame Iris said she wished to reflect the gravity of the crime and the public's legitimate concern, though she had also listened carefully to the arguments in mitigation. She proposed to impose custodial sentences and, in one instance, a financial penalty as well. A fair quantum for the fine, she said, had been difficult to establish, because the nature of the fraud was so unusual; she had gone deep into history to look at the precedents on both sides of the Atlantic. The landmark frauds she had studied included those perpetrated by American investment banks (Goldman Sachs being the most well known) and large pharmaceutical companies who had falsified their academic partners' research results to favour their own products. In the light of these and other precedents, Lukas Parn was fined £3.8 billion. He was further sentenced to four years in prison.

She took into account, she said, the fact that the other defendants had already suffered irremediable professional damage. Nevertheless, Malik Wood received a four-year sentence and Delmore Redding two years suspended.

The court rose.

*

Before the last person had left, there was a message on Talissa's handset. 'Arriving in New York tomorrow. Have told no one. Need to escape. Am staying at the Bakehouse Inn on East 10th Street near Avenue A. Hope that means something to you. Have never been to NY. Can you meet me in the lobby at 6pm? I need some help. Seth'.

She hadn't seen Seth since they'd gone to the park in Ashers End, when he'd been twelve or thirteen. And now the kid needed her. She felt something like elation at the thought of it. For roughly a quarter of a century, she had denied a natural curiosity about him and a sense that, however unrelated they might be, scientifically speaking, there might be a kind of kinship. It had not been for her to make a move, but now that it had come from him . . .

With the trial over, she felt a new lightness of spirit. She took a shower and dressed in a grey skirt with the knee-high leather boots she'd had since postdoc days and a white blouse under a maroon sweater. It was overcoat weather, too, as she headed for the subway to emerge half an hour later on the corner of First and 14th Street.

The wind droned in the wide, empty avenue where once upon a time the motor traffic had fought its way uptown. Some of the low-rise buildings were still let to businesses, but the Greek taverna and the crab shack with its trawler-netted windows were empty. The giant mural of a singer once loved, then reviled, gazed out from the wall of a red-brick building on the corner of 11th. It was a part of town Talissa had known well, coming to seminars at an outpost of the university. In the cross street, with its spindly gingko trees thrusting up through the sidewalk, you could still believe in a neighbourhood of kinds; the florist was open and the Chinese café had customers.

She went past the steps up to the old Russian and Turkish baths and saw the sign for the Bakehouse Inn a little further on. She lingered by some shop windows to pass the time till six, then pushed open the revolving door into the lobby. It was more like a youth hostel than an inn, with maybe twenty people among the piles of luggage waiting to be moved on.

In her mind, Talissa was still searching for a teenage footballer. As she looked round the busy space, she recognised no one, but her eye caught on a man in black jeans and a T-shirt talking to the desk clerk.

Her response to seeing him was like nothing she had felt in her life. Her mind became empty, but every other atom in her body cried out to possess, to own, to consume this being: the body, the skin. Especially the skin. It was more than desire, it was as if her transactions with all other humans to this point had been only a dance or a playground game. She couldn't place her feeling under love or lust or exhilaration. She did want to make love to this man, but it was more than that. She had to own him totally, to consume his flesh or be swallowed by him, gladly, never to return to the light. He was young, too young, but that was part of the poignancy. He had so much time to live.

She sat down on a hard bench. She made herself look down at the marble floor of the lobby, but found her eyes dragged back to the figure at the desk. He turned and started to walk towards her, taking a coat from the arm of a chair as he approached.

He held out his hand. 'Talissa. Thank you for coming.'

Half an hour later, they were in an empty restaurant twenty blocks uptown. 'I have money,' Talissa had said, as she ushered him out of the lobby and called an autonomous cab to the kerbside. She wanted to get him away, before someone could feel what she had felt and take him for themselves. No one else must see him.

It was a French place, Manhattan's version of the old Auvergne, with clean napkins and glasses of ice water poured before the waiter recited his specials.

As he spoke, Talissa became aware that the feeling that was overwhelming her was less like love than a form of excruciating pity. She pitied Seth for the weight of his existence. The intolerable molecular sensation of being a living human that was his to deal with every second till he died.

'We need a minute,' said Talissa. 'Can I get a martini? Straight up with an olive. Seth?'

'OK. Thanks. The same.'

Seth pulled the crust from a piece of bread in a wicker basket.

'Thank you for coming,' he said.

She smiled back. Go on, she thought. Keep talking. I can't.

'It's been difficult,' said Seth. 'The deal was that the press would leave me alone. That's what I was told. But the lawyers couldn't make it stick.'

Be more normal, thought Talissa. Or say something crazy. Misuse a word and break this spell.

The waiter brought the drinks. 'Any questions on the menu, folks?'

'Just give us five minutes.' She could talk to this man at least, it appeared. Words came.

'No problem.'

'My parents refuse to move house, but they have a police guard. I think things are getting a little better now.'

'And you?' She had spoken to him at least, uttered words.

'I've had to move. This man Clive Brewer was no good. The PR guy. He delegated everything to his virtual assistant. Just kept on talking about algorithms and "reach". But he had a colleague called Liz Sitchell. She was smart. She and Catrina. You remember Catrina Olsen?'

Talissa nodded.

'They've found me different places to live. Mostly in London. Flats here and there. All over the place.'

The waiter was hanging back a pace or two from the table. 'Have you people had a chance to . . .'

'Yes, I'd like the snails and the special. The meat dish,' said Seth.

'Excellent. And for you?'

'The soufflé.'

Seth began to talk, to unload, as if he had had no confidant in England.

'I took shelter with a guy called Martin Gosling. I'd known him at university. He lives on a farm in Yorkshire. That held out for a couple of weeks until he got a call. From a news site, I mean.'

Talissa nodded and gestured with her hand for him to carry on. She stuck a fork into the salad that the waiter slid in front of her, but found her throat was closed. She put the fork back on the table.

'They want to look at me, I think. To just, like, stare. Take pictures. The only thing they want to ask is how it *feels*.'

Taking a sip of water, Talissa said, 'And?'

'And what *does* it feel like, you mean? It feels like everything else that happens to you.'

'So?'

'Like nothing much.' Seth paused. 'What I want is to find a new life. Or rather a new identity. I'm happy with my life, with who I am. But no one else is.'

'And?'

'I'd like to live in a normal way, see how I manage with what I've got. Isn't that what everyone wants? I want to see what I can make of it. But I need to be left alone to work it out. So I have to hide who I am.'

Seth pulled a snail from its shell with a wooden-handled pin.

'And then,' he said, 'after Martin's, I went to a house in Newcastle. Another friend from college. Rosalie. She'd not been in touch before, but suddenly I got this message. "Weren't you going to call us, pet?" That's how she talks.'

There was a good deal to say about Rosalie, it seemed. Seth had met her parents for the first time, and her brothers, who'd taken him to a bar, where no one showed any special interest in him. They drank Newcastle beer. Newcastle, it seemed, was the kind of place he liked. The people, the buildings from an age of coal and ships, the bridges, a lot about the bridges, especially the Tyne Bridge, one of whose builders had been the first woman engineer to belong to the society of something or other, but even more about this Rosalie. Talissa became aware that her teeth were clamped tight together.

'But then Rosalie had another call and we decided I should move on. Liz and Catrina found me another place, a room in an inn in Cumbria where they said no one cared about the news, only sheep farming and rain. I used to go out on the fells and walk all day.'

Talissa looked away.

'Are you listening?' said Seth. 'You see, I think I'm going to be found in England. Tracked down. They want to put me on

293

display. They say it's a duty to science or something. They want to sacrifice my . . . peace of mind for what they call the greater good. One of them called me the chance of a lifetime. I'm the Rosetta Stone, he said.'

Seth finished the last of his main course and wiped the plate with bread from the wicker basket. 'You haven't eaten anything,' he said, looking at Talissa's fallen soufflé.

She shook her head and took another sip of water. 'Would you excuse me a minute?'

Pushing back her chair, she went unsteadily to the back of the restaurant, where she could see a sign to the bathroom. Inside, she went into one of the four cubicles, locked the door and sat down. She took a small mirror from her bag and looked at her face. It was paler than usual and there was a tiny line of perspiration on her upper lip. She took a packet of tissues from her bag and opened them. Her fingers were trembling as she placed a leaf of paper against her skin. She leant her head against the wall of the cubicle, then lowered it between her knees. The world became a little steadier. She breathed in several times, stood up and brushed down her skirt.

With a determined step, she made it back to the table and sat down.

'I think you need to meet my friend Susan Kovalenko.'

'Who's she?'

'She can help. But you need to come with me now. To Harlem.' She didn't know what she was saying.

'Why?'

'You can't stay in that awful place.'

'Why not?'

'It's got roaches. Bugs.'

'What?'

'And reporters. It's too risky. I'll settle the check.'

'I paid in advance. One night.'

'OK. We'll go and get your bag then.'

'This is it,' he said, holding up a crumpled pack.

They took the subway north, then walked across town to Talissa's brownstone, where she settled Seth in the living room with a beer.

'There's a dog wants to be let out,' said Seth.

'What? Oh yes. I shut him in the kitchen. He wasn't barking, was he?'

'No.'

'So how did you . . . Never mind.'

After opening the door for Pelham, Talissa went into the bedroom and sat down hard, looking at the half of the queen-size mattress that had for a long time been unoccupied.

'Kojak? It's me. Can you come over? Yes, it's urgent. Well, tell Leon I'll make it up to him. I'll cook him that thing he likes with the shrimp.'

Back in the living room, she found Seth talking to Pelham, who was sitting upright on the sofa next to him.

'How old is he?' said Seth.

'I don't know exactly. But he can't be less than fourteen.'

Stroking the dog's head, Seth said, 'He has another year in him. Not more.'

Twenty minutes later, Susan was at the door of the apartment. Talissa kissed her on the cheek, then held on to her arm for a moment as she showed her in.

'You OK?' said Susan, stopping to look at her.

'Yeah,' said Talissa, showing her into the living room. 'This is Seth.'

'Wow. Fuck . . . I mean, great to meet you, Seth,' said Susan. 'I've heard a lot about you.'

Talissa was beginning to feel a little more normal with Susan in the room, but didn't dare to look in Seth's direction. She opened a bottle of wine and poured two glasses, then emptied some roasted macadamia nuts into a dish and put them on the table.

Susan and Seth were in conversation about his plans, but Talissa could tell he wasn't sure how much he should let on.

'The thing is,' he was saying, 'I want to go and live somewhere remote for a time. But I don't know how long I could last. I might go crazy on my own.'

'I could come with you,' said Talissa.

'But you've managed to keep out of it,' said Susan. 'No one knows who you are.'

'That won't last,' said Talissa. 'They'll find out. Anyway, Susan, what I thought was that you could get Seth into some sort of witness protection thing. Not literally, because he's not a witness, but you must know people in the DA's office who—'

'Hold it right there,' said Susan. 'I have a job to look after, you know. A career. If I start doing that kind of thing, I'll be in big trouble.'

'I don't mean officially. But maybe you could find out how people can hide and reinvent themselves.'

'You mean an Amish settlement?'

'Whatever. And easy ways to change how you look.'

'Listen, T, if you think I'm going to fix a fake ID for this young man, even if—'

'We're not looking for trade secrets, Susan. Just a couple of hints.'

Susan looked away. 'OK. I wasn't going to tell you this, but the Vector people are making a lot of weird noises. The phrase "human purity" has been used. A lot of talk about "alien contamination".'

'What's Vector?' said Seth.

'Don't ask,' said Talissa

'I have a vague idea,' said Susan. She sighed. 'But it's nothing you heard from me. And it's nothing I had from work. Understand?'

'Got it,' said Talissa. 'But if I'm included in your vague idea, remember I can't fly again till August. I've used up my long-haul allowance.'

'We'll talk tomorrow. Your guest looks kind of punchy.'

'Punchy?' said Seth.

'Yeah. Punch-drunk. Tired.'

'The flight, I suppose.'

'Seth, if you want to use the bathroom, I'll make up a bed for you here,' said Talissa.

'Thank you,' said Seth. 'I'll get my bag.'

'Be careful, T,' said Susan as she left.

There was the sound of a shower running while Talissa laid out a sheet, a pillow and a duvet on the couch. She switched on a brass library lamp on the table behind and stood waiting. When there was no sign of the shower ceasing, she went reluctantly to her bedroom.

She undressed, put on a T-shirt and lay down in the darkness. Need had disabled her capacity to think. Questions of right or wrong seemed trivial, like someone wondering – as a hurricane ripped the doors and roof off the house – whether they had shut the cat flap.

Awaking from a shallow, sudden sleep, she went through

into the living room. Seth was lying on his side, quite still, with Pelham asleep beside him. One of his arms lay uncovered by the duvet and Talissa lowered her hand so she could, as lightly as possible, touch the skin.

PART FOUR

2056

1

Two days later, Talissa went with Seth to Penn Station and put him on the train to Boston. From the terminus, he took a cab to the address of a car rental firm in a warehouse near the Charles River, where he waited his turn at the desk.

'Simon Green,' he said. 'You have a reservation for me.'

'Sure do,' said the clerk, a young man in a black cap. 'It's paid up front. Just need to see some ID.'

Seth's hair had been shaved to a number-two length by a barber in Harlem. He wore brown-rimmed spectacles with a plus-one vision adjustment he'd picked off the shelf in a pharmacy. There was a third-day crust on his face where he hadn't shaved.

'Gee,' said the clerk, looking at Seth's proffered handset. 'You have the same birthday as me. What are the chances?'

'I don't know.'

'You're all set. You can pick out any one of the three at the back of the lot there.'

'They just start?'

'Sure. Just give this number and the zip code you're heading for. Speak into the dash. There's enough charge to get you five hundred miles. You connect to a point in the trunk.'

'Got it.'

He picked out a white one. Somehow it seemed to stand out less. It had two cushioned seats in the middle and a bench behind. He strapped himself in and gave his instructions.

The car went back stealthily along the river before heading up for Chelsea, through the northern suburbs and out onto the old interstate. Seth turned off his handset to avoid being traced and followed his progress on a paper map Susan Kovalenko had given him.

He felt like a pioneer, a man from an older time. Some names were recognisable – Ipswich, Portsmouth, York. Maybe it was just that they had English versions. It all felt different, even when it was familiar. Wood-fired pizza. You wouldn't see a sign for that by the side of a road in England. Or a big wine and liquor store standing in its own lot.

'Pull over to the right and park,' he said.

The car did as it was told. 'Here you go, Simon.'

'Don't call me that.'

'What name shall I use?'

Seth thought for a second. 'Ken,' he said. It was his second name, a popular one in Mary's Japanese family.

'Thank you, Ken.'

He went into the shop. Susan had warned him that the house, when he got there, would have a full larder but no drinks, only water from the tap, so he picked out two demijohns of Chardonnay and one of Cabernet. He hesitated, but, feeling the wealth of Talissa's dollar transfer in his blipper, added a twenty-four-pack of beer and two bottles of bourbon to his cart. The woman didn't ask for ID when he held his wrist against the reader. Maybe in his new guise he looked older.

Why should she care anyway? He loaded the drink into the trunk and carried on up the coast, high on the woman's indifference.

There were yellow lines in the middle of the asphalt. On the verge, old orange signs warned of floods or skidding, but, apart from delivery trucks, there was hardly anyone to read them. It became more wooded. Then they were slowing in the town of Bath, whose clapboard houses looked like flats from a film set. There was a sign for the old navy dockyard, now a museum. Seth just wanted to be in his refuge, somewhere in the woods where no one would see him.

Decisively, outside a coffee shop, they swung right and began to head south into the peninsula. The smooth surface of the blacktop belied the gradient and adverse camber as the car roller-coastered on. The villages grew smaller, then the settlements petered out into woodland, into rocks and dunes where the road engineers had given up.

Down a one-lane path, hard left into dense woods, then onto a sloping track towards the sea, where as if by a seventh sense the car found an opening, just wide enough, down which it trickled, twigs and leaves grabbing at the doors, to an eventual halt.

Seth expected the car to tell him they'd arrived, but it remained silent. Rude, he thought. He seemed to be at the back of the house. He discovered the loose brick five courses up from the crawl space and pulled it out to reveal a key with which he let himself into a storeroom. He went through the house, opening doors onto a kitchen, living room and study with a screen rigged up to an ancient DVD player. As Susan had said, there were no computers and no internet connection. On the shelf were books about local history and weather.

At the front of the house there was a veranda with a couple of wicker chairs pointed towards the thin light of the sea, though any view was blocked by pine woods.

He went back to the car and brought in his backpack and the drinks. He put one of the demijohns of Chardonnay into the refrigerator. There was an old carton of UHT milk in the door, but nothing else. The freezer compartment held only desserts and pizzas. The main store cupboard had tuna, meat-flavoured products and vegetables in cans, as well as mayonnaise, ketchup and herbs. The packets of spaghetti looked old.

Going through the house, Seth hunted for a bedroom in which to base himself. There were two on the first floor and possibly more in an attic space above, up a staircase he hadn't climbed. A door in the lobby opened onto wooden steps down to the cellar.

He opted for a ground-floor room with a comfortable bed and a light by which to read. There was a shower room next to it, probably intended for people on their way back from the beach, but it would do.

It was starting to grow dark as he pushed a pizza into the oven. Into a gas-station glass tumbler with a print of a cartoon lobster wearing a monocle he poured some bourbon, then added a lump of bearded permafrost from an ice tray in the freezer. He chucked the tray in the sink, where it could melt.

He ate his dinner in front of the screen, on which he watched an unmarked movie he'd slotted into the DVD player. After some whirring and thumping, it seemed to work fine. It was an old western and the shopfronts of the pioneer town looked like the houses in Bath.

Seth wanted to message Talissa to tell them he was all right.

He ought to be in touch with his parents as well. They didn't know he was in America. The last time he had spoken to them was ten days earlier, when he had called from a place in Scarborough. Mary had been out at a function, but he had told Alaric he was fine and would see them soon, when it was safe. Meanwhile, Susan Kovalenko had been strict: he was to switch off his handset completely for the time he was in Maine.

Although it was early summer, the air was cold and he was reluctant to undress after he had brushed his teeth. A shower could wait. He made sure the back door was locked and drew an extra bolt at the front. He latched the window in his room and closed the curtains before climbing into bed with some pyjamas over his underwear.

He felt sure he'd need to get up in the night, that someone would hammer at the door. Probably only the nearest neighbour come from a mile away to ask if he was OK, but he needed to be ready. He fell asleep at once, only to be woken by the sound of a crash. A window breaking or a vase falling.

The house was too big to investigate. God knew what was in the attic or in the workshops underground. He went into the hall and made sure the door to the cellar was locked.

Back in his own room, he put on a sweater and jammed a chair under the door handle.

Not sleeping was a new experience. At bedtime he normally just closed his eyes and lay on his side without moving for eight hours. That was his habit.

But the fear wouldn't let him sleep. In each as yet unvisited corner of the house, behind every tree in the woods and in the shadows of the unexplored terrain beyond, there were threats he couldn't accurately sense.

*

In the morning, he got up early and made coffee in a stove-top pot. There seemed to be no breakfast foods, so he sat at the table and started to make a list. Fetching the paper map from the car, he figured out where the nearest supermarket was likely to be.

Looking up from the basin in the shower room, he hardly recognised his sleepless face in the mirror. Good. He wouldn't grow a beard. It would be like saying, Look at me, I'm in disguise. But perhaps he'd try a moustache, which, along with the unneeded glasses and the haircut, might be enough.

He went out onto the veranda and down the steps to the lawn. The lack of sunlight under the trees meant the grass was patched with moss and weed. He walked into the woods and on towards the light of the ocean. After a few minutes the evergreens thinned enough for him to see the water. The lawn began again in the better light and ran on down to stony sand among the rocks, at the end of which was a wooden landing stage.

Now he could see straight ahead across a bay to a wooded island, or perhaps another point of the jagged, many-fingered peninsula. The view to left and right was curtailed by trees and the uneven shoreline. His own private bay was about fifty yards across, no more, but the seawater was shallow and clear. It nudged up against the land like a half-teasing cat. He went onto the jetty, pressing with his foot to see if the wood was rotten. It held firm, and he sat at the end to survey his new world.

Later in the morning, he took the car and headed off. He didn't have a zip code, but, once he'd made his accent more American, the car understood the name of the town. On the road leading in, there was a mall built in Roman style with pillars and pediments of beige synthetic stone. He parked on the lot and went inside. The air smelled of burnt coffee.

He found the supermarket and pushed his trolley down the aisles. The choice was overwhelming, apart from meat, which was hidden behind a small manned counter. The cheese looked better than at home and he bought four different kinds, piling them in with the peanut butter and breakfast cereals. He didn't dare approach the butcher in case he had to show a doctor's certificate, like a certified alcoholic in a dry state.

He blipped the reader and carried out his armful of swag in old-style paper bags.

I've been exaggerating things, he thought. No one cares about 'the Parn' or 'genomes' here. They wouldn't even recognise the words. I can be free.

He spoke the zip code of his hidden house.

'Is this Home, Ken?' said the car.

'Yes.'

In the afternoon, after a bland but heavy lunch, he slept on the veranda.

When he awoke, he went into the kitchen to boil a kettle. The teabags produced a pale liquid that tasted of cinnamon. He'd have another look through the hundred different brands in the supermarket. He took a blue 'Freeport' mug down through the woods to his landing stage. If the weather held, he could bring a chair and a book down and spend a day looking out over the sea. Almost all the titles in the small study seemed to be about the Maine coast, its climate and its natural history. Perhaps in the burnt-coffee mall there'd be a store that had a wider selection. Talissa had lent him a volume of short stories, set in Tamil Nadu, but he'd left it behind.

Seth let his mind linger on Talissa. If he himself was nearly twenty-five, she must be about fifty. But she seemed much younger, nearer to his own age. She moved quickly, both on her feet and in her thoughts. She was slim where Mary had become stout. But then again, Mary was older. Talissa had this nervous energy and drive, he thought. A bit like Rosalie in that way.

In New York, he'd seen the way she interacted with her old high school friend. You could tell how close they were beneath the banter. Susan was more outspoken, but she deferred to Talissa. On the other hand, it was clear that Susan was also a little worried for her. Maybe she'd had to rescue her from time to time. Talissa was someone you'd want to hang out with, though – so you could see what underlay that clarity, that speed, how they joined up.

A small boat was approaching the jetty. It was too late to disappear, so Seth stood up and waited for it. He was wearing sunglasses anyway.

The man on board killed the outboard motor as he came alongside. He threw a looped rope over an upright on the jetty.

'You guys interested in any lobster today?' He bent down and pulled a live specimen from a small tank on board. Its claws were held with elastic bands.

'Sure. What else you got?' Seth made his accent more American.

'I have some striped bass. And some shad, but it's a bony little guy, to be honest. I could fetch you some roe. That's the best. Shad roe.'

'Can I get a lobster?' The idea of something fresh appealed to him when he thought of the row of cans at home.

'Sure thing. How many for?'

'Just me.'

'I'll let you have junior here, then.' The man put a small lobster in a bag and passed it across. He held out an electronic receiver to Seth's wrist. 'You like fish?'

'I do. I like tuna.'

'Too big for me to carry. But you can get some at the dock. At the top of the village. I can stop by tomorrow if you like. Name's Bill.'

'OK.'

The boat puttered off into the bay again.

Back at the house, Seth remembered he had no idea how to cook a lobster. But he'd seen something about it on the plastic placemats in a drawer. Sure enough, on one there was a recipe for clarified butter and on another a step-by-step guide to cooking 'Mr Pincers', written in a children's style.

He boiled a deep pan of water, dropped in the blue-black lobster with its coral spots and replaced the lid while he set about making a salad. He was still tearing up the lettuce when he noticed that the cover was coming off the pan as the lobster fought for its life. He had to hold the lid down with a cloth over his hand until the struggle stopped. Nothing on the placemat had warned of this.

His attempt at clarifying butter resulted in something dark brown, so he decided to put the cooked lobster in the fridge and eat it cold with mayonnaise later.

While he waited, he took a glass of Chardonnay out onto the veranda and began to make another list. Books, fresh tuna, friends . . . Company at least. He wasn't meant to make friends.

The lobster tasted as good as he'd hoped, and the bottled mayonnaise went fine with it. The salad, however, tasted of . . . What was it . . . ? He tried the shining lettuce and the bright tomatoes, the fresh carrot and, for comparison, a green apple. Then he sampled them with his eyes shut. The carrot was harder than the tomato, but the taste of all three was interchangeable. They had no flavour.

He turned back to the lobster and finished it off, wiping the plate with a piece of bread. At least the bottle of bourbon he took through to the study had some Kentucky fire in its belly. He put on another old, unlabelled DVD and found it was the story of a rich man who bought dresses for a woman with a big mouth and friendly eyes. He took her to a horse-racing track in her new clothes.

In the night, Seth heard no noises in the woods around the house and there was no crash from upstairs. But he sensed that there were people nearby, more than one of them, and was glad when the sun came up.

Back at the mall the next day, he discovered a bookstore, or at least a place that had some books for sale among its racks of souvenirs. Seth had read little outside his course at university (and not much on it), but he was open to the idea of stories. He bought half a dozen, some fact, some fiction and some he wasn't sure of. He avoided local history since he had that covered back at the house.

There were eight weeks till he was due to meet Talissa in London. He ought to have a project, at least a way of speeding up the time till he could leave. Perhaps he could become expert in something. The saltwater fish of Maine, for example. He looked at the books in the bag. *Ten Ways to Change Your Life*; *The Shadow Line*; *Dead of Night*, a Stig Mallett mystery; *The Twelve Caesars*. He noticed that some of them were second-hand. The *Peanuts Annual* was antique.

It was hard not just to drink all day and listen to the feeble kiss of water on the stones where his garden met the sea. Bill came by at the same time most afternoons and about the fifth time, as he was paying for his catch, Seth asked him if he'd like a cup of tea. 'Or something else. Beer. Bourbon.'

'Not while I got a boat to get home. I'll take a soda.'

'You want to come up to the house?'

'Sure thing. The skiff'll be safe enough. No pirates here.'

They sat on the veranda, Bill with some iced tea Seth had found in a giant bottle in the store cupboard, Seth with a bourbon and water.

'You on vacation?'

'Kind of.' Seth glanced behind him into the study. 'I'm a meteorologist. Doing a little fieldwork.'

'Where you from, kid?'

'Boston.'

'You sound kind of . . . British.'

'I studied there. Three years. Rubbed off on me. Kinda.'

'You going to be here for a while?'

'I guess.'

'If you wanted, you could join us for dinner? There's a clam place just up the coast. They do real good steamers. What's your name, by the way?'

'Ken,' said Seth.

They agreed to meet in a week. It was everything Seth was not meant to do, but he could no longer stand the solitude and strange noises of the house.

In the afternoon of the agreed day, he went on a tourist visit to an old lighthouse. The history of it was told by two young women in summer dresses, probably students, he thought, making money on the side. They were good at invoking the life of a lonesome keeper, seeing no one for weeks on end. Like me, Seth thought.

There were a dozen other tourists standing round. The tickets were cheap and you didn't have to give a name to buy one. Seth was in his sunglasses and a cap with a lobster logo he'd bought at the burnt-coffee mall. He felt anonymous. Perhaps the guides were sisters, he thought. They both had short noses and fair hair drawn back from their faces.

Then came the climax of the show, when the sisters knocked at the door of the lighthouse. And out came a nineteenth-century keeper with a brass lamp and full period costume. The audience smiled as he launched into stories of wrecks and rescues.

As the keeper told his tale, Seth felt both student sisters looking at him. He couldn't risk smiling back, even if he would have liked to have a drink after the show with one of them – or both if that was the deal. He looked away. It was dangerous to engage, he knew. How had Rosalie defused it all?

'Hey, mister, want to get an ice cream?' asked one sister when the thing was over.

'Thanks, but I gotta head,' said Seth, trying to sound like a Mainer as he went back to where the car was parked.

Bill had wanted to meet at six, so Seth still had time to kill. Driving towards the diner, he found a bar by the road. He went in, ordered a beer and took it to a dark corner. Two young men were playing a machine. A group of three old-timers were looking at a ball game on a screen above the bar.

If he was recognised, things would become unbearable. But if no one bothered him, his hermit life was all unnecessary.

People wanted to be known, acknowledged, reassured that

they were more than nothing. He'd seen that. It was natural. If no one knew your name, you began to lose the edges of your outline. You could start to disappear.

Kantor's Crab and Lobster House was a grey-shingled building on Main Street. At the back was a landing stage and a long walkway down to the stony foreshore. Like everywhere else nearby, it was a fishing not a leisure place. 'Kantor's — Food — Spirits' said the rear awning, so you were in no doubt.

Bill was waiting at a table inside and introduced his wife, Marilyn, a woman in a pink polo shirt and wide jeans. It hadn't occurred to Seth that Bill would have a wife. He'd pictured him living on his boat, spending the night in a bunk at the fish houses. Marilyn was too big for her chair but seemed at ease with how much of her was not supported. Seth kept his eyes on her face as she talked brightly. Another couple, Chuck and Barbara, joined them.

'So,' Barbara told him, 'with steamers, the shells are soft, not like regular clams, and they have this siphon here. It's what they use to breathe or feed, or something. First you have to take the sock off.'

'The *sock*?'

'Sure. The cover of the siphon. Like so. Put it in this bowl. You can eat the siphon or you just use it as a handle when you dip the clam in the butter here. Look at him, Bill. He's a natural.'

'So what brings you to our part of the world?' said Chuck.

'I'm on a project. I'm a climate scientist.'

'Bill says you have the old Rodgers house up the coast. Kind of quiet.'

'Yes, it's ideal.'

Seth had flipped through a couple of books in the study and hoped he'd grasped enough about rainfall and erosion. Fishermen tended to know a hell of a lot about weather, but he could always say his work was too scientific to explain.

'What do you do, Barbara?' he asked.

'I used to work in real estate,' she said. 'Then I stopped when we had kids. Now they're grown-up, I'm looking for something new.'

'Barbara's a real good artist,' said Marilyn. 'She does these beautiful seascapes.'

'In oil,' said Chuck.

'Do you like painting, Ken?' said Marilyn.

'No. I mean, not really. I don't see the point.'

The world was what it was.

'Home,' he said to the car. 'Please.' He'd enjoyed the evening more than he'd expected. To follow the steamers, he'd ordered something called 'scrod', and Bill explained it was not a species but a name for whatever white fish they were trying to shift that day. It was good, though, whatever it was, fresh and with a pile of salted fries. Bill had a steak, which seemed odd, though maybe not so much when you thought about it. Barbara insisted on desserts. She and Marilyn both had deep quadrants of cheesecake with mugs of white coffee.

'Those Vector people are making a nuisance of themselves again,' said Barbara.

'Schmucks,' said Bill.

'Yeah, they're all wound up about this White Van guy,' said Chuck. 'Spitting blood.'

'No one listens to those crazies,' said Marilyn.

'I guess the White House had to. Eventually,' said Bill.

The four Americans became thoughtful. Seth coughed and said, 'Do you guys know a good vegetable store? The stuff in the supermarket is—'

'I know a little farm store, honey,' said Barbara.

She told him where to find it and gave his arm a squeeze when they all said goodbye.

It was still only eight thirty when Seth got back to the house. He poured red wine into a beer glass and went into the study.

He wondered why they'd exchanged glances when they found out where he was living. Did they think the house was haunted? Did it have a reputation as a hideout for criminals?

It didn't matter. He'd come to like it. The study was his favourite room. For a start, there was the lottery of the uncased, unmarked DVD in the evening. He didn't know whether to ready himself for an old Scarlett Johansson picture or a thing about concentration camps. He promised himself he would sit through whatever came on. That was the game. Different occupants had left the marks of their taste, long ago.

The furniture in the study was cheap bentwood from a chain store, mismatched antiques, but someone had loved it once. The cushions had home-made crochet covers. There were rugs and knitted throws in clashing colours, little pots, ashtrays and souvenirs on the shelves. Despite its position, no one had tried to make much of the house, to up its real-estate value – even to clear the woods for a view to the sea.

Seth was not in the habit of noticing such things, but he made himself think about the house and its previous inhabitants as a way to defeat the loneliness. Some days, he tried to remember facts from school. The periodic table, rudiments of programming, French words. After a few weeks, some of it

315

came back. He could visualise pages from books, and, if he tried hard enough, the sentences would take shape in his mind – or not so much in his mind as in front of his eyes. He could see stories from the Bible that Mary had left in his room when he was eight or nine. Like the soldiers who had to say the word 'shibboleth' to cross the Jordan, because how they pronounced it, lisp or not, showed if they were from the right tribe. Thousands were killed on the spot for being from the wrong place.

He knew it was risky to meet people, and refused Bill's next offer of dinner. It was another two weeks before, as he bought his lobster at the jetty, he suggested a return visit to Kantor's. He had read a long way into some books on local weather systems so felt he could withstand any questions about his 'research'.

There were days when he tested the limits of the car's co-operation by giving it instructions he knew it couldn't understand. 'Take me somewhere people will be kind to me but not ask too many questions.' It dropped him at the burnt-coffee mall anyway. 'Take me where the carrots taste of carrot.' Fifteen minutes later, they were at the roadside farm store. Seth sat inside in the car and complained that the place was closed. 'I just wanted some of those ugly potatoes to boil for the lobster tonight. And the shit-covered eggs from the real hens. Sometimes I'm so lonely I think I'll kill myself. I just want someone to call me by name. To hear someone say it.'

'You want to go home now, Ken?' said the car.

On other days he found it hard to remember who he was. He saw himself from the outside, as 'Ess', the creature he had first become aware of as a child. He talked to himself as he paced

316

up and down the garden, wondering if it was too early for a beer.

It was probably best not to see Bill and Marilyn again. The idea of lobster no longer drew him down to the jetty. Never imagined I could be lobstered out, he told the car.

Unable to hypothesise a future, he didn't think how things might go with Talissa when he met her again in London and they set off for the Scottish wilds. Nor did he conjecture what might happen if he changed his mind. All he knew was that to hold himself together, he must focus on some other person. Not I or me or even he, but *they*.

Talissa was the fixed point of his future. He barely knew her, but there was a bond. She knew his name, who he truly was, and could stop him being erased from the world.

One evening, he drove into town and ate dinner at Mabel's Famous Pizza. Although it was only eight o'clock, he had the sense that the rush was over and there wouldn't be many customers after him. He read a little of the book he had brought and ordered another beer. He managed to spin out the time until it was at least growing dark. The waitress was quick to bring his check.

It was a twenty-minute drive back to the house. He began to wonder what would be on the DVD. Perhaps he'd drink wine with it tonight. As he turned off the road towards his house, he saw smoke coming from the woods. He went down the track with the branches grabbing at the doors. When he came into the clearing, he saw that his house had burned down. One end wall was still standing and a couple of internal partitions had resisted the flames. But the upstairs had vanished, and from the remains of the ground floor a few thin columns of smoke were still rising. The front door had been wrenched off and lay a few yards away. On it was painted a black plus sign in a circle: the Sun Cross.

Seth stayed in the car. 'Airport,' he said.

'Logan Airport, Ken? Portland?'

'Logan. Go.'

2

Talissa was in Boston, at a conference about the future of human teaching in an age when almost all high school classes were run by AI tutors. Like most such events she'd been to, it was interesting and dispiriting in equal measure.

In the morning, she got an autonomous cab to the Airtube 4 Terminus in Boston for the return journey to New York. She had never used a hyperloop before and was feeling nervous.

'It's easy,' Susan Kovalenko had told her. 'You must have seen film of those things they used to have in hospitals and department stores? When someone shoves a little canister into a pneumatic tube and it kind of whooshes away to another part of the building?'

'I guess so. In an old movie maybe.'

'Well, it's like that.'

This wasn't reassuring. When Talissa arrived at the terminus she felt rather as she had done on going to have her first medical tests in London all those years ago: determined but powerless. There was a well-ventilated atrium with tall potted plants and, every seventy seconds, the bleep of air exchange. She stood in line for ten minutes, impressed by the calm of her fellow passengers. Some were absorbed by their headsets, others were chomping through odourless food as they waited. There were no human staff.

When her turn came, Talissa walked through a beam, which read her metrics and scanned her case contents. A voice directed her to a seat on the descender. She was clasping her bag to her midriff rather like an old lady, she thought, as the slick paternoster conveyed her down to platform level. It'll be no worse than the old subway, she told herself, though the tunnels on the downtown express from the Bronx had always had a reassuring space between the train and the wall.

She was on Canister 5, seat 39, a place that had been selected for her on the grounds of weight distribution throughout the Loop. Larger passengers were seeded evenly for balance. A display in the headrest confirmed her name; the retractable safety straps had been set to her size and short instructions came on repeat through the wraparound that dropped from the rack above.

Trussed and ready, she closed her eyes, still for some reason thinking of Dr Worthington and her 'holiday snaps' in Russell Square. There was a thunderous clank as the vacuum sealed; then, beneath her seat, she felt a hydraulic pillowing. The entertainment screen lit up, offering a choice of recent animations. There was no Fearless Frieda story, sadly, to take her mind off the sensation of travelling at 550 miles per hour, her spine driven against the seat back.

From the Bronx terminus, she got a cab home and packed for the supersonic flight to London. Plans for a Transatlantic Passenger Hyperloop had been put to one side because of cost overruns, though a smaller tube could carry goods beneath the seabed. With hand baggage only at Obama Airport, the travel process had become easier; the flight time to London was only a little over two hours. The drawback was that, for weight reasons, the plane had no windows, so the passengers were invited to watch a film of the outside world on their screens instead.

Talissa closed her eyes. In the months since the trial, the public discussion had focused on the scientific value of the data gathered from Seth's life. There seemed to be a wide understanding that it was only molecular chance that had led to the existence of modern humans; and how it could have been subtly otherwise, with a similar but saner and more integrated creature evolving from the same raw material. There had been broadcasts and essays and public discussion, debates in the US Senate and in the Second Chamber in Britain, that had understood the issues and argued for a greater tolerance as a result: for the acceptance of variety, for the dignity of all humankind — or at least for its sole surviving expression.

The trouble was that hardly anyone read or watched these things. They were too complicated. To judge from the virtual chatter, the thing that caught people's imagination was the sci-fi possibilities of an 'improved' genome, more sex and a longer life. At least there was the resolution just passed by the UN's new medical council, which had required its member states to sign up to a ban on laboratory hybridisation. In a largely deregulated and money-driven world, such treaties were unlikely to stop another Lukas Parn, but they were something positive to point to, some consolation.

The cabin staff brought some water. Talissa settled back in her seat and tried to imagine what an uninhabited Scottish island would feel like.

Late the next morning, after a night at Kavya Gopal's, she stood on the concourse of Euston International station, as arranged. She tried to make herself more visible, moving away from people who might be concealing her. Unable to eat since leaving Boston, she was starting to feel weak.

Come to me now, she thought. I am here. Her gaze went over shopfronts, trade names, to the entrances from the street and the Underground. Probably, he'd come from the pontoon where the water transport docked, but the sweep of her eyes couldn't cover every corner of the station. She breathed out and looked at the ground. Come to me, now. There was a hand on her elbow, a polite brushing of her cheek. She sprang back, then forward as she held him, feeling his skin on hers.

'I thought you weren't coming.'

'No, no. I just got a bit delayed saying goodbye to my parents.'

'We need to move. I have seats at the front, where there won't be so many people.'

'My God, what have you got in there?' said Seth, pointing to Talissa's outsize pack.

'Sleeping roll, lightweight tent, soluble food, fuel blocks . . . I'm an expert camper, don't forget.'

'Wasn't it heavy?'

'No, I sent it on by hyperloop.'

'I'll carry it. You take my little bag.'

As the train edged out through the Victorian cuttings, Talissa found herself opposite Seth with a strip of table between them. She wanted to stare and stare, but found it hard to meet his eye.

'So,' she said, pretending to look at her handset. 'Are we all set for your little island?'

'Yes,' said Seth. 'I spoke to John Rockingham and he's been in touch with the local boatman. A man called Brodie. He says it should be OK at this time of year. Not too much of a swell.'

'Good. You look a little different.'

'Must be the moustache.'

'I think you maybe need to lose that.' It was hiding his skin.

'Oh, I thought it was good.'

'It looks like you bought a complete disguise from a shop. In with the glasses.'

'Right.'

Talissa felt a little stronger. 'Have you ever been to Glasgow?' she said.

'No.'

'I booked a place. It looked quiet. Only five rooms.'

'OK.'

'Are you quite sure about this, Seth?'

'I've always wanted to go to this island. To escape and be alone. And now I think . . . This is the moment.'

'After the interview, were there any leaks about your appearance? No one took a picture of you?'

'No. But . . .'

'But what?'

'At the interview place . . . I did forget my mask and hat and glasses. For a second.'

'And people saw you?'

'Yes. But they were nice. Diane, the woman in the FAT lab. And the others.'

'But someone could have taken a picture.'

'I suppose it's possible. Or I'm on the security footage or something, just for those few moments.'

'Have your parents been troubled?'

'No. But Catrina says she gets messages from scientists.

Begging her. She says she gets followed. And . . . other things.'

A caterer came by with a trolley. Seth asked for a sandwich and some beer. Talissa looked away. 'Water, please.'

She sat back and watched rectangles of England going by. 'Have you switched off your handset?' she said.

'I left it with Catrina.'

'Good. We're going up the west coast. I have some paper maps. Susan got them for me.'

'The house in Maine had a lot of those. I used to spread them out on the floor. They're kind of . . . fascinating.'

'Did you meet people there?'

'I tried not to. But it was lonely.'

'I'm sorry.'

'My best friend was the talking car.'

Talissa had the impression he was holding something back.

Near Stafford, she became aware that a couple across the gangway were staring at them. They spoke quietly to each other, as if comparing notes, then looked back at Seth. It could be that they were passing the journey in harmless speculation: the age difference between Seth and her, the possible relationship . . . But their gaze seemed too intent.

Talissa leant across the table to whisper in Seth's ear. 'Don't look now. Pretend you're staring out the window . . .'

After a moment, she let go of his wrist and let him turn. When the train slowed down for Penrith, Talissa said quietly, 'I think we should get off. I'll find a place to stay.'

On the platform, she searched the options on her handset. They were on the edge of the North Lakes and everywhere seemed full for the holidays.

'The only place with a room is this inn. Near Keswick. The Fox and Hounds.'

'Keswick,' said Seth. 'That's how they say it here. Not Kess-wick.'

From the cab, Talissa booked the last free room. The inn was in a small village at the bottom of a fell and the door opened on to a dark, empty bar with a flagged floor. They rang a handbell and waited until a man in an apron came through from the kitchen.

'Kovak?' he said. 'You're in room six. On the second floor. Do you need a hand with . . . All right. Just call down if you need anything.'

As they opened the bedroom door, Seth said, 'Kovak?'

'Can't be too careful,' said Talissa. 'And it's a homage. To Susan. Or nearly.'

'There's only one bed,' said Seth.

'Only one room,' said Talissa. 'Last one in the Lakes. But I'll take the floor if you like.'

'No, no. I will. It's fine.'

At dinner downstairs, Talissa said, 'I think it's better that we take a car from here. More private.'

'It'll cost a fortune,' said Seth.

'Parn's paying. He gave me money.'

'Catrina said Parn's lawyers have appealed against his sentence.'

'I heard that, too,' said Talissa. 'They're confident they'll get it suspended. They'll increase the fine to compensate, but that won't hurt him.'

They drank a bottle of wine with dinner and it made Talissa more relaxed. Her appetite returned and she ordered dessert, an apple tart, to counteract the wine. When they climbed the stairs, she felt resigned. The assault of emotions she had never known and couldn't name had left her unsure of what to do.

'You can have the duvet as a mattress,' she said. 'It's hot, so I won't need it on the bed.'

In the bathroom, she stood beneath the strong, warm shower with her eyes closed. She thought of Susan watching her with that look of quizzical concern. When she was as clean as a newborn, she brushed her teeth and gargled with two different products. She arranged her black hair casually and put on a long T-shirt that reached almost to her knees.

'All yours,' she said, taking a book from her bag. While Seth was in the bathroom, she turned off the overhead light. The bedside lamps gave a softer glow as she settled back against the pillows.

She heard the shower and the basin, then the sliding lock. She looked over the top of her reading glasses. 'All good?'

'Yes. I borrowed some of your toothpaste. Hope that's OK.'

He had shaved off the moustache so she could see the skin of his face. He wore pyjama trousers and a T-shirt. He lay down on the duvet.

'Shall I turn off the light?' said Talissa.

'Sure.'

She rolled across the bed to reach the far lamp, feeling her own T-shirt rise up her thighs while she fumbled for the switch.

At Keswick the next morning, they hired a car from the station and strapped themselves in side by side.

'Best if I give the instructions,' said Seth.

The car took them silently up the old motorway into the Lowlands.

'Lanarkshire,' said Seth. 'Famous for its coalfields. Once upon a time. Dad said.'

'I don't see any. And I don't see any people either. Just a few sheep.'

Shortly after Glasgow, the narrow road began to run among woods by an inland sea. Seth looked up from his map. 'Loch Lomond,' he said.

'It's gigantic,' said Talissa. 'And how come you're so good with maps?'

'I did a year in the Scout cadets at school. Dad insisted.'

After another hour, the landscape began to change again, into a moorland of russet and sage. There were patches of heather and yet more lochs, smaller ones. The weather seemed to cast a different light at almost every bend in the road, showers yielding to sunshine, then low cloud as rain beat the windscreen again.

'So many lochs,' said Seth. 'There's even one called Loch Lochy. Do you think they ran out of names?'

Talissa kept looking out of the window. Now there were mountains – not just hills but monsters with cascades above the treeline. At one moment it reminded her of Yosemite, the next it looked more like Wyoming.

They stopped in a village – though why there was a village here, rather than at any other spot in the empty landscape, was impossible to say. Once a marketplace for farmers, she imagined . . . Except there was no farming, no crops or signs of cultivation.

'Perhaps before the Highland Clearances,' Seth said when she asked. 'Crofters had their own smallholdings and might meet up here. Who knows? At least there's a bar.'

Inside, Seth ordered pizza from the menu on a board. There was nothing that Talissa wanted. A group of men sat at a table, watching horses race on a screen. They were drinking beer from huge glasses they brought back to the bar to be refilled. They hardly talked. Seth watched and plumped for number five in the paddock.

As Talissa sipped her drink, she felt the eyes of two of the men on her. It was hard to know if it was a reflex estimation of her appeal, or if there was something else that drew their gaze. It made her uneasy. If these men in this wilderness, in the midst of their gallons of beer and betting, had somehow recognised Seth, then how much more remote would they need to be until they were safe?

The car took them onwards to the north. Still the terrain kept shifting with the swoop and roll of the road. There were coniferous forests growing up the mountainsides, abandoned ski stations on snowless slopes, then in a moment silvery rivers pouring over white boulders. Sheep with black faces stood in the middle of the road, sensing no danger.

Seth was asleep, perhaps tired from his night on the floor or from the glass of black beer he had drunk. His head leant against Talissa's shoulder. For an instant she felt maternal – if tenderly protective was what mothers felt. Perhaps her desire to consume him body and soul was in some way immoral or taboo. Yet they were less related by blood than any two humans on earth for tens of thousands of years. They could not be any more unrelated. So she told herself, again, as she touched his thick hair.

After seven hours in the car, they found the guest house a short way outside the port. Again, it was the only room

Talissa had been able to find: the cooler weather of Scotland was making it more popular each year. There was no reception area or desk, just the windowless hallway of someone's downstairs, with the scent of old cooking.

'I'm Olivia,' said the owner. 'Follow me upstairs, please.'

On the landing there were three numbered doors. Olivia turned a handle. 'Here we are. It's a double bed. Is that going to be all right?'

'Yes,' said Talissa, looking away.

'The fan's not working, but you can open the window. It's a nice view over the loch.'

'It's a *very* nice view.' A vertical herringbone of cloud rose from a blue hill over the water.

'You close the blind with this little chain. It can be temperamental.'

On the window sill was a pink paper orchid in a plastic pot.

'The shower works on an electric heater, so you just turn it on. We don't use the bath.'

'What time is breakfast?' said Seth.

'Did you book in for it?' said Olivia.

'Not specifically,' said Talissa. 'I thought we'd—'

'In that case, it's not included. I'm on my own here.'

'I see,' said Talissa. 'We'll get something in town.'

When Olivia had gone, Seth said, 'How many people does it take to boil a kettle?'

'I guess there'll be food on the boat. Don't you think?'

'Maybe haggis.'

'What's that?'

'Sheep's innards. With oats. You won't like it.'

Talissa was looking at the bed. 'It's my turn to take the floor,' she said.

'The bed's quite wide,' said Seth. 'I could guarantee not to move around. I fall asleep at once. So everyone says.'

'Everyone?'

'Mum. Rosalie. Wilson, when I shared a tent with him in the Scouts.'

'I'll ask Olivia where's good for dinner,' said Talissa, her voice bright with relief.

They walked into the port. There was a single string of whitewashed houses along the shore of the loch, which, a mile or so to the west, opened on to the sea. Although there were signs of activity at the deep dock, an air of farewell hung over the town, an end-of-continent sadness.

A few other alleys had sprung up behind the front, and at the foot of one was the place that Olivia had recommended. It was a big, open room, with bare floorboards and Scottish music, live bands twice a week according to a board. Seth ordered a venison burger and Talissa some ravioli.

'Shall we drink wine again?' said Seth. 'I liked what we had in Keswick.'

'I don't know much about wine,' said Talissa. 'Let's ask the guy.'

The waiter spent a few minutes at the table and talked about varietals and growers in more detail than the brief list seemed to need. A man of about sixty with glasses and a high voice, he seemed reluctant to leave. He looked hard at Seth as he asked what kind of wine he liked.

'Maybe just the cheapest red,' Talissa said. 'So long as it makes us feel drunk.'

The waiter didn't smile at her joke, but did at last head off to the bar. The wine when it came tasted of vanilla and blackcurrants. After they'd eaten and the waiter came to take their plates, he lingered and said, 'I hope you don't mind me asking, but are you the laddie who—'

'No!' said Talissa, loudly through the wine. 'He's not. Please bring the check now.'

As they walked along the front, Talissa muttered, 'What an asshole.'

'Yeah,' said Seth. 'What an utter dick.'

She found that she had taken Seth's arm and that, courteously, he had not resisted. For a hundred yards or so, they traded insults for the waiter.

'Cocksucker,' said Seth. 'Sorry. Was that too much?'

'No. Not for that schmuck.'

Seth stopped suddenly. 'There's something I have to tell you,' he said. He put his face close to hers and she could smell the sweet blackcurrant of the wine and some toffee ice cream on his breath. 'Something that happened in Maine.'

When he had finished the story of the fire and his flight from Boston, they stood staring over the water in silence.

'Where did you go?'

'Cleveland. It was the first flight I could get on. I didn't know anything about the place, but I was there for a week before I came to London. I moved each day. I tried to fit in, but I felt I looked different. I ended up in a room near the lake.'

'You did the right thing.'

'I don't know if I can survive feeling constantly . . . pursued. I'm not sure it's worth living like that.'

She held his arm. 'We're going to our own island now.'

They let themselves back into the guest house, using a code on the door, and went quietly upstairs. Seth took the first shower while Talissa arranged the bed, stacking a pair of

331

pillows on either side, with a wide neutral space between. When it was her turn in the bathroom, she noticed he had once again helped himself to her toothpaste. She dried her skin carefully and pulled on a clean T-shirt. It was not as long as the previous one, so she slipped on some underpants. The first ones that came out of her bag happened to be new, ivory with a lace trim. Seth's bedside light was out when she went back and he seemed already to be in a state of motionless sleep.

Talissa left her book unread and turned off her own light, moving delicately so as not to wake him. She closed her eyes and tried not to inhale the fresh smell of him or to think of that glowing skin.

'Are you OK?' she heard him say a few minutes later.

'Yes,' she said thickly.

'I thought you were crying. I thought I felt a sort of trembling through the springs.'

'No. Sleep well.'

It was still dark when they started the car and drove the short way to the ferry port. Three lines of vehicles, most of them delivery trucks, had already been boxed into lanes by men in fluorescent bibs and were waiting, their headlights holding the fine drizzle. Talissa had booked ahead and now went over the road to the terminal building to buy a ticket for her foot passenger. She hoped in this way to avoid giving his name. In the strip-lit hall, two women sat behind a desk, sipping from cardboard cups. Clearly they had been at work for hours. One of them put down her coffee and tapped on a keyboard till a ticket shot across the pass.

Back in the car, they were next to a truck of baled hay, four rows of eight identical fat cylinders, in two tiers lashed to attention. The islands were barren, Talissa had read, but the livestock needed to be fed. When they boarded the ferry, the top of the hay truck passed under the gantry with a foot's clearance. The efficiency impressed her, but her main question was unanswered. In a country whose terrain was so harsh and unpopulated, why had some chosen to make their lives yet more difficult by settling on an island even less hospitable than the mainland? The mad Sapiens drive.

They climbed the metal stairs to a passenger lounge, where Talissa sat by a window and Seth went to explore the chance of breakfast.

Dawn was breaking as the ferry lumbered out of the port. Talissa looked at the thin line of whitewashed houses as they started to recede. She thought of grandmothers hundreds of years ago waving a last goodbye to children and grandchildren they would never see again as their slow ships began the crossing of the Atlantic. There had been no day in her adult life when she had not wondered at humans and their journeyings.

Seth came back to the table, carrying a tray of food.

'I got you some porridge,' he said. 'I thought you'd like that. And tea.'

'Did they have haggis?'

'No.'

'What's that thing?'

'Black pudding.'

'Is that also made from sheep's guts?'

'No, it's pig's blood.'

'Oh. Is that better?'

'I'll let you know.'

They could see the swell of the sea around them. To the north was a run of blue-brown hills that rose from the water like the vertebrae of a half-submerged monster.

'I'm going up above,' said Talissa. 'On deck.'

It was harder to walk than she'd expected and she had to hold on to screwed-down tables as she crossed the lounge to the stairs. Out on the top deck were rows of empty plastic seats and some orange lifeboats hanging from the side. She was starting to make out the island ahead of them when she saw five dolphins in an arrowhead, pursuing them. There seemed a driven purpose in their movements as they followed their target, part fish, part torpedo, shouldering the waves.

The port on the island was like an ordinary town, with schools and parks, but a mile to the south all signs of civilisation disappeared. There were still fingerposts on the road, but no settlements they could see. The rain intensified and the car seemed wary, dropping its pace. Two sheep huddled together in an old bus shelter.

'I think we'll be alone here,' said Seth.

As the rain retreated, they saw the treeless landscape more clearly. There were large hills and small lakes. But more striking than either were the dark boulders that lay over all the countryside, as if thousands of years ago a generation of giants had been interrupted in a game and had had no time to clear up. They had vanished from the earth and no subsequent inhabitants had had the strength to move their granite playthings.

After an hour of driving, they saw some buildings. 'I'm hungry,' said Seth. 'Let's see if we can find something here.'

There was a cluster of houses, one of which was a shop,

though it was closed. A little way up the hill was what looked like a hotel.

At the reception desk, behind some glass, a woman asked if they were looking for a room.

'No, we wanted to eat. Is it too late for lunch?' said Seth.

'We're waiting for a food delivery from the mainland just now.'

'Do you have, like, potato chips?' said Talissa.

'We have a bar. Through that door.'

They went into a small room with wood-panelled walls. Above the bar were hundreds of bottles of whisky.

'This is great,' said Seth. 'Do you have any crisps?'

'I think so,' said the barmaid, bending down to look.

'I'll bring them,' said Talissa. 'And some drinks. You sit down.'

She brought over some whisky for him and some beer for herself. The crisps were soft. Seth looked at the packet and saw that they were two months out of date.

'There *is* plenty of food on our own island, isn't there?' said Talissa.

'Yes. In the bothy. So Brodie said. But let's see if we can get some supplies of our own. If we see a shop.'

'A shop?' Talissa raised an eyebrow.

Half an hour later, they arrived in the village where they had arranged to meet their man. A dozen houses were clustered round a stone jetty that stuck out into the bay. There were a few small boats moored against it and a larger one with a wheelhouse and an inboard engine.

'That'll be us,' said Seth.

There was a corrugated iron shack selling tweed and, next to it, a closed café. In something called the An Clachan community centre, among the souvenirs and craftworks, there was a food section, where they loaded a basket with tins of tuna and fruit, beans and sealed packets of biscuits, cakes and tea.

'Can you eat eggs?'

'Yes,' said Talissa. 'If it's that or canned peas.'

'But how are we going to cook them?'

'I have ways.' Talissa pointed at her weighty pack. 'And a pan in there.'

They left the car in a deserted area at the end of the road. Then they took their box of food and their bags down onto the jetty to wait for their boatman. They were to meet at four and it was a two-hour trip to the island, where the tide needed to be high when they docked. The rain had cleared, at least for five minutes, and the sky to the west was blue.

'God, this is beautiful,' said Talissa, her legs dangling against the stonework of the jetty. She thought of the grid of Harlem streets round her brownstone as she leant her head for a moment on Seth's shoulder.

To their surprise, the boatman arrived on time. A small, muscular man in a yellow waterproof jacket, he shook hands and helped them load their bags. He smiled often, but struggled to keep a note of incredulity from his voice.

'And you'll be staying how long?'

'We don't know,' said Seth. 'As long as it takes.'

'You've got enough stores,' said Brodie, looking at Talissa's pack.

'Will we be left alone?' she said.

'No one's lived there for a hundred years,' said Brodie. 'In the beginning there were priests.'

'But there are visitors, right?'

'Only twice a year. When they go and cull the deer.'

'Is the weather going to stay fine?' said Talissa.

'Aye. It's much warmer than when I was young. Though it never settles for long. Some things don't change.'

'We've noticed. Every hour a new adventure.'

The boat's motor made a gurgling, bass sound as Brodie backed off the jetty. When he was clear, he swung round and headed west, towards the open water, the engine pitch rising.

Once they were out of the bay, they began to notice the swell. Brodie's thudding boat was less stable than the ferry, but it ploughed on with a will of its own. The noise drowned any hope of speech, so they stayed silent, with their eyes on the horizon.

After about an hour, a tiny rock came into view, then grew bigger as they approached. No other land was visible in the ocean, not the island they had left, not the mainland, not even a gull-tormented outcrop, nothing but their own last refuge. Brodie brought the boat close to a cliff, and as they came alongside they saw a flat surface with some iron rings driven into the rock. Brodie cut the engine and jumped onto the natural platform, holding a rope with which he secured the boat. They passed up the packs and the box of food, then he helped them ashore. 'Follow me,' he said.

The cliff was not as steep as it had looked from the sea and there was a path with bits of shingle and broken stone that helped their grip. At the top, they paused for breath and Brodie pointed inland.

'You see that wee building in the distance there? That's the bothy. On the far side, after a couple of minutes' walk, it goes down to a beach. You can swim if you like, but watch the current. Don't go out deep.'

'How far is it?'

'The island's three quarters of a mile at the widest. But you'll get a good walk if you go round the hill there. You can drink the water from the wee stream. You may see some cattle. Keep away. They're wild. They can trample you.'

'OK,' said Talissa. 'So we just . . .'

'Aye. You're on your own. I'd come with you, but I have to catch the tide. I'll see you in six days. Same time.'

Brodie disappeared from view under the rim of the cliff.

'I'd like to sleep outside tonight,' Talissa said. 'But let's take a look at this bothy place.'

Seth hitched her pack onto his back and picked up the box of food.

The path across the top of the island was damp with the recent rain, but there were no human footprints, only the marks of some cloven hooves and the paws of rabbits. There were no gates or fences, no claim on the land. Halfway across, they stopped to look around them. There was nothing to see but the occasional edge of white foam in the infinite grey sea.

A little out of breath, they dropped their bags outside the building and pushed open the plank door. Inside was a single room, with an improvised fireplace and chimney at one end. The floor was flagged with the same stone as the walls, with grass instead of mortar in the joints. A raised divan with wooden sides, hardly a bed, had some straw in it. There was a table and a metal tank fed by water from a pipe connected to the gutter on the roof. Someone had nailed some shelves to upright pieces of timber and on these were some supplies for the deer cullers – tinned foods, candles, soap and two bottles of whisky.

'I like it,' said Seth. 'I'm going to find the beach.'

'Did you bring matches?' said Talissa.

'Shit. I forgot.'

'I'll take a look around. Don't be away too long.'

'Are you frightened?'

'Hell yeah. I'm a city girl.'

'But you said you loved camping.'

'With a car and a freeway close at hand.'

'I'll be ten minutes.'

In his absence, Talissa tried not to behave like a wife, or a mother. She prepared no welcome tea for his return, though she did find some matches on a ledge inside the chimney. Now that it had stopped raining, it was a warm August evening. It ought to be possible to sleep outside, she thought, away from the torment of his closeness, so long as the insects weren't too bad.

He took a little more than the ten minutes, but was smiling when he came in. 'There's a beach,' he said. 'It's got sand and lots of stone, seaweed, quite rough. But it seems sheltered. The ground goes down quite slowly, so we could swim off it.'

Talissa frowned. 'Please don't laugh at me, Seth, but I never learned to swim. The public pool was miles away when I was a kid. We never went on holiday to a beach or anything like that. My dad died when I was young and—'

'Don't worry,' said Seth. 'I can't swim either.'

'Oh.' Talissa looked down at the table. 'Shall we try to make a fire? To cook something?'

'Yes, I'll find some fuel. There's a pile of something over there. Is it peat? I'll make you a bed outside if you still want that?'

'What with?'

'Any soft stuff I can find.'

339

'Maybe we should try sleeping on the beach if there's enough sand.'

'Good idea,' said Seth.

Unlike the place from which they'd come, where all the new growths and saplings were eaten by sheep, the new island did have a few stunted conifers. Seth found twigs and branches, some of which were dry enough to start a fire. They fried eggs in butter, using Talissa's pan, and heated some beans. Seth took a bottle of whisky from the shelf.

'We'd better get down to the beach while it's still light,' said Talissa. 'Do you think it'll get cold at night?'

'No, but it's sure to rain, don't you think?'

'Then we'll come back inside. I'm taking a sweater anyway.'

The beach had black stones among the volcanic rocks but enough sand for Seth to clear a dry place for Talissa to sleep.

'You could use sea wrack as a pillow,' he said.

'You won't stay?' she said.

'I was thinking of the straw on the bed indoors.'

'It's getting dark.'

'I'll stay. Are you all right?'

She sighed. 'Yes.'

'It's like the end of the world here. It's like no one's been here for a million years.'

'I know.'

They lay down next to each other on the sand as the darkness fell.

3

When Seth awoke, he looked to see if Talissa was still there. She was asleep, turned away from him. It was cold, and he wanted to drape the sweater over her shoulders, but she was using it as a pillow.

The sun was bright but still low, striking a dim pathway over the sea. He guessed it was about six o'clock, and the best thing he could do was fetch some water from the stream. He had slept well and felt no stiffness as he climbed the bank to the peaty grass behind.

In the bothy was a bucket, which he took to where the stream trickled out of the hillside. He could dig a hole in the stony bed later to get the bucket in at less of an angle. There was an old pan in the chimney and he managed to coax the fire back to life, blowing on the peat embers, feeding in some dry pine needles, then sticks. Very slowly, the water began to heat up.

Talissa was at the door, smiling. 'I thought you'd left.'

'No. I'm making tea.'

'I'm going to wash in the stream.'

With the tea, when the water had finally boiled, they ate some biscuits.

'We need more eggs,' said Talissa.

'Maybe I'll find a gulls' nest,' said Seth. 'We have to explore.'

'Be careful. Gulls are savage, aren't they? We can last till Brodie comes back.'

Afterwards, they climbed the hill to survey the island. Their sheltered beach was on the north-east, and further down the same side was a wooded area – a few wind-whipped larches at any rate – then open ground that seemed as if it could once have been cultivated for oats or root crops, supposing the Celt or Norse farmers had known how. The west of the island, where they'd docked, looked barren in the Atlantic gales.

Talissa began to laugh. 'It's so wonderful. To be alone.'

'Finally.' Seth put his face towards the wind.

For a few minutes they stood in silence, till Seth pointed. 'Let's look down there.'

'What are we looking for?'

'Eggs, rabbits. I don't know.'

'You go. Be careful. I'll see you back at the bothy.'

Seth went alone towards the southern headland, a place between the bleak and the habitable. Past the remains of a drystone wall, he noticed that the ground was marked with hoof prints. The wind veered and began to blow hard in his face. A shower stung his eyes, and he crouched down behind a boulder, knowing how quickly it might pass. As it eased, he emerged to find an animal gazing down at him from above. He recoiled for a moment, but saw that it was just a cow. It held his gaze and snorted.

The rain began again, but harder, and Seth pressed back against the boulder. The cow came and stood beside him. He crawled under its belly, smelling its hot, wet flanks until the rain stopped again. Then he stood up and continued to walk towards some open grass, where there was a herd, perhaps thirty of the creatures, with shaggy red coats, bulls with dangling testes and half-grown calves among the females, of which only two had milk. These were not the creatures who'd once fed burger chains and dairies, but something closer to their Neolithic ancestors. They'd gone backwards in time. He watched them from a distance as he went on towards the sea.

When he had put the cattle from his mind and was coming close to the water, he sensed something strange. And then, as he rounded a corner, he saw it – pulled up and secured by a chain to a solitary tree above the rocky shore, a rowing boat. When he got near, he saw it was made of some rugged compound, with wooden oars lying on the deck. He felt affronted by its presence – by the thought that other humans had been to this remote point of his island. Presumably it belonged to the people who came to cull the deer. He turned to go back to the bothy.

The wind was getting up again and the noise of seabirds began to oppress him. He wished he'd paid more attention as a child when Alaric had talked to him about different species on their holidays. He was fairly sure that the shrieking came from an oystercatcher. The only consolation he could take was that if there were oystercatchers then there might be oysters, too. He could search among the rocks. First, he'd build a shelter on the beach so that if it rained at night they could still sleep out with the stars and the moon above them.

He felt an urge to look after Talissa. Although she was far from home and seemed unsure of what to do, she was his lifeline. He needed her. She understood who he was, accepted him and asked no questions. She loved him, obviously.

But that was what frightened him. How was he meant to respond to the depth of her feeling? It was not that he was unmoved by her. Her skin was beautiful to him, as was the deep brown of her eyes and her swift physical movements. He was drawn to the fragile certainty of her manner – the sense she gave of knowing what was hers by right while having access to it only sometimes, and by chance. But he would never be able to satisfy the alien hunger that he sensed in her.

In the evening, when they ate dinner inside, he told her about the cattle.

'I suppose they're feral,' she said. 'Domestic animals no longer being shaped by humans. They can rediscover some genes that have been dormant for hundreds of generations. But they can't go back to being wild aurochsen. It's too late. We've changed them.'

'Do you know this from your work?'

'I don't know that much about genetics, to be honest. But I do know some Germans early in the last century thought they could recreate the original cows, which were these huge aur-ochs things. I think they were Nazis. The scientists, I mean.'

Neither of them spoke for a while.

'Are you going to sleep on the beach again?' said Seth eventually.

'Yes. It looks dry.'

'Tomorrow I'll try to build a shelter so you won't get wet.'

'What with?'

'I suppose . . . with . . .'

'Animal hides? On sharpened poles? A palisade?'

'Whatever comes to hand.'

Talissa laughed. 'Have some whisky.'

344

He went and fetched a bottle from the shelf. Talissa lit some candles and let a few drops of wax drip onto the table so she could anchor them.

'Do you like it here?' she said.

'Yes. I feel free. I feel I can be myself. And nothing matters.'

'Will it take a long time? To work out who you are and what to do?'

'I don't know. I might need to come and live here for a time. A year or more. Put a bed in. Bring some hens. And beer.'

'Could I come too?'

'What about your job?'

'They owe me a sabbatical. And my freshman course is already taught by AI.'

'Really?'

'Can I try some whisky?' said Talissa. 'Boy, that's fierce. Tell me, what do you really want?'

'Well . . .' Seth looked up for a moment, to the roof of the shelter, then back to Talissa's worried face. 'I can tell you what I *don't* want. I don't want my whole life to be about who or what created me. I don't want my life to be all about who my parents and their parents were. Where they came from and what that makes me.'

'I understand.'

'I'm a man. Can't we leave it at that?'

'I can. But what would you like your life to be about instead?'

'Bridges and engineering. Work.' He smiled. 'The manufacture of concrete generates huge carbon emissions, but we've discovered a process that consumes more than it emits. It's what they call carbonederous.'

'That sounds exciting. And what else?'

'Horses. Privacy. Just seeing how my life turns out. How my story goes.'

Talissa said nothing.

'What about you?' said Seth.

'Oh, pretty much the same. But for the bridges, read anthropology. Thinking about who we are and how we got here. The how, and the how strange.'

There was another silence, in which they could hear the wind.

'Not horses, then,' said Seth, to break the quiet.

'Maybe I could learn to love them too.'

'I don't suppose you've had to spend all your life being fixated on where your family came from. You could always just be an American.'

Talissa smiled. 'Yeah. I'm American OK. My four grandparents came from three different continents. But the way you are . . . There's always someone who won't like it.'

'Aren't all Americans like you? From all over?'

'Some more than others. But I can't complain. I might have had Iraqi parents. Or Russian. Or from somewhere even more despised.'

'Shall we go down to the beach while it's still light? So we can see the way.'

'All right. I'm going to bring another sweater.'

They sat against the rocks behind their sleeping place. The sun had set on the other side of the island, but in the moonlight they could still make out where the sea was turning back on itself, slack and restless on the black stones.

'Do you know how old these rocks are?' said Talissa.

'No.'

'About three hundred and fifty million years, I'd say. That's

346

roughly when the plates beneath the earth collided and forced up the mountains. This kind of rock's called gneiss.'

'Niece?'

She spelled it for him.

'Are you all right?' said Seth. 'You seem . . .'

'I'm fine. You mentioning your parents made me think about mine.'

'Do you remember your father?'

'Not very well. I remember a kind of . . . attitude more than a man. Of kindness and routine. Of doing things his way. He did love me. I do know that, thank God. I haven't had to carry *that* doubt. He was . . . amused by me. I made him laugh. But his death was hard to take in at that age. For years I dreamed he was alive and we were going off to do normal things as a family. Every week I'd have these dreams. Then one day, maybe five years after he died, I had to break it to him that he was in fact dead. It was so hard to do.'

Talissa felt her throat closing down on a buried feeling that was trying to escape, trapping the air in her lungs till it exploded in a sob. Through her clouded eyes, the rocks and hills, the caves and the sea seemed to break into black fragments, millions of years old, shattering into some dust in the stars above them. She closed her eyes and Seth held her in his arms.

When the spasms had subsided, she moved away a little and began to breathe evenly.

Seth said, 'What's it like to dream?'

Talissa stood up and looked at him, dry-eyed.

'Do you mean . . . that dream? My dream? It was . . .'

'No. Any dream. I've never had one.'

*

When Talissa woke in the morning, she looked over the calm sea. She was alone. She levered herself up from the sand and walked back to the bothy, where Seth was making tea. The wind had dropped and the sun was already hot.

It was hard to understand the turmoil she had felt the night before. It had been replaced by a feeling of serenity, as if nothing could touch her now. She was in a place beyond pain.

When they had had breakfast of more tea and some cake from a packet, Seth said he was going to swim. 'Or paddle, anyway. Get myself wet. I'm too hot.'

They walked back to their beach and he took off his clothes.

'Are you going to come in?' he said.

She hesitated.

'Are you embarrassed?'

'I don't think I know how to be,' said Talissa. 'Not any more.'

She pulled off her dress and underwear and they walked down to the water together. There were seals in the shallow water and, a little way off, a pair of them lumbering onto the beach. For all the heat of the sun, the sea was colder than she'd expected and they went in gradually, stopping when it was waist-high. He seemed unsure if he was allowed to look at her breasts and their dark circles just above the waves. She leant over and kissed him.

When they were starting to grow cold, they went back and lay down on the sand. The sun dried them quickly and Talissa lay with her head on Seth's shoulder. The back of her hand brushed against him, where he was aroused.

'I'm sorry,' he said.

'It's all right. What would you like to do?' she said.

He looked troubled, as if trying to guess what she wanted.

348

'To kiss you here,' he said, touching her. 'Would you turn round?'

She knelt and let him spread her flesh apart with his thumbs. The movement of his tongue reduced her to a single point of longing. It went on till it seemed this sense of dying was all she'd ever wanted. She crawled away, breathing hard, and turned round. 'Will you stand up?' she said.

She knelt and used her tongue in turn, then stopped and looked up at him. 'These,' she said. 'They remind me of the pods on a sycamore.' She smiled. 'But heavy.'

She thought of the mixed seeds they carried, the weight in her palm. She said, 'If you want to, you can . . .'

'Not if you don't—'

'I want you to. But don't finish. Stop just before.'

She knelt down on the sand again and he did as he was told. It was not long before he began to gasp. 'I think it's nearly . . .' Talissa moved away, stood up and took him in her hand.

When it was done, they looked down at the sand and the piece of rock where the first spurt had landed.

'So,' said Talissa. 'And after all that . . .'

'I know.'

They stared at the pools of sticky, mundane fluid heating in the sun.

'It's just like . . . It's the same as . . .'

'What did you expect, Talissa?'

The next day was equally hot and they wore no clothes. Although they made love again, it didn't cure or sate Talissa's longing. It didn't seem enough.

They walked towards the wooded side of the island,

through grass and camomile and buttercups. At a sheltered part of the hill, they sat down and looked over the sea.

'I wish we had wine,' said Seth.

Talissa laughed. 'Water's all we need. Here.' She'd filled an empty whisky bottle at the stream.

He stroked the back of her hand, then turned it over and admired the colours of her skin.

'Do you love me?' he said.

'Oh yes,' said Talissa. 'But much more than love. Alas.'

Seth looked puzzled. 'I thought that was the best that we could feel.'

'So did I. Till I met you.'

'And now what do you think?'

'When I look at you, or touch your face, like this . . . I feel beyond myself. As if every atom of my body was in yours. I feel you *are* me. You are more me than I am.'

Seth stroked her hand again. 'And does that make you happy?'

'No. The weight of being you is more than I can bear.'

'You mustn't say that.'

'All my life force, every nerve, is on fire with pity for you. For us. Me too. For all of us for having to be alive. And die.'

That night, it became cooler and the clouds lowered. They ate the best things they could find among the tins on the shelf. Seth persuaded Talissa to drink some whisky with him, diluted with water from the stream.

'What's that noise?' said Seth.

'I can't hear anything.'

They went outside, and a minute later she heard the nervous thud of a helicopter.

'Do you think they've come to rescue us?' said Talissa. 'Maybe Brodie knows the weather's turning and he's had to get help.'

Seth looked up into the clouds. 'If it was an air-sea rescue thing it would be marked, wouldn't it?'

'Yes. A logo saying Scottish Coastguard or something.'

'This one isn't marked. I'm going to put out the fire so there's no smoke for them to see.'

'Good idea.'

'It's starting to rain,' said Seth, once they were inside. 'At least that'll make it harder for them to make out anything.'

'Who do you think it is?' There was a note of panic in Talissa's voice.

'Press. Galatia. Maybe even scientists. Or those Vector people.'

'It'll be all right, Seth.' Now she was pleading. 'You must believe me. We can find a way to outflank them. To manoeuvre our way. If not here, then at home next week we can make a plan to get through this together.'

'I don't understand.'

After a few minutes, Seth went out again. The helicopter had gone. Either it had done what it wanted or had been frustrated by the low cloud. In its place he could sense the presence of numerous small drones.

Seth turned his face up into the rain and let the water run down over his neck and shoulders. He had made up his mind.

They put on some clothes and slept close together, entwined in the straw of the wooden bed.

When Talissa awoke the next morning, she was alone.

Something made her think that this time he was not coming back. On the table was a pencil note that said, 'Thank you for loving me. Please thank my parents too. S'.

He must be on the island somewhere. Unless he'd somehow made a deal with the helicopter people. Talissa dressed and drank some tea, trying to stay calm. It had stopped raining when she went to the stream to brush her teeth, but the cloud was still low.

First, she climbed to the top of the hill so she could survey the island in the small hope that she would spot him. She walked for hours, till the sun was high. It was late in the afternoon when she approached the southern headland. Past the remains of a drystone wall, she noticed that the ground was marked not just with hoof prints but by human feet. A few minutes later, she came across a herd of wild cattle. She remembered Brodie's warning as well as Seth's description as she pressed on towards the sea.

The footprints petered out a few yards short of the water. She looked around and called his name. Her voice was drowned by the screech of birds.

She saw a chain on the ground. One end was attached to a solitary tree above the rocky shore, the other end was free.

The birds were circling in a frenzy above her head. Why did they hate her so much? They mustered like airborne troops, peeling off in ones and twos and diving down towards her where she stood, calling his name. The flap of wings and screeching drove her back.

In the bothy, she drank and drank, until the whisky was finished. She lay down on the straw and felt the world spin about her head.

She was awoken by a hammering on the door. Pushing back her hair, unsteady on her legs, she went to open it.

'I've come to take you back.' It was the boatman in his yellow jacket. It was early morning.

'I thought we had more time.'

'Yes, but the port's crawling with people. One of them tried to get me to bring him over here. Some American folk, too. I think they're chartering a helicopter. Where's the young laddie?'

As well as she could, Talissa explained what had happened.

'I can get a signal on the hill,' said Brodie. 'I'll call for help. But we only have a short time to catch the tide. Get your things together.'

An hour later, she sat crouched in the stern as the boat ploughed on with a will of its own.

Brodie put his mouth to her ear. 'The rescue team are on the way. They're the best in the islands. They'll find him.'

She wrapped her arms round her knees.

Next day, a ferry took her back to the mainland. No dolphins escorted them, though she could smell the black pudding from the galley. She looked through the window at the blue vertebrae of island rocks heaving through the seas. From the dock, she told the rental car to take her to an airport.

One day, many hundreds of years into the future, on a beach in a remote Scottish island, two observant youngsters might see a bone and have their curiosity aroused. A genome test would say that this was a hybrid human and the definitive twenty-first-century date would send the world into a spin, upending all previous beliefs about interbreeding and extinction. Some would claim it was a new species and would go to look for others in the sediment and in the caves. No one would have heard of Seth.

What she felt for him had registered on her nerves and in her mind, making her think that the feeling was hers. But it was his existence she had experienced, not her response to it. It no more belonged to her than a tree belonged to the silvered glass of a mirror that reflected it. And he – was he cursed or blessed, she couldn't say – was not able, in return, to feel her compassion and despair.

In the car, she calculated she could be in London that night. When Seth had told her that he didn't dream, perhaps he meant only that, like Pelham, he didn't remember his dreams. And in the end that came to the same thing. She'd spend one night in London, she thought, talk to Kavya, then be in New York the next day. There she could see Susan, her friend. She could connect with some colleagues and students and with what seemed to be her life. She'd call Mark, maybe, check in on Felix and her still-living mother. In the evening she would sit on the couch with Pelham, lame now, feel his head on her shoulder, hold his aching ribcage in her arm, and think about the thousands of years in which their forebears had come to rely on one another, one with speed and one with spears, sharing the kill that came from it, till reliance had mutated into love.

She believed that Seth was in a better place by being dead. His life would not have been tolerable and her own burning pity could now sleep. She thought of Kavya telling her about Sanjiv, the child she'd loved, and how he no longer existed. And Kavya had been stoical about the fact. Love passed, lives ended; and if you thought that only what was permanent had value, you were lost.

When she was back home she would tell no one, not even Susan, about her feelings for Seth or about their time on the island. There were no words for such things. They would remain between the two of them, so private as barely to exist.

In the bothy, the day before, Seth had sensed the dawn coming when he climbed from the straw.

He looked down at Talissa, breathing evenly. When he saw the rise of her chest, the black eyelashes on her cheek and heard in his mind her low voice speaking, he felt the beginnings of a new emotion in his belly. It was a hard and frightening thing, however, something that might crush him. He strode towards the door.

It grated on the stone as he pulled at it. Looking back into the room, he had a moment's remorse. He scribbled on a piece of paper on the table, then went out into the morning.

Past the broken stone wall he pressed on, walking swiftly, not weighed down by doubt. The red cattle were nowhere to be seen, but he remembered his course easily enough. He found the rowing boat, unhooked the chain and dragged it over the shingle to the sand.

He had never rowed before, but he didn't think it could be hard. To go backwards was the thing, that much he knew. When the water was up to his knees, he climbed in, put the oars through the rowlocks and began. It took a few minutes of splashing before he was able to make the boat move steadily away from the island. As he left the shelter of the cove, the waves began to mount. But by then he had a rhythm and could force the boat onward through the swell.

When he felt he was far enough away, a hundred yards or so, he pulled the oars in. Drowning, he'd once read, was not as bad as you might think. Apparently you fainted or your heart failed before you swallowed all that water.

Seth lowered himself over the side, then with both feet kicked the boat as hard as he could towards the shore. He splashed as he sank and for a moment the saltwater buoyed him up. Then he went under, feeling the sea at first cold on his scalp, then warmer as it claimed him.